Dear Reader,

Over the next two years Dell will be publishing my older, out-of-print books in five two-in-one volumes. Many of you for a number of years have been asking me where you can find these books, and I have been unable to offer very helpful answers. Until now!

The problem was choice. How did I pick just ten of the fifty or so books that are just begging to be republished? I listened to you. Those of you who have read those old books have your favorites, and some titles pop up over and over again. Other readers like the books with connected characters, since series are very popular at the moment.

We are starting with both categories of readers in mind. *Dark Angel* and *Lord Carew's Bride* are the first two of five connected books—the other three will be out soon. *Lord Carew* has always been a particular reader favorite. And both books have the same villain, Lionel, whom readers love to hate. But please note that the answer is still going to be no—I am not going to redeem him in a story of his own. Some villains are just too villainous!

I hope you will enjoy (re)reading these two books and will come back soon for the next two. For more detail and a publishing schedule, see my web site at www.marybalogh.com.

Mary Balogh

# PRAISE FOR THE NOVELS OF
# MARY BALOGH

## SEDUCING AN ANGEL

"With her inimitable, brilliantly nuanced sense of characterization, elegantly sensual style, and droll wit, best-seller Balogh continues to set the standard to which all other Regency historical writers aspire while delivering another addictively readable addition to her Huxtable family series." —*Booklist*

"One of [Balogh's] best books to date."
—A Romance Review

## AT LAST COMES LOVE

"Sparkling with sharp wit, lively repartee, and delicious sensuality, the emotionally rewarding *At Last Comes Love* metes out both justice and compassion; totally satisfying." —*Library Journal*

"*At Last Comes Love* is the epitome of what any great romance should be.... This novel will leave you crying, laughing, cheering, and ready to fight for two characters that any reader will most definitely fall in love with!"
—Coffee Time Romance

## THEN COMES SEDUCTION

"Exquisite sexual chemistry permeates this charmingly complex story." —*Library Journal*

"Balogh delivers another smartly fashioned love story that will dazzle readers with its captivating combination of nuanced characters, exquisitely sensual romance, and elegant wit." —*Booklist*

"Mary Balogh succeeds shockingly well."
—Rock Hill *Herald*

### FIRST COMES MARRIAGE

"Intriguing and romantic . . . Readers are rewarded with passages they'll be tempted to dog-ear so they can read them over and over." —McAllen *Monitor*

"Wonderful characterization [and a] riveting plot . . . I highly recommend you read *First Comes Marriage*."
—Romance Reviews Today

"Peppered with brilliant banter, laced with laughter . . . and tingling with sexual tension, this story of two seemingly mismatched people struggling to make their marriage work tugs at a few heartstrings and skillfully paves the way for the stories to come."
—*Library Journal*

"The incomparable Balogh delivers a masterful first in a new trilogy. . . . Always fresh, intelligent, emotional and sensual, Balogh's stories reach out to readers, touching heart and mind with their warmth and wit. Prepare for a joyous read." —*Romantic Times*

## SIMPLY PERFECT

"A warm-hearted and feel-good story . . . Readers will want to add this wonderful story to their collection. *Simply Perfect* is another must-read from this talented author, and a Perfect Ten." —Romance Reviews Today

"With her signature exquisite sense of characterization and subtle wit, Balogh brings her sweetly sensual, thoroughly romantic Simply quartet to a truly triumphant conclusion." —*Booklist*

## SIMPLY MAGIC

"Absorbing and appealing. This is an unusually subtle approach in a romance, and it works to great effect." —*Publishers Weekly*

"Balogh has once again crafted a sensuous tale of two very real people finding love and making each other's lives whole and beautiful. Readers will be delighted." —*Booklist*

## SIMPLY UNFORGETTABLE

"When an author has created a series as beloved to readers as Balogh's Bedwyn saga, it is hard to believe that she can surpass the delights with the first installment in a new quartet. But Balogh has done just that." —*Booklist*

"A memorable cast . . . refresh[es] a classic Regency plot with humor, wit, and the sizzling romantic chemistry that one expects from Balogh. Well-written and emotionally complex." —*Library Journal*

## SIMPLY LOVE

"One of the things that make Ms. Balogh's books so memorable is the emotion she pours into her stories. The writing is superb, with realistic dialogue, sexual tension, and a wonderful heart-wrenching story. *Simply Love* is a book to savor, and to read again. It is a Perfect Ten. Romance doesn't get any better than this."
—Romance Reviews Today

"With more than her usual panache, Balogh returns to Regency England for a satisfying adult love story."
—*Publishers Weekly*

## SLIGHTLY DANGEROUS

"*Slightly Dangerous* is the culmination of Balogh's wonderfully entertaining Bedwyn series. . . . Balogh, famous for her believable characters and finely crafted Regency-era settings, forges a relationship that leaps off the page and into the hearts of her readers." —*Booklist*

"With this series, Balogh has created a wonderfully romantic world of Regency culture and society. Readers will miss the honorable Bedwyns and their mates; ending the series with Wulfric's story is icing on the cake. Highly recommended." —*Library Journal*

## SLIGHTLY SINFUL

"Smart, playful, and deliciously satisfying . . . Balogh once again delivers a clean, sprightly tale rich in both plot and character. . . . With its irrepressible characters and deft plotting, this polished romance is an ideal summer read." —*Publishers Weekly* (starred review)

## SLIGHTLY TEMPTED

"Once again, Balogh has penned an entrancing, unconventional yarn that should expand her following." —*Publishers Weekly*

"Balogh is a gifted writer. . . . *Slightly Tempted* invites reflection, a fine quality in romance, and Morgan and Gervase are memorable characters." —*Contra Costa Times*

## SLIGHTLY SCANDALOUS

"With its impeccable plotting and memorable characters, Balogh's book raises the bar for Regency romances." —*Publishers Weekly* (starred review)

"The sexual tension fairly crackles between this pair of beautifully matched protagonists. . . . This delightful and exceptionally well-done title nicely demonstrates [Balogh's] matchless style." —*Library Journal*

"This third book in the Bedwyn series is . . . highly enjoyable as part of the series or on its own merits." —*Old Book Barn Gazette*

## SLIGHTLY WICKED

"Sympathetic characters and scalding sexual tension make the second installment [in the Slightly series] a truly engrossing read. . . . Balogh's sure-footed story possesses an abundance of character and class."
—*Publishers Weekly*

## SLIGHTLY MARRIED

"*Slightly Married* is a masterpiece! Mary Balogh has an unparalleled gift for creating complex, compelling characters who come alive on the pages. . . . A Perfect Ten." —*Romance Reviews Today*

## A SUMMER TO REMEMBER

"Balogh outdoes herself with this romantic romp, crafting a truly seamless plot and peopling it with well-rounded, winning characters." —*Publishers Weekly*

"The most sensuous romance of the year." —*Booklist*

"This one will rise to the top." —*Library Journal*

"Filled with vivid descriptions, sharp dialogue, and fantastic characters, this passionate, adventurous tale will remain memorable for readers who love an entertaining read." —*Rendezvous*

## WEB OF LOVE

"A beautiful tale of how grief and guilt can lead to love."
—*Library Journal*

# Dark Angel

# Lord Carew's Bride

MARY BALOGH

A DELL BOOK  NEW YORK

2010 Bantam Books Mass Market Omnibus Edition

*Dark Angel* copyright © 1994 by Mary Balogh
*Lord Carew's Bride* copyright © 1994 by Mary Balogh
Excerpt from *Seducing an Angel* copyright © 2009 by Mary Balogh

BANTAM BOOKS and the rooster colophon are registered trademarks of Random House, Inc.

Originally published in paperback in the United States by Signet, an imprint of New American Library, a division of Penguin Books USA Inc.

ISBN 978-0-440-24544-5

Cover design: Lynn Andreozzi
Cover photograph and retouching: Herman Estevez
Cover lettering: Iskra Johnson

Printed in the United States of America

www.bantamdell.com

2 4 6 8 9 7 5 3 1

# Dark Angel

# 1

*L*ONDON WAS SOMEWHAT OVERWHELMING TO the two young ladies who entered it in an imposing traveling carriage late one April afternoon. Instead of talking and exclaiming over it as they might have been expected to do considering the fact that they had chattered almost without ceasing during the long journey from Gloucestershire, they gazed in wonder and awe through opposite windows as the crowded, shabby, sometimes squalid streets of the outskirts gradually gave place to the elegant splendor that was Mayfair.

"Oh," one of them breathed on a sigh, breaking a long silence, "here we are at last, Jenny. At last! And suddenly I feel very small and very insignificant and very . . ." She sighed again.

"Frightened?" the other young lady suggested. She continued to gaze outward.

"Oh, Jenny," Miss Samantha Newman said, turning her head from the window at last to look at her companion, "it is all very well for you to be so calm and complacent. You have Lord Kersey waiting here to sweep you off your feet. Imagine, if you will, what it must be like to have no one. What if every gentleman in town takes one look at me and grimaces in distaste? What if I am a total wallflower at my very first ball? What if . . ." She stopped in some indignation when the other young lady laughed merrily, and then she joined in reluctantly. "Well, it could happen, you know. It could!"

"And pigs might fly south for the winter," the Honorable Miss Jennifer Winwood said quite unsympathetically. "One has only to remember how all the gentlemen at home tread all over each other's toes in their haste to be first at your side at the local assemblies."

Samantha wrinkled her nose and laughed again. "But this is London," she said, "not the country."

"And so the crushed-toe malady is about to spread to London," Jennifer said, looking in affectionate envy, as she frequently did, at her cousin's perfect beauty—short and shining blond curls, large blue eyes framed by long lashes darker than her hair, delicate porcelain complexion saved from even the remotest danger of insipidity by the natural blush of color in her cheeks. And Sam was small without being diminutive and well shaped without being either voluptuous or its opposite. Jennifer often regretted her own more vivid—and less ladylike—self. Gentlemen admired her dark red hair, which she had never been able to bear to have cut even when short hair became fashionable, and her dark eyes and her long legs and generous figure. But she often had the uncomfortable notion that she looked more like an actress or courtesan—not that she had ever seen either—than a lady. She longed to look and be the perfect lady. And she never really craved gentlemen's admiration.

Except Lord Kersey's—Lionel's. She had never spoken his name aloud to anyone, though she sometimes whispered it to herself, and in her heart and her dreams he was Lionel. He was going to be her husband. Soon. Before the Season was out. He was going to make his formal offer within the next few days or weeks and then after her presentation at court and her come-out ball their wedding was to be arranged. It was to be at St. George's in Hanover Square. After that she would have to be presented at court all over again as a married lady.

Soon. Very soon now. It had been such a long wait. Five endless years.

"Oh, Jenny, this must be it." The carriage had turned sharply into a large and elegant square and was slowing outside one of its mansions. "This must be Berkeley Square."

They had indeed reached their destination. The double front doors were opened wide even as they watched and liveried servants spilled forth. Others jumped down from the baggage coach that had followed closely behind their traveling carriage throughout the journey. One of them lifted two maidservants down while the coachman himself was handing the young ladies down the steps of their carriage. It seemed a great deal of fuss and bustle for the arrival of two rather insignificant persons, Jennifer thought in some amusement. She had spent all her twenty years in the relative informality of country living.

But she was very willing to adapt. Soon she would

be a married lady, the Viscountess Kersey, and would be lady of her own London home and country estate. It was a heady thought for someone who was only just now arriving in London for the first time. She was so very old to be doing that, so very old not to be officially out. But two years ago when she was eighteen and her come-out was planned and also the engagement and marriage that had been arranged three years before that by her papa and the Earl of Rushford, Viscount Kersey's father, the viscount had been detained in the north of England by the severe illness of an uncle. Jennifer had shed many a tear that spring and summer, not so much at the lost Season as at the delay in her marriage. She had seen Lord Kersey so few times. And then last year disaster had struck again in the form of the death of her grandmother in January. There had been no question of either a Season or a wedding.

And so here she was, arriving in London for the first time at the advanced age of twenty. The only consolation was that her cousin Samantha, who had been living with them for four years, since the passing of her own parents, was now eighteen and able to come out at the same time as Jennifer. It would be good to have company and a confidante. And a bridesmaid at her wedding.

It had seemed an eternity, Jennifer thought, stopping a moment to gaze up at her father's London house. She had not even seen Lord Kersey for over a year and even then only very briefly and formally in the presence of others at various Christmas parties and assemblies. She had dreamed of him every night since and had day-dreamed about him every day. She had loved him passionately and singlemindedly for five years. Soon dreams would be reality.

Her father's butler bowed to them with stiff deference from the doorway and conducted them to the library, where Jennifer's father, Viscount Nordal, was awaiting them, standing formally before the desk, his hands clasped behind his back. He would, of course, have heard the commotion of their arrival, but it would have been out of character for Papa to have come out to meet them.

Samantha rushed toward him so that he was forced to bring his arms forward to hug her. "Uncle Gerald!" she exclaimed. "We have been speechless with the splendor of all we have seen. Have we not, Jenny? All we could do was peer out of the carriage windows and gawk with hanging jaws. Was it not so, Jenny? How lovely it is to see you again. Are you well?"

"I gather the speechlessness was not a permanent affliction," he said with a rare sally into humor. He turned from her to hug his daughter. "Yes, quite well, I thank you, Samantha. It is a relief to know you have both arrived safely. I have been wondering if I should have come for you myself. It does not do for young ladies to travel alone."

"Alone?" Samantha chuckled. "We had a veritable army with us, Uncle. Any highwayman would have taken one look and decided in despair that it would be certain suicide to risk an attack. A pity. I have always dreamed of being borne off by a handsome highway-man." She laughed lightly to dispel her uncle's frown.

"Well," he said, looking closely at both of them, "you will do. You both look healthy and pretty enough. A tri-fle rustic, of course. I have a modiste coming here to-morrow morning. Agatha arranged it. She has come to stay and take charge of all the faradiddle of your presentations and the rest of it. You are to mind her. She will know what is what so that you are both suitably decked out for the Season and so that you will both know how to go on."

Jennifer and Samantha exchanged rueful smiles.

"Well," Lord Nordal said dismissively, "you will be tired after your journey, I daresay, and will be glad to rest for a while."

"Aunt Agatha!" Samantha said a short while later as she and Jennifer were being conducted to their rooms by the housekeeper. "The dragon herself. I always have diffi-culty understanding how she and Mama could have been sisters. Will we have any enjoyment out of this Sea-son, Jenny?"

"Far more than we would without her," Jennifer said. "Without Aunt Agatha, who would take us about, Sam, and introduce us to Society? Who would see to it that we receive and accept the proper invitations? And who would see to it that we have partners at the balls we at-tend and escorts to the theater and opera? Papa? Can you really see Papa so exerting himself?"

Samantha chuckled with her at the mental image of her stern and humorless uncle playing the part of social organizer for their Season. "I suppose you are right," she said. "Yes, she will see to it that we have partners, will she not? She will see to it that my worst nightmare will not be realized. Dear Aunt Aggy. Not that you have to worry about partners, Jenny. You will have Lord Kersey."

The very thought was enough to turn Jennifer's heart over in a somersault. Dancing with Lionel. Attending the theater with Lionel. Perhaps being alone with Lionel for a few moments whenever it could be arranged and exchanging kisses with him. Kisses—her knees had turned to jelly at Christmas last year when he had kissed her hand. Would her knees bear her up if—no, *when*—he kissed her lips?

"But not all the time," she said. "It would be most indecorous to dance with the same partner more than twice at one ball, Sam, even if he were one's betrothed. You know that."

"Perhaps you will meet someone even more handsome, then," Samantha said. "And someone who is not cold."

Jennifer felt the old indignation against her cousin's assessment of Lord Kersey. He was very blond and very blue-eyed and had features of chiseled excellence. And to Samantha he seemed cold—although she shared his coloring. Of course, the warmth of her complexion would always save Sam from such an accusation even apart from the liveliness of her face and the eagerness with which she approached life.

Lord Kersey—Lionel—was not cold. Sam, of course, had never had the full force of his smile directed her way.

It was a smile of devastating attractiveness. It was a smile that had enslaved Jennifer ever since at the age of fifteen she had met for the first time the husband her father had picked out for her. She had never resented the arranged match. Never once. She had fallen in love with her intended husband at first sight and had remained in love with him ever since.

"If I do meet someone more handsome," she said as they reached the top of the stairs and were led in the direction of their rooms, "I shall pass him on to you, Sam. If he has not seen you first, that is, and fallen prostrate at your feet."

"What a delightful idea," Samantha said.

"Not that it would be possible to meet anyone more handsome than Lord Kersey, of course," Jennifer said.

"I will grant you that," Samantha agreed. "But maybe somewhere in this vast metropolis there is a gentleman who is equally handsome and who admires blond hair and blue eyes and insignificant stature and a nondescript figure."

Jennifer laughed and turned to enter the room the housekeeper was indicating as hers. "And Sam," she said just before they parted, "do be careful not to call our aunt Aunt Aggy to her face. Do you remember her expression when you did so last year at Grandmama's funeral?"

Samantha chuckled and pulled a face.

———

"STUBBORNNESS WILL BE YOUR undoing one of these days, Gabe," Sir Albert Boyle remarked to his companion as they rode in Hyde Park unfashionably early in the afternoon. "But I must say I am glad you are back in town for all that. It has been dull without you for the last two years."

"But you will note that I do not quite have the courage to take to Rotten Row at five o'clock on my first full day back," Gabriel Fisher, the Earl of Thornhill, said dryly. "Perhaps tomorrow. *Probably* tomorrow. I'll be damned before I'll stay away altogether, Bertie, merely because I can anticipate being looked at askance and watching very proper matrons draw their sweet young charges behind their skirts and away from my contaminating influence. It is a pity hooped skirts fell out of fashion several decades ago. They would be able to hide their daughters more effectively."

"It may not be half as bad as you expect," his friend said. "And you could always proclaim the truth, you know."

"The truth?" The earl laughed without any trace of humor. "How do you know that the truth has not been told, Bertie? How do you know that I am not the heinous villain I have been made out to be?"

"I know you," Sir Albert said. "Remember?"

"And so you do," the earl said, fixing his eyes on the approaching figures of two young ladies, still some distance away, who were strolling beneath frilly parasols, their maids walking at a discreet distance behind them. "People may believe what they will, Bertie. To hell with the *ton* and their scandalmongering. Besides, it is altogether possible that I will be more in demand this year than I have ever been before."

"Scandal does often add fascination when it attaches to a man's name," his friend agreed. "And of course the fact that you are now an earl whereas two years ago you were a mere baron will help. And as rich as Croesus to boot. At least, I assume you are. That is how you always used to describe your father."

The Earl of Thornhill was apparently paying no attention. His eyes were narrowed. "You will never know, Bertie," he said, "how I have pined during the past year and a half on the Continent for the sight of an English beauty. There is nothing to compare in Italy or France or Switzerland, you know, or anywhere else either. Tall and short. Dark and fair. Well endowed and more delicate. But each exquisite in her own very English way. Will they pretend not to notice us, do you think, and direct their eyes downward? Or will they look up? Will they blush? Will they smile?"

"Or frown," Sir Albert said, laughing as he followed the direction of his friend's gaze. "Exquisite, yes. And strangers, unfortunately. Of course at this time of year London is always full of strangers. After a few weeks one will have seen them a dozen times at a dozen different entertainments."

"Frown? I think not," the earl said softly as their horses took them closer to the two ladies, who really should have waited a few hours if they hoped to be ogled as they deserved to be, he thought. He swept off his hat and inclined his head, almost forcing them to raise their eyes.

The small blonde blushed. Very prettily. She was true English beauty personified. The sort of beauty one dreamed of acquiring in a bride when one's thoughts must eventually bend that way. The tall dark-haired girl did not blush. Her hair, he noted with interest, was not dark brown, as he had first thought. When the light of the sun caught it as she raised her head and the brim of her bonnet no longer shaded it, he saw that it was a dark, rich red. And her eyes were dark and large. Her figure— well, if the other girl could turn the thoughts of even a fancy-free twenty-six-year-old to matrimony, then this one could turn the thoughts in another direction altogether. She was the sort of British beauty he had dreamed through tedious months of duty and a type of self-exile abroad of having naked beneath him on a bed.

"Good afternoon." He smiled, directing the full intensity of his dark gaze not at the blond beauty who had first taken his eye and who had stopped walking in order to curtsy, but at the greater challenge of her luscious companion, who was making no response at all beyond a candid stare and a slight pause in her walk. It was a pity, he found himself thinking, that she was very obviously a lady.

"Good afternoon," Sir Albert said beside him while the one girl curtsied, the other waited for her before moving on, and the maids stepped closer.

The two gentlemen rode on and did not look back.

"Eminently bedworthy," the earl muttered. "Lusciously, mouth-wateringly so. I am going to have to set up a mistress, Bertie. I have had no one since leaving England, if you will believe it, beyond one reckless encounter with a whore and then several weeks of terror at what she might have given me apart from an hour of strenuous and moderately satisfying sport. I did not repeat the experiment. And taking a mistress seemed somehow disrespectful to Catherine. I shall have to take a look-in at the theaters and opera houses and see who is available. It will not do to salivate in the park every afternoon, will it?"

"Hair the color of pale moonbeams," said Sir Albert, waxing poetic, "and eyes like cornflowers. She is going to have armies of suitors before many days have passed. Especially if she has a fortune to match the face."

"Ah," the earl said, "you fancied the blonde, did you? It was the lady of the long and shapely legs who had my mind turning determinedly in the direction of mistresses. Oh, to have such legs twine about one's own, Bertie. Yes, I must say I am glad to be back in England, scandal or no scandal."

He knew he should be spending the spring at Chalcote instead of postponing his return until the summer. His father had been dead only a little over a year—since his own removal to the Continent with Catherine, his father's second wife. His title and his property were new to him. He should have hastened home as soon as the news reached them, but bringing Catherine back had been out of the question and he had felt himself unable to leave her at that particular time. Staying with her had seemed more important than hurrying home too late to attend his father's funeral anyway.

Now he knew he should go home. But Bertie had been right. There was a great deal of stubbornness in him. Coming to London for the Season was madness when doing so meant facing the *ton*, who believed almost without exception that he had eloped to the Continent with his father's wife after impregnating her. And now, of course, he had abandoned her to live alone in Switzerland with their daughter—or so the story doubtless went. Catherine was indeed living there quite comfortably with the child. He had given her the protection of his company during her confinement and for almost a year following it. Now she was quite capable of living independently—and he had been almost desperately homesick.

It would have been far better to have gone straight home to Chalcote. It was what he should have done and what he had wanted to do. London would be better faced—if at all—next year or the year after when the scandal had cooled somewhat. Except that scandal never cooled in London. Whenever he went there for the first time—whether it was now or ten years hence—it would flare about him.

It had never been his way to avoid scandal or to show that he cared one way or another for what people said of him. He did care as much as anyone, he supposed, but he would go to the devil before he would show that he cared. He had not made any attempt to correct that erroneous conclusion that had been jumped to when he had taken his pregnant stepmother away from his father's fury after she admitted that she was with child. It was as Gabriel had suspected—his father, sickly since before his second marriage, had never consummated that marriage. He had been afraid that his father would harm Catherine or her unborn child or would openly deny paternity and ruin her forever. The old earl had not done so, but gossip had blossomed into a major scandal anyway when her flight to the Continent with her stepson and her condition had become common knowledge.

Let people think what they would, the present Earl of Thornhill had thought. He had been established in Switzerland with Catherine before she told him who the father of her child was.

He should have returned to kill the man, he had thought often since. But as Catherine had explained to him, what had happened had not been rape. The foolish woman had loved the villain who had so carelessly impregnated her—the wife of a man who would know that he had been cuckolded—and had then made himself very scarce as soon as his sins had threatened to find him out.

And so the Earl of Thornhill was back, fifteen months after the sudden death of his father, almost one year after the birth of the child who bore his father's name despite the very public conviction that she was not his father's.

Back and foolishly thrusting his head straight into the

lion's mouth. And eyeing British beauties who were obviously in town for the annual spring marriage mart. There would be one or two parents who would be outraged and foaming at the mouth if they knew that the Earl of Thornhill had just made his bow to their daughters—and had imagined one of them naked on a bed beneath him, her long legs twined about his.

He smiled rather grimly.

"Tomorrow, Bertie," he said, "weather permitting, we will come for the fashionable squeeze. And tomorrow I shall send back acceptances to some of my invitations. Yes, I have had a surprising number. I suppose my newly acquired rank, as you say, and, even more important, my newly acquired fortune do a great deal to make some people turn a blind eye to my notoriety."

"People will flock to view you," Sir Albert said cheerfully, "if only to see if you have acquired horns and a tail during the past year, Gabe, and if they can see any signs through your stockings and dancing shoes of cloven feet. I revel in the irony of your name. Gabriel of the cloven foot." He laughed loudly.

What would that dark red hair look like without the bonnet, the earl wondered, and beneath the light of hundreds of candles in their chandeliers? Would he find out? Would he ever be allowed close enough to her to see quite clearly?

He looked back over his shoulder, but she and her companion had passed out of sight.

"There," Samantha said, twirling her parasol, well pleased with life. "We are not to be quite ignored, Jenny. I even read admiration in their eyes. I wonder who they are. Will we find out, do you think?"

"Probably," Jennifer said. "They are undoubtedly gentlemen. And how could they fail to admire you? All the gentlemen at home do. I do not see why London gentlemen should be any different."

Samantha sighed. "I just wish we did not look so rustic," she said. "I wish some of the clothes we were measured for this morning had been made up already. Aunt Aggy was a positive love, poker face or not, to insist on so many clothes for each of us, was she not? I could have hugged her except that Aunt Aggy is not quite the sort of person one hugs. I wonder if our Uncle Percy ever . . . Oh, never mind." She laughed lightly. "I wish I were wearing the new blue walking dress that is to be finished by next week."

"I am not sure," Jennifer said, "that those gentlemen should have spoken to us. It would have been more proper if they had merely touched their hats and ridden on."

Samantha laughed again. "The dark one was very handsome," she said. "As handsome as Lord Kersey, in fact, though in entirely the opposite way. But I think I liked his companion better. He smiled sweetly and did not look like the devil."

Jennifer would not own that the dark gentleman was as handsome as Lionel. He was too dark, too thin-faced, too bold. His eyes had bored into hers as if he saw her not only without her clothes but even without her skin and bones. And his eyes and his smile, she had noticed, had been directed wholly and quite improperly on her. If he had deemed it polite to sweep off his hat and to smile and even pass the time of day, then he should have made it a gesture to the two of them. Not just to Samantha, and not just to her. His behavior had been quite unmannerly. She suspected that perhaps they had just encountered one of the rakes with whom London was said to abound.

"Yes," she said, "he did look like the devil, did he not? As Lord Kersey looks like an angel. You were quite right to say they are handsome in quite opposite ways, Sam. That gentleman looks like Lucifer. Lord Kersey looks like an angel."

"The angel Gabriel," Samantha said with a laugh, "and the devil Lucifer." She twirled her parasol. "Oh, this walk has done me the world of good, Jenny, even though Aunt Aggy has strictly forbidden us to show our faces at anything that might be called fashionable until next week. Two gentlemen have raised their hats to us and bidden us a good afternoon and my spirits have soared even though one of them looks like the devil. A handsome devil, though. Of course, you don't have to wait a week, you lucky thing. Lord Kersey is calling on you tomorrow morning."

"Yes." Jennifer went off into a dream. Word had come during the morning that Lionel was back in town and that tomorrow morning he was to call on her father—and on her.

Sometimes it was very difficult to remember that one was twenty years old and a dignified lady. Sometimes it was difficult not to set one's parasol twirling at lightning speed and not to whoop out one's joy to surrounding nature. Tomorrow she would see Lionel again. Tomorrow—perhaps—she would be officially betrothed to him.

Tomorrow. Oh, would tomorrow ever come?

## 2

*L*ADY BRILL, JENNIFER AND SAMANTHA'S AUNT
Agatha, was merely a baronet's widow and daughter and sister of a viscount, but she had a presence that a duchess might have envied and a self-assurance acquired during many years of residence in London. It should have been impossible for any self-respecting modiste to produce even a single garment less than twenty-four hours after her first call upon a client. And yet, thanks to the cajolery of Lady Brill, early in the morning after Madame Sophie had spent several hours at Berkeley Square with the Honorable Miss Jennifer Winwood and Miss Samantha Newman, a morning dress of pale green was delivered to the former by Madame's head assistant, who made sure that the fit was perfect before she left again.

Jennifer was to be fashionable when she received her first formal town visit from Viscount Kersey.

And she must be demure and ladylike, she told herself as she brushed cold and unsteady hands lightly over the fabric of her new dress, smoothing out nonexistent wrinkles. Her heart fluttered. She breathed as if she had just run for a mile nonstop and uphill. Samantha had just darted into her dressing room with word that the

Earl and Countess of Rushford and Viscount Kersey had arrived.

"You look splendid," she said, stopping just inside the door and gazing at her cousin with mingled admiration and envy. "Oh, Jenny, how does it *feel*? How does it feel to be about to go downstairs to meet your future husband?"

It felt rather as if her slippers had been soled with lead. If she had been able to eat any breakfast, she would now be feeling bilious. She felt bilious anyway.

"Do you think I should have had my hair cut?" she asked, and stared at her image in the glass, amazed that she could think of nothing more profound to say on such a momentous occasion. "It is really very long, yet short hair is all the crack, according to Aunt Agatha."

"It looks very elegant piled like that," Samantha said. "And very pretty too with the trailing curls. I thought you would be bounding with excitement."

"How can I," Jennifer asked almost in a wail, "when I cannot lift my feet from the floor? It has been over a year, Sam, and even then we were never alone together and never together at all for more than five minutes at a time. What if he has changed his mind? What if there was nothing to change? What if he never did want this match? It was arranged by our papas years ago. It has always suited me. But what if it does not suit him?" Panic clawed at her.

Samantha clucked her tongue and tossed a look at the ceiling. "Men are not forced into marriage, Jenny," she said. "Women sometimes are because we are rarely given a say in the ordering of our own lives. That is the way of the world, alas. But not men. If Lord Kersey did not like this match, he would have said so long ago and there would have been an end of the matter. You are merely giving in to the vapors. I have never heard you express these doubts before."

She had had them, Jennifer supposed, suppressed so deep that even she had been scarcely aware of them. Fears that all her dreams would come to nothing. She did not know what she would do if that happened. There would be a frightening emptiness in her life and a painful void in her heart. But he was here—downstairs at this very moment.

"If I am not summoned soon," she said, clenching her hands into tight fists and then stretching her fingers wide, "I shall crumple into a heap on the floor. Perhaps this is only a courtesy visit, Sam. Do you think? After all, we have not seen each other for over a year. There will be a few visits before he can be expected to come to the point, will there not? I am being unnecessarily foolish. In which case, I am doubtless very overdressed and Lord and Lady Rushford and Li—and their son will laugh privately at me. His mama and papa would not have come with him if this was it, would they?"

Samantha tossed a look at the ceiling again, but before she could say anything more there was a knock on the door behind her and a footman announced that Miss Winwood's presence was requested in the rose salon.

Jennifer inhaled slowly and deeply through her nose before being subjected to her cousin's hug. A minute later she was walking downstairs with a quiet dignity that belied the wild beating of her heart.

She was about to see him again. Would he look as she remembered? Would he be pleased with her? Would she be able to behave like the mature woman of twenty that she was?

Three gentlemen rose to their feet when she was admitted to the salon. A lady remained seated. Jennifer curtsied to her father and then to the Earl and Countess of Rushford when her father presented her to them. The earl was large and as haughty-looking as she remembered him. Samantha had once remarked that he was an older version of his son, but Jennifer had never been able to see any likeness. Lionel could never grow into someone so—unappealing. The countess was dumpy and placid-looking. It was hard to believe that she could have produced such a handsome son.

The earl inclined his head to her and looked her over appraisingly from head to toe, his lips pursed, rather as if she was inanimate merchandise he was considering purchasing, Jennifer thought. But she saw approval in his eyes. The countess smiled reassuringly at her and even rose to hug her and set a cheek against hers.

"Jennifer, dear," she said. "As lovely as ever. What a very pretty dress."

And then her father indicated the third gentleman in the room and she turned her head at last and looked at Viscount Kersey as she curtsied to him. On the rare occasions she had been about to see him in the five years since their marriage had been arranged, she had always wondered anxiously if he would be as splendid as she remembered him. And each time she had been jolted by the fact that he was even more so. The same held true now.

Viscount Kersey was not only handsome and elegant. He was—perfect. There was no feature of his face, no part of his body that could possibly be improved upon. It was the impression Jennifer had again now as her eyes took in the silver blondness of his hair, the deep blue of his eyes, his chiseled features and perfectly proportioned body beneath the immaculately fashionable clothes. He was still a few inches taller than she. She had been terrified that she would grow beyond him, but the danger was now past.

He bowed to her, his eyes on her the whole while. Cold, Samantha always called him. It was the uneasy impression Jennifer had of him now. He did not smile, though he said all that was proper and took his part in the conversation that followed when they had all seated themselves. But then she did not smile either. Doubtless she appeared cold to him. It was difficult to smile and to look and feel comfortable under such circumstances. She sat with stiff and straight back, mechanically taking her part in the conversation, aware of the critical appraisal of his parents.

It was merely a social call after all, then, she thought after a few minutes. It was foolish of her to have expected the event to have greater significance when they had not met for so long. Ridiculous of her. She hoped her appearance and her manner would not cause them to realize that she had expected more. How rustic they would think her.

And then her father got to his feet.

"I'll show you the new section of my library I mentioned at White's last week, Rushford," he said, "if you would care to come and see it now. It will take but a few minutes."

"Certainly," the earl agreed, rising and crossing the room to the door. "My own library is sadly out of date. I shall have to set my secretary to it."

His countess followed him. "And I shall call in on Lady Brill while I am here," she said. "It is always a pleasure to see Agatha when I am in town. Jennifer, my dear, perhaps you will entertain my son for a short while?" She smiled and nodded at both of them.

Jennifer had lulled herself with the conviction that she had been wrong about the purpose of this visit. She felt now almost as if she had been taken unaware. Panic threatened. But gazing down at her hands, which rested in her lap, she was relieved to find that they were neither trembling nor fidgeting.

Viscount Kersey stood up when the door closed behind their parents. It was, Jennifer realized, startled, the first time they had ever been quite alone together. She looked up to find him gazing down at her. She smiled.

"You are very lovely," he said. "I trust you are enjoying London?"

"Thank you." She blushed with pleasure at the compliment, though the words had been formally spoken.

"We arrived only two days ago and have been out but once since, for a walk in the park yesterday afternoon. But yes, I intend to enjoy it, my lord." Her mind grappled with the realization that the moment had finally come.

"Is it an encumbrance?" he asked. "This match that was forced on you when you were far too young to know quite what was being arranged on your behalf? Do you wish yourself out of it now that you are here for the Season? Do you wish you were free to receive the attentions of other gentlemen? Do you feel trapped?"

"No!" She felt her flush deepen. "I have never for a moment regretted it, my lord. Apart from the fact that I trust my father to arrange for my future, I . . ." . . . *fell in love with you at first sight*. She had been about to say the words aloud. ". . . I find that it also suits my own inclination to accept his plans," she said.

He inclined his head in a half-bow. "I had to ask," he said. "You were but fifteen. I was twenty and the circumstances for me were a little different."

And then she remembered her earlier doubts. He had been twenty. Only twenty. Now at the age of twenty-five did he regret what he had agreed to then? Had he been hoping that she would answer his questions differently? Had he been hoping that she would offer him a way out? He still had not smiled. She had.

"B-but perhaps," she said, "this planned match is an encumbrance to you, my lord?" Now it was not the soles of her slippers that felt as if they were made of lead, but her heart. It seemed so altogether likely suddenly. He was so very handsome and—fashionable. He did not know her at all. He had not set eyes on her since Christmas of last year.

For a moment he looked at the door through which his parents had just passed and half smiled. Then he took a few steps closer to her and leaned down to possess himself of her right hand. "It was my pleasure when it was first suggested," he said, "to consider you as my future bride, and it is my pleasure now. I have looked forward impatiently to this moment. Shall we make it official, then? Will you do me the honor of marrying me?"

All doubts fled. She looked up into his blue, blue eyes and knew that the moment had come when all her dreams were being realized. Lionel was standing close before her, holding her hand, gazing into her eyes, asking her to be his wife. And then he smiled, dispelling any fear there might have been of coldness in his addresses, revealing perfect white teeth. She felt the old welling of excitement and love.

"Yes," she said. "Oh, yes, my lord." She got to her feet, not having planned to do so, not knowing quite why she did so.

"Then you have completed the happiness that began in my life five years ago," he said, and raised her hand to his lips.

She knew suddenly why she had stood up. They were standing very close. They were alone together for the first time. He had just proposed marriage and she had just accepted. She wanted him to kiss her lips. She

blushed at the realization of just how improper her unconscious wish had been. She hoped he had not guessed.

He behaved with the utmost propriety. He returned
her hand to her side and took a step back. "You have
made me the happiest of men, Miss Winwood," he said.

She wanted him to call her Jennifer and wondered
if she should say so. But perhaps it would be too forward. She wanted him to invite her to use his given name
as she had used it in her dreams for five years. But she
realized suddenly that the stiffness and formality of his
manner must be the result of embarrassment. It must be
so much more of an ordeal for a man to make an offer
than for a woman to receive it. The woman's role was
passive while the man's was active. She tried to imagine
their roles reversed. She tried to imagine how she would
have felt earlier this morning waiting for him to arrive if
she had known that she must take the initiative, that she
must speak the words of the offer. She smiled at him in
sympathy.

"And you have made me happy too, my lord," she
said. "I shall devote my life to your happiness."

They were saved from further conversation by the return to the salon of their parents, expectant looks on
their faces. In all that followed, Jennifer held on to her
happiness, to her knowledge that now, after so long, it
was finally official, irrevocable, that her happiness had
been signed and sealed.

They were to be married at the end of June. In the
meanwhile they were to spend a month enjoying the activities of the Season in company together—or as much

in company as propriety would allow—before their betrothal was officially announced and celebrated in a grand dinner and ball at the Earl of Rushford's mansion. And then another month would follow before the wedding would actually take place.

The end of June. Two months. In two months' time she would be the Viscountess Kersey. Lionel's bride. And during those two months she was to dance with him at balls and assemblies, sit with him at dinners and concerts, attend the theater and the opera with him, drive out with him, walk out with him. Get to know him. Get to feel comfortable with him. Become his friend.

And then his wife forever after. His lifelong companion. The mother of his children.

It was too much like heaven, she thought, glancing across the room at him while their fathers talked. He was looking back, unsmiling again. Two months during which to dispel the slight discomfort that made this morning just a little less than perfect. Except that it was perfect, she told herself determinedly. The awkwardness was to be expected. They scarcely knew each other despite the fact that for five years they had been intended for each other. They had not even met for over a year. And a proposal of marriage would be a strained occasion even in the most ideal of circumstances.

Oh, yes, everything was perfect. Except that perfection was an absolute state, and she knew that what had begun this morning was going to get better during the following two months and even better at the end of June.

She was the happiest woman alive, she told herself.

She was in love with the most handsome man in the world and she was betrothed to him—officially betrothed at last. He had smiled at her and told her she had made him the happiest of men. She was going to see to it that that held true for the rest of their lives.

He kissed her hand again when he and his parents took their leave a few minutes later. So did the earl. The countess hugged and kissed her again and even shed a few tears.

Jennifer, dismissed by her father, refused to feel flat and depressed. How ridiculous! But how natural when she had just been offered for and had just accepted and had no one at the moment with whom to share her joy. She forgot herself as far as to take the stairs two at a time to Samantha's dressing room.

THE EARL OF THORNHILL put into effect his promise to ride in the park at the fashionable hour the day after he had ridden there early. He was accompanied by Sir Albert Boyle, as before, and by their mutual friend, Lord Francis Kneller.

This time the park was as crowded as it always was at such an hour during the spring. He was not as embarrassed as he had half expected to be, though, he found. Many of the gentlemen he now saw, he had met at White's yesterday or this morning. Men tended not to be swayed greatly by scandal when it concerned one of their own.

Many of the ladies in the park did not know him—yet,

anyway. It was a long time since he had been in London. Those who did—mostly older ladies—looked haughtily at him and would have given him the cut direct if he had given them the opportunity, but they were far too well bred to make a scene.

It all went rather well, he thought, and he was glad after all that he had come to town first before going to Chalcote. The next time he came he would be old and stale news. Other scandals would long ago have supplanted the one in which he had been involved.

"A shame," Sir Albert said, looking around the crowd carefully. "Not a sight of her, Gabe—of *them*. The most delightful little blonde you have ever set eyes on, Frank. And her companion had long legs that Gabe admired. Fancied them twined about his own, or something like that. But they are not here."

Lord Francis guffawed. "I hope you did not tell her so, Gabe," he said. "Maybe it is common courtesy to a Swiss miss to tell her such things, but an English miss would have twelve fits of the vapors and her papa and all her brothers and male cousins and uncles would separately challenge you. You would have appointments at dawn for a month of mornings."

"I kept my thoughts to myself," the earl said, grinning, "until I was foolish enough to confide them to Bertie. They must be otherwise engaged this afternoon, Bertie. Or perhaps they have not been presented yet. That would explain yesterday's solitary walk."

He too had looked about hopefully for them—in particular for the redhead. He had surprised himself by dreaming of her last night, but she had been telling him, alas, that he should go home where he belonged.

And then his grin faded and he completely missed the witticism of Lord Francis's that set Sir Albert to laughing. Yes, he thought. *Yes!*

There had been another reason for his return to London. He had hardly acknowledged it to himself and it might very well have come to nothing. But yes. He felt something strangely like elation. He had come at just the right time. He could not have timed it better if he had tried.

He had always known that he must confront Catherine's former lover somehow. The Gothic notion of challenging the man to a duel and putting a bullet between his eyes had passed long ago. But there had to be something. His father was dead. He was the head of the family that had been dishonored. More important, he had always been fond of Catherine, and he had been with her through much of her pregnancy and confinement. She had had to bear the whole burden alone, not the least part of which had been a deeply bruised heart. And though she was now passionately devoted to her daughter, nevertheless all the responsibility and stress of bringing up the child was hers alone and would be for years and years to come.

The father, as was the nature of things, had suffered nothing but physical pleasure from the affair.

The least he could do, the Earl of Thornhill had decided some time ago—the very least—was inform the man that he knew. Catherine had kept his identity a closely guarded secret for a long time and even then had told only her stepson.

And now the father of Catherine's child was riding in the park, bowing gallantly over the hand of a lady in a phaeton and flashing the whiteness of his handsome smile at her. He had not a care in the world. The earl amused himself for a moment with the mental image of his fist shattering those white teeth into a million fragments.

"You are blocking the path, Gabe," Lord Francis said.

"What?" he said. "Oh, sorry." Catherine's former lover had tipped his hat to the lady in the phaeton and was riding away from the crowd into the more open spaces of the park. "Excuse me, will you? There is someone I must talk to."

Without waiting for their answer, he maneuvered his horse around vehicles and pedestrians and other horses until he was clear of them and could close the gap with the other rider.

"Kersey," he called when he was within earshot, "well met."

Viscount Kersey turned his head sharply, a slight frown between his handsome brows, and then smiled. "Ah, Thornhill," he said, "you are back in England, are you? Facing the music and all that?" He laughed. "Sorry about your father. It must have been a shock to you under the circumstances."

"He had been ill for several years," the earl said. "Your daughter is going to be blond like you, though she does not have much hair to speak of at the moment. Did you know, by the way, that it was a daughter, not a son? So much better, I always think, when the child cannot be acknowledged as one's heir anyway."

It was as if a curtain came down just behind the blue eyes, he noted with interest.

"What are you talking about?" Viscount Kersey asked, his voice both chilly and haughty.

"Lady Thornhill is now established comfortably in Switzerland with her daughter," the earl said, "and is in a fair way to recovering her spirits. I do not suppose you are much interested in hearing about her, though, are you?"

"Why should I be?" Lord Kersey frowned back at him. "Beyond the fact that I met the countess once or twice while I was attending my uncle during his sickness. I rather gather that you are the one who should be most concerned with her well-being, Thornhill."

The earl smiled. "I have no desire to prolong this exchange of civilities," he said. "And I am not about to slap a glove in your face. Suffice it to say that I know and that for the rest of your life you will know that I know. If I can be of any disservice to you, Kersey, it will be my pleasure to oblige. Good day to you." He touched his whip to the brim of his hat and turned to ride unhurriedly away in the opposite direction from that taken by Kersey.

He was satisfied, he thought. He had accomplished what he had always planned to do. Perhaps Kersey would suffer some discomfort from the knowledge that his secret was not quite so secret after all.

And yet, the earl thought, there should be more. His

father had been cuckolded and his stepmother dishonored and he himself had had his reputation ruined. A child was to grow up unsupported and unacknowledged by her real father.

There should be more.

For the first time in a long while the urge really to hurt Kersey burned in him. He should be made to suffer—just a little. He could not be publicly exposed without stirring up the old scandal for Catherine again. Lord Thornhill would not do that to her even though she was far away. No, he would have no satisfaction from hurling mud at Kersey and watching him as like as not ducking out of its aim.

But there should be some way.

He would watch for it, the earl decided. If there was anything he could do to see Kersey suffer, then he would do it.

Without the slightest qualm.

# 3

*A*LTHOUGH HE HAD BROKEN THE ICE, SO TO speak, by riding in the park and facing the *ton*, two weeks passed before the Earl of Thornhill attended his first social function. He considered not doing so at all. He had proved a point to both himself and them, and he had confronted Kersey with his knowledge. He was very tempted to leave London and go home to Chalcote. But he supposed that since he had made his stand, he might as well complete the process. Riding in the park was not quite the same as attending an entertainment of the Season.

He decided to attend a ball. He had plenty of invitations to choose among. It appeared that his title and wealth were of greater significance after all than his notoriety. Every hostess during the Season liked to grace her ballroom with as many men of fortune as possible and as many titled gentlemen as could be persuaded to attend. Young, unmarried gentlemen were particularly courted, especially where there were young daughters or nieces or granddaughters to be brought out and married off. The Earl of Thornhill, being twenty-six years old, had every required attribute.

He decided on Viscount Nordal's ball in Berkeley

Square for the simple reason that both Sir Albert Boyle and Lord Francis Kneller were going there. Nordal had a daughter and a niece he was bringing out—though it would be more accurate, probably, to say that his sister, Lady Brill, was doing the bringing out. She was one of Society's dragons. But the earl, seated in his carriage on the way to Sir Albert Boyle's rooms to take him up before proceeding to Berkeley Square, shrugged his shoulders. Her brother had invited him, and if she chose to snub him, then he would put on an armor of cold haughtiness and make free with his quizzing glass.

He did not really want to be attending this ball, but it seemed the wise thing to do.

"What do these girls look like?" he asked Sir Albert when the latter had joined him in the carriage. "Does Nordal have a difficult task on his hands?"

Sir Albert shrugged. "I've never seen 'em," he said. "They must have made their curtsy to the queen this week and it is Society's turn this evening. Five pounds say they are not lookers, though, Gabe. They never are. Every maidservant in sight tonight will have oceans of beauty, but every lady will look like a horse."

The earl chuckled. "Unkind, Bertie," he said. "Perhaps they will not like the look of us either. One is supposed to look beyond outward appearance, anyway, to the character within."

Sir Albert made an indelicate noise, rather like a snort. "Or to their papas' pockets," he said. "If they are well lined, the girl's looks are insignificant, Gabe."

"You have become a cynic in my absence," the earl

said as his carriage slowed to join the line of carriages outside the house on Berkeley Square.

The hall, when they entered it, was brightly lit, and both it and the staircase were crowded with guests and humming with sound. The two gentlemen joined the line on the stairs. The earl fancied that several raised lorgnettes and several poker faces and outright frowns and whispers behind hands and fans were occasioned by his arrival. But there was nothing openly hostile.

Viscount Nordal, at the beginning of the receiving line, was affable, and even Lady Brill, playing the grand lady as her brother's hostess, nodded graciously before presenting her nieces. Lord Thornhill had an impression of two young ladies of *ton* dressed in virginal white, as was to be expected. The white gown was an almost obligatory uniform for unmarried young ladies.

And then he recognized the one standing beside Lady Brill. Miss Samantha Newman. Looking tonight more the personification of English beauty than ever. She positively sparkled with blond loveliness and was refreshingly free of the pretense of ennui that so many young ladies affected in order to make themselves appear more mature.

The Earl of Thornhill bowed to her and murmured some platitude before turning his head expectantly toward the other young lady. The Honorable Miss Jennifer Winwood.

Yes. Oh, yes, indeed. He had exaggerated nothing in memory. He was a tall man, but her eyes were on a level with his chin. And fine dark eyes they were too, more amber than brown. All the glorious dark red hair he had merely glimpsed beneath her bonnet in the park was now piled on her head with cascades of curls over her neck and temples. And she was as shapely as a dream, though he did not lower his eyes from her face to confirm the impression. Her coloring and her figure made her look as vivid as if she were dressed in scarlet. And every bit as enticing.

He bowed over her hand, murmured that he was charmed, looked deeply into her eyes to be sure that she had recognized him—how mortifying if she had not!—and moved on into the ballroom.

"Well, Bertie," he said, coming to a pause inside the doors and raising his quizzing glass to his eye to survey the scene about him, "you owe me five pounds, my dear chap. The Season has at least two lookers to offer."

"I had convinced myself," Sir Albert said, "that they must have been a figment of our imagination, Gabe. I am smitten to the heart."

"By the blonde, I suppose," the Earl of Thornhill said. "I intend to dance with the other. We will see if I have been invited merely as an aristocratic ornament, Bertie, or if I am to be allowed within striking distance of one of Society's daughters."

"Five pounds say you will be allowed close, Gabe, and encouraged to stay close," his friend said. "I'll win my money back easily."

"Ah," the earl said. "Here comes Kneller. Wearing lavender. You look too gorgeous to be real, Frank. You are out to slay the ladies, not singly, I see, but by the dozen."

IT HAD BEEN AN exciting and a frustrating fortnight. Exciting in the sense that they had prepared for their presentation at the queen's drawing room and, amidst great trepidation, had accomplished the task. And exciting too in that there had been their come-out ball to look forward to and a dizzying number of invitations to read and choose among—though that had usually meant agreeing to the events that Aunt Agatha approved and rejecting others that they might have found more tempting. And there had been fittings to enjoy and newly delivered garments to try on and exclaim over.

But it had been frustrating too. At long last they were in London and the Season had begun and all around them the *ton* were enjoying themselves with furious determination. Yet they must remain in seclusion until they had been presented and then until their come-out ball. It was enough to give even the cheeriest of mortals the dismals, Samantha had declared on more than one occasion.

It had been frustrating for Jennifer in another way too. Viscount Kersey had been to tea once. Once! He had come with his mother and had sat drinking tea and conversing for half an hour—with Jennifer, Samantha, and Aunt Agatha. He had smiled just for Jennifer as he took his leave and had kissed her hand.

But that was all she had had of the first two weeks of

her official betrothal. Yes, it was all very frustrating. And all very proper, of course. And there had been the excitement of everything else that was happening.

But at last the evening of the ball had arrived and Jennifer felt almost sick with excitement. She despised herself heartily since she was twenty years old and long past the age for such girlish reactions. But she was excited and there it was. She was not going to pretend otherwise.

She had not realized there could be so many people in all London as the numbers who passed along the receiving line into the ballroom in a seemingly endless stream. Young ladies all in white, like Samantha and herself, older ladies in brighter colors with turbans and nodding plumes, older men who bowed and smiled and paid lavish compliments, younger men who bowed and murmured all that was proper and looked assessingly. Oh, she could understand why all this was known as the marriage mart, Jennifer thought, and was glad anew that she was not really a part of it. Lord Kersey had arrived early and was already in the ballroom. He had solicited the opening set with her as was only right and proper.

There were very few people Jennifer recognized. A few of the girls and ladies who had been at the queen's drawing room. One or two of her father's friends who had called at the house during the previous two weeks. Two younger gentlemen—the two who had ridden past them and greeted them in the park that first afternoon.

Yes, he did indeed look like the devil, she thought

when her eyes alit on the dark gentleman and she recognized him instantly. He was very dark and very tall and, unlike any other gentleman she had seen, he was dressed in black—coat, waistcoat, and knee breeches. His shirt and neckcloth and cuffs and stockings looked startlingly white in contrast. He made a perfect Lucifer to Lionel's Gabriel, she thought, remembering her conversation with Samantha in the park.

He was the Earl of Thornhill. A very exalted personage indeed. He looked at her very boldly with his dark eyes—as he had done that other time. Perhaps gentlemen of his rank felt justified in taking greater liberties than other gentlemen did. She felt doubly grateful for Lord Kersey's presence in the ballroom and for the official nature of their betrothal. The Earl of Thornhill made her feel—uncomfortable.

The gentleman who had been with him in the park—Sir Albert Boyle—came after him. He smiled and bowed and went on into the ballroom. He behaved as all the other gentlemen guests had done.

But Jennifer quickly forgot about the only two young gentlemen who had been familiar to her. For actually they were not the only two. There was Viscount Kersey, who surely outshone every other gentleman in the ballroom enough to make it seem that the light from the hundreds of candles in their chandeliers shone only on him while every other gentleman stood in the shade.

It was a fanciful and ridiculous thought, she knew. She smiled at it and at him as he bowed finally over her hand and led her onto the empty floor to signal the formation of the opening set. Lord Graham, one of her father's younger acquaintances and one who had received a nod of approval from Aunt Agatha, was leading Samantha out, Jennifer knew, but she had eyes for nothing and no one except her betrothed.

He was all ice blue and silver and white. And blond. He made her heart turn over and beat with uncomfortable rapidity. She savored the moment with all her heart. It was the moment she had so long awaited. She would remember it for the rest of her life, she decided quite deliberately.

"You look extremely lovely tonight," he murmured to her as they waited for the sets to form around them and the music to begin.

"Thank you, my lord." She smiled, realizing that she had been about to return the compliment and stopping herself just in time. Though the thought struck her that she should be able to say such a thing to her betrothed. But she had seen so little of him. They would grow more comfortable in time. Now that she was out and could move freely in society, they would be together almost daily. Soon they would be comfortable together. They would be friends. She would be able to speak her thoughts to him without having first to stop to consider if they were proper.

Now, at this moment, she was in awe of him and despised herself for being so. She was being gauche and rustic. She was behaving like a seventeen-year-old fresh from the schoolroom. She consciously put on her cloak of quiet dignity, and decided to enjoy the moment for what it was worth. Everything else that she longed for would come in its own time. She must not spoil the present by longing for what would come if she but gave it time.

They danced the steps of the opening country dance in silence. Jennifer was partly glad of it. Although she had attended numerous assemblies at home and was an accomplished dancer, nevertheless she had never before danced in such surroundings and in such company. And she felt eyes on them, as was only to be expected since this was her come-out ball, and Samantha's. She was thankful for the absence of conversation so that she could concentrate on her steps. And of course the intricate patterns of the dance separated them frequently so that any sustained conversation would have been impossible.

As she became accustomed to the steps and relaxed a little, her eyes sometimes strayed beyond the confines of the set in which she danced. All these grand and richly clad lords and ladies were gathered in her honor and Sam's. It was a heady thought. And a wonderful one. At last. At last she was in London and out and officially betrothed. Her betrothal would be publicly announced in two weeks' time, and in six weeks' time she would be married.

She glanced again at the splendid blond god who was to be her bridegroom. How all the other young ladies must envy her. She wondered how general was the knowledge that they were betrothed and guessed that it was very general. Not many things remained secret for long in London society, she had heard. And this was no little thing.

And then beyond her betrothed her eye was caught by that one point of incongruity in the ballroom—by the black-clad figure of the Earl of Thornhill, who stood alone on the sidelines. No, not really alone, she saw when she focused her eyes on him. Two other gentlemen were standing with him, including Sir Albert Boyle. He just appeared to be alone because he looked so different from everyone else around him. So tall and so dark. He was watching her quite steadily, she realized. She lowered her eyes hastily and returned her attention to the dance.

He was the very antithesis of Lionel. It was so remarkable that she wondered foolishly why others were not exclaiming about it. Day and night. Summer and winter. Angel and devil. She smiled again and again wished that she was comfortable enough with her betrothed to share the joke with him.

KERSEY! THE EARL OF Thornhill noticed him a few moments after he had finished teasing Lord Francis Kneller about his lavender and silver evening clothes and then could not understand why he had not noticed the man immediately. His eyes narrowed on the viscount and he felt an unexpected surging of hatred for him.

Perhaps, he thought, he should have left London for the North and home after all. Perhaps London was not big enough for the two of them. But he would be damned before he would allow himself to be driven away by the likes of Kersey.

He forced his attention away from the man and continued his light, bantering conversation with his friends.

But his attention did not remain diverted for long.

"The devil!" he muttered when the whole assembly seemed finally to be gathered and the members of the receiving line entered the ballroom and the orchestra began its final tune-up. The first set was about to begin and the two young ladies whose come-out ball this was were being led first onto the floor by their partners. He spoke another obscenity beneath his breath.

"I could not agree more, Gabe," Sir Albert said, mock gloom in his voice. "Graham has cut me out and broken my heart. But that is not what ails you, is it? Kersey has done the like for you. Perhaps we should go home and put bullets in our brains."

Viscount Kersey was leading out the delicious redhead—Miss Jennifer Winwood. The devil himself, looking rather like an angel in his pale splendor, was bending over innocence, murmuring something into her ear. Lord Thornhill found that he had clamped his teeth together. He wondered what Nordal would do if he knew. Probably nothing. It was, after all, merely a dance, even though Kersey had been chosen to partner Nordal's daughter in perhaps the most important dance of her life. Anyway, there were not many men who would condemn another for making sport with someone else's wife. To say it was common practice was hardly to exaggerate. It was not even uncommon for one man to impregnate another man's wife. The only unpardonable indiscretion would be to do so before the wife had presented her husband with a legitimate male heir. Kersey had not been that indiscreet, although Catherine herself had borne no other child. And of course, far more unpardonable was to make sport with one's own father's wife. Kersey had not done that either.

"They look rather like something come straight down from heaven, do they not?" Sir Francis Kneller said at Lord Thornhill's side. He nodded in the direction of Kersey and Miss Winwood. "While the rest of us ordinary mortals have to settle for what is left. A lowering thought, eh, Gabe? Though there is nothing ordinary about you, it must be admitted. The choice of black tonight was inspired, old chap. You look positively satanic. The ladies will think it very appropriate—and will doubtless be panting all over you." He chuckled merrily.

"One wonders," the earl said, his eyes following the couple as they began to dance, "what Kersey has done to be so in favor with Nordal that he has been granted such an honor. Apart from being rather beautiful, of course." He did not try to hide the contempt in his voice. It really was not difficult to understand why Catherine, married to his elderly and infirm father, had fallen so recklessly in love with the viscount.

Sir Francis laughed again. "You have not heard?" he said. "It is a crying shame, if you were to ask me, when she is one of the few beauties in this year's crop. But it is ever thus, is it not?" He sighed and raised his quizzing glass the better to watch Miss Winwood dance.

"What is ever thus?" the earl asked. "Never tell me she has the pox, Frank. What a waste."

"Betrothed to Kersey," Sir Francis said gloomily. "Wedding to take place some time before the end of the Season, if gossip has the right of it. At St. George's with the flower of the *ton* present, I would not doubt. Of course, there is still her cousin, the equally delectable Miss Newman. More delectable, in fact. I have always had a soft spot for blondes, as what red-blooded blade has not? She has a more than respectable dowry too, so I have heard. It may be just a lure, of course, and will dwindle alarmingly as soon as one has committed oneself to showing a definite interest."

"The blonde is spoken for," Sir Albert said. "I spoke her name—though actually I did not know it at the time—in the park two weeks ago, did I not, Gabe? Do you think I should slap a glove in Graham's face at the end of the set?"

"Why wait until the end?" Sir Francis asked and the two men chuckled with hearty amusement.

The Earl of Thornhill was not listening to them. Betrothed! Poor girl. He pitied her deeply. And felt a certain anger on her behalf. She deserved better. Though perhaps not. He did not know her, after all, and had been given the impression of a certain haughty reserve both in the park and in the receiving line tonight. Perhaps possessing Kersey's title and fortune and beauty would be enough for her. Perhaps she was in love with him.

*Probably* she was in love with him. There was something in the way she looked at him that suggested it.

And perhaps he loved her, the earl thought cynically, or the dowry that would come with her. Nordal was reputed to be wealthy enough. Perhaps Kersey was now ready to settle into a dull and blameless married life. It would not be difficult to settle for the redhead of the long legs, the earl thought, his eyes watching that last feature as she danced. Long and obviously shapely as outlined against the soft silk and lace of her high-waisted gown. And surely it would not be difficult to be satisfied with such loveliness and such voluptuousness for a lifetime.

Yes, perhaps it was appropriate, he thought, as he continued to watch them dance. They matched each other in beauty and in a certain icy aloofness.

And then his eyes met the girl's across the room as she danced. She did not immediately look away and he deliberately held her eyes with his own until she did. Lord, she was a desirable woman. There was a certain incongruity between that glorious red hair and well-endowed body on the one hand and the virginal white and the air of aloofness on the other. Miss Jennifer Winwood did not look either virginal or cold. At least, she did not look as if she should be. That hair should be loose and spread over a pillow. Those breasts should be bared and lifting from a bed to touch a man's chest.

Of course, she would not be virginal for much longer. That hair would indeed be released and those breasts bared and those legs twined—about Kersey's. There was something almost obscene in the thought, and definitely unseemly. His mind was not in the habit of wandering into other men's beds.

He wished Kersey and Miss Winwood happy in their forthcoming marriage, he thought, his eyes narrowing on them. Or rather, to the contrary, if he was to be more honest with himself, he wished their marriage to the devil. Unwilling hatred festered in him as he watched them dance and his two friends continued to chuckle over the witticisms they were exchanging.

What he would really like was to see Kersey suffer as Catherine had suffered, Lord Thornhill thought. Or even a fraction as much as she had suffered. He would like to see the redhead break his heart or otherwise make his life miserable. Though that hardly seemed fair to her. His eyes rested on her again. He did not know her at all and should take his own advice about looking beyond outward appearances to the character within, but she was gloriously beautiful. Kersey did not deserve the happiness of possessing such beauty.

The earl watched the girl for the rest of the set, his eyes narrowed in speculation. He was certainly going to dance with her himself before the evening was out if it could possibly be arranged. The beginnings of an idea were niggling at the corners of his mind.

Yes, he thought, revenge would be sweet. Even just a little revenge. And there just might be a way to get it.

"Is this not the most heavenly night you have ever lived through?" Samantha asked Jennifer later in the evening during one of the rare moments when they were able to exchange a private word. "Four sets and four different partners apiece. Mr. Maxwell is going to dance with me again later. He is not the most handsome gentleman here, Jenny, but he does make me laugh. He says the most outrageous things about everyone around us."

She was glowing, Jennifer saw, and looking even lovelier than usual if that were possible. Only someone with Samantha's modesty could possibly have doubted that she would take the *ton* by storm, as the saying went. There was not another lady present to match her in loveliness.

"Yes, so is Lord Kersey," she said with a sigh. "Going to dance with me again, that is. I hate this rule that one can dance with the same partner no more than twice. It was the first dance and I was nervous and watching my steps. I feel as if I have spent no time with him at all." In imagination, in her dreams of what tonight would be like, she had danced the night away with Lionel, both of them aware only of each other. It had been an enchanted night—in her dreams. But of course she had known that propriety would keep them apart much of the evening. Sometimes she almost hated propriety.

Viscount Kersey had danced with Samantha and then had disappeared, presumably to the card room, which everyone knew no one but the dowagers and elderly gentlemen were meant to use. But even if he had stayed in the ballroom, he could not have danced with her again. Or if he had, she would have nothing left to look forward to for the rest of the evening.

In her dreams too she had pictured them alone together. Just for a short while. Just long enough so that they could smile into each other's eyes quite privately and exchange their first kiss. Ah, it had been a wonderful dream—and a rather silly one, she supposed.

But perhaps it really would happen later in the evening. Perhaps he would claim the supper dance—surely it would be strange if he did not, and the supper dance was next. And perhaps he would contrive to lead her from the dining room a little sooner than everyone else.

She had looked at his mouth as they danced. She had imagined his lips touching hers and had felt hot all over at the thought. It was ridiculous. By the age of twenty she should at least know what a man's lips felt like.

And then her thoughts were very effectively distracted. A gentleman was bowing before her and soliciting her hand for the next set—for the supper set. A tall gentleman dressed all in black and white. The Earl of Thornhill. Jennifer looked around, startled. Her aunt had brought all her other partners to her. But Aunt Agatha was some distance away, her attention monopolized by a very large and imposing elderly lady in purple.

This was the supper dance. Where was Lionel? She had set her heart on dancing it with him. But he was nowhere in sight. How mortifying!

"Thank you, my lord," she said, dropping a slight curtsy. "It would be my pleasure." She wished there had been a way of refusing. There must have been a way—but she did not know it.

She did not enjoy the dance. He was very tall, far taller than Lionel, and somehow—threatening. No, not that, she told herself when the word leapt to mind. *Disturbing* was perhaps a better word. He watched her constantly, and his dark eyes somehow compelled her to look back so that for several measures of the dance, when they were face-to-face, she found herself gazing into his eyes and feeling somehow enveloped in something to which she could not put a name at all. He spoke occasionally.

"I was beginning to believe," he said, "that I had imagined you."

He was referring to that afternoon in the park, she supposed.

"Until tonight," she said, "I have not been out and have been unable to attend parties."

"I gather that after tonight," he said, "you will be seen everywhere. I must make sure, then, that I am everywhere too."

Perhaps she should tell him that she was betrothed, she thought uneasily, but she stopped herself from doing so. His words were the typical gallantry that she must expect in London. He would be amused if he thought she had misunderstood.

"That would be pleasant," she said.

He smiled suddenly, and his severe, satanic features were transformed into an expression that was undoubtedly attractive. "I can almost hear you saying the same words to a tooth-drawer," he said. "In just the same tone of voice."

The idea was so ludicrous and unexpected that she laughed.

"I was wrong," he said softly. "I thought that perhaps you had never been taught to smile. But better than that, you know how to laugh."

She sobered instantly. He was flirting with her, she thought. And she found him a little frightening, though she had no idea why. Perhaps because at heart she was still just a gauche little schoolgirl and did not know how to handle gentlemen who had a great deal of town bronze.

Soon after they had started to dance, she caught sight of Lord Kersey, who had returned to the ballroom. Their eyes met briefly and she fancied that he looked annoyed. Indeed, that was perhaps an understatement. For one moment he looked furious. But he had no right to be either. He had not asked for this set and had come late to claim it. Surely he must know how she longed to be dancing it with him. Oh, surely he knew. She tried to tell him so with her eyes, but he had looked away.

A few moments later she saw that he was dancing with Samantha—again. She could have cried with frustration and disappointment. And quite unreasonably she hated the dark gentleman—the Earl of Thornhill—though he could not have known that she had been waiting hopefully for just this set with her betrothed.

He led her in to supper when the set came to an end. She had hoped against reason that somehow he would excuse himself and Lord Kersey would come to take his place. But Lionel, of course, was obliged to lead in

Samantha, having danced with her. She could stamp her foot in bad temper, Jennifer thought, but fortunately the foolishness of the mental image of herself doing just that restored her sense of humor and she had to struggle with herself not to laugh aloud.

The Earl of Thornhill found her a seat at a table in one corner that was so crowded with flowers that there was not really room for anyone but the two of them. Indeed, it seemed that the table had not been intended to be sat at at all. Aunt Agatha had intended that she sit at the central table with Lord Kersey and Samantha and her escort, Jennifer knew, but somehow the plan had gone awry. Her aunt was frowning at her now, but what was she to do? Aunt Agatha should have been attending to her duty before the last set and then this would not have happened. Samantha and Lord Kersey sat together at the central table.

"I gather," the Earl of Thornhill said, "that a presentation to the queen is easily the worst ordeal of a young lady's life. Is it true? Do tell me about your presentation."

Jennifer sighed. "Oh, the ridiculous clothes," she said. "I will never know why we are not allowed to wear the sort of clothes we would wear to—well, an occasion like this, for example. All those fittings and all that expense for a few minutes of one's life. And the curtsy, practiced over and over again for months on end and all over and done with in a few seconds. Perhaps it was the worst ordeal of my life, my lord. It was also the most ridiculous."

He looked amused. "You may find yourself in a closely guarded cell in the Tower awaiting execution at the chopping block if you shout that opinion into the wrong ears," he said.

She felt herself coloring. What on earth had possessed her to speak so candidly?

"Tell me about it," he said. "I have always wanted to know what happens at those drawing rooms, and I believe I have always been rather thankful that I am male."

She told him all about it and he told her that he had been traveling for the past year and more and described parts of France and Switzerland to her. There could be no part of the world lovelier than the Alps, he told her, and she believed him, listening to his descriptions.

She was unaware of what she ate or did not eat during supper. And she was unaware of how much time passed or did not pass before the people around them began to leave their tables and wander back in the direction of the ballroom.

It was not fair, she thought as the Earl of Thornhill conducted her back there and then bowed over her hand before removing himself both from her presence and from the ballroom, that that time and that splendid opportunity for conversation should have been wasted with him when she might have been with Lionel. She grudgingly admitted that she had enjoyed both talking and listening to him. But it was what she had dreamed of doing with Lionel. And now the opportunity was gone for the night. Lord Kersey would dance with her again, but there would be no chance to talk with each other, to laugh together, to get to know each other a little better.

The evening was spoiled. The Earl of Thornhill had

spoiled it for her, though that was an unfair condemnation. It was not his fault that Aunt Agatha had been delayed by the lady in purple and that Lord Kersey had been late returning to the ballroom. And he really had made an effort to make himself agreeable to her. Under any other circumstances she might have been gratified by his attention, for he was without a doubt as handsome in his own way as Lionel was in his.

Devil and angel. No, that was not fair.

Oh, but she had so longed for a conversation of just that nature with Lionel. He was approaching her now with Aunt Agatha. She smiled at him and felt her heart flutter.

# 4

*H*OW COULD SHE POSSIBLY BE FEELING DEPRESSED? She was not, Jennifer told herself firmly late the following morning. It was just that she was still a little tired. The downstairs salon was almost laden with flowers, roughly half of them hers and half Samantha's. But despite all the excitement of the day before and the very late night, Sam was bubbling with exuberance.

"So many gentlemen sending us flowers, Jenny," she said, her arms spread wide eventually so that she looked as if she were dancing in a garden. "Some of the names I can scarce put faces to, I must confess. This is so very wonderful. I know it is the thing to send ladies flowers the morning after their come-out, but at least some of them must have come from genuine admiration, must they not?"

"Yes." Jennifer touched her fingers lightly to a leaf on the largest bouquet of all. She felt a little like crying and could not at all understand herself—or forgive herself. She had every reason to be gloriously happy. The evening had been a wonderful success—for both of them. There had not been enough sets to enable them to dance with all the gentlemen who had asked them.

"That one, for example." Samantha laughed. "Lord Kersey must have ordered the very largest bouquet the shop was able to provide. You must be ecstatic. You looked very splendid together, Jenny. Everyone was saying so. And everyone knows that you are betrothed. The announcement might as well have been put in the papers already."

"He looked marvelously handsome, did he not?" Jennifer asked wistfully, thinking back to her disappointment of the evening before—though she would not openly admit anything had been disappointing. As she had expected, Lionel had danced with her again after supper, but there had been little opportunity to talk. Dancing was not conducive to conversation, except perhaps the waltz. But there had been no waltzes last night because she and Samantha and many of the other young ladies would not have been allowed to dance it. There had been no chance yet for them to be approved by any of the patronesses of Almack's. A lady was not allowed to waltz until one of them gave the nod.

"And he even sent me a nosegay," Samantha said, lifting one and smelling its fragrance. "Was that not kind of him? I am sorry I ever called him cold. I shall never do so again. A gentleman who sends me a nosegay cannot possibly be cold." She laughed once more. "Do you suppose we will have callers this afternoon? Aunt Aggy said it is to be expected. I keep wanting to pinch myself to prove this is all real, but then I stop myself from doing so in case it is not."

Jennifer touched one of her own nosegays but did not

pick it up. Roses. Red roses. It must not be easy to find roses at this time of year.

He had not returned to the ballroom. He must have gone home after supper or else spent the rest of the evening in the card room. She still resented the fact that the half hour or so she might have spent with Lionel during the supper break had been spent with him instead, that the conversation she might have been having with her betrothed had been had with the Earl of Thornhill instead. But then, if she had been with Lionel they would have been at the central table and would still have had no chance for private conversation. And Viscount Kersey had not been traveling in Europe for the past year and more and would not have been able to entertain her with all those stories and to fill her with longing to see it all for herself.

It had not been the earl's fault. She knew that. But she resented him anyway. It was unfair, but it was sometimes impossible to be fair when the heart was involved. She touched the tip of one finger to the petal of a rose and bent her head to breathe in the scent.

Actually she did have positive reason for feeling resentment—against both him and Aunt Agatha. Aunt Agatha had told her at the end of the evening that she ought not to have danced with the Earl of Thornhill and that she certainly ought not to have allowed him to maneuver her to a table in the dining room where no one else could join them.

"I cannot understand my brother's inviting him," Lady Brill had said. "He is an earl, of course, and has a vast fortune besides being the owner of one of the most prosperous estates in England. But even so he is not a suitable guest at a ball with young and innocent ladies. I would have discouraged him quite adamantly if he had asked you or Samantha to dance in my hearing."

"I did not know, Aunt," Jennifer had said. "And he did ask most politely. How could I have said no?"

"He has an unsavory reputation," Lady Brill had said, "and should have had the grace to stay away from you. You must have nothing more to do with him, Jennifer. If you see him again, you must nod politely but in that way all ladies must acquire of indicating that you wish no further acquaintance. If he persists, you will be obliged to give him the cut direct."

She would not say what had given the earl an unsavory reputation and appeared shocked that Jennifer had even thought to ask.

He should not have asked her to dance. He should not have steered her to that particular table. But it would not happen again. She would do what Aunt Agatha had directed if he should approach her again. In less than two weeks' time her betrothal would be announced and then she would be quite safe from any other gentleman, however savory or unsavory his reputation.

"It is a fine day," Samantha said, wandering to the window and staring upward, "even though the sun is not shining. Do you suppose we will have invitations to drive in the park, Jenny? If any gentlemen call on us this afternoon, that is. Oh, I do hope so. On both counts. Of course, you need feel no anxiety. Lord Kersey is bound to call and he will take you driving. But I must live in suspense."

Jennifer linked her arm with her cousin's and they left the room together. "Before you complain further," she said, "think back one month, Sam, and one year and two years. Then the most exciting thing we had to look forward to was a walk to the village to change the floral arrangements on the altar in church."

"Oh, yes," Samantha agreed. "Yes, that is true, is it not? If there are no visitors this afternoon and no drive, there is still tomorrow, of course, and the Chisleys' ball."

And Lionel would surely come, Jennifer thought.

HE HAD SENT HER a nosegay during the morning. Nothing too lavish, merely what any gentleman might be expected to send the morning after attending her come-out ball. But he did send roses, exorbitantly expensive at this time of year, and he did deliberately neglect to send flowers to the little blonde although normal courtesy would have prompted him to do so.

He did not pay a call at Berkeley Square during the afternoon, though he pondered the idea and was very tempted when he discovered that Sir Albert was going to do so. Attending a ball at the house among hundreds of other guests and attending a drawing room among perhaps only a dozen or so were vastly different matters. He might be made to feel actively unwelcome in the drawing room. At the very least he would be frozen out by the dragon who was the girl's aunt and who had let down her guard over her charges for only that one moment of which he had taken full advantage the night before.

No, he would not call at Berkeley Square. But he would ride in the park at the fashionable hour and hope to see her there. She was almost sure to be there the day after her come-out ball. It was, after all, the fashionable thing to do. Kersey would doubtless take her driving there. It would be perfect.

He would take things slowly, Lord Thornhill decided anew this morning as he had decided last evening when the idea had first come to him. The woman was reserved and neither silly nor empty-headed. Indeed, he had been amused by her wit as she had described the queen's drawing room. He guessed that she was older than most of the young girls currently making their come-out. She seemed older. She would not be easily led astray. Especially from Kersey. Even sensible ladies would not find it difficult to fall in love with Kersey, he guessed. Catherine had done so and she had always appeared to him to be a woman of sense.

But lead her astray he would, the long-legged, voluptuous redhead. The fact that it would not be easy made it a more exhilarating challenge. She was betrothed even though no public announcement had yet been made. Probably it would be made soon. According to Kneller, the wedding was to take place before the end of the Season. It would be better if the announcement had been made. A public scandal, a broken engagement in the middle of the Season—it would be a nasty humiliation for Kersey. It would not be exactly an eye for an eye. But it would be satisfying enough.

Revenge—even a small amount of revenge—would be very sweet. And the desire for it at the moment was so consuming him that it was even drowning out conscience.


VISCOUNT KERSEY HAD COME to call at Berkeley Square, along with an amazingly large number of other gentlemen—and some ladies. It was very gratifying, especially for Samantha, who still had not learned that her beauty and vitality would draw gentlemen like bees to flowers. Jennifer was pleased for her, and both pleased and frustrated for herself. Pleased because several of the visitors made a point of sitting close to her and conversing with her, frustrating because Lionel stood back and let others monopolize her attention.

But he had asked soon after his arrival if she would drive with him in his curricle to the park later. And so during the hour or so when her father's drawing room was crowded with visitors she could console herself with the sight of him, as splendid in elegant day clothes as he had been in silk and lace the evening before. And with the knowledge that at last—oh, at last—they would be alone together afterward for an hour or more, driving out in the fresh air and the beauty that was Hyde Park.

It was a naive hope. She realized it quite early in the outing. Hyde Park at five o'clock in the afternoon was not the place one went to in order to be alone with someone or to enjoy some private conversation. Rotten Row proved to be an even greater squeeze than her father's ballroom had been last evening. All the fashionable world was there, strolling or riding or driving in a variety of fashionable conveyances.

But it was wonderful, nevertheless, to be riding up beside Lionel, almost shoulder to shoulder with him, to be seen there, to know that most people were well aware of the connection between them.

"This is amazing," she said. "Samantha and I walked here a couple of weeks ago but earlier in the afternoon. There was no one here." Except for two gentlemen on horseback, one dark and bold-eyed.

"There is a fashionable time for taking the air," Viscount Kersey said. "There is no point in being here at any other time of day."

"Except really to take the air and exercise," she said with a smile and a twirl of her parasol.

He looked at her uncomprehendingly and she felt foolish. One always felt foolish when one made a joke that the other person did not understand. But it had admittedly been a feeble joke.

"Do you ever find at the end of the Season that you long to return to the country in order to see and enjoy nature without all the distractions?" she asked.

"I prefer civilized living," he said.

It was almost the extent of their conversation. One came to Hyde Park, Jennifer soon realized, not in order to drive or ride or walk, but in order to bow and wave and smile and converse and gossip. It was amazing, considering the fact that she had been officially out for less than twenty-four hours, how many people she now knew and how many of them stopped to exchange pleasantries with her and Lord Kersey.

He was a great favorite with the ladies, of course. It became quickly apparent to Jennifer that those who stopped did so more to gaze at and talk with him than to converse with her. But the realization amused rather than annoyed her. She felt a wonderful possessive warmth, knowing that he was hers, knowing that all these women must be green with envy because he had chosen her as his bride.

And if the ladies stopped for his benefit, several gentlemen stopped for hers. It was flattering to know that she had attracted notice even though it must be common knowledge that she was betrothed. Unlike Samantha, she had not wondered incessantly for the last several months and even years if she would be attractive to gentlemen. She had been concerned only with being attractive for Lord Kersey. She had assumed that no other man would afford her a second glance knowing that she was not part of the great marriage mart.

The Earl of Thornhill was riding in the park, looking less satanic than he had last evening in a blue riding coat and buff pantaloons and Hessians. But he had a powerful presence. Even amid the crush of fashionable persons she saw him when he was quite a distance away. And hoped that he would not come close so that she would not have to treat him with the chill courtesy Aunt

Agatha had directed. She wished she knew what had given him an unsavory reputation. Though it was unladylike to want to know any such thing.

Her attention was distracted by Lord Graham, Samantha's first partner of the evening before, and another gentleman, who stopped to pay their respects. When they rode on, Jennifer found that the earl was close by and looking directly at her—as he seemed always to be doing. She inclined her head to him, hoping that he would ride on past.

He stopped and touched his hat. "Miss Winwood, Kersey," he said. "Fine day."

"Thornhill," the viscount said stiffly and made to move on with his curricle. But the earl had laid a careless arm along the frame below the seat on which Jennifer sat.

"I trust you are rested after your success last evening," he said, looking directly into her eyes, ignoring the viscount.

"Yes, I thank you." How did one maintain the proper chill when such dark eyes gazed into one's own and when they were the type of eyes it was almost impossible to look away from? "Thank you for the nosegay," she said, without having intended to mention it. "It must have been difficult to find roses at this time of year. They are lovely."

"Are they?" He did something with his eyes so that they smiled though the rest of his face did not. It was quite disconcerting, Jennifer found.

"Yes," she said lamely, and wondered if she was blushing. She hoped not, but her cheeks felt hot.

He withdrew his arm from the curricle and sat upright in the saddle again. Jennifer wondered idly if it was just that his horse was larger than anyone else's or if it was his superior height that made it seem that he towered over everyone else in the park.

"But not more lovely than their recipient," he said, his voice making it sound as if they were quite alone together, and he touched his hat again and inclined his head, without looking at all at Lord Kersey.

It had all happened in a few seconds. Several other people had spent longer beside their curricle. And yet she felt ruffled, disturbed, conspicuous. She felt that everyone must be looking at her and wondering why the Earl of Thornhill should be showing a particular interest in her when she was betrothed to Viscount Kersey. She was being foolish, she knew. She twirled her parasol and looked about her. Samantha, riding up beside Mr. Maxwell in his phaeton, was laughing gaily at something a trio of young riders were saying. Mr. Maxwell was laughing too.

"I do not believe it is wise," the viscount said beside her, his voice stiff with something that sounded almost like fury, "to allow the Earl of Thornhill to make free with you, Miss Winwood."

"What?" She turned her head sharply to look at him. "Make free, my lord?" She bristled.

"I was surprised and not altogether pleased that your father saw fit to invite him to your come-out ball last evening," he said. "I was even less pleased that your aunt allowed you to dance a set with him and accompany him in to supper."

"Aunt Agatha did not allow it," she said. "She was otherwise engaged when he asked me. I did not know there was any reason to say no. He was an invited guest in Papa's house, after all."

"You must have known," he said, "that I would come to claim your hand for the supper dance."

"How was I to know?" she asked. "You had not mentioned it. And you were not in the ballroom when the set was about to begin. It was what I had hoped for, but you were not there. It would have been unmannerly not to have accepted Lord Thornhill or anyone else who asked at that particular moment."

"Now you know that he is not respectable," he said, "you will be able to avoid him in future. It is my opinion that he should not be admitted anywhere with respectable people. I especially do not like him to be in company with my betrothed."

Jealousy. The irritation Jennifer had been feeling melted instantly. He was jealous. And possessive of her. He did not want her exposed to an influence that he felt to be less than proper. Or to the attentions of a gentleman who was undoubtedly handsome. She gazed at him and wished that he would turn to her and take her hand in his or show some definite sign of his affection for her.

And then he did both. And smiled. "You are such an innocent," he said.

She winced inwardly. She was twenty years old and

did not like being treated as if she were still a child. But she did like to be the object of his solicitation. Her eyes strayed downward to his mouth. They had driven away from the crush on Rotten Row and were almost private together—a rare moment. Would he have found the opportunity to kiss her last night? she wondered. He really had intended to dance the supper dance with her. There would have been the opportunity—if they had lagged behind everyone else on the way to the dining room or if they had left it ahead of everyone else.

"What has he done that has put him so far beyond the pale?" she asked. She was not so naive that she did not know it was fairly common practice for young unmarried gentlemen—and some married ones too—to consort with women of a certain type. Perhaps even Lionel—but no, she could not think that of him. She would not. He was too proper a gentleman. But she could not believe it was just that with the Earl of Thornhill. It must be something more unusual, something worse—if there was anything worse.

He looked at her and frowned. "It would not be seemly for you to know," he said. "Suffice it to say that he is guilty of one of the most heinous sins man is capable of. He should have been forced to stay on the Continent where he was instead of contaminating England's shores by returning."

Exile? It had been exile, then, that had driven the Earl of Thornhill to his almost two years abroad? And what was one of the most heinous sins? *Sin* was the word Lord

Kersey had used, not crime. What had he done? It was not seemly that she know. But curiosity gnawed at her.

The viscount lifted her down when they returned to the house on Berkeley Square, his hands at her waist. For a moment his hands lingered there and when Jennifer looked up into his face she thought that he was going to kiss her. In full view of the houses across the street and of the footman who had just opened the doors into the house. But he released her and raised her hand to his lips instead.

"Until tomorrow evening," he said. "You will reserve the opening set for me at the Chisleys' ball?"

"Yes, of course," she said.

"And the supper dance?" His smile had never failed to make her insides somersault.

She smiled back. "Yes," she said. "And the supper dance, my lord."

She was still smiling as she entered the house alone and ran lightly upstairs to her room. Tomorrow night. Tomorrow night he would kiss her. Everything in his look and his smile had said so. She felt a surging of renewed happiness. She could scarcely wait for tomorrow evening.

IT WAS QUITE BY accident that the Earl of Thornhill saw Jennifer entering the library with her cousin and a maid late the following morning. He was with two acquaintances but excused himself and followed the ladies inside. It was too good an opportunity to be missed.

A few people were reading the papers. Some of them looked up to see who the new arrival was. A few more people were browsing over the shelves of books. Miss Winwood was among them, at a different shelf from her cousin. The maid stood quietly inside the door, waiting for her charges to choose books.

The earl waited until Jennifer turned a corner and paused to look at a case of books that conveniently hid her from the front of the library.

"Ah," he said softly, stepping up behind her, "a fellow reader."

He had startled her. She whirled about to face him so that her back was to the bookcase. He was glad that he had stood so close. Even amidst the semidarkness of the shelves and the dust of books she looked startlingly lovely. He still had not satisfied himself as to the exact color of her eyes. But they were wide and beautiful eyes.

"Good morning, my lord," she said. "I am borrowing a book."

He smiled and waited until she realized the absurdity of her own words and smiled unwillingly back—he guessed that it was unwillingly. He guessed too that she had been warned against him. She had looked guilty and almost terrified when she first turned. He wondered what they had told her of him. In particular, he wondered what Kersey had told her.

"So I see." He took the book that was tucked under her arm and raised his eyebrows. "Pope? You like his poetry?"

"I do not know," she said. "But I mean to find out."

"You like poetry?" he asked. "You have tried Wordsworth or Coleridge?"

"Both," she said. "And I love both. Mr. Pope is quite different, I have heard. Perhaps I will love him just as well. I do not believe that liking one type of literature means that one will not like another type. Do you? It would give one a very narrow scope of interest."

"Quite," he said. "Do you like novels? Richardson, for example?"

She smiled again. "I liked *Pamela* until I read Mr. Fielding's *Joseph Andrews*," she said, "and realized how he had made fun of the other book and how right he was to do so. I was ashamed that I had not seen for myself how hypocritical Pamela was."

"But that is one purpose of literature, surely," he said. "To help us see aspects of our world that we had not thought of for ourselves. To broaden our horizons and our minds. To make us more critical and more liberal in our thinking."

"Yes," she said. "Yes, you are right." And then she blushed and looked around her and licked her lips and he guessed that she had just remembered she was not supposed to be talking with him.

"I do not attack young ladies in dark corners of libraries," he said. "But I understand that you must go."

"Yes," she said, looking warily at him. He had not stood back to enable her to pass.

"You will be at the Chisleys' ball this evening?" he asked.

She nodded.

"You will reserve a set for me?" he asked. "The second, perhaps? Doubtless you will dance the first with your betrothed."

"You know?" she said.

"Perhaps you have not been in town long enough to realize how impossible it is to keep a secret," he said. "And I do not believe your engagement is even meant to be an official secret, is it?"

"No," she said.

"You will dance the second set with me?"

She hesitated and swallowed. "Thank you," she said. "That would be pleasant."

"It would," he agreed. "But I wish you would not keep looking at me when you say so as if you saw me as an executioner with his hood on and his ax over his shoulder."

He held her eyes with his until she smiled.

"Until this evening," he said, stepping back at last. "Every minute until then will seem an hour long and every hour a day."

"How absurd," she said.

"Most things in life are," he agreed.

She hesitated and then whisked herself past him.

"Your book," he said.

She looked back at him, mortified, and held out one hand for it. He placed it in her hand, making sure that his fingers brushed against hers as he let it go.

A very fortunate encounter, he thought. Luck was on his side. He had no doubt it would rattle Kersey to see him dance with Miss Winwood this evening. It would be a pleasure to rattle Kersey.

He just wished, the earl thought as he left the library five minutes later, after the ladies had already done so, that it was a different lady. He had the uncomfortable feeling that beneath the vividly beautiful and desirable body that housed Miss Winwood was a rather likable person. An intelligent one with a sense of humor. Someone whom in other circumstances he might have liked to befriend.

But he shut his mind to conscience. He did not want to be deflected from his purpose. The prospect of making Kersey look a fool was just too tempting for the present.

# 5

THE DAY HAD BEEN UNSEASONABLY WARM. THE evening was cooler, but the indoors still held the heat of the day. The French windows along the length of the Chisley ballroom had been thrown back to admit as much air as possible and to allow the guests to dance or stroll on the wide balcony beyond and even to descend to the lantern-lit garden below if they so chose.

It was a great squeeze of an event, it being the come-out of the middle Chisley girl. The Earl of Thornhill made his bow to her in the receiving line after passing by her mother, whose manner dripped ice almost visibly. It was quite unexceptional for his lordship to attend and add luster to her ball, that manner said quite audibly, but let him not expect to dance with Miss Horatia Chisley. Not this evening or any other evening of the Season.

"Well, I am for dancing," Lord Francis Kneller said as they looked about them in the ballroom. "I promised my sister that I would lead out Rosalie Ogden—younger sister of her particular friend, you know. The girl has not taken well." He grimaced. "Nothing for a dowry and nothing much for a face either."

"It is admirable of you to be willing to do your civic duty, Frank," the earl said, raising his quizzing glass to his eye. Yes, they had arrived already, and were being closely guarded by Lady Brill. He wondered if he would after all be able to get past the redoubtable old dragon. Would she agree that a promise given at the library this morning must be honored? "And how about you, Bertie? Have you come with the intention of tripping the light fantastic?"

"Not all night long," Sir Albert replied. "One does not mind being seen to be browsing at the marriage mart, Gabe, but one would not wish to be thought to be shopping in earnest. The very prospect makes me nervous. Point out Miss Ogden to me, Frank, and I'll dance with her too. I like your sister. Miss Newman promised me a set when I called at Berkeley Square yesterday afternoon. I had better claim it early. She is going to be besieged."

"And you, Gabe?" Lord Francis asked as their friend strolled away to join the group of young men beginning to gather about the little blond beauty.

"Later," the earl said. The ball was about to begin. Miss Horatia Chisley was being led onto the floor by a young gentleman whose shirt points looked in imminent danger of piercing his eyeballs, and sets were beginning to form. "I intend to stand here and ogle the ladies for a while."

Lord Francis chuckled and moved away.

She was wearing white again—of course. She would wear it all through the spring. And yet she had a way of making white look like the most vivid of colors. Tonight's gown was rather lower in the bosom and more heavily flounced at the hem. It shimmered with lace overlaying satin. She was dancing with Kersey, who was looking startlingly gorgeous in silver and pink. The earl surveyed the viscount through his glass with some distaste. Pink! There was something distinctly feminine about the color. It was worse even than Frank's lavender at the Nordal ball. And yet Kersey was drawing female admiration as he always did.

Jennifer Winwood had eyes for no one else. She smiled with unfashionable warmth at her betrothed. Despite the intelligence and sense and wit that Thornhill had seen in her, she was not immune to the beauty and charm of Kersey, it seemed. She was very probably in love with the man. He hoped not. Not that he would balk at the challenge if she were. He just hoped she was not.

He just wished that, having decided upon some small measure of revenge, he did not have to involve a third person. Especially an innocent.

It would be as well for this particular innocent in more ways than one if her feelings were not deeply engaged. Persistent inquiries over the past few days had revealed that Kersey kept two mistresses, one a dancer of recent acquisition, the other a former seamstress who had already borne him two children. He was also known to frequent brothels more often than one would expect of a man who had established mistresses on whom to slake his appetites.

It seemed unlikely that such a man would suddenly become a model husband on his marriage. It would be as well if Miss Winwood, like most wives, did not expect either fidelity or devotion. It would be disastrous for her if she loved Kersey.

Though that would be her problem, not his, the earl thought grimly, turning his glass on her for a moment before lowering it. But good Lord, how could any man, betrothed to such a woman, contemplating marriage with her within the next few months, need anyone else? And how would any man after marriage with her have energy left or desire to expend on another woman?

The Earl of Thornhill waited with some impatience and some trepidation for the set to end and for the second to form. Though trepidation waned after Miss Newman, dancing the intricate steps of a vigorous country dance right before his eyes, had her hem stepped on by some clumsy oaf and a ruffle dragged too awkwardly to enable her to continue the dance. A few moments later, just as the music was drawing to a close, she left the ballroom with Lady Brill, obviously bound for the ladies' withdrawing room and a quick repair there by the maids and seamstresses who would be kept on hand for just such an emergency.

The fates appeared to be on his side, the earl thought. And Kersey, aware that his fiancée's chaperone had disappeared, was remaining at her side like a true gentleman and watchdog. It was perfect!

JENNIFER WAS NOT ABLE to enjoy the opening set even though she was dancing it with Lord Kersey and he had smiled at her and complimented her on her appearance and reminded her that she was to save the supper dance for him. And even though, as usual, he was looking quite splendidly handsome in pale colors that made his blondness dazzling.

She could not draw her mind free of the foolish promise she had given at the library. She had been warned against the Earl of Thornhill by both Aunt Agatha and Lord Kersey. Lionel had said that the earl was guilty of some heinous sin. And her own instinct warned her against him. She did not like the way he looked at her so directly and so boldly with his dark eyes. She did not like the look of him, handsome as he undoubtedly was. He was so very different from Lionel. Besides, she had no interest whatsoever in any man but her betrothed.

And yet she had allowed herself to be drawn into conversation with him at the library. She had allowed herself to laugh with him. It somehow seemed unseemly to laugh with another man—almost intimate. And worst of all—a brief conversation was quite unexceptionable, she supposed—she had agreed to dance the second set at the Chisley ball with him.

The knowledge of her foolishness had weighed heavily on her ever since. And to compound her foolishness, she had not even told anyone. Not even Samantha, who should have been easy to tell since she had seen him in the library and had commented on his presence there. She had not told Aunt Agatha or Lord Kersey. She positively dreaded the moment when he would come to claim his dance. If Aunt Agatha tried to steer him away, then Jennifer was going to have to admit that she had promised the set to him during what was now going to seem to have been a clandestine meeting at the library.

Why, oh why, had she not gone home and openly complained of how she had been maneuvered into accepting, of how she could not have refused without seeming discourteous, of how she intended to dance with him and make it very obvious to him that she wished for no further acquaintance with him? Why had she not done so? But it was too late now.

The opening set of country dances was a vigorous one. Jennifer felt hot and breathless when it came to an end and the viscount escorted her to where Aunt Agatha should have been waiting. She fanned herself in a vain attempt to cool her cheeks and calm her agitation. Aunt Agatha, someone told her, had gone to the withdrawing room with Samantha because Sam's hem was down. It was a small relief, but Lord Kersey lingered.

"Mama is not here either," he said. "I shall do myself the honor of remaining at your side, Miss Winwood."

She knew there would be no reprieve. The Earl of Thornhill was there and had been from the start. He had not danced the opening set but had stood on the sidelines, quizzing glass in hand. She knew, even though she had not once looked at him, that he had watched her through most of the dance. She had been aware of him with every nerve ending in her body and had resented the fact when she wanted to be free to feel awareness of no one but Lionel.

But it was her own fault. She must learn not to behave

so rustically. She must learn not to allow others more accomplished in the social niceties to maneuver her.

The Earl of Thornhill came to claim his dance while the viscount was still at her side. The latter set a hand beneath her arm and closed it possessively about her elbow.

"Miss Winwood is otherwise engaged for this set," he said with chilly hauteur when the earl bowed.

"Really?" Lord Thornhill's eyebrows rose with a matching haughtiness. "I understood that this set had been promised to me." His eyes caught and held Jennifer's. "Following a pleasant but all too brief discussion of books at the library this morning."

She mentally kicked herself again for not mentioning it to anyone. Just as if there were something to hide. But he need not have mentioned it either. It was almost as if he was delighting in embarrassing her.

"Why, yes," she said, sounding surprised, as if she had just remembered something so insignificant that it had slipped her mind. "So it is, my lord. Thank you."

But she had concentrated so hard on the tone of surprise that she had forgotten also to sound chilly. She was not good at dissembling. And why should she dissemble? Why should she feel as if she had been caught out in some dreadful indiscretion? She resented deeply having been put in such a position. She would certainly see to it that such a thing never happened again.

Viscount Kersey released her elbow and bowed stiffly before moving away without another word.

"I do not blame him," the Earl of Thornhill said. "If

you were mine, or soon to be mine, I too would be unwilling for any other man to pry you from my side. But he must be aware that it would not be at all the thing for him to remain with you all evening."

"Viscount Kersey is well aware of what is socially correct, my lord," she said, fanning herself again and hoping that the music would start and the set be in progress before Aunt Agatha returned.

"The dance has made you overwarm," he said. "And the ballroom was stuffy to begin with. Stroll on the balcony with me until the set begins. It is cooler out there." He held out his arm for hers, an arm that shimmered gold. He looked quite as striking in gold and brown and white as he had in black, she thought. It was perhaps his height and bearing and coloring that made him stand out in a crowd quite as much as Lionel did. He was taller than Lionel.

"Thank you." She laid her arm along his. The prospect of breathing in fresh air was too tempting to be resisted, as was the desire to be out of sight of her aunt until the dancing began. Though she would have to be faced afterward, of course. Doubtless there would be scolds. And what about Lionel? What would he say when he claimed the supper dance? Anything? There was nothing improper about her dancing with other gentlemen. It was quite the correct thing to do, in fact. But he had warned her particularly against the Earl of Thornhill. And he now knew that she had talked with the earl in the library this morning.

"Well," the earl said as they passed the French windows to the delicious coolness of the balcony, "do you like Mr. Pope?"

"Oh," she said with a laugh, "I have not had a chance even to open the book yet. I have been busy."

"Preparing for a ball," he said. "And the result has been worth every minute."

He looked down at her, warm appreciation in his eyes, and she was very aware of the low cut of her gown, a cut she had protested during her fittings. But even Aunt Agatha had approved the low décolletage and called it fashionable. She had, of course, worn something slightly more demure for her come-out ball. But not tonight. Jennifer was very well aware that she had more of a bosom than many other women. It was a physical attribute that made her uncomfortable.

"Thank you," she said.

"I suppose," he said, "that almost every moment of every day is taken up with busy frivolity. Are you enjoying your first Season?"

"It has hardly begun yet," she said. "But yes, of course. I have waited so long. Two years ago when Papa was planning to bring me out we had to change our plans because Lord Kersey was attending his sick uncle in the north of England. We have been intended for each other for five years, you see. And then last year I was unable to come because my grandmother had died."

"I am sorry," he said. "Were you close to her?"

"Yes," she said. "My mother and her own mother died when I was very young. Grandmama was like a mother to me. She apologized to me when she was dying." The memory could still draw tears. "She knew that she was going to spoil my come-out, as she put it, and cause my official betrothal to be put off yet another year."

"You are positively ancient," the earl said with a smile.

"I am twenty," she said and then remembered that a lady never divulged her age.

"But at last," he said, "you have achieved your dream. You are enjoying a Season."

"Yes. And with Samantha. That at least has worked out well. She is almost two years younger than I." It was not so much the Season she was enjoying, though, as what it meant. Lionel. An official betrothal. Marriage. "Frivolity is good for a while. I do not believe I would like it as a way of life."

Most of the other couples who had been strolling had returned to the ballroom. The music was beginning for the second set. The Earl of Thornhill made no move to take her inside, and Jennifer was tempted by the coolness and the escape from the squash of guests inside the ballroom.

"Ah," he said. "You are not frivolous by nature, then. How have you spent your life until now? How do you envisage spending it after your marriage?"

"In the country, I hope," she said, "That is where real life is lived. I have managed Papa's home for a few years since Grandmama became too infirm to do it for herself. I like visiting my father's people and doing what I can to make life more comfortable for them. I like to feel useful.

I was born to wealth and privilege—and to responsibility. I look forward to managing my husband's home. I am glad I have had some experience."

They had strolled along the balcony and back. He drew her now to sit on a bench and she knew that he had no intention of joining the set. She did not really mind, though she did wonder if her absence would be noticed. They were not alone, though. There were a few other couples still taking the air rather than dancing.

Jennifer took her arm from his when they sat down and rested her hands in her lap. He said nothing for a while. They listened to the music and the sounds of voices from beyond the French windows.

"What do you do?" she asked. "When you are not in London, that is. Or traveling on the Continent." She wished when it was too late that she had not asked. She did not want to have her ears regaled with shocking improprieties.

"I have led a rather useless life," he said. "For several years I gave myself up to every conceivable pleasure, imagining that I was really living, that everyone who led a more staid existence was to be pitied. The proverbial wild oats, one might say. That life was curtailed rather abruptly and thereby perhaps a few more years of my life were saved from uselessness. My father died a little over a year ago and precipitated me into my present title and all that goes with it. My estate is in the north of England. I have not been there since my return from Europe. But there are enough duties awaiting me there to keep my life staid and blameless for the rest of my days, I believe."

Wild oats. One of those oats was far worse than the typical indiscretion of young men, if Lionel was to be believed. But he had changed? The death of his father and the responsibilities it brought had caused him to turn over a new leaf. But the *ton* could be unforgiving, she knew. She wondered why he had come to London when he might have gone straight home to begin his new life—if indeed he was serious about doing so.

"Why have you come here instead of going home after such a long absence?" she asked. "And if there is so much to do there."

"I had something to prove," he said. "I would not have it said that I was afraid to show my face here."

Ah. Then there really was something beyond just the ordinary. She looked down at her hands.

"And under the circumstances," he said, "I am very glad that I am here."

His voice was softer. He did not explain his meaning. He did not need to. His meaning spoke loudly in the tone of his voice and in the silence that followed. But she was betrothed. He knew it. Perhaps he was merely speaking with meaningless gallantry. Perhaps he thought she liked to be flattered. And indeed there was treacherous pleasure to be gained from his unspoken words.

"The music is loud," she said—the first words she could think of with which to break the silence between them.

He stood up and offered his arm again. "So it is," he said.

She assumed, when she stood up and set her arm

along his again, that he intended to stroll along the balcony with her once more. Instead he turned to the steps leading down into the garden and took her down them. She went without protest, knowing that she was allowing herself to be manipulated again, knowing that she should very firmly hold back and demand to be taken into the ballroom. Even her absence on the balcony might be construed as an indiscretion. Especially considering the identity of her partner and the heinous sin that everyone else except her seemed to know of.

But she went unprotestingly. It was so difficult to make a stand when one did not know exactly why one was supposed to do so. The garden was lit by lanterns. It was intended for use by guests during the evening. And it was not deserted. There was a couple seated on a wrought-iron seat to one side of the garden. The earl turned her to stroll in the other direction.

"There is something about England and English gardens," he said, "that is quite distinctive and quite incomparable. One can see brighter, gayer, larger flowers in Italy and Switzerland. But there is nowhere like England."

"You did not stay away so long out of choice, then?" she asked. She was prying, she knew. And rather afraid that he would answer all her unasked questions.

"Oh, yes," he said, smiling at her, "entirely from choice. Sometimes there are more important things to be done than admiring flowers. And new places and new experiences are always to be welcomed. I came back as soon as there was no further reason to be away."

"I see," she said, watching the patterns of light and shade the lanterns made on the grass before her feet.

"Do you?" He laughed softly. "At a guess, I would say that they have not considered the lurid details fitting for a maiden's ears but have hinted at dark crimes and bitter exile. Am I correct?"

She wished the darkness could swallow her up. He was quite correct. But she felt foolish, young and gauche. She felt as if she had been caught searching his room or reading through his letters or doing something equally incriminating.

"Your life is none of my concern, my lord," she said.

He laughed again. "But you have been warned against me," he said. "Your aunt and your father will scold you for granting me this set. They will be even more annoyed that you have allowed me to take you from the ballroom. Kersey will be angry too, will he not? You must not allow this to be repeated, you know. You will be in serious trouble if you do."

He echoed her own thought—and gave her the opportunity she needed. She should agree with him, tell him that yes, this had been very pleasant, but she really must not dance with him or converse with him again. But his words made her feel as if she were a child instead of a woman of twenty. As if she could not be trusted to act for herself within the bounds of propriety. He had done something dreadful, but since then his father had died and he had been forced to grow up and change his ways. He could not go back and change whatever it was he had done wrong. But surely he should be allowed a chance to prove that he had changed. And surely she was old enough to make some decisions for herself instead of obeying blindly when no reason was given for restricting her freedom.

"I am twenty years old, my lord," she said. "There is nothing improper in my dancing with you or even strolling with you in a designated area." At least, she did not think it was improper. Though she had the uneasy feeling that others might not agree. Like Aunt Agatha and Lionel, for example.

"You are kind." He touched a hand lightly to hers as it rested on his arm. He had long, elegant fingers, she saw, looking down. It looked a capable and powerful hand. She resisted the instinct to pull her hand away. She would look like a frightened child after all. He spoke softly. "Is there anyone in this world whom you envy so much that it is almost a physical pain?"

She considered. "No," she said. "Sometimes there are aspects of appearance or behavior that I envy, but never seriously so. I am happy with my person and with my life as they are." It was true, she thought. For years, since she was fifteen, she had been happy, and now her happiness had reached its culmination. Or almost so. There were a few weeks during which to enjoy Lionel's company and to get to know him better. And then their wedding and the rest of their lives together. Happiness was soon going to turn to bliss. She felt an unexpected twinge of alarm. Life could not be that wonderful, could it? Or proceed quite so smoothly?

"Well," the Earl of Thornhill said softly, "I have felt

such envy. I *feel* such envy. I envy Kersey more than I have ever envied any man."

"No." She looked up at him in some distress, her lips forming the word rather than expressing it out loud. "Oh, no, that is absurd."

"Is it?" His hand had closed about hers.

But in drawing her hand free at last and turning to make her way back across the garden and up the steps to the safety of the balcony, she made the mistake of turning in toward him. And of looking up into his eyes. And of pausing. And of noting that there was gentleness and something like pain in his eyes.

He kissed her.

Only his lips touched hers. His hands did not touch her at all. It would have been the easiest thing in the world to break away. But she stood transfixed by the wholly novel feeling of a man's lips against her own. Slightly parted. Warm. Even moist.

And then he stopped kissing her and she realized the full enormity of what had happened. She had been kissed. By a man. For the first time.

Not by Lionel.

By the Earl of Thornhill.

And she had not stopped him or pulled back her head.

And she did not now slap his face.

"Come," he said, his voice very quiet, "the set must be almost at an end. I will escort you back to the ballroom."

She set her arm on his and walked beside him just as

if nothing had happened. She neither protested nor scolded. He neither justified himself nor apologized.

Just as if a kiss was a normal part of a stroll a man and woman took together instead of dancing.

Perhaps it was. Perhaps she was even more naive than she realized.

But of course it was not. A kiss was something a man and woman shared when they were going to marry. Perhaps even only when they were actually married.

She was going to marry Lord Kersey. She had looked forward so eagerly to his kissing her for the first time. To his being the first—and only—man ever to do so.

And now it was all spoiled.

The earl had timed their return very well. The music was just drawing to a close as he led her through the French windows to Aunt Agatha's side. He bowed and took his leave, and she stood beside her aunt feeling like a scarlet woman, feeling that everyone had but to look at her to know.

Everything was spoiled.

VISCOUNT KERSEY FOUND THE Earl of Thornhill outside the ballroom, at the head of the staircase. He was apparently leaving even though the ball had scarcely begun.

"Thornhill," the viscount called. "A moment, please." He smiled his dazzling white smile at Lady Coombes, who was passing on the arm of her brother, and joined the earl on the stairs.

"Yes?" The earl's hand closed about the handle of his quizzing glass.

Lord Kersey reined in his temper, conscious as he always was of his surroundings. "It was not wisely done," he said. "You must know that my betrothed, my soon-to-be wife, is not to be seen in your company, Thornhill. Certainly she is not to be seen stepping out of a ballroom with you."

"Indeed?" The earl's eyebrows rose. "Perhaps it is with Miss Winwood you should be having this conversation, Kersey. Perhaps you have some influence with her."

"She is an innocent." The viscount's nostrils flared, but he recalled the fact that they were in full view of anyone both abovestairs and below who cared to look. "I know what your game is, Thornhill. I am on to you. You would be wise to end it or it will be the worse for you."

"Interesting." The earl raised his glass to his eye and surveyed the other unhurriedly through it from head to toe. "You mean there will be a challenge, Kersey? The choice of weapons would be mine, would it not? I have a little skill with both swords and pistols. Or would you merely ruin my reputation? It cannot be done, my dear fellow. My reputation has sunk as low as it will go. I am reputed to have seduced my stepmother, got her with child, and run off with her, leaving my father to die of a broken heart. And if that was not quite devilish enough, I then abandoned her in a foreign land, leaving her among strangers. And yet here I stand as an invited guest at a *ton* event in London. No, Kersey, I do not believe there is a great deal you can do to my reputation that you have not already done."

"We will see." The viscount turned abruptly to go back upstairs. "Two can play at your game, Thornhill. It will be interesting to discover which of us plays it with the greater skill."

"Quite fascinating," the earl agreed. "I begin to enjoy this Season more and more." He bowed elegantly and continued on his way down the stairs.

# 6

$I$T WAS DIFFICULT TO THROW OFF THE FEELING that everything had been spoiled. Merely because the Earl of Thornhill had kissed her, Jennifer told herself, trying to minimize the importance of what had happened. All he had done was touch his lips to hers for a few seconds. It was really nothing at all.

But it was everything. Everything to spoil the pattern of life as it had been building for five years. Everything to upset her and everyone around her—not that everyone else knew the whole of it.

Aunt Agatha scolded in the ballroom. Very quietly and quite expressionlessly so that no one, not even anyone standing within a few feet of them, would have known that she was scolding. But she made it clear that if dancing with the Earl of Thornhill was not indiscreet enough to raise the eyebrows of society, leaving the ballroom with him, being absent with him for all of half an hour, was enough to ruin her reputation. She would be fortunate indeed if her absence had not been particularly noted and if she did not become the *on dit* in fashionable drawing rooms tomorrow.

It was in vain to protest that both the balcony and the garden were lit and that other couples were outside. The balcony and the garden were not for the use of a young unchaperoned girl who happened to be with a man who was neither her husband nor her betrothed, she was told. Especially when that man was a rake of the lowest order.

Jennifer now believed that he was indeed a rake. It was unpardonable of him to have stolen that kiss. And unpardonable of her to have allowed it, not to have protested her shock and outrage. She was unable to argue further with Aunt Agatha or to wrap herself about with righteousness. She felt horribly guilty.

Viscount Kersey danced the supper set with her and led her in to supper, but his manner was cold. Icy cold. He said nothing—that was the worst of it. And she was quite unable to bring up the topic herself. She was powerfully reminded of Samantha's opinion of him. But she could not blame him for his coldness this time, though she would have far preferred to be taken aside and scolded roundly. She felt very much as if she had been unfaithful to him. She felt unworthy of him. She had kissed another man when she was betrothed to Lord Kersey.

And yet Lionel was the only man she had ever wanted to kiss. She had so looked forward to the supper dance and to the supper half hour spent with him. But it had all been totally ruined—entirely through her own fault.

After supper Lord Kersey returned her to Aunt Agatha's side and engaged Samantha for the coming set. He took her out onto the balcony and kept her there the whole time—as punishment, Jennifer supposed. And it worked. It was agony knowing he was out there, even though it was only with Sam. She danced with Henry Chisley and smiled at him and chattered with him and was all the time aware of the absence of Lionel.

Yes, it was suitable punishment. If she had made him feel like this when she had gone outside, then she deserved to be punished. And it was the Earl of Thornhill with whom she had gone outside. And she had allowed him to kiss her.

She went home and to bed some time early in the morning, weary to the point of exhaustion, only to find that she could not sleep. She tried wrapping herself about with the warmth of the knowledge that in just a little over a week's time there was to be the dinner at the Earl of Rushford's and her betrothal was to be announced. After that all would be well. She would spend more time with Lionel and get to know him better. He would kiss her. There would be all the excitement of their approaching wedding. She pictured him as he had appeared this evening, handsome enough to bring an ache to her throat. He was hers—the man she loved, the man she was to marry.

And yet her mind kept straying to dark, compelling eyes and long, artistic fingers. She kept feeling his mouth on hers and reliving her surprise at the discovery that his lips had been slightly parted so that she had felt the soft moistness of the inside of his mouth. She kept remembering the physical sensations that had accompanied the kiss—the strange tightening in her breasts, the aching throb between her legs.

She kept remembering that she had talked to him and listened to him. She had revealed far more of herself than she had ever done with Lionel, and had learned more of him than she knew of her own betrothed. He had convinced her that whatever had been in his past he had now reformed his ways and was prepared to live a responsible life. And then he had kissed her.

She felt sinful and spoiled. And unwillingly fascinated by the memories.

The morning brought with it no relief. Tired and dispirited, she wandered into Samantha's room only to find her cousin sitting quietly at the window, heavy-eyed.

"Have you been crying?" she asked, alarmed. Samantha never cried.

"No," Samantha said, smiling quickly. "I am just tired after last night. We were warned that the Season would be exhausting, Jenny, and it sounded marvelous, did it not? It has hardly started yet, and already it is simply—exhausting."

Jennifer sat down beside her. "Did you not enjoy last night's ball?" she asked. "You had a partner for each set. You danced twice with a few of them." Lionel, for example.

"I enjoyed it." Samantha got to her feet. "Let's go down to breakfast, shall we? And perhaps for a walk in the park afterward to blow away the cobwebs? I can feel them just clinging to me. Ugh!"

Samantha was not her usual exuberant self. Jennifer

had counted on her being so. She had expected to find her cousin eager to talk about last night, to discuss her partners, to reveal her favorite. But she seemed unwilling to talk about last night. Jennifer felt her own spirits dip even lower.

"Sam," she said, "I thought you would cheer me up. You know that I was in disgrace last night, I suppose?"

"Yes." Samantha bit her lip. "I think he likes you, Jenny. He has never tried to dance with me. Yet he has danced with you twice. I think he really is the devil. He must know that you are betrothed. Lionel was upset."

"Lionel?" Jennifer frowned.

Samantha flushed. "Lord Kersey," she said. "You upset him, Jenny. You ought not to have gone off with Lord Thornhill like that."

"You are scolding now too?" Jennifer asked quietly.

"Well, it was not right, you must admit," Samantha said. "You have a man, Jenny, and you have claimed forever that you love him. It was not right to step outside with the earl. Who is to know what you were up to, the two of you, out there?"

They were halfway down the stairs. But Samantha had stopped in order to stare accusingly at her cousin. And then, under Jennifer's dismayed gaze, she bit her upper lip, her eyes filled with tears, and she turned without another word to hurry upstairs again.

"Sam?" Jennifer called after her. But she was left alone in the middle of the staircase. Feeling wretchedly miserable and as much like eating breakfast as she felt like jumping into a den of lions.

It had really not seemed like such a dreadful indiscretion at the time. Had it been? Why had the French windows been open and lanterns lit both on the balcony and in the garden if guests had not been expected to stroll out there?

But guilt prevented her from feeling indignation against everyone who was condemning her—even Sam. For of course it had turned into an indiscretion. They were right and she was wrong. She had allowed a man who was not even her betrothed to kiss her in the garden.

SAMANTHA THREW HERSELF ACROSS her bed and sobbed into the pillow she held with both hands against her face. It had taken her a long while to erase all traces of last night's tears. Now she would have to begin all over again—after she had stopped crying again, that was.

She felt wretchedly guilty and wretchedly something else too. She would not put that something else into words.

She had a number of admirers already. She determinedly stopped sobbing and turned her head sideways so that she could breathe. She began to list them and picture them in her mind. There was Sir Albert Boyle. He was very ordinary, very kindly. There was Lord Graham, who was very young but quite dashing too. There were Mr. Maxwell, who made her laugh, and Sir Richard Parkes and Mr. Chisley, all quite worthy of her consideration. Perhaps a few of her new partners from last night would show further interest and become regular admirers too. Perhaps soon one or two of those admirers would turn into definite beaux. Perhaps soon she would be involved in a courtship. Perhaps Jenny would not be the only one married by the end of the summer.

But the thought of Jennifer distracted her.

He really had been very upset. Very angry. She had felt it as soon as supper was over and he had asked her for the next set. She had been annoyed, wondering why she should be expected to dance with him and smile at him and spend half an hour in his company when his eyes were so cold and his lips so compressed and his mind so obviously distracted. There were other gentlemen she could have been dancing with who would actually have looked at her and appreciated her.

She had been even more indignant when Lord Kersey had made it clear that he was not going to dance with her but expected her to step out onto the balcony with him.

"I am not sure, my lord," she had said to him, "that it is proper for me to leave the ballroom without a chaperone." She had suspected that he was doing it in order to punish Jenny. She did not want to be caught in the middle of a lovers' quarrel—if, indeed, that was what it was. If she was going to walk on the balcony instead of dancing, she would have preferred to do so with one of her admirers.

"It is quite proper," he had assured her. "You are the cousin of my betrothed."

And so she had allowed herself to be led outside—and straight down the steps to the garden below, where he took her to sit on a wrought-iron seat that was out of sight of the balcony and the ballroom.

"What a mess," he had said. "What a bloody mess."

She would have felt more shock at the word he had used in her hearing if she had not been in the process of removing her hand from its resting place on his arm and if his own had not come shooting across his body to hold it where it was. She had felt remarkably uncomfortable—and still angry at being drawn into something that was none of her concern.

"Does she love me?" he had asked abruptly. "Do you know? Does she confide in you?"

"Of course she loves you," she had said, shocked. "She is your betrothed, is she not?"

"Yes," he had said. "Forced into it five years ago when she was no more than a child. When I was no more than a boy. She seems remarkably interested in Thornhill."

"She danced with him once at our ball and once at this," she had said, being drawn against her will into this quarrel or whatever it was between her cousin and her betrothed. She was still feeling angry that she was missing half an hour of the ball.

"Except that here they did not dance," he had said.

"They came out here," Samantha had said. "Or perhaps only out onto the balcony. There is no great indiscretion in that. We are out here. We are committing no indiscretion."

"No," he had said. "There is nothing even remotely indiscreet about a couple's being outdoors unchaperoned during a ball, is there?"

And as if to prove his point, which he had made obvious through the sarcasm of his tone, he had drawn his arm from beneath hers, circled her shoulders with it, raised her chin with his free hand, and kissed her.

Samantha had been so shocked that for a moment she had sat rooted to the spot. And then she had struggled to be free. She pushed at his shoulder, her palm itching to crack across his face. She was furiously angry.

But he had not let her go. He had used his superior strength to imprison her hands against his chest and had drawn her closer to him with both arms. His head had angled more comfortably against hers and he had kissed her again—with greater heat.

She had stopped struggling. And then she had stopped being passive. She had kissed him back. And somehow one of her arms had worked its way loose of its prison and was about his neck. For perhaps a minute she had mindlessly reveled in her first kiss.

He had looked down at her silently, his eyes glinting in the moonlight, when he finally lifted his head, and she had gazed back, only gradually realizing what had just happened, with whom she had shared her first kiss. Only gradually remembering that she had never greatly liked him, that she had always thought him cold.

"My lord," she had said uncertainly. She had wanted to be angry again, but anger had seemed inappropriate after her minute of undeniable surrender.

"Lionel," he had whispered.

"Lionel." She had spread one hand over his chest. She had not been able to think what to say to him.

"You see," he had said, "why chaperones are such a necessary evil?"

She had stared mutely back at him. Had he merely been demonstrating what might have happened between Jenny and the Earl of Thornhill? Was that what this was all about? But her mind refused to work quite clearly.

"Samantha." He had touched the backs of his knuckles lightly to her cheek. "I could wish that you had gone to live with your uncle a year or two sooner than you did. Perhaps he and my father would have chosen me a different bride. One more congenial to my tastes."

"I think you should take me inside," she had said, feeling a little sick suddenly.

"Yes," he had agreed. "Oh, yes, indeed I should."

But he had not immediately got to his feet. He had lowered his head and kissed her again. And to her everlasting shame, she had allowed it to happen even though this time she could not plead the shock of the totally unexpected.

They had climbed the steps to the balcony and strolled there in silence for the rest of the set. But his free hand had rested the whole time on her hand as it lay along his arm.

All night Samantha had not known what to make of the encounter. Except that he did not love Jenny and regretted the promise that had led him into the betrothal that was so soon to be announced. She did not know what his feelings were for her or even if he had any at all.

All night she had been tortured by guilt. She had allowed herself to be kissed—twice—by Jenny's betrothed. Worse than that—he was the man Jenny loved to distraction and had loved for five years. And Jenny, as well as being her cousin, was her very dearest friend.

Perhaps the kiss had meant nothing to him. Undoubtedly it had not.

Samantha wished the same could be said of her. If it had meant nothing, if she could shrug it off, perhaps she could feel simple anger and simple sorrow over the fact that Jenny's betrothed did not love her.

But the kisses had meant something. She had lain awake all night, and cried through much of it, fearing that she was in love with Lord Kersey—with Lionel. That perhaps she always had been and had protected herself from what had seemed so very undesirable and improper a passion by looking for faults in him.

But perhaps she was not, either. Perhaps she was merely reacting in a thoroughly silly and predictable way, falling in love with the first man to kiss her. As if kisses and love were synonymous terms. Yes, that was it, of course. She did not love him or even like him. She was angry with the way he had behaved to her last night. What he had done was unpardonable.

"Lionel," she whispered, closing her eyes and hugging the damp pillow to her bosom. "Lionel." Oh, dear Lord, how she hated him.

THE EARL OF THORNHILL rather wished over the coming days that he had not conversed with Miss Jennifer Winwood at the Chisley ball. She was a beautiful and a very desirable woman. He wanted to know only those facts about her—the only sort of facts one needed to know about any woman. He had never felt in any way guilty about any of the women he had hired for casual sexual encounters or about any he had employed for longer periods of time as mistresses. When a woman was only a beautiful sexual object one did not have to have feelings for her beyond the physical.

He had no intention of even trying to make Miss Winwood his mistress, of course. He was not quite that base even if he had allowed the desire for revenge rather to obsess him. But he did intend to lead her astray, to compromise her, to cause her to break off her betrothal or, failing that, to cause Kersey to end it. Either way the resulting scandal and humiliation to Kersey would be marginally satisfying to himself.

It would have been far better to have seen to it that she remained to him just the luscious long-legged redhead whom he had dreamed of bedding from the first moment he had seen her—long before he had known of her connection to Kersey. And to have concentrated his mind on the numerous attractions of her person between that red hair and those long legs.

It had been foolish to allow her to become a person to him. She saw her life as one of privilege. She felt that she owed something in return. She felt that she had some responsibility to her father's dependents and would have to her husband's after she was married. She preferred the country to town. She felt that was where real life was lived. She did not often envy other people. She considered herself a happy person.

Damnation! He did not want to know any of those things.

Except that he could use them to soothe his conscience, he supposed. He could convince himself that he was about to do her a favor. She deserved better than Kersey. But perhaps after the scandal of a broken engagement she would be able to get no one else.

He had been surprised at her reaction to his kiss—though it could scarcely be called that when he had merely touched his lips to hers for a few seconds and had kept both his hands and the rest of his body deliberately away from hers. Even so he had been surprised that she had neither drawn away nor scolded afterward nor burst into tears. She had accepted the kiss, even pushing her lips back against his own for those brief seconds. And afterward she had behaved as if nothing untoward had happened between them at all.

It was gratifying. It had all been very easy so far.

He just wished that in order to soften her up, to make her comfortable with him and susceptible to his advances he had not had to converse with her. He just wished that he did not know she had taken that book of Pope's poetry to read just because she did not want to be narrow in her reading tastes.

He saw her the evening after the Chisley ball at the theater and bowed to her from his own box when he caught her eye. He had the impression that she had known for a long time that he was there but had deliberately kept her eyes averted. He did not make any attempt to call at Rushford's box, where she was seated with her party.

He saw her again the following afternoon in the park, where she was driving in a landau with Kersey, Miss Newman, and Henry Chisley, and touched his hat to her without either stopping to pay his respects or looking at any of the four of them except her. And he saw her the same evening at Mrs. Hobbs's concert. He sat on the opposite side of the room from her and Kersey and the Earl and Countess of Rushford and watched her for much of the evening though he did not approach her at any of the times when there was a break in the recitals and the other guests were generally milling about.

But at Richmond the next afternoon, at old Lady Bromley's garden party, he decided that he had left her alone for long enough. He was fortunate, he supposed, to have been invited to such a select gathering, but Lady Bromley was Catherine's grandmother and knew that he was not the father of Catherine's child—though clearly she did not know who was, or Kersey would doubtless not be among her guests.

Lady Bromley took his arm and strolled with him down by the river, which she was fortunate enough to have as one boundary of her garden. She walked very slowly, but he was quite content to match his pace to hers. The sun was shining, there was not a cloud in the sky, and somehow he intended before the afternoon was over to get Miss Jennifer Winwood alone again. To move one step closer to achieving his revenge—to winning the game, as Kersey termed it.

"I had a letter from Catherine just yesterday," Lady Bromley said. "The child is well and she is well. The climate seems to agree with her. And the company. She is doing well there, Thornhill?"

"She seemed remarkably contented when I left there two months ago, ma'am," he assured her quite truthfully. "Indeed, I would say she has found the place in this world where she best belongs."

"In a foreign country," she said with a click of the tongue. "It does not seem right somehow. But I am glad. She was never happy here. If you will pardon me for saying so, Thornhill, my son-in-law, the impecunious fool, should never have married her off so young to a man old enough to be her father."

Yes, the earl thought. Catherine was four months younger than himself. She had been his father's wife for more than six years before fleeing to the Continent with him. Yes, it had been criminal, especially given his father's ill health even at the time of his marriage and his consequent ill humor.

"Who is the German count?" Lady Bromley asked.

"German count?" The earl raised his eyebrows.

"With an unreadable and doubtless unpronounceable name," she said. "Mentioned twice in the course of the letter."

"I do not believe I met him," the earl said with a smile. "But it was only a matter of time before someone was taken into Catherine's favor, ma'am. She attracts a great deal of interest."

"Hm," she said. "Because Thornhill—your father, that is—left her a small fortune. And the child too."

"Because she is lovely and charming," he said.

Lady Bromley looked pleased, though she said no more. They were down by the river and three boats were out on the water, three gentlemen rowing them while their ladies sat at their ease looking picturesque. Jennifer Winwood, in a boat with Kersey, trailed one hand in the water and held a parasol in the other.

"A handsome couple," Lady Bromley said, seeing the direction of his gaze. "Recently betrothed, so I have heard, and to be married at St. George's before the Season is out."

"Yes," the earl said, "I had heard. And yes, a handsome couple indeed."

Kersey pulled the boat in to the bank a few minutes later and handed his lady out. She looked younger than her twenty years this afternoon, the earl thought, with her delicate sprigged muslin dress and straw bonnet trimmed with blue cornflowers and the frivolous confection of a blue parasol.

"Miss Newman?" The viscount smiled at his betrothed's cousin, the small blonde, who was standing close by in company with a few other young people. "Your turn. May I have the pleasure?"

It looked as if Miss Newman did not want the pleasure at all, the earl thought. Poor girl. But she stepped forward and set her hand in Kersey's. At almost the same moment Colonel and Mrs. Morris engaged Lady Bromley in conversation, and the Earl of Thornhill took advantage of the moment, perhaps the best the afternoon would provide.

"Miss Winwood," he said before she had had a chance to move from the bank to join the group with which her cousin had been conversing. He held out his arm to her. "May I escort you up to the terrace? There are cool drinks being served there, I believe."

The situation could not have been more perfect. There were several people observing them, including Kersey, who was powerless to do anything about it, short of making a scene. And she was powerless to refuse without seeming quite ill-mannered. She really was looking incredibly lovely—a point that had no particular relevance to anything.

She hesitated for only a moment before taking his arm. But of course she was a gently bred young lady and quite inexperienced in the ways of the world. She really had no choice at all.

"Thank you," she said. "A glass of lemonade would be welcome, my lord."

The Earl of Thornhill, looking down appreciatively at her, wondered with some interest if he was playing the game alone this afternoon. Had Kersey not seen him on the bank with Lady Bromley? If so, why had he not kept Miss Winwood out longer? Or failing that, why had he not relinquished the boat to someone else and kept his betrothed on his arm?

It seemed almost as if Kersey had conceded this round of the game.

Unless somehow he was a more active participant in it.

Fascinating! It truly was fascinating.

But what, he wondered, *was* the game exactly?

# 7

$S$HE HAD BEEN AWARE OF HIM STANDING ON THE bank of the river and had willed him either to move away by the time Viscount Kersey had brought in the boat or else to continue talking with Lady Bromley. But she saw Colonel and Mrs. Morris move up to join them and she remembered that when Lionel had taken her out he had kindly offered to take Samantha next, though Sam had protested strangely that she was not very happy on water. She was certainly happy swimming, something she did a great deal of at home during the summer.

Jennifer knew how matters were going to develop, almost as if all their actions were part of a play she had read or seen and all the people actors in that drama. She was quite powerless to change anything. She could only keep her eyes averted from Lord Thornhill and hope to lose herself among the group of acquaintances with whom Samantha had been conversing.

But of course the arrival of the colonel and his wife gave him the chance to extricate himself from the company of their hostess and he stepped forward as Lord Kersey was handing Samantha into the boat.

"Miss Winwood," he said, "may I escort you up to the

terrace? There are cool drinks being served there, I believe."

She could hardly refuse without making an issue of it. His tone was civil and he was holding out an arm to her. But what alarmed her more than that fact was the realization that she did not really want to refuse. She had been very aware of him ever since the evening of the Chisley ball—and even before that—and always knew almost with a sixth sense when he was present at the same entertainment as she. She was always aware of him at every moment even though she rarely looked at him and even then did so unwillingly.

She did not want to be aware of him. She disliked him and even hated him. She wanted everything within her to concentrate on Lionel and these longed-for weeks with him before their wedding. It was not an easy time. Although they were spending more and more time in each other's company, they were not yet relaxed enough with each other to talk freely. It was because they were betrothed and everyone knew it but there had not yet been an official announcement, she told herself. After the Earl of Rushford's dinner next week all would change and everything would be as wonderful as she had imagined.

She did not need or want the distraction of the Earl of Thornhill. And she deeply, deeply resented the fact that he had kissed her while Lionel had not. And yet he was like a magnet to her eyes and her senses. Even when she could not see him, she thought about him almost constantly.

Now, forced into company with him again, she felt almost relief. Perhaps if she took his arm and walked up to the terrace with him and drank a glass of lemonade with him, the dreadful memory of the Chisley ball would be dispelled and the terrible unwilling . . . attraction would be over. There. She had never used that word before. But it was true, she thought with some dread. She was attracted to the Earl of Thornhill.

"Thank you," she said as coolly as she was able, taking his arm. "A glass of lemonade would be welcome, my lord."

Touching him again, standing close beside him again brought a vivid memory of that night and a rather frightening physical awareness with which she was so unfamiliar that she did not know quite what to do with it.

She would walk and converse, she decided. It was broad daylight. There were lawns and trees and flowers to be admired and a clear blue sky to gaze up at. It was only as she walked that she realized she had not looked back for one last sight of Lionel. He had looked so splendidly handsome and virile rowing her on the river. She concentrated her mind on her love for him.

"Do I owe you an apology?" the Earl of Thornhill asked.

"An apology?" She looked up at him, startled. His dark eyes were looking very directly back into hers.

"For kissing you," he said. "Don't tell me that it was a thing of such insignificance that you have forgotten about it." He smiled.

She could feel herself flushing. And could not for the life of her think of anything to say.

"I have not forgotten it," he said, "or forgiven myself for giving it. I could use the quietness of the garden and the moonlight for an excuse, but I had taken you down there and should have realized the danger and guarded against it. I am deeply sorry for the distress I must have caused you."

She had not been mistaken in him, then. Whatever he had been in the past, he was no longer a man without honor and conscience. He was a kind gentleman. She was glad. She had been saddened by her disillusionment. And yet she was disappointed too. She had the uncomfortable feeling that she would be altogether safer if he really were the unprincipled rake that kiss had made him appear to be. She could guard herself more easily against a rake.

"Thank you," she said. "It did cause me some distress. I am betrothed and only my intended husband has the right to—to—"

"Yes." He touched the fingers of his free hand lightly to the back of her hand. "If my apology has been accepted, let us change the subject, shall we? Tell me what you think of Pope's poetry."

"I admire it," she said. "It is written with great polish and elegance."

He chuckled. "If I were Pope listening to you now," he said, "I would go out and shoot myself."

She looked at him and laughed and twirled her parasol. "I meant precisely what I said," she told him. "I feel no great emotional response to his poetry as I do to Mr. Wordsworth's, for example. But I feel an intellectual response. That does not mean I like it less. Merely differently."

"Have you read 'The Rape of the Lock'?" he asked.

"I loved it," she said. "It was so amusing and clever and so . . . ridiculous."

"It makes one feel uncomfortable at every frivolity society has ever led one into, does it not?" he said. "Do you enjoy humor and satire in literature?"

"*She Stoops to Conquer* for humor and *Gulliver's Travels* for satire," she said. "Yes, I enjoy both. And emotion and sentimentality too, I must confess, though gentlemen immediately look very superior and politely scornful when a woman admits as much."

The Earl of Thornhill threw back his head and laughed. "I dare do no such thing now, then," he said. "Your tone made it sound as if you were throwing down the gauntlet and daring me to take up the challenge. Besides, I have been known to shed a surreptitious tear or two over *Romeo and Juliet*. Not that I would ever admit as much even if I were being stretched on the rack."

"But you just did." She laughed.

They spoke about literature during the rest of the stroll up the long lawns to the terrace and about dogs while they drank blessedly cool lemonade. Jennifer did not know how they had got onto the latter subject, but she found herself telling the earl about her collie who loved to eat the cakes she smuggled to him and who sensed when he was about to be taken for a walk and tore around in circles and yipped and otherwise demonstrated wild and undignified enthusiasm until his expectations were met.

"I miss him," she ended rather lamely. "But life in town would not suit him. He is unaccustomed to being walked on a leash."

"Come," he said, taking her empty glass from her hand and offering his arm again after setting the glass on the table, "let us stroll into the orchard. There will be no fruit to see at this time of year and we are too late for the blossoms, but there will be relief from the heat of the sun for a while until tea is served."

Jennifer had no idea how much time had elapsed since they had left the riverbank. It could have been ten minutes or it could have been an hour. But for the first time in however long it had been she looked about her with awareness and noted that there were a few other people, in couples or small groups, on the terrace and others in larger numbers strolling on the lawns. One group was playing croquet while others watched. Lionel and Samantha were nowhere in sight. They had not yet come up from the river. They must be still out in the boat or else standing on the bank as part of the group with whom they had all gone down there.

She should be down there too, she thought, feeling disoriented for a moment, realizing how absorbed she had been in her conversation with the earl. She should be with Lionel. She wanted to be with him. She had looked forward to this afternoon, especially when she had woken up and seen how lovely the weather was. Perhaps there would be the chance to wander alone with him, she had thought, as she was wandering with the Earl of Thornhill now. It had seemed like a wonderful opportunity. Lionel was escorting both her and Samantha at the garden party. Aunt Agatha was otherwise engaged, as was the Countess of Rushford.

"Perhaps," she said, "you should escort me back to the river, my lord. I believe my cousin and Lord Kersey must still be there."

"If you wish." He smiled. "Though the thought of shade and quietness for a few minutes is definitely appealing, is it not?"

It was. And—treacherously—the lure of his company for a few minutes longer. Being with Lionel was not nearly as comfortable at present. There were too many tensions surrounding the facts of their betrothal and its announcement and their impending marriage. In time they would be this comfortable together. But not yet.

"Wonderfully so," she said, smiling conspiratorially at him. "Parasols are made to look pretty, my lord, but accomplish very little else."

"I had always suspected as much." He grinned at her. "But heaven forbid that women should ever admit it and become practical beings. How ghastly to think that the time may ever come."

She took his arm and allowed him to lead her toward the orchard. "Do you believe that women should be only ornaments to brighten a man's life, then?" she asked. "Nothing else?"

"I would have to take exception to the word *only*," he said. "All men—and women too—like to be surrounded by lovely ornaments. They make life more pleasant and more elegant. But life would be unbearably dull and lonely if there was nothing but the ornaments. They would soon lose their appeal and be fit for nothing else but to be hurled for the relief of frustration. A woman would quickly lose her appeal, no matter how lovely and ornamental she was, if she had nothing else to offer."

"Oh," she said. "Fit only to be hurled in a fit of temper."

He chuckled. "It is the reason for the failure of so many marriages," he said. "So many couples are trapped into a lifetime of boredom and even active misery. Had you noticed? And very often it is because they once thought that what pleased the eye would satisfy the emotions and the mind for the rest of their lives."

"You do not look for beauty in a prospective bride, then?" she asked.

He laughed again. "I do not yet know what I look for," he said. "I am not yet in search of a bride. But you are twisting my words. Lovely ornaments are important to life. There must be aesthetic pleasure to make it complete. But there has to be more too. Much more, I believe."

The wife the Earl of Thornhill would choose eventually would be a fortunate woman, Jennifer thought. She would also have to be a special person.

It was indeed blessedly cool among the trees of the orchard. The branches overhead did not block the sun but muted its rays and gave a strange air of seclusion, though the lawns and the garden party guests were close by. It was almost like being back in the country, Jennifer thought and closed her eyes briefly against an unexpected stabbing of nostalgia.

"And what about you?" the Earl of Thornhill asked. "Your impending marriage is an arranged one. Did you have any hand in the choice?"

"No," she said. "Papa and the Earl of Rushford are friends and decided years ago that a match between their children was a desirable thing."

"And you did not fight against their decision tooth and nail?" he asked, smiling.

"No," she said. "Why should I? I trust Papa's wisdom and I approved his choice."

"And still do?" he asked.

"Yes."

"Because he is beautiful?" he asked. "He will certainly be a wonderful ornament for you to look at for the rest of your life."

She felt that she should be offended that he had somehow insulted Lionel. But there was a teasing gleam in his eye when she looked up at him. She thought of his belief that there had to be more than beauty to attract if a marriage was to have a hope of bringing a lifelong companionship and happiness. Yes, Lionel was beautiful and it was his beauty that had caused her to fall headlong in love with him. But there was more. There was his cool courtesy and sense of propriety. There was—oh, there was a whole character to be discovered over the next weeks and months. They were going to be wonderfully happy. She had waited five long years for the happiness they were soon to know.

"Do you love him?" he asked quietly.

But the conversation had become far too personal. She had not yet told Lionel that she loved him. He had not told her that he loved her. She was certainly not going to discuss her feelings with a stranger.

"I think," she said, "we should talk about poetry again."

He chuckled and patted her hand. "Yes," he said. "It was a dreadfully impertinent question. Forgive me. In a very short acquaintance I have come to think of you as a friend. Friends talk to each other on the most intimate of topics. But friends are usually of the same gender. When they are not, there must always be some barrier to total friendship, I suppose, unless they share a relationship that is intimate in all ways. I am unaccustomed to having a woman as a friend."

Were they friends? She scarcely knew him. And yet she found it remarkably easy to talk with him. But she ought not even to be with him. Lionel did not like it and Aunt Agatha had warned her quite severely against him. He was not quite respectable. And there was something about him that stopped her from being quite at her ease with him. Some . . . attraction. There was that word again.

"I have never had a gentleman as a friend," she said. "And I do not believe it is a possibility, my lord. I mean between you and me." She was surprised to feel a certain sadness. And surprised too and a little uncomfortable to find that they had stopped walking and that somehow she had come to be standing with her back against a tree while he stood before her, one hand resting against the trunk above and to one side of her head. "I am going to be married soon."

"Yes." He smiled down at her. "It was a foolish and impulsive notion, was it not, that we could be friends. But it is true for this afternoon, nevertheless. You feel it too, do you not? We are friends. Am I wrong?"

She shook her head. And then wondered if she should have nodded. And was not at all sure with which of his questions she had agreed.

"And so," he said, "I am forgiven for my indiscretion of the other night?"

She nodded. "It was as much my fault as yours," she said almost in a whisper.

She wondered, gazing at his smiling face and friendly eyes, why she had ever agreed with Samantha's comparison of him to the devil. Or had she been the one to suggest it? She could no longer remember. But it was only his very dark coloring in comparison with Lionel's blondness that had made her think so. Now that she knew him a little, she found that he was a man she liked. She regretted that there could be no real friendship between them.

"No," he said. "I am more experienced in these matters than you. I should have known better, Jennifer."

It took her a moment to understand why she felt suddenly as if something intimate had passed between them—almost like the kiss they had shared in the Chisleys' garden. And then she realized that he had used her given name, as Lionel had still not done. She opened her mouth to reprimand him and then closed it again. He was her friend—for today anyway.

"Ah," he said. "Another indiscretion. Pardon me. Yes, I was quite right. It is impossible for two people of opposite gender to be true friends. There are other feelings that interfere with those of pure friendship. Alas. I could never be your friend, Jennifer Winwood. Not under present circumstances."

She saw her hand, as if it belonged to someone else, lift to his face and both saw and felt her fingers touch his cheek. And then she lowered it more hastily to lay it flat against the bark at her side, and bit her lip.

Tension rippled between them. But though her mind knew it and knew where it was likely to lead, the rest of her being seemed powerless to break free of it. Or perhaps did not really want to do so. She wanted—she needed—to feel his mouth against hers again. She wanted to feel his arms about her, his body against hers. Her head knew quite clearly that she wanted no such thing, but her body and her emotions were ignoring that knowledge.

"You have just forgiven me," he said softly, his mouth only a few inches from her own, "for a sin I am sorely tempted to repeat. And for one I knew would tempt me again if I had you alone and unobserved once more. No, there is not the smallest possibility of a friendship between you and me. And none of any other relationship.

You are betrothed—to a man you love. I found you five years too late, Jennifer Winwood. Had I not, I would have fought him for you—every inch of the way. Perhaps I might even have won." He took a step back and removed his hand from the trunk of the tree.

"You could have anyone you want," she said, still gazing at him. At his darkly handsome features and tall, athletic physique. She did not care what he had done. Any woman would fall in love with him if she but got to know him a little. Any woman whose heart was not already given elsewhere, that was.

He chuckled and looked genuinely amused for a moment. "Oh, no, there you are wrong," he said. "There is at least someone I cannot have. Let me escort you back to the terrace. It must be teatime and it is probable that everyone has come up from the river."

"Yes." She felt depressed suddenly. She should be feeling relief and gratitude—relief at having escaped another dreadful infidelity and gratitude that he had had greater control and better sense than she had had. But she felt sad. Sad for him because he seemed to care for her but could do nothing to attach her interest because she was betrothed. And sad for herself because she had dreamed of just such encounters as she had had with the Earl of Thornhill—but with Lionel. How perfect—how utterly perfect—life would be if it was he who had kissed her at the ball and almost kissed her in the orchard and if it were with him that she had talked so comfortably and so freely on a variety of topics both important and trivial. If it were he with whom she was becoming friends.

She loved Lionel so very, very dearly. But she knew by now that it was no fairy-tale love that they had. It was a very real human relationship that did not come easily to either of them. They had both agreed that they wanted the marriage and she believed they both loved. But building companionship and friendship was something they would have to work on. Perhaps it would be easier once they had the more intimate relationship of marriage, once they lived together and shared responsibilities. But the dream of meeting in London and proceeding from that moment to living happily ever after had not become reality. She would admit it to herself now.

And yet it might have if they had had characters that were more compatible. She knew that it was possible to be comfortable with a man and to find it easy both to talk and to listen to him. But Lionel was not that man.

She loved him but he was not yet her friend. Perhaps it was as well, she thought. Making him her friend would give her a goal to work toward after her marriage. One always needed goals in order to give purpose to life.

Viscount Kersey was on the terrace with Samantha and a group of other people. It seemed to Jennifer as if they all turned to watch her progress across the lawn from the orchard. And it seemed to her now, when it was too late, that after all it had been indiscreet to go just there.

The Earl of Thornhill did not linger when he had returned her to Lionel's side. But he took his leave in such a way as to embarrass her deeply, though she was sure that had not been his intention. He took her right hand in both his, gazed at her with intent eyes, as she remembered his doing that first afternoon in the park, and spoke quietly, but quite loudly enough for the whole group to hear since they had all fallen silent at their approach.

"Thank you, Miss Winwood," he said, "for the pleasure of your company."

The words were quite innocuous. They were meant to be. They were merely a courtesy, the type of words any gentleman could be expected to say to any lady after he had danced with her or walked with her. And yet somehow they came out sounding alarmingly intimate. Or perhaps it was just that she was feeling guilty at what had almost happened again, Jennifer thought, and was hearing his words with the ears of guilt. His words made it sound as if they had been very much alone together and very pleased with each other's company. She had to stop herself from turning to the gathered company to explain that he had not meant his words that way at all.

And then to make matters worse—though it was a gesture as innocent as the words had been—he raised her hand to his lips. She wished he had not kept his eyes on hers as he did so. And she wished he had not kept her hand there for what seemed like several seconds. He meant nothing by it, of course, but—oh, but she was afraid that that would not be obvious to all those who watched. To Lionel in particular.

The earl walked away without a word to Lord Kersey or Samantha or any of the others. She felt the discourtesy and was surprised by it and disappointed in him.

She did not watch to see where he went. She smiled at her betrothed and felt horribly uncomfortable.

"You were very brave to have gone walking with the Earl of Thornhill, Miss Winwood," Miss Simons said, wide-eyed. "My maid told me, and she had it on the most reliable authority, that he was forced to run away to the Continent with his stepmother when his father discovered them together in compromising circumstances."

"Claudia!" Her brother's voice cut across hers like a whip, so that she had the grace to blush even as she giggled.

"Well, it is true," she muttered.

"I see that tea is being served," Samantha said gaily. "I am starved. Shall we lead the way, Jenny? I am not shy." She laughed as she linked her arm through her cousin's and led her away to the tables, which a long line of footmen had just laden with platefuls of various appetizing-looking foods.

## 8

WHAT DID MISS SIMONS MEAN," JENNIFER ASKED, her voice low, her eyes directed at the grass before her feet, "when she said that he fled to the Continent after being caught in a compromising situation with his stepmother?" She blushed at her own words, but Lionel had started it, taking her off to walk alone when they had scarcely even started their tea. He had told her coldly that he was extremely displeased with her behavior.

"The question is an improper one," Viscount Kersey said, "coming from a young lady I have been led to expect to be well bred. But I believe Miss Simons's words spoke for themselves."

She was silent for a moment, digesting his words, anger warring in her with guilt. How dare he scold her as if she were a child, one part of her mind thought. And how dare he suggest in that cold voice that she was ill bred. And then the other part of her mind reminded her that she had once let the Earl of Thornhill kiss her and that perhaps she would have allowed it again this afternoon if he had cared to press the point. Yet another part of her felt like crying. The spring was not proceeding at all as she had expected.

"But he took her to the Continent with him?" She

could not leave it alone. She had to know. Perhaps in knowing she would finally be able to shake herself free of the totally unwilling attraction she felt toward the earl. Not that it could really be called that. How could she feel an attraction to him when all her love was given to Lionel? "He took his stepmother? Without his father? Or was it after the death of his father?"

"It was before his father's death," Lord Kersey said, his words clipped. "It was the probable cause of his father's death. He fled with the countess because she was in no fit condition to be seen by decent people in this country. There. Are you satisfied?"

There was a buzzing in her head and a coldness in her nostrils. No. She would not believe it. She must have misunderstood what Lionel had said. The earl had done . . . *that* with his own stepmother? He had caused her to be with child? And had taken her away for her confinement? And . . . and then what?

"Where is she now?" Her voice was a whisper.

He laughed. But when she looked at him, she saw that he was sneering, an expression that marred his good looks. She frowned and looked away again.

"Abandoned, of course," he said. "He grew tired of her and came home alone."

"Oh."

They had walked all the way to the bank of the river, she saw. There was one couple out in a boat, no doubt enjoying the luxury of being together while everyone was at tea. There was no one else on the bank.

"So you see," Viscount Kersey said, "why being seen in

company with such a man can do irreparable harm to a lady's reputation. And why I must forbid you ever to speak with him again."

Jennifer turned her parasol slowly above her head while she watched the boat out on the river. "My lord," she said quietly, "I am twenty years old. And yet people persist in treating me like a child and telling what I must do and what I must not do."

"You are a young lady," he said, "and an innocent."

"I will no longer be an innocent in a little over a month's time," she said, turning to face him.

"You will be my wife." A muscle was twitching in his jaw.

Ah, yes. She would owe him obedience as she now owed obedience to her father—and to Aunt Agatha acting in her father's stead during her come-out. It was the lot of women. Only love could sweeten the pill. And she and Lionel loved each other. Did they not?

"Should I not at least be given a reason?" she asked. "If you must give me a command, my lord, should I not know why that command is given so that I may follow it as a rational choice of my own as much as from the need to obey? I have been warned several times to shun the Earl of Thornhill's company, but until now I have been given no reason to do so. I am a rational being even though I am a woman."

He gazed back at her, his handsome face tight with some emotion she could not read.

*He does not understand,* she thought. She felt a twinge of alarm, of uneasiness for her future, for the rest of her life.

*He does not understand that I am a person, that women have minds just as men do.*

She loved him. She had loved him totally and passionately for five years. But for the first time—and she felt panic at the thought—she wondered if a blind, unreasoned love would be enough for her. She had thought that love would be everything. She had lived for this spring and for this betrothal and for her marriage. Was love everything?

"Of course you have a mind," he said. "If it is a good mind, it will recognize the wisdom of deferring to the greater experience and better judgment of the men who have the charge of you and of women considerably older than yourself. I hope you are not going to be difficult."

He might as well have slapped her face. She felt as dazed as if he had, and as humiliated.

"Difficult?" she said. "Do you wish for a placid, docile wife, then, my lord?"

"I certainly expect one who knows her own place and mine," he said. "I assumed from my knowledge of your upbringing and the fact that you have always lived in the country that you would suit me. So did my mother and my father."

And she did not? Because she had danced with the Earl of Thornhill and walked with him when no one had thought it necessary to explain to her why she should not? Perhaps, she thought—but the thought bewildered her because it was so new and so strange—perhaps Viscount Kersey would not suit her.

She gazed at him. At her beautiful Lionel. The man

she had dreamed of daily and nightly for so long that it seemed she must have loved him and dreamed of him all her life. What had gone wrong with this Season?

"You seem rebellious," he said. "Perhaps you are regretting your acceptance of my offer three weeks ago. Perhaps you would like to change your answer now before the official announcement is made."

"No!" The answer and the sheer panic that provoked it were purely instinctive, but they came to her rescue and completely drowned out the strange doubts she had been having. "No, Lionel. I love you!"

And then she froze to the sound of her own words even as she gazed, horrified, into the very blue eyes that looked intently back. She had called him by his given name before she had been invited to do so. She had told him she loved him before he had said the words to her. She was deeply embarrassed. And yet she had spoken the truth, she thought. She bit her lip but did not lower her eyes.

"I see," he said. "Well, then, we have no quarrel, do we?"

Had they been quarreling? She supposed they had. There was a feeling of relief in the thought. It was natural for lovers to quarrel. Not that they were lovers exactly—not yet anyway. But they were betrothed. It was natural. He had been jealous and annoyed and she had been on the defensive. Now it was over. Now it was time to make up—as she supposed they would do dozens or hundreds of times during the course of the rest of their lives. This was real life as opposed to the life of perfection she lived in dreams. It was nothing to worry about.

"I do not even like him," she said. "He is bold and . . . a-and unmannerly. I danced with him at Papa's ball and at the Chisleys' only because I could not get out of doing so without seeming quite ill-mannered. And I walked with him this afternoon for the same reason. I would have far preferred to be with you, but you had promised to take Sam out in the boat. I do not like him, and now that I know what he has done, I shall certainly never speak with him again."

"I am glad to hear it," he said.

She twirled her parasol, feeling all the relief and light-heartedness that came at the end of a quarrel. She smiled. "Don't look as if you are still cross with me, then," she said. "Smile at me. These are such beautiful surroundings for a garden party, and I have so looked forward to being here—with you."

She blushed at her own boldness, but her heart was full of her love for him again. He had been jealous and she was touched—though she would never again give him even the whisper of a cause.

"And I with you," he said rather stiffly.

But then he smiled and Jennifer's heart performed its usual somersault. She held out her hand to him, realizing she had done so only when he took it and raised it to his lips. She wished—oh, she wished they were in some secluded spot, the orchard, perhaps, so that he could kiss her on the lips. It seemed such a perfect moment for their first kiss. The warmest, most relaxed moment they had yet shared.

"Almack's tomorrow evening," she said, "and the Velgards' costume ball the evening after. And then your father's dinner and ball two nights after that." She still smiled at him.

He squeezed her hand. "I can scarcely wait," he said. And he took her hand to his lips yet again.

She had heard it said, Jennifer thought, that it was good for couples to quarrel, that quarrels often cleared the air between them and made the relationship better than ever. It was so very true. She felt the warmth of his arm through his sleeve as they strolled up the lawn again, back in the direction of the house, and felt so happy that the old cliché of the heart being about to burst seemed almost to suit. It was all behind them, the rather slow, uncomfortable beginning to their betrothal. And any last-minute doubts—if they could be called that—had been put to rest.

She would determinedly avoid the Earl of Thornhill for the rest of the Season. She felt ashamed now of the ease she had felt in his company just this afternoon and the feeling she had had that there was indeed a certain friendship between them. She felt more discomfort than ever over the fact that she had allowed him that kiss at the Chisleys' ball. Knowing what she now knew of him, she would not find it at all difficult to snub him quite openly if necessary. His own stepmother! He had done *that* with his father's wife.

She closed her mind quite firmly to twinges of guilt

over the fact that she was no longer making allowances for the possibility that he had finished sowing his wild oats and was now trying to make amends. Some things were unforgivable. Besides, he had abandoned his stepmother and their child and left them alone somewhere in a foreign land. He was not making amends at all. He was quite despicable. Quite loathsome.

"And so you see," Sir Albert Boyle said as he sat over an early afternoon dinner at White's with his friend, the Earl of Thornhill, "I have been caught. Past tense, it seems, Gabe. Not even present tense, and certainly not future."

The earl looked at him keenly. "But you have made no declaration yet?" he asked.

"Good Lord, no." Sir Albert gazed gloomily into his port for a moment before taking a drink. "I said it would happen, Gabe. Appear one too many times in a ballroom and dance one too many sets, and someone will get it into her head that you are out shopping when in truth you are just browsing. Rosalie Ogden!"

"I thought that if you fell victim to anyone this year it would be to Miss Newman," the earl said.

"Ah," his friend said. "The delectable blonde. Every red-blooded man's dream." He looked down into his glass. "And the plain and ordinary and rather dull Miss Ogden, with whom I have danced and whom I have taken driving because Frank said she had not taken well, poor girl."

"And she is expecting a declaration? And her mother is expecting it?" The earl frowned. "You don't have to do it, Bertie. You have not compromised the girl, have you?"

"Lord, no," Sir Albert said. "She is not the type of girl one goes slinking off into grottoes with, Gabe. I thought about calling tomorrow actually. Before my nerve goes."

The Earl of Thornhill dabbed at his mouth with his napkin and set it down beside his empty plate. He wondered what he was missing. He and Bertie had been close friends for years—since their schoolboy days.

"Why?" he asked. "You are not in love with the girl by any chance, are you?" He could not imagine any man being in love with Miss Rosalie Ogden, though the thought was unkind. She seemed so totally without any quality that any man might find appealing. Bertie, on the other hand, was young and good-looking and wealthy and intelligent and could surely attach the affections of almost any lady he cared to set his sights on.

Sir Albert puffed out his cheeks and blew air out through his mouth. "It's like this, Gabe," he said. "You dance with a girl because you feel sorry for her and imagine how sad and humiliated she would be going home and to bed knowing that she had been a wallflower all evening while the prettier girls had danced. And then you take her driving for the same reason, and walking and boating at a garden party and then dancing again at Almack's last evening. And then you start to realize that there is someone hiding behind the plainness and the quietness and the—the dullness. Someone sort of sweet in a way and someone who—well, who would bleed if she cut herself, if you know what I mean. Someone who loves kittens to distraction and cries over chimney sweeps' climbing boys and likes to slip up to her sister's nursery to play with her nieces and nephews instead of sitting in the drawing room listening to the adults converse. And then you realize that she is not quite as plain or as quiet or as dull as you had thought."

"You *are* in love with her," the earl said, intrigued.

"Well, I don't see stars whirling about my head," Sir Albert said. "So it can't be that, Gabe, can it? It is just that I am—well, a little bit fond of her, I suppose. It sort of creeps up on you. You don't notice it and you don't particularly want it or welcome it when you discover it. But it's there. And there seems to be only one thing to do about it. No, two, I suppose. I could leave London tomorrow—go visit my aunt in Brighton, or something like that. But I would always wait for word of her marrying some oaf and then I would always wonder if he was allowing climbing boys into their house and keeping kittens out. And if he was giving her children for her own nursery. Gabe, I think I must have been touched by the sun. Has it been hot lately? I have known her for less than a week. I cannot even realistically talk about anything creeping up on me, can I? Creeping is a slow process. Galloping, more like."

"You are in love with her," the earl said again.

"Well," Sir Albert said. "Whatever name you care to give it, Gabe. But I think I am off to call tomorrow. Brigham is her uncle and guardian. I'll have a word with him first. And with her mother too. I'll do the thing properly. I'll probably even go down on one knee when the moment comes." He winced. "Do you think I will do anything so unspeakably humiliating, Gabe?"

The earl chuckled.

"There is nothing for a dowry, by the way," Sir Albert said. "Or so Frank says, and he should know since his sister is a friend of her sister's. So I cannot be accused of acting in such haste out of any greed for her fortune, can I? Besides, it must be well-known that my own pockets are well enough lined that I don't have to snatch at dowries."

"It will never be known for anything other than what it is," the earl said. "A love match, Bertie."

His friend grimaced and drained off his glass of port. "I have to be going," he said. "I am to drive her with her mother to the Tower this afternoon. I shall have to see how I feel afterward. Perhaps I will change my mind and be saved. Do you think, Gabe?"

The earl merely smiled.

"Are you coming?" Sir Albert got to his feet.

"No," the earl said. "I think I'll stay and drink another glass of port, Bertie. I shall drink to your health and happiness. Go and make yourself pretty for your lady love."

Sir Albert grimaced once more and took his leave. The Earl of Thornhill did not drink another glass of port, but he did sit alone at the table for a long while, turning his empty glass absently with the fingers of one hand, his pensive manner discouraging both acquaintances from joining him and waiters from clearing the table.

*And then you start to realize that there is someone hiding . . .*

*someone who would bleed if she cut herself . . . it sort of creeps up on you.*

It was something entirely between him and Kersey, he thought. He had taken the fall for Kersey's evil, and he had watched Catherine suffer as a result of it. And now he saw a chance for a little revenge and had found himself consumed by the desire to accomplish it. Kersey knew it and had issued his own challenge. It was just between the two of them.

Except that Jennifer Winwood was caught in the middle. She was the pawn he would use to upset Kersey's life, to bring scandal and humiliation to his name. Very publicly. There was no better arena for this particular type of revenge than London during the Season.

Jennifer Winwood was unimportant. She would find someone else more worthy of her than Kersey. In fact, as he had told himself before, he was doing her a favor. If he could bring about an end to her betrothal, he would have done her a favor even if she did not realize it. Not that it really mattered. Having some measure of revenge on Kersey was all that was important.

Except that . . .

*. . . someone who would bleed if she cut herself.* When he had apologized for having kissed her in the Chisleys' garden, she had admitted that it had disturbed her. *It did cause me some distress,* she had said.

*. . . you start to realize that there is someone hiding . . .* She enjoyed emotion and sentimentality in literature as well as humor and satire. She had a collie whom she missed, one that yipped and demonstrated wild and undignified

enthusiasm when a walk was imminent. She had never had a gentleman friend. She had lifted her hand and touched his cheek when he had pretended sadness over the fact that her engagement made it impossible for them ever to be friends.

*. . . someone who would bleed if she cut herself.*

Damnation! He had no wish to hurt the girl. None whatsoever. And no wish to deceive her. And yet he had done nothing but deceive her, pretending to friendly and even tender feelings for her when he felt none.

Except that . . .

*It sort of creeps up on you. You don't notice it and you don't particularly want it . . .*

The Earl of Thornhill got abruptly to his feet and had to reach back a hasty hand to stop his chair from toppling backward. He needed air and exercise.

He needed to steel himself for the costume ball at Lady Velgard's this evening. He needed to remind himself how all-consuming the desire for revenge had become to him since seeing Kersey again.


"DO YOU SUPPOSE THERE will be any waltzes tonight?" Jennifer asked. Although it was a warm day outside, she was sitting on the floor of the sitting room she shared with her cousin, her back to a fire, drying her long hair. Her arms were clasped about her knees. She had the kind of beauty that Samantha had always envied. She could have been an Amazon warrior or a Greek goddess or a— or a Queen Elizabeth I. It was as Queen Elizabeth that she was going to the costume ball this evening. Samantha, on the other hand, saw only a milk-and-water miss when she looked in her own mirror, and she was to dress up tonight as—of all things—a fairy queen.

"I believe there almost certainly will be," she said. "There usually are, so I have heard, except sometimes if it is someone's come-out ball."

"I hope so." Jennifer rested one cheek on her knees. "Sam, was it not wonderful beyond belief to be granted permission to waltz at Almack's last evening? It was the happiest moment of my life—well, one of them, anyway."

"And I was stuck dancing it with Mr. Piper," Samantha said. "To say he has two left feet is unduly to insult left feet, Jenny."

Her cousin laughed. And looked wonderfully happy, as she had been looking for a few days now. Their roles seemed almost to have been reversed. Jenny was the sunny one, always on the verge of laughter. Samantha, on the other hand, was having to force her mood, to try to convince everyone else as well as herself that her first Season was all she had expected it to be.

"That was a pity," Jennifer admitted. "Whom would you have liked to dance it with, Sam? If you had your choice of any gentleman?"

Lionel, Samantha thought treacherously and quelled the thought instantly. Out on the river at Lady Bromley's garden party Lionel—Lord Kersey—had apologized for what had happened at the Chisley ball. He had been out of temper, he had claimed, and had forgotten that he was a gentleman. And then he had rowed her silently on the river, his eyes occasionally becoming locked with hers. When he had handed her out onto the bank, he had retained her hand in his for a second or two longer than was necessary and had squeezed it so hard that she had almost cried out in pain and had whispered hastily and fiercely to her.

"I wish," he had said, "I could forget again that I am a gentleman. Samantha, I wish . . ." But his voice had trailed off and his eyes had gazed into hers with dismay and remorse.

"Oh, I do not know," she said now with a shrug. "Sir Albert Boyle, maybe. Or Mr. Maxwell. Or Mr. Simons. Someone with both a left foot and a right foot and some feel for music." She laughed lightly.

Jennifer's eyes were steady on her. "Is there no one special yet, Sam?" she asked. "It is strange. Somehow I expected that you would fall wildly in love with some impossibly handsome gentleman with forty thousand a year after our first ball. You have a large court of admirers. Indeed, it seems to grow every day. But you seem to favor no one in particular."

"Give me time," Samantha said airily. "I intend to settle on no one less handsome than Li—than Lord Kersey."

"Or the Earl of Thornhill," Jennifer said, and then she flushed and turned her head to rest the other cheek on her knees. "I mean, someone as handsome as he."

If only the earl did not have that dreadful reputation, Samantha thought, her treacherous thoughts breaking free again. And if there was not the betrothal. He seemed to like Jenny and she . . . Well, she had been alone with him on two separate occasions. If only . . . If only Lionel were free. But she jerked her mind back to reality.

"He was not at Almack's last night," she said. "I wonder if he will be at the ball this evening."

"I hope not," Jennifer said. "Did you know that what that unspeakably stupid Claudia Simons said about him at the garden party was true? He did run off with his stepmother. She was increasing, Sam. And then he abandoned her and the child to come back here alone."

"His own father's wife?" Samantha felt genuine horror. "Oh, Jenny, we were right about him that very first time. Lucifer. The devil. He really is, is he not?"

"Except that he does not seem evil when one talks with him," Jennifer said. "He seems warm and friendly. But I suppose that is the nature of the devil, is it not? Oh, but I do not want to talk about him, Sam. I hope there are waltzes tonight. I want to waltz again with Lord Kersey and feel his hand at my waist. I want to dance just with him for half an hour." She had her eyes closed, Samantha saw. "I can hardly wait."

Samantha's spirits had sunk so low that she felt as if definite physical leaden weights were pressing down on her. Lionel, she thought. Oh, Lionel. How she too would love to be waltzing with him tonight. And . . . Oh, thought was pointless.

She hated her cousin suddenly. And then she turned her hatred against herself. And against Lionel. If he had tender feelings for her—and she was sure that he did—how could he be contemplating marriage with Jenny?

But he was trapped into that by an unwritten agreement made five years before, when he had been only twenty.

Only Jenny could break the engagement. It would be horribly scandalous even for her to do it, but it would be impossible for him. An honorable gentleman just did not break such a promise. But Jenny had no reason to break off her betrothal. She would never do so, unless—unless she knew that he loved someone else.

Samantha tried to break the trend of her thoughts.

"Oh, Sam," Jennifer said, hugging her knees more tightly, her eyes still closed, "you really must find someone soon. You must find out for yourself what this happiness feels like."

Samantha rested her head against the back of the chair on which she sat and closed her own eyes. She felt suddenly both dizzy and nauseated.

# 9

SHE WORE A GOLD MASK, BUT IT DID NOTHING TO hide her identity. Nor was it meant to. It was a mere convention of a costume ball. She was all in gold and white and unmistakably dressed as Queen Elizabeth I. The rich, heavy gold and white brocade of her dress and the stiff ruff that fanned out behind her head were carried with a suitably regal bearing. Her dark red hair was set severely back from her face and curled all about her head.

She would have drawn eyes even if she had stood alone. But she stood with an Elizabethan courtier whose clothes matched her own in color and splendor. His own gold mask gleamed pale against his blond hair.

They were by far the most attractive couple in the ballroom.

The Earl of Thornhill, watching them after the courtier had joined his queen and her cousin and aunt after their arrival at Lady Velgard's costume ball, was not sorry about the fact that they drew such universal attention despite the presence of other clever and attractive costumes on other guests. And he was not sorry that they were so easily recognizable. It would all work to his advantage.

"Bertie is not coming tonight," Lord Francis Kneller said at the earl's elbow. "Do you know why, Gabe?" His tone suggested that he certainly did even if his friend did not.

She was glowing, Lord Thornhill thought, gazing across the room—as many other people seemed to be doing. Her mouth was curved into a smile. Something about the whole set of her body and head suggested that she was excited and happy. Happy with her partner. In love with him. Damnation. "Why?" he asked.

"Because Rosalie Ogden's mama thinks a costume ball too racy an event for her daughter to attend," Lord Francis said, emphasizing the girl's name. "Rosalie Ogden, Gabe. Bertie is not coming because she will not be here."

"He took her sightseeing to the Tower this afternoon, I believe," the earl said.

"Good Lord," Lord Francis said. "Good Lord, Gabe, is he touched in the upper works?"

"I believe," the earl said, looking at him at last and grinning, "it is called love, Frank."

"Well, good Lord." His friend seemed to have been rendered inarticulate.

"I suppose," the earl said, "it is only natural that we feel a twinge of alarm when one of our number turns his mind toward matrimony, Frank. It reminds us that we too are getting older and that responsibility and the need to be setting up nurseries are staring us in the eyeball."

"The devil!" Lord Francis said. "We are not even thirty

yet, Gabe. Or even close to it. But Rosalie Ogden! He is seriously thinking of offering for her?"

"I have it on the best authority," the earl said, "that there is rather a sweet girl hiding behind the plainness and the quietness."

"There would have to be," Lord Francis said. "There is not even anything much for a dowry. Ah, a waltz. The opportunity to get my arm about some slender waist is not to be wasted, Gabe—I hope you noticed the pun. The fairy queen, do you think? No, she is swamped by her usual court. Cleopatra, then. I was presented to her at Almack's last evening so I can just stroll along and ask." He walked away without more ado, Roman toga notwithstanding, to claim the set with the lady of his choice.

The Earl of Thornhill stood where he was and watched. And assured a few fellow guests, who approached him in mock terror, that no, his pistols were not loaded. He was dressed as a highwayman of bygone years, all in black, including his mask. He wore a powdered wig, tied and bagged with black silk at the neck, and a tricorne hat.

Ah, he thought, so she had been granted permission to waltz. She was dancing it now with Kersey and smiling up at him, her attention wholly on him. And Lord, she was beautiful. Every time he saw her he seemed to be jolted anew by her beauty, as if he had forgotten it since his last sight of her. He was glad she was able to waltz. And if one was being danced this early in the evening, there must be several more planned for the rest of the night.

He intended to dance one of those waltzes with Miss Jennifer Winwood. It might not be easy to get past the defenses of Lady Brill and Kersey. And even the Countess of Rushford, Kersey's mother, was present tonight and keeping a proprietary eye on her son and his affianced bride. But somehow he would do it. He had no real fear of failure.

IF LIONEL WAS IRRESISTIBLY handsome as a gentleman of the present age, Jennifer thought, as a gentleman of Queen Elizabeth's court he was—well, there were not words. He was irresistibly handsome. She waltzed with him and felt that her feet scarcely touched the floor. It was surely the most divine and the most intimate dance ever invented. He was drawing all eyes just like a magnet, of course, as he always did. She basked in the fact that it was with her he danced and to her that he was betrothed. She felt that she was somehow picking up some of his re-flected splendor.

*He* was there—the Earl of Thornhill. At first she had thought he was not. Most of the guests were recognizable despite ingenious costumes and masks. But he was not easy to recognize, except for his height, which first drew her eyes his way. His hair was white and long and tied back beneath his hat. He made an alarmingly attractive highwayman, she thought. She was sure it was he when he stood beside a pillar instead of dancing the first set—and when he watched her the whole while. He was, of course, wearing a wig, she realized. A powdered wig, old-fashioned like the tricorne and the skirted coat and the long topboots.

She wished he had not come. Although she did not look directly at him, she saw him constantly nevertheless and was aware of him at every moment, as she always was. And yet there was a certain horror in the fascination she felt for him, knowing what she now knew of him. His stepmother! He was a father. He had a child, abandoned somewhere on the Continent with the child's mother. She wondered if he had left them quite destitute or if at the very least he had taken some measures to support them.

And she tried not to think about him at all.

It was easy to avoid him. Lionel, although he danced with her only once, hovered close between sets, and Aunt Agatha kept careful watch over her choice of partners and Samantha's. She did not, as so many of the chaperones did, find a cozy seat in a corner and while away the time gossiping with other ladies. And Lionel's mother engaged her in conversation between each set. It was like having a small army of bodyguards, Jennifer thought in some relief. She was not going to have to face the embarrassment of refusing to dance with him.

But then he made no move toward her, either.

It was unalloyed relief she felt, she told herself, refusing to recognize a certain feeling of inexplicable depression.

And then, well into the evening, events became so

strange that Jennifer was left feeling bewildered and exposed and not a little frightened. The Earl of Thornhill had moved closer. She sensed it without having to look to be sure. But Lionel looked long and consideringly in the direction where she knew the earl stood, though he said nothing. He would redouble his watch over her, she thought in some relief. But instead, he turned to his mother and to Aunt Agatha with a smile, commented on the heat in the ballroom, and suggested that they go to the dining room in search of a drink. He would do himself the honor of watching over their charges until their return.

They went.

Samantha, close by, was surrounded by her usual court of admirers. Some of them were talking with Jennifer too, though Lord Kersey continued to stay close beside her. But then he was gone, without a word or a sign, and he was smiling warmly at Samantha and taking her by the hand and leading her onto the floor for the waltz that was about to begin.

No one had yet asked Jennifer to dance, and it seemed that every gentleman turned to watch in chagrin as Sam was taken from beneath their very noses. In a moment, Jennifer thought afterward, one of them would have turned back and solicited her hand. Lionel must have thought that one of them already had. He must have thought that it was safe to leave her side, even though his mother and Aunt Agatha had left the ballroom.

But there was that moment when she stood alone, bewildered and exposed and a little frightened.

And in that moment a gentleman did indeed step forward and bow and reach out a hand for hers. A tall, black-masked highwayman in the fashion of the previous century, his long, powdered hair and tricorne hat making him look quite devastatingly attractive.

"Your majesty," the Earl of Thornhill said, "will you do me the honor?"

It was so much easier to tell oneself that one was going to issue a cold snub than actually to do it, Jennifer found. That, of course, was why she had been content to be hovered over all evening. She found it almost impossible to look into his eyes and refuse him.

"I—I—" she said.

He smiled at her. His hand was still extended. She felt as if eyes were on them but could not look about her to see. She felt doubly exposed and bewildered. She had promised Lionel. But it was merely a dance. A waltz. If she refused the Earl of Thornhill, she would not be able to dance it with any other gentleman.

She set her hand in his. "Thank you," she said.

But she would not leave the ballroom with him. The French windows were open, as they had been at the Chisley ball, and the ballroom was warm. But she would not set one toe out onto the balcony.

She had thought the waltz intimate when she had danced it with Lionel. It seemed even more so with the earl. It was his superior height, she decided. And his hand, warm and strong against the back of her waist, was holding her a little closer than Lionel had done—and a little closer than her dancing master had done. He was holding her just a little too close. If she swayed toward him even slightly in the course of the dance, she would touch him—with her breasts.

She should have said no, she thought, now that it was too late. A very firm, chilly no. She darted a look up into his eyes. They were looking steadily back, as she had expected they would. They looked even darker than usual and more compelling through the slits of his mask. She looked down sharply.

"I thought we were almost friends," he said quietly.

"No." She drew breath to say more, but left the one word to stand alone.

"They have been warning you against me again," he said. "I should not have taken you into the cool seclusion of the orchard, should I? Was he very angry with you? Would it help if I explained to him that nothing improper happened?"

"Is it true," she asked, and she blushed, knowing what she was about to say, "that you fled to the Continent with your stepmother?"

"Ah," he said, "they really have been busy. I would not use the word *fled*. It gives the impression of running in panic or guilt. But yes, I accompanied the Countess of Thornhill, my father's second wife, to the Continent." He was watching her keenly, she saw when she looked up briefly again. His head had bent slightly toward hers. People were watching. She could feel them watching.

"She had your child," she said. She did not know how she got the words past her lips. She did not even know why she would want to say them.

"She gave birth to a daughter in Switzerland," he said.

"And you abandoned them there." She was breathless. Her voice was accusing. She wished—oh, she wished she had said no. Why had Lionel been so careless after protecting her all evening and after telling his mother and Aunt Agatha that he would look after her?

"I left them in their new home there," he said, "while I came back to mine."

Another couple twirled close to them and his arm tightened about her, drawing her even closer. He did not relax it after the couple were safely past.

"Do you have any other questions?" he asked.

"No." She was being almost overpowered by that same feeling she had had when he kissed her in the Chisleys' garden. At a totally inappropriate time. When he had just admitted ... "Please do not hold me so close. It is unseemly."

She raised her eyes unwillingly to his as his hold relaxed just a little. And then found that she could not look away again.

"You should not have asked me to dance," she said. "Not that first time or any time since. It is not right. You should have stayed away."

"Why?" His voice was very quiet. It sounded like a hand would feel slowly caressing its way up her back. "Because I am not respectable? Or because you find it impossible to say no?"

She bit her lip. "You just admitted—"

"No," he said. "That is a poor choice of word. I just gave you a few facts. Gossipmongers love to take facts and twist them and squeeze them and sensationalize them until they are almost unrecognizable as truth."

"But you cannot deny the facts," she said.

"No," he said, and he smiled.

"Are you saying, then," she said, "that the facts do not mean what they appear to mean?"

"I am saying no such thing," he said. "I will leave the facts with you and the interpretation of those facts that Kersey and others of your family or acquaintances have put upon them in your hearing. But you have liked me, have you not? We were almost friends at the garden party, were we not?"

His eyes held hers, and his voice beguiled her. She wanted to believe in his innocence. When she was with him, she could not believe him the villain everyone else thought him and that even she had concurred with. When she was with him, he was . . . her friend. And something else—something more. But she was afraid of the direction her thoughts were taking and brought them to a stop.

"Tell me," she said, gazing earnestly at him, "that you are innocent of those things people say about you."

"My father's wife was never my mistress," he said. "Her child is not mine. I left her in comfort and security in Switzerland because there was no further need for me to stay with her. Do you believe me, Jennifer?"

She drew in a sharp breath at the sound of her name on his lips—again. And she swayed toward him until the tips of her breasts touching his coat brought her jolting back to a realization of where she was. But they were very close to one set of opened French windows, and he waltzed her through them before she could look about her to see if she had been observed. She felt dazed, almost as if she had been in some sort of trance. She had forgotten for perhaps seconds, perhaps minutes, that she was dancing with him in a crowded ballroom and that in the nature of things their every look and gesture were being observed.

She was thankful after all for the comparative privacy of the balcony. And for its coolness.

"Yes, I believe you," she said. "Yes, I do."

"Gabriel," he said, his head close to hers. "It is my name."

"Gabriel." She looked at him, startled. Gabriel? He was the angel Gabriel, she thought foolishly. Not Lionel, but this man whom she and Sam had called Lucifer.

"On your lips," he said, "my name sounds like an endearment." He closed the gap of inches between their mouths and touched hers with his own for a few brief moments.

It was hardly a kiss. It was even less a kiss than the other one had been. But he had continued dancing on the balcony and now they were at the next set of French windows and reentering the ballroom. But whereas he had probably intended the light touching of mouths to happen out of sight on the balcony, it actually happened a fraction of a second too late—they were fully in the doorway and fully in view of any of a few hundred people who happened to be looking their way.

Jennifer froze, terrified to turn her head to the right or the left, terrified to look away from his eyes.

He did not look away from hers. "If you dare to look into your heart," he said, "and find that it has changed since last you looked, pay heed to it. It is not too late—yet. But soon it will be."

Her eyes widened as the meaning of his words hit her. "Nothing has changed," she said. "Nothing at all. I am going to be married in a month's time. It is all arranged. I love him."

His eyes smiled a little sadly. "You would not admit to that the last time we spoke," he said. "It is true, then? What I have felt since meeting you, what I feel, is entirely one-sided?"

She bit her lip again. "You must not say such things," she said. "Please. You say that we are almost friends and yet you try to upset me. You try to make me feel doubts when I feel none. You try to make me admit that I—"

"No," he said softly. "Not if it will upset you to do so, Jennifer. Not if it will hurt you, my love."

There was such an aching stab of . . . longing? deep in her womb that for a moment she closed her eyes. But the music was drawing to a close. Blessedly the set was coming to an end.

Oh, blessedly.

*My love. My love.*

He bowed over her hand when he had returned her to the edge of the floor and they were flanked by Aunt Agatha on the one side and the Countess of Rushford on the other, and raised it to his lips.

Aunt Agatha was tight-lipped and smiling all at the same time. Lionel had not yet returned from the floor with Samantha. The countess was smiling and linked her arm through Jennifer's.

"It is hot in here, my dear," she said. "Come, stroll with me about the ballroom and onto the balcony. Let us be seen smiling and conversing together. Sometimes, I know, these things happen, and it is almost invariably not the young lady's fault. Smile, dear. We have a great deal of smoothing over to do."

Her arm was not as relaxed as her person appeared to be, Jennifer noticed. She also noticed that her smiling future mother-in-law was angry.

Jennifer smiled. And looked about her as the two of them strolled around the perimeter of the room in the direction of the French windows to find that everyone seemed to be looking at them. At her. It seemed hardly an exaggeration.

"Some cool air would be pleasant," she said, holding onto her smile with a conscious effort.

*My love. My love.* The words, spoken in the voice of the Earl of Thornhill, echoed and reechoed in her head.

"WELL, MY ETHEREAL FAIRY queen." His blue eyes smiled at her through the slits of his golden mask. "Are you able to grant wishes?"

Samantha looked at him warily. Although she had been chatting brightly with several gentlemen since the last set ended, because she loved Lionel she was always aware of him when they were in a room together. She had seen him send his mother and Aunt Aggy away and had heard what he had said to them. He had sent them away so that he could ask her to dance, she thought a few minutes later. But he did not need to send them out of the way in order to do that. It was quite unexceptionable for him to dance with her. In doing so now, though, he had left Jenny alone for the moment. But only for a moment. Then she was dancing with the Earl of Thornhill. Had Lionel not seen the danger? Was it not his duty to protect Jenny from the attentions of that man?

"Jenny is dancing with the Earl of Thornhill," she said. "She could not help it. She could hardly have said no without appearing rude."

"Yes." He glanced over his shoulder. "So she is."

He was neither surprised nor annoyed. Almost, Samantha thought, as if he had planned it. But that made no sense. He had warned Jenny to stay away from the earl. He had made her promise never to speak with him again.

"You must be looking forward to the evening after tomorrow," she said brightly.

"Must I?" His eyes were back on her. He was smiling in a perfectly sociable manner. He was dancing at the perfect distance from her. No one looking at him would realize that there was that special light in his eye, the one that had been there during their outing in the boat.

"Don't," Samantha said. "Don't look at me like that."

"How can I help it?" he asked. "But I am sorry."

Samantha felt intensely unhappy. She was deeply and

quite unwillingly in love with him. And he seemed to share her feelings. But it was not right. He had made his offer to Jenny and had been accepted. Perhaps he had been more or less forced into it, but he had done it nevertheless, and now he was honor-bound to live by it. It was not right that he look at her in this way and speak in this way. It was not fair—either to Jenny or to her.

In the last couple of days she had come to see Lionel as a weak, perhaps even dishonorable man, and the knowledge hurt and confused her. She loved him. But she would love him in the secret of her heart for the rest of her life, she had decided. She would not share sighs and lovelorn looks with him behind Jenny's back.

She could not.

"I have made you unhappy," he said.

"Yes." She looked into his eyes. "Jenny is my cousin and my closest friend. She is like a sister to me. I want to see her happy."

"So do I," he said. "I care for her. Sometimes—" He looked away from her and they waltzed in silence for a while. "Sometimes we have to be cruel in order to be kind. Sometimes trying to protect other people from hurt only succeeds in bringing them greater and longer-lasting pain in the end."

She did not know what he was trying to say. But despite herself she felt the stirrings of hope, the beginnings of a response that she had been quite determined to keep at bay tonight and forever in the future.

He looked directly into her eyes, still smiling, still waltzing with studied elegance. "If you and I protect her from pain now," he said, "do you believe that we can hide the truth from her for the rest of our lifetimes? Do you believe she will not be more hurt by it in the future, when it is too late for anything to be done about it?"

Samantha felt as if she was about to faint. "The truth?" she said. "What is the truth?"

He looked at her and twirled her about the corner of the ballroom, saying nothing. But looking everything.

"But we cannot tell her," she said.

"I cannot." His smile faded for a few moments while he gazed deeply into her eyes. "I am a gentleman, Samantha. A gentleman cannot do such a thing even to prevent a lifetime of unhappiness for three people."

"You want *me* . . . ?" He wanted her to tell Jenny that she loved Lionel and that he loved her. That only Jenny and the betrothal that had not yet been officially announced stood between them and happiness. Oh, no. No. "No," she said. "No, I could not possibly. This is not right. It is not right at all."

A part of her—a base part that horrified her—was tempted. Another part was repelled, repelled by him and repelled by her reaction to him. She could not love him, surely. He was no gentleman. Not really. A gentleman could not suggest such a thing. Not even when the alternative was to marry the woman he did not love.

Jenny. Oh, poor Jenny. She loved Lionel to distraction. And she deserved happiness. She did not deserve this sort of deceit and trickery.

"I will not do it," she said firmly. "I could not. But for Jenny's sake, if you feel that you cannot give her your full loyalty even if not your heart, you must tell her yourself. An honorable man would do that. An honorable man would not expect me to do it for him."

"For us," he said. "But it does not matter. I see that I have asked too much of you. And you are right. It was a dishonorable and ungentlemanly suggestion. I am ashamed that my heart tempted me into making it on the spur of the moment."

Samantha was suddenly very aware of her youth. She was only eighteen years old. She resented it when people sometimes called her young and innocent and naive. And yet she felt all three at this moment. She had the feeling she had been caught up in something beyond her experience and beyond her ability to handle. She had fallen in love with Lionel because he was handsome and because he had kissed her—was there any other basis for her feelings if she was strictly honest with herself? And he had fallen in love with her because . . . *Was* he in love with her? Why? Why so suddenly? Could his feelings be so deep that he was willing to upset the plans of five years and cause scandal in doing so?

She felt bewildered and frightened.

"I would rather," she said quietly and unhappily, "that we changed the subject, my lord."

"Ah," he said. "Yes. Of course."

They began to exchange opinions on the various costumes about them.

# 10

SIR ALBERT BOYLE FOUND HIS FRIEND THE EARL OF Thornhill at home late in the afternoon of the following day. He was in the sitting room of his own apartments abovestairs, drunk.

It was neither the place nor the time of day in which to be inebriated. And Lord Thornhill was not the type of man to let himself get thoroughly foxed. Especially at home alone during the daytime. Not that he was very obviously drunk. Apart from the slight dishevelment of his clothes and hair and his slouching posture and the fact that there were two empty decanters in the room, one on a desk and the other on the hearth at his feet, and an almost empty glass dangling from one hand, he looked quiet enough. He was not dancing on tables or roaring out bawdy ballads.

But Sir Albert, waved to a chair by a careless hand—the one that held the glass—knew his friend well. He was drunk.

"Well," the earl said. There was no slurring in his speech. "Is the deed done, Bertie? You have come here to celebrate? Ring for another decanter, my dear chap. These two seem to be empty."

"She accepted me," Sir Albert said. He did not approach the bellpull. He eyed his friend warily.

"Of course." The earl refrained from adding that the girl would have had to be a blithering idiot to refuse. "My felicitations, Bertie. You are floating on clouds of bliss?"

"She had tears in her eyes the whole time I talked with her," Sir Albert said, ruining his fashionably rumpled hair by running the fingers of one hand through it. "And she put her mouth up to be kissed when I was only intending to kiss her hand. She kisses prettily." He flushed.

The earl regarded his friend through the inch of brandy left in the bottom of his glass. "Ah, the innocence of true love," he said. "So you have a slave for life, Bertie. That will be comfortable for you."

Sir Albert got to his feet and crossed to the window, where he stood, gazing out. "I am terrified, Gabe," he said. "The tears. The look of surprise followed by hope followed by happiness and adoration. It was enough to turn any fellow's head. It is enough to make me conceited for life."

"But you are terrified." The earl chuckled.

"It is such an enormous responsibility," Sir Albert said. "What if I cannot make her happy? What if I come to take her for granted just because she was so easily won? What if she accepted me only because she cannot expect many such chances? What if—"

The earl swore, using language so profane that there could be no further doubt that he was severely inebriated.

"Bertie," he said, reverting to decent English, "if you

cannot see the stars clustered about your head, old chap, you have to be blind in both eyes."

"It is just the responsibility," Sir Albert said again. "The power we have over other people's lives sometimes, Gabe!"

"Well." The earl laughed. "Am I to wish you happy, Bertie, or am I to commiserate with you?"

"Wish me happy, if you will," his friend said, turning from the window to look at him. "What is the occasion for the private party, Gabe?"

The earl laughed again and raised his glass. "You have been busy today," he said. "You have not heard?"

Sir Albert frowned. "I called in at White's," he said, "and came on here when you were not there. Yes, I heard. You have to expect that people will grasp at any straw to break your back, Gabe, when your reputation is on such shaky footing. Was there a quite ghastly mixing of images there? No matter. Take no notice of it. Of the malice, I mean."

"One wonders—" The earl paused to drain off the brandy that remained in his glass. "One wonders if Miss Winwood is able to take no notice of it."

"Well, there is that." His friend resumed the seat he had been waved to at the start of his visit. "And it is unfortunate with her betrothal to Kersey about to be officially announced—not that there is a member of the *ton* or a footman or a groom who does not know of it. Gabe, you did not actually kiss her in the Velgards' ballroom last evening, did you? The truth can get vastly distorted in the retelling."

"Yes, I did." The earl chuckled. "In the doorway to the balcony, actually. I imagine we were far more easily seen there and by far more people than if I had done it in the middle of the dancing floor."

"Then you owe her an apology, do you not?" Sir Albert looked troubled. He had defended his friend against a large group at White's, all of whose members had insisted that it really had happened and that before it had, the two had had eyes only for each other and had waltzed indecorously close and had disappeared onto the balcony with the obvious intention of getting closer. It had been the joke of White's, the day's story in which everyone delighted. The Lord only knew what was being done to the poor girl's reputation in the drawing rooms of London, where the ladies would delight in the story in an entirely more vicious manner.

"Do I?" The earl narrowed his eyes on his glass before hurling it onto the hearth and watching in apparent satisfaction as it shattered. "I think not, Bertie. She did not exactly fight me off. Besides, it was merely a kiss. Hardly even that. A momentary meeting of lips."

"In full sight of the gathered *ton*," Sir Albert said.

"Life becomes dull when the Season is a few weeks old," Lord Thornhill said, his voice cold and cynical. "The *ton* needs some sensation to gossip about. Miss Winwood and I have obliged them."

"But it will be far worse for her than for you, Gabe." Sir Albert was indignant at his friend's apparent unconcern at what had happened—and what was happening. But he knew the impossibility of talking sensibly with a man who was very far from sober despite his quiet manner and articulate speech. "I know you fancied her from the first, but she is spoken for. There must be some other beauty you can flirt with if you feel that way inclined. The blonde, for example. Miss Newman."

"No one but the delicious redhead will do," the earl said. "Today she and I are being gossiped about. Today her betrothal is on shaky ground. Today Kersey will be feeling foolish at the very least. I am well content." His tone was almost vicious.

"Good Lord, Gabe." Sir Albert leapt to his feet again. "You are not trying to end the girl's betrothal, are you? Are you that desperate for her? You will ruin her, that's what you will do. Will you be proud of yourself then?"

"Sit down, Bertie, do," the earl said. "It hurts my eyes to look up at you. But ring for another decanter before you do. I am thirsty if you are not."

"You are foxed," his friend said, glaring at him.

"And so I am," the earl agreed. "But not nearly foxed enough, Bertie. I am still conscious. Send for more, there's a good chap."

"If you weren't drunk," Sir Albert said, "I would draw your cork, Gabe. I swear I would. But if you weren't drunk you would not be saying such insane things. So you fancy her but can't have her. So you were a little indiscreet last night—no, more than a little. It can be patched up provided Kersey or Rushford don't lose their heads. Apologize to the lot of them, Gabe, or at the very least stay away from them. Leave London. It is the only decent thing to do."

"But . . ." The Earl of Thornhill narrowed his eyes and spoke so quietly that he sounded almost menacing. "I am not expected to be decent, Bertie. If I can debauch my own stepmother, I am capable of any outrage."

Sir Albert stared down at him. "There is no talking to you in your present state," he said. "If I were you, Gabe, I would get your man to bring up a very large pot of very strong coffee. And a large bowl of very cold water for you to plunge your head into a few times. I shall leave instructions to that effect on my way out. Good day." He turned to leave the room.

The earl, still sprawled in his chair, chuckled once more. "She is a fortunate woman, Miss Rosalie Ogden, Bertie," he said. "She will be acquiring a mother hen to care for her for the rest of her days."

Sir Albert Boyle, his back bristling with indignation, left the room.

THE EARL OF THORNHILL rested his head against the back of his chair and stared upward. Closing his eyes was not a comfortable experience. He could not summon up enough energy to get to his feet to pull on the bell rope and order up more brandy. Besides, he had the feeling that he had had altogether too much already. Oceans too much, if the truth were known.

He had made a curious discovery in the course of the afternoon. Self-loathing was the perfect antidote to the effects of liquor on one's system. Even if he drank another ocean or two of brandy, he would not be able to drink himself into insensibility, he suspected. His body might become more and more foxed. His mind would remain coldly, coldly sober.

He could not possibly have slapped a glove in Kersey's face and been content to put a bullet between his eyes or the tip of a sword through his heart. Oh, no, that would have been altogether too easy and too unsubtle. And it would have renewed the scandal against Catherine and brought her further dishonor.

No, no, he had taken the far cleverer and more devious course of tampering with the man's life, making him look like a fool before the *ton*. Showing the world that Kersey, despite his title and his prospects and his wealth and good looks, could not keep a beautiful woman. Causing him the embarrassing scandal of a broken engagement.

And like the upright, honest, honorable man he was, he had tackled the task indirectly, working on Kersey's betrothed so that at the very least she would so compromise herself that Kersey would feel obliged to turn her off, or at the best she would feel so compromised that she would break with Kersey. Either way, Kersey would be embarrassed and humiliated.

Fine revenge indeed. Oh, very fine and admirable.

*Yes, I believe you*, she had said last night. *Yes, I do.* He could see her eyes now, gazing at him with earnest trust through the slits of her golden mask as he had waltzed her through the French windows, toward which he had carefully maneuvered her. And then at his prompting, she had spoken his name.

He wished he could drown out the echo of her voice and the words she had spoken. He wished he could close his eyes and no longer see hers. But the room spun about him when he tried—and he could still see her eyes.

*I love him*, she had said. *I love him. I love him. I love him.*

Today she was doubtless in deep trouble with her family and with Kersey and the Rushfords. Today she was doubtless the subject of eager and malicious gossip the length and breadth of fashionable London. Today she was doubtless in deep distress.

*Yes, I believe you.*

*Gabriel.*

*I love him.*

The earl turned his head from side to side against the back of his chair, but he succeeded only in making himself feel dizzy and nauseated. The sound of her voice, soft and earnest, would not go away.

He wondered if she would be able to weather the storm, if he had gone just too far last night and forced her to go too far. . . .

*The power we have over other people's lives,* Bertie had just said. It was a relief to hear Bertie's voice in his mind instead of hers for a while. Until he really heard the words, that was, repeating themselves over and over again, just as her words had been doing all afternoon. *The power we have over other people's lives.*

His plan was proceeding perfectly. Even better than he could have hoped. It was poised for completion tomorrow night. The Earl and Countess of Rushford's ball was surely the event at which the betrothal of their son was to be announced. And though he had not been invited to the dinner that was to precede the ball, he had unexpectedly had an invitation to the ball.

It was there he had planned his most outrageous assault on Jennifer Winwood. It would be quite perfect. He would ruin the ball—except for the gossipmongers—wreck Kersey's betrothal, and humiliate him in the most public manner possible. The fact that he would also ruin his own reputation once and for all had seemed immaterial to him. He really did not care.

But there was Jennifer Winwood, caught in the middle. The one who would probably suffer the most. No, the one who *would* suffer the most. The innocent one. The one it was so easy to mislead because she was so ready to believe the best of other people. Because she wanted to believe the best of him. Because she wanted to be his friend.

*Yes, I believe you. Yes, I do.* If he had not been drunk, the Earl of Thornhill would doubtless not have put his hands to his ears to stop the sound of her voice. But he was drunk.

*Gabriel.*

She made his name sound like an endearment, he had told her. The one spontaneous truth he had spoken to her. It did not sound like an endearment now. It sounded like a curse straight from hell.

No, he could not proceed. It was perhaps too late now to give in to a crisis of conscience, but better now than not at all. Perhaps last night's indiscretion could be smoothed over. Apparently Lady Rushford had walked about with the girl during the set following the one she had danced with him, and had smiled and looked unconcerned. Wise woman! It was far better to have done that than to have whisked her home in disgrace.

Perhaps, with Kersey's mother behind her and the grand dinner and ball before her with its public announcement of her betrothal, today's scandal would become tomorrow's stale and forgotten gossip.

If he stayed out of the way.

If he left town and remained away for the rest of the Season. If he kept himself out of her life and out of sight of the *ton*.

He would set his servants about packing his things and send word ahead to Chalcote and arrange for the journey, he decided. He should be able to leave within three or four days, perhaps sooner. In the meanwhile, he would stay at home.

The Earl of Thornhill got to his feet, relieved now that his decision was made, now that he had pulled himself back from committing a great evil before it was quite too late. But the combination of a change in position and a releasing of his self-loathing was too much for him. He staggered and fell to his hands and knees while the room spun about him at dizzying and unrelenting speed.

Lord, how much had he drunk, anyway?

The door of his sitting room opened quietly to admit his valet, who was carrying a large pot of coffee on a tray.

Bless Bertie, mother hen par excellence.

———

JENNIFER WAS RIDING IN the park, seated in an open barouche beside Viscount Kersey, the Countess of Rushford opposite her, Aunt Agatha beside the countess. Jennifer was wearing a white muslin day dress of fashionable but modest design, chosen carefully for her by Aunt Agatha, and her straw bonnet. She was smiling brightly and looking steadily into the eyes of anyone who cared to look into hers and conversing with all who drew near and with all to whom they drew near. Her left hand rested on Lionel's sleeve. His left hand covered it.

It was what must be done, the countess had said briskly and quite firmly when she had called earlier at Berkeley Square with her son. It would be nonsense to behave as if there were something to be ashamed of merely because the Earl of Thornhill, who was a disgrace to his name and his rank, had chosen to behave with such outrageous vulgarity. Rushford, she had explained, was to make it quite clear to Lord Thornhill that despite his invitation to tomorrow evening's ball, he would be unwelcome there.

Lionel had stood quietly behind his mother's chair while she had said all this, and Jennifer had studiously not looked at him. But she had got together her courage finally to ask the countess and Aunt Agatha, who had also been present, if she might have a private word with Lord Kersey.

It was necessary, she had felt. Her father had summoned her during the morning and scolded her roundly—which was a mild way to describe his blazing anger—

and told her to be prepared to return to the country for a very long stay if the Earl of Rushford decided that she was no longer worthy of his son's hand. He and Rushford had quite a quarrel over this business, he had explained, and he would be damned before he would be put even more in the wrong by a chit of a daughter. She had better be very careful. Aunt Agatha had been tight-lipped and curiously quiet all day. Sam had not emerged from her room.

Last evening's incident—the kiss at the French windows—had burst into scandal this morning, Jennifer gathered. She was the *on dit* of fashionable drawing rooms. She was in disgrace. Everything was in ruins. Lionel would no longer want her. Nor would any other respectable gentleman. Not that she wanted any other gentleman. If she lost Lionel, she would want to die. It would be as simple as that.

Curiously, she did not really blame the Earl of Thornhill. Not really. He had protested his innocence and she had believed him. His kiss—if it could be called that—had been meant for the privacy of the darkness out on the balcony. It had been a kiss of friendship. Except that he had called her—Jennifer had tried all through a sleepless night not to remember what he had called her. But the words had spoken themselves over and over to her weary mind.

*My love,* he had called her.

Yes, she needed to talk with Lionel. There was enormous relief in the discovery that the countess had not had a change of heart since last evening but was still willing to face down the scandal and make light of what had happened. But it was not quite enough.

"Very well," Lady Rushford said, getting to her feet. "For five minutes, dear. Kersey and I must leave soon so that we can all get ready to be seen in the park when everyone else is there. Lady Brill?" She left the room with Aunt Agatha.

Viscount Kersey stayed where he was and said nothing.

Jennifer forced herself to look at him. He was very pale. Very handsome. "There was nothing in it," she said. "He explained to me that he did not do those dreadful things that everyone believes he did, and I believed him. That was all."

His eyes met hers finally and she was reminded again of what Sam had always said of him. She shivered involuntarily. "What did he tell you?" he asked.

"That his stepmother was never his mistress," she said, her cheeks hot. "That the child she had was not his."

He gazed at her in silence for a few moments. "And you believed him," he said. "You are incredibly naive."

"My lord," she said, moving steadily ahead into her greatest nightmare, "do you wish to continue with our betrothal? Would you prefer that I changed my answer now, before any announcement has been made?"

Again the brief silence, while Jennifer died a little inside. "It is too late for that," he said. "The announcement is a mere formality. Everyone knows."

"But if it were not too late," she persisted, "you would prefer that I cried off?"

She thought he would never answer. Silence stretched between them. "The question is academic," he said. "We are betrothed. If you cry off, I will not have you say that you did so at my request. My mother has her heart set on the match—as do my father and yours."

"And you?" She was whispering.

"And I," he said.

She searched his eyes. But they were blank. Cold. He did not love her. He would be quite happy if their betrothal came to an end. Except that he felt they had proceeded too far with it. And his parents and her father had their hearts set on it, as they had for five years.

And his heart was set on the match. So he said. But did he mean it? Could she bear it if he did not? Could she bear to be married to him, fearing as she now did that he was marrying for appearance's sake and for his parents' sake? Fearing as she now did that he did not love her?

But could she bear to lose him? To give him up entirely of her own will—against the will of everyone else concerned? She could teach him to love her. She could love him into loving her. She could show him that despite what had happened in the last days and weeks with the Earl of Thornhill, she was capable of loyalty and fidelity and devotion. It would not even take any effort on her part. It was what she wanted more than anything else in the world.

Before either of them could say anything else, Aunt Agatha and the Countess of Rushford were back in the room and the countess was taking charge of the situation again with great energy and calm good sense. Her general air of placidity was quite deceptive, Jennifer was discovering. They were to drive in the park, the four of them, and show the fashionable world how ridiculous was any gossip that had been making the rounds during the course of the day.

"We will confound and disappoint all the tabbies," she said with a laugh. "Oh, my dears, you look so very handsome together. Tomorrow night's ball will be the greatest squeeze of the Season. The greatest success. And I am going to be the happiest mother in town."

And so at the fashionable hour they were driving in the park. It was not so very difficult after all, Jennifer found. No one was so ill-bred as to cause any scene either by look or by word or by gesture. And playing a part gradually developed into living the part. She really was feeling happy. A crisis in her life was passing, thanks to the good advice of her future mother-in-law. And Lionel, sitting beside her, was smiling at others and smiling at her. And touching her hand. And once or twice raising it to his lips. There was warmth in his eyes again.

She had been very foolish. It had been all her fault. She was, as Lionel himself had said, incredibly naive. But finally she had learned her lesson. From now on there was only Lionel and what she owed him. If he was disappointed in her now, she would teach him to be proud of her. If he did not love her now, he would in future.

She turned her head and smiled at him, her heart in her eyes. He smiled back, his eyes roaming her face and fixing themselves on her lips. He leaned a little toward her and then straightened up for good manners' sake, his smile more rueful. .

His mother, watching closely from the seat opposite, nodded her approval and turned her smile on the occupants of a landau that was passing.

# 11

THERE WAS AN ATMOSPHERE OF GAIETY AND and an air of expectancy among the forty guests who sat down to dinner at the Earl of Rushford's table. Everyone knew what announcement was to be made at the end of it, but the knowing did not dampen enthusiasm. Neither did the near scandal of a few days before, which had blossomed gloriously for a few hours only to die down again, as so many would-be scandals did. Not that the dying was to be much lamented. There was always a new one eagerly waiting to take its place.

Samantha smiled, as everyone about her did, and conversed with Mr. Averleigh on her left, and even flirted with him a little. One quickly learned how to flirt in fashionable society, how to hide behind smiles and blushes and sparkling eyes and witty responses. How to draw compliments and admiration and then hold the gentleman concerned at arm's length. Not that that always worked. She had had to refuse a marriage offer that very morning from Mr. Maxwell and was very much afraid that she might have hurt him. And Aunt Aggy had been puzzled and her uncle had been annoyed with her— both had approved his suit.

Samantha continued to smile—indeed, she redoubled her efforts—when the dreaded moment came and the Earl of Rushford got to his feet to make the announcement they had all been waiting for. She did not hear his actual words. But there was a swell of sound as many pretended surprise, and applause and laughter— and Lionel was on his feet and drawing Jenny to hers and kissing her hand. And the two of them were smiling radiantly into each other's eyes and looking as if happily-ever-after were not a strong enough term to describe what their future was to be.

And yet, Samantha thought, withdrawing her eyes from them under the pretense of lifting her wineglass, Lionel did not love Jenny. And Jenny—well, Jenny did love him. But also she had been unduly upset over the incident with the Earl of Thornhill. And Samantha? Well, her feelings were immaterial. Except that she constantly felt wretched and could not at all concentrate on becoming especially fond of one gentleman from her flatteringly large group of admirers. And she was not even sure that Jenny was going to be happy. She herself could have borne it, she felt, if only she knew that the two of them loved each other. She would know then that her own feelings were quite wrong and must be put firmly behind her.

Well, she thought when Lady Rushford got to her feet finally to signal the ladies to leave the dining room, it was done now. Finally done. Now it was quite official and unalterable. Any faint and absurd hope that might have lingered somewhere far back in her brain was now firmly dashed.

It was a relief. Yes, it really was.

She drew close to her cousin in the drawing room, no easy matter when it seemed that all the ladies, without exception, were trying to do the same thing. Jennifer saw her and turned with shining eyes to hug her tightly.

"Oh, Sam," she said, "wish me happy." She laughed. "Wish me what I already have in such abundance that I believe I may well burst with it."

Samantha could not afterward remember what she said in reply. But she did wish it. Oh, she did. She wished Jenny all the happiness in the world. Her own feelings did not matter in the slightest.

IT WAS MUCH LATER in the evening. Jennifer was hot and flushed and footsore. But happier than she could remember being. Now, tonight, at last, the dreams she had had for five long years of what this Season would be like were coming true.

She was the focus of attention and admiration—not that these things were important in themselves, she knew. But every woman has some hidden vanity and enjoys attention, even when there is one single gentleman who holds her heart. The Earl of Rushford had danced with her and made it clear that he was pleased with her. Even Papa—wonder of wonders—had led her into a set.

And Lionel—oh, Lionel had danced with her twice, both waltzes, and had declared his intention of dancing the final set with her. A man was to be excused the minor impropriety of dancing with his betrothed three times in one evening, he had said, his head bent close to hers, his eyes smiling warmly. And if the *ton* did not agree, well, then, the *ton* might go hang.

She had laughed with delight at his outrageous words.

And everyone was watching them. It was no vanity to believe that. It was true. Everyone could see that Lionel was looking at her as if he would devour her. And she did not care that they would see too that she adored him.

All doubts—if there had been any doubts—had been put to rest tonight. He had been angry and hurt yesterday. Understandably so. It had all been her fault. But now, tonight, he had put that anger aside and his true feelings for her were there for all to see—on his face and in his eyes.

*He* had not come to the ball. It was no surprise—she was sure that Lionel and his father would have made sure that he did not come. But it was an enormous relief. She dreaded seeing him again. It was certainly wonderful that she did not have to do so tonight of all nights. Tonight she could no longer even hear his voice in her head. Tonight she was finally free of him.

The Earl of Rushford had been called from the ballroom a short while ago. Not that Jennifer particularly noticed, but then a footman came to ask Viscount Kersey to join his father in the library, and Lionel left her side after smiling regretfully at her and squeezing her hand.

He was gone through most of the next set, which Jennifer danced with Sir Albert Boyle. She found his company interesting since he told her with a smile that she must wish him happy as he wished her. He had recently become betrothed to Miss Rosalie Ogden. She always felt a special interest in Sir Albert because he was the first gentleman she and Sam had met in London. She hastily closed her mind to the other gentleman who had been with him in the park that day.

But despite her interest in Sir Albert, she was disappointed in the long absence of her betrothed. Even if they could not dance together all evening, she could at least gaze at him much of the time. He was dressed tonight in varying shades of light green to match the color of her own gown. Aunt Agatha had thought a pale color suitable for a young lady who was now officially betrothed. Jennifer smiled secretly to herself. She wondered if five years from now or ten she would still be restless when Lionel was out of her sight for longer than a few minutes.

And then he was there again, in the doorway with his father, his face as pale as his shirt, his smile completely gone, his expression severe. What had happened? Something clearly had. Bad news? Was that why first the earl and then he had been summoned from the ballroom? His father, she saw when she shifted her glance to him, was looking decidedly grim. The set was coming to an end, but she could not hurry toward them to ask what it was. It would not be seemly. She was forced to allow Sir Albert Boyle to escort her back to Aunt Agatha's side and to wait for Lionel to come to her. What was wrong? Oh, poor Lionel.

Whatever it was, he would be glad that the evening was almost at an end. There could be no more than one or two sets remaining.

Jennifer watched in some concern, fanning her hot face, as the Earl of Rushford, followed closely by his son, made his way toward the raised dais on which the orchestra sat, climbed onto it, and stood there, his arms raised for silence. He was holding a single sheet of paper in one hand. Lionel stood beside him, his expression stony, his eyes downcast.

A hush descended on the ballroom as the guests gradually became aware that their host was waiting to address them. Jennifer took one step forward but stopped again.

"It distresses me to make any announcement to destroy the mood of the evening and put an abrupt and early end to the festivities," the earl said, his voice stern and clear. "But something disturbing has been brought to my attention this evening, and after consultation with my son and careful deliberation, I have decided that I have no choice but to speak out publicly and without delay."

The hush in the ballroom became almost loud. Jennifer, for no reason she could fathom, felt her heart beat faster. She could hear it beating in her ears.

"This letter was delivered to the house an hour ago," the earl said, holding the sheet of paper he held a little higher. "And one of my servants was bribed to deliver it into the hands of one of my . . . guests. Fortunately, my servants are loyal. Both the letter and the bribe were put into my butler's hands and then into mine."

Whatever could it be, Jennifer thought in the murmuring that followed, that it had necessitated this public display? She started to fan herself, but she stopped when she realized that everyone about her was still.

"I will read this letter," the earl said, "if you will indulge me for a few moments." He held the sheet of paper up before him and read. " 'My love, Your ordeal is almost at an end, this farce of an evening that you felt obliged to suffer through. Tomorrow I will contrive to see you privately, as I have done many times before. I will hold you again and kiss you again and make love to you again. And we will make plans to steal away together so that we may kiss and love whenever we wish. Forgive my incaution in sending you this tonight, but I know you will be disappointed at not seeing me there. I have been advised to stay away after our almost open indiscretion of a few evenings ago. I will be sure that my messenger gives a large enough bribe that this will be placed in your own hands—and next to your heart after you have read it. Would that I could be there too. Until tomorrow, my love. Thornhill.' "

Jennifer stood very still. She was beyond thought.

"My servant was bribed," the Earl of Rushford said, "to deliver this into the hands of Miss Jennifer Winwood."

She had become a block of stone. Or a block of ice. Sound—sounds of shock and of outrage—swelled about her. It was something that was happening at a great distance from her.

"In the last week or so," the earl said, having somehow imposed silence on his gathered guests again, "my son has more than once overlooked what was apparently the unfortunate but harmless indiscretion of youth and innocence. As a man of honor and sensibility, he has stood by his commitment to Miss Winwood and shielded her name from scandal and dishonor. It appears that he has been much deceived. And that the countess and I have been much deceived. We have been deceived in a friendship of many years' standing. I will make it clear here and now that there will be no further connection between my family and Miss Winwood's, that the betrothal announced earlier this evening is no longer in existence. Good night, ladies and gentlemen. You will excuse me, I am sure, if I feel that there is no longer anything to celebrate tonight."

Lionel was standing beside his father, looking stern and dignified and very handsome. It was as if the part of Jennifer that was not her body had detached itself from that body and was observing almost dispassionately. It was as if what had been said and what was happening had nothing to do with her.

The Earl of Rushford stood, feet apart, on the dais, watching his guests depart. None of them approached him. They were perhaps too embarrassed to do so. Or perhaps they were in too much of a rush to get ouside so that they could glory in the retelling of what had just happened. Lionel continued to stand there too, straight-backed and pale, his gaze directed downward. Everyone was leaving. Most people did not look at her. Again, it seemed as if they were in the grip of a massive embarrassment.

Then someone grabbed her wrist with painful tightness—Aunt Agatha—and someone else grasped her other elbow in a grip that felt as if it might grind her bones—Papa. And together they turned her and propelled her from the room faster than her feet would move, or so it seemed. Somehow, although everyone was leaving, nothing impeded their progress. Everyone fell back to either side of them, almost as if they had the plague.

And then—she did not know how it could have been brought up so fast—she was inside her father's carriage, Papa beside her, Aunt Agatha across from her, Samantha next to Aunt Agatha, and the carriage was in motion.

"I have a horse whip in the stables," her father was saying, his voice so quiet that Jennifer knew he was more than angry. "Prepare yourself, Miss. I will be using it when we arrive home."

"Oh, no, Uncle," Samantha wailed.

"Gerald—" Aunt Agatha said.

"Silence!" he said.

They all stayed silent during the remainder of the journey home.

———

"I AM SORRY, MY lord."

His valet's voice somehow got all mixed up with his dream. He was trying to leave London, but no matter which street his carriage turned along, there was always a press of traffic ahead of them and tangled vehicles and angry, excited people arguing and gesticulating. And no way past. And then his valet was standing at the door of the carriage, addressing him in his most formal manner. "I am sorry, my lord."

"Sorry, dammit. Out of my way. Get up, Gabe. Get up before I throw a pitcher of cold water over you."

For a moment Bertie was there too, adding confusion to the melee by trying to force a high-spirited horse past his carriage. And then the Earl of Thornhill woke up.

"I am sorry, my lord," his valet said again. "I tried to—"

"Get up, Gabe."

Bertie, resplendent in ball clothes, pushed the valet unceremoniously aside, grasped the bedclothes, and flung them back. He was quite furiously angry, the earl realized, shaking off the remnants of sleep and waving off his man.

"Go back to bed," he told him. "Good Lord, Bertie, what the devil are you doing here at this time? What time is it, by the way?" He swung his legs over the side of the bed, sat up, and ran his fingers through his hair.

"Get up!" Sir Albert ordered. "I am going to give you the thrashing of your life, Gabe."

The earl looked up at him in some surprise. "Here, Bertie?" he said. "Is the space not rather confined? And you do not have a whip, my dear chap. Will you at least allow me to put on some clothes? I have an aversion to being thrashed, or even to holding a conversation, while I am naked." He got to his feet.

"You are slime," Sir Albert said, his voice cold with contempt. "I have always defended you from all who have defamed you, Gabe. But they have been right and I have been wrong. You were probably giving it to your stepmother after all. You are slime!"

The earl turned, having not quite reached his dressing room door. "Have a care, Bertie," he said quietly. "You are talking about a lady. About a member of my family."

"You disgust me!" his erstwhile friend said. "You are slime."

"Yes." The earl disappeared into his dressing room and came back a moment later tying the sash of a brocaded dressing gown about his waist. "So you said before, Bertie. Would it be too much to ask that you explain the reason for the violence of your feelings—at this time of the night, whatever time it is?"

"Your bribe was not high enough," Sir Albert said very distinctly. "Your letter fell into the wrong hands."

The earl waited, but clearly Bertie had finished. "Next time I try to bribe someone," he said, "I must remember to double the sum. Corruption is more expensive than it used to be, it seems. My letter, Bertie? Which one is that? I have written four or five in the last few days."

"Don't play stupid," Sir Albert said. "She has doubtless been at fault too, Gabe, meeting you in private, allowing intimacies. But she is basically an innocent, I believe, just as Miss Ogden is and all the other young girls who have just made their come-out. They are no match for experienced rakes bent on seducing and ruining them. It was Rushford himself who intercepted that letter, you may be interested to know. He read it aloud to the whole gathering. She is ruined. I hope you are satisfied."

The Earl of Thornhill looked at him silently for a while. "I think we had better go into my sitting room, Bertie," he said at last, turning to lead the way, and lighting a branch of candles when he got there. "You had better tell me exactly what happened tonight."

"How could you!" Sir Albert said. "If you had to be seducing a lady of virtue when there are all sorts of women of another class who would be only too pleased to earn the extra income, did you also have to be so mad as to risk exposing her to the whole *ton*? Did you have no fear that the letter would fall into the wrong hands?"

"Bertie." The earl's tone had become crisp. "Assume for a few minutes, if you will, that I do not know what you are talking about. Or pretend you are recounting the story to a stranger. Tell me what happened. In what way have I ruined Miss Winwood? I assume it is she I have ruined?"

Sir Albert would not sit, but he did calm down enough to give a terse account of what had happened in the Rushford ballroom less than an hour before.

"Did you see the letter?" the earl asked when the story had been completed.

"Of course not," Sir Albert said. "Rushford was holding it. He read it in its entirety. Why would I want to see it?"

"For a rather important reason actually," the earl said. "You know my handwriting, Bertie. That letter would not have been in it."

"Are you trying to tell me that you did not write the letter?" his friend asked, incredulous.

"Not trying," Lord Thornhill said curtly. "I am telling you, Bertie. Good Lord. You believe I am capable of that?"

"You are capable of kissing the girl in sight of the whole *ton*," Sir Albert reminded him.

Ah, yes. Righteous indignation was denied him. Yes, this was something he might well have done. It was rather clever actually. And had obviously worked like a dream.

"Gabe," his friend said, frowning, "if you did not write it, who did? It makes no sense."

"Someone who wanted to embarrass me," the earl said. "Or someone who wanted to ruin Miss Winwood."

"It makes no sense," Sir Albert said again.

"Actually," the earl said, smiling rather grimly, "it makes a great deal of sense, Bertie. I believe I have just been outplayed in a game over which I thought I had complete control."

Sir Albert looked his incomprehension.

"It is time you were in your bed," Lord Thornhill said. "Staying up all night and tripping the light fantastic through much of it can be ruinous on the complexion and the constitution, you know, Bertie."

"I may be a fool and a dupe, but I believe your denials," Sir Albert said. "However, it does not change the fact that she is totally ruined, Gabe. She will never be sent another invitation. She will never be able to show her face in town again. I doubt that her father will be able to find her a husband even in the country. It is a shame, I rather like her. And if you are to be believed, she has done nothing to bring on her own ruin."

"Sometimes," the earl said, indicating the door with one hand, "these things happen, Bertie. I need the rest of my beauty sleep."

"And you will not be able to show your face here either," Sir Albert said, moving toward the door.

"Now that," the earl said as his friend was finally leaving, "I would not count upon, Bertie."

Very cleverly done, he thought grimly, alone again at last. He did not bother to move back into his bedchamber. He knew that there would be no more sleep for him tonight.

Very cleverly done indeed.

WHEN VISCOUNT NORDAL'S BUTLER opened the library door the next morning to announce the arrival of the Earl of Thornhill, the viscount at first refused to see him and instructed his servant to throw him out. However, when that nervous individual reappeared less than a minute later with the news that the earl intended to stay in the hall until he was admitted, the viscount directed that he be shown in.

He was standing behind his desk when the earl strode in.

"I have not a word to say to you, Thornhill," he said. "Perhaps I should have sent you a challenge this morning. You have brought ruin on me and my whole family. But fighting a duel with you would suggest that I was defending my daughter's honor. As I understand it, there is no honor to be fought for."

"I will buy a special license today," the earl said curtly, wasting no time on preliminaries, "and marry her tomorrow. You need not concern yourself with a dowry for her. I have fortune enough with which to support her."

The viscount sneered. "Not quite what you anticipated being forced into," he said, "when you have been enjoying the pleasures of the marriage bed without benefit of clergy and expected to go on doing so. Is it possible that you care enough for the opinion of your peers to do the decent thing, Thornhill?"

The Earl of Thornhill strode across the room and rested both hands flat on the desk before leaning across it to address himself to his prospective father-in-law. "I will make one thing clear," he said. "To my knowledge Miss Winwood is as pure as she was on the day her mother bore her. And if I am to marry her, I will meet anyone who wishes to assume otherwise. Yourself included."

The viscount bristled. "Get out!" he said.

"Your daughter's name and honor seem to mean nothing to you," the earl said, "except as they reflect upon your own. Very well, then. The only thing that can happen today—the *only* thing—is for her to affiance herself to me, for us to marry without delay. With your daughter safely and honorably married, you will be able to hold your head high again, Nordal. And eventually so will she."

Viscount Nordal looked back at him with silent loathing.

The earl removed his hands from the desk and took a step back. "It is early for a lady to be up and dressed the morning after a ball," he said, "but I do not imagine Miss Winwood has been troubled by too much sleep. I will see her now, Nordal, before I leave about other business. Alone, if you please."

Viscount Nordal's hand went to the bell rope behind his left shoulder.

"Have my daughter sent alone to the rose salon," he told the butler, who appeared almost immediately. "While we wait, Thornhill, I believe we have a little business to discuss. Have a seat."

The Earl of Thornhill sat, both his expression and his mood grim.

# 12

JENNIFER AWOKE FEELING SOME AMAZEMENT that she had slept at all. In fact, she seemed to have slept quite deeply and dreamlessly. But she awoke quite early without any of the illusions one so often has that the unpleasant events of the day before were merely dreams. Perhaps it was the soreness of her back and derrière when she moved. Sam's tears and pleadings and Aunt Agatha's admonitions had had their effect on Papa. He had not sent to the stables for a whip. He had used a cane instead and bent her over the desk in the library just like a naughty child while he did so.

It was all over. Everything that made her life worth living. Over when she was still only twenty years old. There was nothing left to make the rest of it worth living and never would be. Curiously, this morning her mind still had that strange detachment of the night before. She knew what had happened and she knew what the consequences were and what they would be for the rest of her days. But only her mind knew. No other part of her had begun to react to them yet.

She sat up gingerly, moving her legs over the edge of the bed. He had done it one more time and this time had ruined her completely. She had trusted him despite all the evidence and all the warnings from older, more experienced people than she. And he had done this to her. Lionel was lost to her. There was to be no more betrothal, no marriage. No more Season.

She realized suddenly what had woken her this early. Through the half-open door into her dressing room she could hear her maid and someone else moving about, opening and shutting doors and drawers. They were packing her trunks. She was to leave some time today for the country. But she was to go home only temporarily. Only until Papa could make arrangements for her to take up residence in some suitably remote location with a lady companion. The lady companion, she had understood, was in reality to be her jailer.

Wherever it was he banished her to, she was to spend the rest of her life there.

Her maid had set a plain morning dress over a chair in her room and a bowl and jug of water on the dresser. Jennifer got to her feet and washed and dressed herself. She brushed her hair and twisted it into a simple knot at her neck. And then she sat down on the edge of the bed again. She could not go down to breakfast, she had just remembered. She was confined to her room until the carriage was ready for her.

She had not been given any chance to defend herself, she realized. But it did not matter. The truth mattered little in such circumstances. The fact was that for reasons of his own the Earl of Thornhill had written that letter and Lionel's father had read it and then exposed her and turned her off publicly. The fact was that she was ruined beyond redemption. Nothing could change that. There was no point in exerting herself to try to get someone to listen to her.

There was a tap on the dressing room door, the murmuring of her maid's voice and a footman's. Perhaps it was her breakfast tray, she thought, wondering if it would hold nothing but dry bread and water. Or perhaps they were ready for her. Papa doubtless wanted to get her on her way as soon as possible.

"You are wanted downstairs, Miss," her maid said, appearing in the doorway, looking nervous. The servants doubtless knew the whole story. Servants always did. "In the rose salon without delay."

It was not the carriage, then. And the summons was not to the library. Of course, that did not necessarily mean that she was not to be caned again. Perhaps Papa had sent for the whip after all this morning. Perhaps she should weep as soon as she saw it and every time he used it. He had been incensed last night when she had remained quiet during her beating. It was not that she had not felt every stroke. It was just that her mind had been too numb to react.

The rose salon was empty. She walked across to the window and gazed out onto the square beyond the railings. She had loved London. There was a sense of energy and excitement here that she never felt in the country, though the country was where she thought she would prefer to do her day-by-day living. She supposed now it was as well she felt that way.

She wondered what Lionel was doing at this precise

minute. Viscount Kersey. She no longer had the right even to think of him as Lionel.

And then the door opened and closed behind her. She did not turn. She was not sure she would not grovel when she actually saw the whip. She was still very sore from the cane.

"Miss Winwood?" The voice came from close behind her.

She spun around, eyes wide, all the numbness and passivity of the past hours gone without trace. "You!" she said. "Get out. *Get out!*"

He looked cool and elegant, booted feet set slightly apart, hands clasped behind his back. She hated him with such intensity that she would have killed him if she had had a weapon.

"I have come to save you from disgrace," he said. "We will marry tomorrow."

Her eyes widened further and her hands clenched into fists at her sides. "You have come to gloat," she said. "You have come to mock me. Well, gaze your fill, my lord. I have not looked in a glass this morning, but I would guess that I am not a pretty sight. This is what you have done to me. Enjoy the sight and then get out."

"You are unnaturally pale," he said, "and have shadows beneath your eyes. Your eyes are wild and unhappy. Apart from that, I see the same beauty I have admired since I first saw you. I will procure a special license today. We will marry tomorrow."

She laughed. "Yes, you mean it," she said. "Of course. It is the only explanation. For some reason you decided that you wanted me. I was unavailable because I was betrothed. But that was not going to stop you. You stalked me and preyed upon my innocence and gullibility and gradually compromised me more and more until last night that lying letter, which you fully intended would fall into the wrong hands, completed your scheme. You are diabolical. We were right to call you Lucifer, the devil. It is an irony beyond humor that you have the name of an angel."

He watched her steadily. She had not even shaken his calm. She itched to take her fingernails to his face.

"I did not write or send that letter," he said.

She looked at him incredulously and laughed. "Oh, did you not?" she said. "It wrote itself and sent itself, I suppose. And I suppose you did not lie with your stepmother or father her child or abandon her in a foreign country in order to return here for fresh prey."

"No," he said.

His calm infuriated her. "And I suppose you did not deliberately set out to free me from my betrothal," she said.

He opened his mouth to speak and then closed it again.

"So that I would marry you." She glared at him scornfully. "Did it not matter to you that I was to marry the man of my choice? Did you imagine that I would gladly give him up for you? Or that I would happily accept the replacement once it was made? Did you imagine that I could ever do anything but despise and loathe you?"

"No," he said.

"But it did not matter," she said. "The state of my heart does not matter to you. My happiness does not matter to you. Possessing me is all. You must very much like what you see, my lord Gabriel."

His eyes moved down her body and up again. She was very much aware of her large breasts and generous curves.

"Yes," he said.

"I suppose it did not occur to you," she said, "that with Lord Kersey lost and my reputation in shreds I would refuse you."

"We will marry in the morning," he said, "and attend the theater in the evening. We will drive in the park the following afternoon and attend Lady Truscott's ball in the evening. We will face down this scandal before I take you to my estate in the North."

"You must be mad." She was whispering. "All this smacks of insanity. I will not marry you. You must be insane to think that I would."

"Consider the alternative," he said.

The alternative was imprisonment in some remote part of the country for the rest of her life. Her earlier numbness gone, the prospect was suddenly terrifying. Her father would do it, too. She had no illusions about him. No sentiment would persuade him to relax the sentence after a year or so and bring her home to the country.

He was going to cut her hair before she left. She had a sudden memory of that detail. He had said it after the caning. And he had meant it. For some reason it became in that moment the most terrifying detail of all that was facing her.

"He is going to have my hair cropped close to my head." She had said the words aloud. She could almost hear the echo of them. And his eyes had lifted to her hair.

"There will be no company," he said, "no pretty clothes. No marriage. No running of a home and attending to those less fortunate than yourself. There will be no one less fortunate than you. There will be no children."

She fought panic and clenched her fists, trying to convert it into fury against him again.

"We will marry tomorrow morning," he said.

It would be worse. A thousand times worse. She looked at him in some horror, at his tall figure, at the breadth of his shoulders, at his dark hair and eyes and aristocratic features. She reminded herself of the villainies of which he was guilty, of the fiendish way he had stalked her and brought her to ruin just so that he would have her for himself. And yet all she could see and feel and hear was the scissors, cold against her head, chopping through the thickness of her hair.

She bit her lip hard.

Her hand was in both of his suddenly, cold and limp in his warm, strong ones. And he was on one knee in front of her. She watched him in shock, her feelings numb again.

"Miss Winwood," he said, "will you do me the great honor of being my wife?"

He gazed up at her, his expression quite unfathomable. Looking handsome and romantic and quite as if he could not possibly be guilty of any of the fiendishness she knew him guilty of beyond a doubt.

The alternative was the scissors. It had all boiled down to that almost farcical triviality. The scissors and the sight of her hair falling in heavy locks to the floor to be swept up and burned. She fought a wave of nausea.

"Yes." She closed her eyes. She was not quite sure she had spoken the word aloud.

But she must have. He was on his feet again and squeezing both her hands very tightly. "I will make it my life's work," he said, "to see to it that you will in time be glad of your answer."

"It would be a waste of your energy," she said, looking deliberately into his eyes. "After tomorrow morning you will possess my body, my lord. It seems to be important to you. You will never possess my heart or my respect or my esteem. I will hate you every day for the rest of my life."

"Well." He kissed the back of each hand in turn, squeezed them again, and released them. His manner was brisk. "There is much I must do today. You will remain at home. I am sure you would not wish otherwise. You will—" He paused suddenly and looked into her eyes. "Were you harshly treated after your return home last night?"

She smiled. "My father is a stern man, my lord," she said. "You brought great humiliation on him."

He frowned. "Did he touch you?" he asked.

"With his hands? No." She was still smiling. "He used a cane."

He closed his eyes briefly. "I will leave instructions," he said, "that you are to be gently treated for the rest of today and tomorrow morning. After that you will be under my protection."

"Do you have a cane too?" she asked. "It is a very effective weapon for imposing discipline, my lord. I am still sore this morning."

"It is the last you will ever feel," he said. "My word of honor on it."

She laughed. "I am enormously comforted," she said. "Your honor, my lord?"

He looked at her steadily for a few moments and then made her a formal bow. "Until tomorrow morning," he said. He turned and left the room, closing the door behind him.

Well, Jennifer thought. Well. But she could not—or would not—force her mind past the single word. She stood where she was until the door opened again several minutes later to admit both Aunt Agatha and her father.

"Well, Miss," her father said. "It seems that total disgrace is to be avoided after all. Though how I am to hold up my head today when I leave this house I do not know."

"Well, Jennifer." Her aunt was smiling rather stiffly. "We have a busy day ahead of us. We have a wedding to prepare for."

A wedding. She was to be married. Not in a month's time in St. George's with half the *ton* in attendance. Tomorrow in some obscure church—she did not know where. And not to Lionel, to whom she had been promised for five years, whom she had loved and longed for for five years. To the Earl of Thornhill.

She was to be the Countess of Thornhill.

His wife.

"Yes." She moved across the room toward her aunt.


THE EARL OF THORNHILL received much the same reception at the Rushford mansion as he had at Nordal's. Except that this time, when he sent the message that he would remain in the hall until he was admitted, he immediately broke his own vow by following the butler up the stairs, despite that servant's protest, and was at his shoulder and able to walk past him when the door to the earl's private apartments was opened by a valet.

"No," he said for the benefit of the servants and both astonished men in the earl's dressing room—Kersey was with him there—"I will not be turned off."

The Earl of Rushford, thin-lipped and furious, nodded his dismissal to the servants, ignoring the apologies of his butler. Viscount Kersey stood where he was and sneered.

"I have come," the Earl of Thornhill said, "for Miss Winwood's property."

"For . . . ? I will have you tossed out for this, Thornhill." Lord Rushford's voice vibrated with fury.

"I believe," Lord Kersey said, raising a quizzing glass to his eye, "he is asking for the letter, Father. By what right do you claim that slut's, ah, property, Thornhill?"

"I have the honor of being the lady's betrothed," Lord

Thornhill said coldly and distinctly. "I am reluctant to slap a glove in your face, Kersey, as I am sure you are well aware. The lady has suffered enough at our hands. But if you utter one whisper of an insult about her from this moment on, you will leave me with no choice. Now, the letter." He held out an imperious hand to Rushford.

The earl drew in a sharp breath. "The letter," he said, "has been burned. My house is sullied by even the ashes of such filth."

"So you are going to marry her." Lord Kersey chuckled until he caught his father's stern eye on him.

"Ah." Lord Thornhill's hand returned to his side. "I feared it. And since it is you who tell me, Rushford, I believe you. It was wisely done, too, though I will pay you the courtesy of believing that perhaps you did not realize it. If the letter still existed, there would be more men than just me who could have vouched for the fact that it was not in my hand."

"You would have been foolish not to have had some lackey pen it for you," Lord Kersey said. "But denial would be pointless. Who else would have had a motive to write it—and sign your name to it? You have destroyed my happiness, Thornhill, and made a good pass to destroy my name. Only the bold action of my father averted that chance and brought me the sympathy of the *ton* instead. My father's name too might have been brought to humiliation. For that fact more than any other I find your behavior unforgivable."

"The bold action of your father destroyed the name of an innocent young lady instead," Lord Thornhill said, "and in the cruelest manner imaginable. For a man newly affianced and apparently deep in love, you have recovered from her apparent defection with remarkable speed, Kersey. If I were you, I would put on a longer face when you go out. You would not wish it said, I am sure, that you were glad to be set free, that perhaps you had maneuvered to be free."

The viscount's eyes flashed. "It would be like you to spread such slander, Thornhill," he said. "I merely ask you to consider whose word is more likely to be trusted among the *ton*. The answer is rather obvious, is it not?"

"I must ask you to leave, Thornhill," Lord Rushford said. "My son has suffered a severe shock at your hands and at the hands of the woman I cannot bring myself to name. And the countess and I have suffered a painful disappointment in her. If you dare to come back, I will have you thrown out bodily. I trust I make myself understood?"

"Assuming that the question is rhetorical," Lord Thornhill said with a bow, "I will leave it unanswered. Good day to you."

It had been a slim hope, he thought as he made his way from the house on foot. If he could have proved that the letter was not in his hand, perhaps he could have set up enough doubt in fashionable drawing rooms that her way back into society would be made a little easier. Though, of course, there was no denying the fact that he was the one who had kissed her openly at the Velgards' costume ball and that she had been the one he had kissed.

No, it had been a slim chance. And he had not really expected that the letter would still exist. If he had been Rushford, he would have burned it. If he had been Kersey, he would have burned the house down too as an extra precaution.

He had paid the call for another reason. He had wanted them to know that Jennifer Winwood was to be his wife, that they would carry on any sort of a campaign against her at their peril. And he had wanted Kersey to know that he understood fully and that the game was not yet at an end.

Kersey had won the first round. There was no doubt about that. Far from suffering humiliation at the loss of his betrothed, he had deliberately arranged matters so that he could be free of her. He had wanted to be free of her. And he had done it in such a way that his adversary was stuck with her instead—though the earl winced away somewhat from the word he had used in his mind. She deserved better than that attitude. She was a total innocent, a victim of the plotting and cruelty of both Kersey and himself.

When he had told her earlier that he would devote his life to making sure that she would one day be glad of her decision, he had meant it. He would see to it that her reputation was restored and that for the rest of her days she would have whatever her heart desired. He would salve his conscience perhaps a little by doing that.

But the game with Kersey was not over. Somehow he would have his revenge. A more satisfactory revenge than a mere humiliation. Somehow he was going to find a way to kill Kersey.

In the meantime there was a special license to be obtained and all sorts of arrangements to be made.

Good Lord, he thought, stopping suddenly on the pavement, this time tomorrow he was going to be a married man.

But there was panic in the thought. He pushed it from him.

SAMANTHA TAPPED HESITANTLY ON Jennifer's door after luncheon. Although Jennifer had not come down for that meal, Samantha had learned that she was no longer in disgrace or in solitary confinement. She had learned to her utter astonishment that Jenny was to marry the Earl of Thornhill tomorrow.

"May I come in?" she asked, peering around the door. "Or would you rather I went away?"

Jennifer was sitting curled up on a chair, a cushion hugged to her bosom. "Come in, Sam." She smiled wanly.

Samantha came into the sitting room and glanced toward the half-open door into the dressing room. There was a great bustling going on in there. "Your things are still being packed?" she asked. Could she have possibly mistaken?

"To be removed to Grosvenor Square tomorrow," Jennifer explained. "I am to be married, Sam. It is a great triumph, is it not? I must be the first of those presented at

Court this spring to be married. And I will be a countess, no less." She bent her head to rest her forehead against the top of the cushion.

"Oh, Jenny." Samantha gazed at her in some distress. "It is better than the alternative, at least."

"That is exactly what he pointed out," Jennifer said with a little laugh. "Do you know why I eventually said yes, Sam? For an enormously important reason. Papa was going to have my hair cropped short before sending me away today. I said yes so that I would not have to have my hair cut."

She buried her face against the cushion. Samantha could not tell whether she was laughing or crying. Not that it really mattered. The emotion was the same.

She could think of nothing to say to her cousin. Nothing that would console her. She seated herself on a sofa and gazed at Jennifer's bowed head and thought back with horrified guilt to the unwilling elation she had felt last night—and still felt today. She did not really feel happy. Oh, no, she did not. It hurt dreadfully to watch Jenny suffering and to know the cruel circumstances that had brought about that suffering. Though Jenny had been so indiscreet . . . perhaps. Something worried her.

"Jenny," she said and then bit her lip. It must be the last thing her cousin wanted to talk about. "When did you have those clandestine meetings with him? We have always been together or with Aunt Aggy."

Jennifer's head shot up. "What?" She was frowning.

"The letter—" Samantha, facing those hostile eyes, said no more.

"That letter was a cruel hoax," Jennifer said. "He is deranged, Sam. He is obsessed with me. It was all lies. He did it to make sure that my betrothal would end and in such a way that I would be ruined and would have no alternative but to marry him instead. He is having his way. I will be marrying him tomorrow. But I have told him that I will hate him for the rest of my life. To such a man that probably does not even matter. I think my b-body must be all he wants."

Samantha stared at her. "I cannot believe that he could be capable of such dreadful cruelty," she said.

"Well, believe it." Jennifer buried her face again. "He denied having written the letter. Can you imagine that, Sam? If he did not, who did, I would like to know? Who else could possibly have wanted to ruin me and to end my engagement?"

"No one." Samantha continued to stare at her bowed head. "No one, Jenny." Except herself. Not that she had ever wished even one moment of suffering on Jenny, of course. Never that. But she had dreamed of the engagement's somehow coming to an end. Lionel had said that if only he had met her, Samantha, before Jenny . . .

And Lionel had wished his betrothal at an end. He had felt trapped by it. He had wished he was free to pay court to Samantha. But Lionel did not wish any harm to Jenny either. Lionel was a man of honor. Samantha frowned.

Jennifer was looking at her and smiling rather bleakly. "I am not very good company today, am I?" she said. "Don't you envy me, Sam? The Countess of Thornhill this time tomorrow?"

"Jenny." Samantha leaned forward. "Perhaps it will not be so very bad. He is very handsome and he has wealth and property. At least you will be able to console yourself with the knowledge that he was willing to go to great lengths to win you. I believe he must love you deeply."

"If you love someone," Jennifer said, "you do not deliberately cause that person deep misery, Sam."

"I did not say he was perfect." Samantha smiled. "I am just trying to help you to see the bright side. I know that at this moment there must seem nothing bright in life to you at all. But think about it. Lionel—Lord Kersey—promised himself to you a long time ago, when he was a very young man. Did he make great efforts to see you in the years following? To press forward your marriage? Has he professed deep love for you this Season or tried to make an earlier wedding date than that arranged by his parents and Uncle Gerald?"

"What are you trying to say?" Jennifer was angry, Samantha saw.

"Only that perhaps in a way the Earl of Thornhill loves you more than Lord Kersey does," Samantha said. "Only that perhaps life might not have turned into the idyll you expected if you had married the viscount and that perhaps it will not turn into quite the nightmare you expect now."

The anger died from Jennifer's eyes and she smiled. "Sam," she said, hurling the cushion, but not with any great force. "You could sell a hat to a milliner. I swear you could. It really does not matter when all is said and done, does it? I'll never know what life would have been like with Lord Kersey. And I dare not think of it now or I will become a watering pot. Aunt Agatha has instructed me to be in my very best looks for tomorrow. For my wedding day."

She smiled again and then spread her hands over her face and broke into wrenching sobs.

"Oh, Jenny." Samantha in her turn clutched the cushion to her bosom and found herself wondering treacherously how long Lionel would deem it proper to leave it before he called on her.

And then she hated herself for thinking of her own hopes when her dearest friend was in such misery.

Growing up was not nearly the pleasant, uncomplicated business she had expected it to be. Sometimes it was downright frightening.

# 13

IT WAS THE FIRST OF SEVERAL WEDDINGS TO UNITE members of the *ton* that were the primary purpose and inevitable result of the Season. It should therefore have been a singular triumph for the bride and her family, something to gloat over with well-bred condescension for the rest of the spring.

But this particular wedding, though it united a peer of the realm with the daughter of a viscount, was not a large, fashionable affair. It did not take place in St. George's or any other fashionable place of worship. It took place in a small church, where the rector was willing to perform the service at such short notice. And it was not attended by a large number of fashionable guests—merely by the groom's two friends, Sir Albert Boyle and Lord Francis Kneller, and by the bride's father, aunt, and cousin.

Jennifer, walking down the cold aisle of an empty, echoing church with her father and coming to a halt beside her bridegroom, tried to hold her mind blank. She tried not to think of the wedding in one month's time that she had been expecting.

She had not looked at her bridegroom, though she saw now in some surprise that he wore buckled shoes and white stockings. He was dressed as if for an evening social event. As was she. Aunt Agatha had insisted on white silk and lace, the finest of her evening gowns. Just as if it were a special occasion.

She supposed it was.

His hand, when it took her own, felt warm. And large and strong. She looked at it, at the long, well-manicured fingers. There was fine lace at his wrist and a blue satin sleeve. His hand squeezed her own slightly.

It was, she realized, a significant moment. A significant symbol. She had placed her hand in his and thereby surrendered all of herself to him for the rest of her life. To a man who had seduced his stepmother and then abandoned her and her child. To a man who was ruthless enough to do anything in order to win the object of his obsession. She was surrendering to him because she did not want to have her hair cut off.

He was speaking, repeating what the rector said to him. He was promising to worship her with his body and to endow her with all his worldly goods. She felt the hysterical urge to giggle and involuntarily gripped his hand more tightly in order to stop herself.

And she promised—she could hear herself as if it were another person—to love, honor, and obey him. To obey him. Yes, it was total surrender. Something he had forced her into. Something for which she would hate him for the rest of her life. Yet she was promising to love him. Solemnly promising before witnesses and before God.

She looked up into his face for the first time. He was

the handsome stranger of Hyde Park, the gentleman whom she had come to like and believe despite herself. The first—and only—man to have kissed her. Dark hair, dark eyes—focused steadily on hers—finely chiseled features. Devil with an angel's name. Her husband. That was what the rector was saying. He was her husband.

He bent his head and kissed her lips. Briefly and lightly as he had done twice before. As on both those occasions, she felt his kiss right down to her toes. His eyes smiled at her—a kindly, reassuring expression that hid the triumph he must be feeling. He had won. In no time at all. He had seen her and desired her and taken her away from Lionel and married her himself.

She wondered suddenly what he would do when he tired of her, as he surely would. He would put her away with as much callousness and as much ruthlessness as he had used to get her, she did not doubt. She felt an inward shiver.

Aunt Agatha was dabbing at her eyes with a confection of a lace handkerchief. Samantha was weeping openly. Her father was looking relieved. They all hugged her and shook the earl by the hand. His friends, smiling and overhearty, shook his hand more firmly and kissed Jennifer's. Lord Francis called her the Countess of Thornhill.

She was. Yes, she was. His countess, his wife, his possession.

He handed her into his carriage—she had a general impression of dark blue velvet and luxury—and a footman closed the door. She had hoped that Sam or perhaps his friends would ride with them. But no, they were to come on to Papa's for the wedding breakfast by other carriages.

She had been alone with him before. There was nothing so very strange about it. She must accustom herself to being alone with him. She was his possession.

At first he drew her arm through his and covered her hand with his own. They sat in silence until the horses had been set in motion. His arm and his hand were warm, but her own hand, sandwiched between the two, could draw no warmth or comfort to herself.

And then he released her arm in order to set his about her shoulders and draw her close to him. "You are like a block of ice," he said. "The church was cold and your gown is thin. Though I do not suppose either of those two facts is the real cause." He lifted her chin with his free hand, his palm warm beneath it, his fingers cupping her jaw. He set his mouth to hers again. "It is not going to be the nightmare you expect. I promise you it will not."

The side of her head was brushing his shoulder. She let it rest fully against the warm satin there and closed her eyes. She must not try to fight her way free. She was his wife. Besides, she was so very weary. She had slept last night in mere fits and starts. She would be inclined to believe that she had not slept at all, except that she could remember bizarre dreams.

"Jennifer." His voice was low against her ear. It was always so hard when she listened to his voice or when she was within the aura of his physical presence to believe that in reality he was the very devil. "We are man and wife, my dear. We must make the best of it. If either of us is to find any happiness in what remains of our lives, we must find it in each other. If we try very hard, perhaps we will not find the task altogether impossible."

Almost, she thought, as if he had been forced into this marriage as much as she had. She felt a flash of anger, but she quelled it. Any strong emotion might precipitate her out of the welcome lethargy that had taken her through the morning. She did not want to wake to full reality yet.

"You look very beautiful today," he said. "I am more proud than I can say that you are my wife."

And then his mouth was on hers again, warm, not at all demanding. His lips were parted. She wondered idly if all men kissed like this—if it was the way to kiss. But she would never know. She felt warmth seep into her flesh and into her bones. She pushed her lips back against his, reaching for greater comfort.

She was half asleep by the time the carriage drew to a halt outside her father's house. Half asleep and half dreaming. But when she opened her eyes and he drew back his head, it was Gabriel, Earl of Thornhill, at whom she gazed, not Lionel, Viscount Kersey.

With a sharp jabbing of pain, which seemed almost physical, she understood that she was married to this man. That there would never again be Lionel. Never again the dream, except perhaps during the kindest—or cruelest—sleep.

———

THE WEDDING BREAKFAST PROCEEDED with surprising ease. Perhaps it was because everyone—except Jennifer—tried very hard. Almost too hard, the Earl of Thornhill thought. The topics of conversation were too trivial and were clung to for too long. There was too much animation over trivialities and far too much laughter, especially from Frank and Bertie, and from Miss Newman. But he was grateful even so. Awkward silences and inappropriate solemnity would have been unbearable.

He was married. Without any chance to make his own choice, without any time to consider and digest what it was he had been forced into, he was married—to a woman who hated him with very good reason. She believed his perfidies far worse than they really were, and perhaps in time he could clear himself of some charges to her satisfaction. But he could not clear himself of everything.

He was horribly guilty. And if she knew the full truth, it would be worse for her than what she now believed. At least now she believed that he had wanted her and had deliberately set about getting her. How would she feel if she ever learned that he had not wanted her at all?

No, that was not strictly true. He had been moved by her beauty and by her innocent charm from the first. And powerfully attracted sexually. Perhaps if he had met her under different circumstances, he would indeed have set about wooing her. But he had not.

Bertie had been coldly satisfied at his news and had held out a hand as a signal that their quarrel was at an end. He had even agreed to attend the wedding. Frank had been incredulous and then inclined to find the whole matter a great lark. He too had agreed to come.

It felt somehow reassuring to have his closest friends at his wedding. He had relatives scattered about the north of England—and of course there were Catherine and the child who was officially his half-sister in Switzerland. But there had been no time to summon any of them, even if it had seemed appropriate to do so.

He took his bride home in the middle of the afternoon. It was perhaps only then that reality began to hit him. He was taking her to his home, now hers too. Her belongings had been delivered there in the morning. Maids had been bustling in the dressing room adjoining his own before he had left for church, unpacking her clothes. His servants, well aware that this was his wedding day and that his bride was coming home with him, were dressed in their best uniforms and had been lined up for inspection in the hall. There was a general buzz of excitement, hastily quelled by one frown from his housekeeper, as he stepped over the doorstep with his countess on his arm.

His servants applauded with an enthusiasm that went a little beyond politeness.

He smiled down at Jennifer and was relieved to see that she too was smiling. Whatever her personal feelings for him—he had not had one smile from her all day— she was prepared to play her part for his servants and hers, it seemed. He walked with her along the row of servants while his housekeeper introduced each to his wife. She smiled at all of them and stopped to talk to a few.

And then his housekeeper was preceding them up the stairs at his direction.

"You will show her ladyship to her rooms, if you please, Mrs. Harris," he said, when they reached the first landing.

She nodded politely and went on ahead to stand a few stairs up the next flight of stairs, out of earshot.

He kissed his wife's hand. "You are exhausted," he said. "You will rest for a few hours, my dear. Alone. I will not disturb you."

She flushed, her eyes on their hands.

"We will leave that for tonight," he said, "after the theater."

It had been arranged during the breakfast that her aunt and her cousin and Frank would share his box at the theater with them this evening.

But she raised her eyes to his. "You cannot really be serious," she said. "I cannot be seen at the theater. Not after what happened just the evening before last. It would be far better if we left for the country."

"No," he said, "it would not, Jennifer. Frank and Bertie will be putting it about this afternoon that we have been wed this morning. By this evening it will be general knowledge. News of you and me will travel faster even than usual under present circumstances. Tonight we must appear in public. And we must smile and look happy, my dear. We will dare anyone to cut our acquaintance. If we creep away now, we may find it impossible ever to come back."

"I do not want ever to come back," she said.

"You will." He released her hand. "If only to bring out our own daughters when the time comes."

She bit her lip.

"Go now," he said, "and rest. We will face the *ton* together this evening, and you will find that it is not impossible after all. Very few things are."

She turned without a word and left him. He watched her climb the stairs behind Mrs. Harris, tall and elegant and shapely, her dark red hair arranged in intricate curls at the back of her head and down over her neck.

Perhaps he would not have chosen a bride quite so precipitately if he had been given the choice, he thought, and perhaps he would not have chosen her. But one thing was sure. His loins ached for her. It was no easy thing to watch her go to her bed in the apartments adjoining his own and to know her his wife, their marriage as yet unconsummated, and yet not go to join her there.

He wished at least as strongly as she did that there was not this infernal compulsion to appear before the *ton* tonight as man and wife. He would give a chunk of his fortune to be able to go to bed with her instead and seek out an evening's entertainment of a different nature.

SHE WAS POWERFULLY REMINDED during dinner of the one vow she had made to him just that morning. She had promised to obey him for the rest of her life.

Somehow, seated adjacent to him at the long table in the dining room, she responded to his efforts to keep a conversation going. A little social training was a marvelous thing, she thought. One was able to talk politely on a variety of topics even when there was nothing to say and even when talking was the last thing in the world one felt like doing.

But one topic was difficult to introduce. She left it until she could not delay any longer without leaving it altogether.

"My lord," she said, looking up into his face for one of the few times since the meal had begun, "will you please excuse me from attending the theater this evening? It has been such a busy day. And I did not sleep very well either last night or this afternoon. I have a h-headache. I do not feel very well." Her voice trailed off. She sounded feebly abject even to her own ears.

"Gabriel," he said, reaching across the table to touch his fingers lightly to the back of her hand. "I will not be 'my lorded' all through life by my own wife. Say it."

"Gabriel," she said obediently. The most unsuitable name there ever was.

"I do not believe you, my dear," he said. "And if I did I would require you to attend the theater anyway. And I will ask you to smile and hold your head high. You have done nothing to be ashamed of. Nothing whatsoever."

"Except," she said softly, "being naive enough to fall into your trap."

He removed his hand from hers. "Tomorrow evening," he said, "we will be attending Lady Truscott's ball. You will find it a great deal easier to do if you keep your courage this evening."

"If?" she said. "I do not believe I have a choice, do I?"

"No," he said, "you have no choice, Jennifer."

She could scarcely move her mind beyond the terrifying ordeal of appearing before the *ton* less than forty-eight hours after being stranded in the Earl of Rushford's ballroom while he read that letter aloud. But if she did try to edge her mind forward to assure herself, as she would normally do, that it would eventually be over and she could creep home to the comfort and privacy of her bed, she realized that there was no comfort to be had there.

Today was her wedding day. Tonight was her wedding night. Before she could expect any privacy or comfort tonight, there was that to be lived through. She looked involuntarily at her husband and shivered. What would it feel like? she wondered. Would the pain be more powerful than the humiliation? She knew what was to happen. She had known for some time, but if she had been in any doubt, Aunt Agatha had put it to rest early this morning by describing the process with brisk and surprisingly graphic frankness.

She owed him obedience. She must let it happen. And she must hope that she could keep her mind as mercifully blank as she had kept it this morning.

"It is time to leave," he said, setting down his napkin on the table, getting to his feet, and reaching out a hand to assist her. "The carriage will be here soon. You certainly do not want the added embarrassment of making a late entrance, I am sure."

Jennifer scrambled to her feet with almost ungainly haste.

IT SEEMED THAT THE very doormen at the theater stared at them askance. It seemed that everyone else who was within the doors or on the stairs or otherwise not yet within the theater moved aside to give them room and fell into an incredulous silence. It seemed that all eyes in the theater, many of them assisted by quizzing glasses or lorgnettes, turned their way as they stepped into the earl's box, and as if all conversations were instantly terminated and others begun after but a moment's pause. Excited, buzzing, shocked conversations.

It seemed—no, it *was*, Jennifer thought. She clung to her husband's arm and looked frequently up into his smiling face, her own mirroring his expression. She responded to what he said to her with words of her own. She had no idea what he said or what she said in reply. She kept her chin high.

Lord Francis Kneller was there already with Aunt Agatha and Samantha. He got to his feet, took Jennifer's hand and kissed it, smiling at her and leading her to the chair which her husband held for her. She seated herself.

"Bravo, ma'am," Lord Francis said and winked at her before resuming his seat beside Samantha.

Her husband sat down beside her and lifted her arm

to rest along his. He bent his head close to her as she directed her eyes on the empty stage.

"You look lovely and wonderful and regal," he said. "Look about you and smile even more if you meet the eye of someone you know."

It was the hardest thing she had yet done. Except that she found when she did it that eyes were not directed at her at all. No one had even as much courage as she, she thought, raising her chin a notch higher. They could not meet her eye to eye and so pretended hastily to be looking elsewhere. She saw Sir Albert Boyle in a box opposite with Rosalie Ogden and her mama and another older gentleman, and smiled warmly at him. He smiled and bowed his head in her direction.

It was working, she thought several minutes later, just as the play was about to begin. Their entrance had obviously caused something of a sensation. Most people would not look directly at them when they thought themselves observed. But there had not been a great booing or hissing. No one had jumped up onto the stage to demand that they leave and not dare to contaminate decent people with their presence ever again. A few people had inclined their heads to her. One or two had even smiled.

Everyone, her husband had said, would know that they were married. Sir Albert and Lord Francis had made it easier for them by making sure that word spread this afternoon. Doubtless they had ridden in the park and made the wedding the sole topic of their conversation.

Two evenings ago, she thought suddenly, perhaps at

about this exact time, her betrothal to Lord Kersey was announced. This evening she was another man's wife.

Before she could shake off the distressing thought and before the play could begin, she was aware of another of those almost imperceptible pauses in the general conversation, followed by a renewed buzz of talk. And she saw instantly why. The box close to theirs in which she had sat one evening last week had been mercifully empty thus far, but now it was filling—with the Earl and Countess of Rushford, another older couple whom Jennifer did not know, and Viscount Kersey escorting Horatia Chisley.

It was perhaps the most intensely painful moment of her life, Jennifer thought. A hand clamped down hard on hers as she was about to get to her feet to flee she knew not where.

"Smile!" her husband commanded. "Look at me while I talk to you."

She smiled and looked. And had no idea what he said to her, his eyes warm on hers.

"Brave girl." She heard his words at last. "It will become easier, my love. You do not think so now, but it will. I promise." He raised her hand and held it to his lips.

She felt intense hatred for him. He had caused this. She should be there in the other box with her betrothed, radiant with the expectation of her coming nuptials. This man had seen to it that that dream was shattered. To be replaced by this.

Samantha leaned close to say something to her. She was flushed and bright-eyed and looked very unhappy,

Jennifer thought. Poor Sam. All this must be ruining her Season too.

And then, as the play began and she turned her attention at last and gratefully to the stage, she heard the echo of Lionel's laugh. Was he too masking heartache with laughter? she wondered.

Oh, Lionel. Lionel.

"THERE. YOU SEE?" HER husband said hours later when they were in the carriage on the way home—Lord Francis had escorted Aunt Agatha and Samantha—"It is all safely in the past. You carried it off wonderfully well."

She set her head back against the cushions of the carriage and closed her eyes. "Gabriel," she asked quietly, "why did you do it? Could you not have simply asked me and if I had said no accepted defeat? Why the letter? I was in the ballroom when it was read, surrounded by half the *ton*. You cannot imagine the horror and humiliation. How could you have done that to me?"

He did not touch her. There was a short silence.

"I know nothing of the letter," he said. "I did not write it or have it written or send it. Someone else did so, knowing that it would be easily believed in light of other things that had happened between us."

"I suppose," she said wearily, "that it was not you who kissed me in full view of everyone at the Velgards' costume ball either? And that you did not deliberately kiss me there instead of out on the balcony or not at all?"

He did not answer.

"It does not matter anyway, does it?" she said. "We are married and I am halfway to being respectable again and there is no point in hankering after what is gone forever."

"Kersey?" he said. "The time may come when you will realize you had a narrow escape from him, Jennifer."

She could not speak for a while. Her teeth were clamped together. "I cannot command anything, can I?" she said. "I would ask you, Gabriel, I would beg you please never to mention his name to me again. If there is one shred of decency in you, do that for me."

They traveled the rest of the way to Grosvenor Square in silence. And entered the house and ascended the stairs together in silence. He stopped outside her dressing room door. The door was ajar and there was light within. Her maid was in there, waiting for her.

"I will join you shortly," he said, bowing over her hand.

"Oh, yes, I have no doubt of that," she said, her voice bitter, knowing that she would be wiser to keep her mouth shut. "It is what you have waited for, is it not? But not really for very long at all. You have arranged all with admirable speed."

She wondered as he set his hands behind him and regarded her quietly if he would break the promise he had made to her yesterday morning. She wondered if he would cuff her. Or if he would set about a more ordered chastisement. She would have no recourse. She was his property. And she had provoked him.

"Yes," he said quietly, "it is what I have wanted. I will be with you shortly, Jennifer, to make love to you."

And there. As she stepped inside her dressing room as he pushed the door open for her, her stomach churned quite as painfully as her face would have done if he had given her the back of his hand. He had put it into words and terrified her.

She heartily despised herself.

Her maid, she saw, had set out her best nightgown and was smiling knowingly at her.

# 14

$I$T HAD NOT BY ANY MEANS BEEN AN EASY DAY. HE still could not quite digest the fact that he was married. The evening had been a dreadful ordeal. He had had to force himself through this twice now, facing the *ton*, refusing to hide from them, daring them to cut him. Except that this time it had been worse because this time an innocent was involved with him, and loss of reputation was always worse for a woman than for a man.

Kersey had basked in the situation at the theater. He had looked tragic and brave and had been gravely attentive to Miss Chisley. He had laughed once early in the evening, seemed to realize that gaiety was not appropriate to the image he wished to project, and had not laughed again. Far from being embarrassed at the ending of his betrothal, he was cleverly enlisting the sympathy of the *ton*.

It would be the greatest pleasure in the world to kill him.

But it was his wedding night, the Earl of Thornhill reminded himself after he had dismissed his valet. And it was difficult to face, much as he wanted her. She hated him. She had not made any secret of that. It was going to feel like violation, like rape. And yet it was something that had to happen. The only chance either of them had for a measure of contentment in their future was somehow to make something normal out of their marriage.

Her dressing room was empty and in darkness. He passed through it, tapped on the door into her bedchamber, and opened it. His wife's room. It felt strange to know that this empty room in his house was now his wife's.

She was not in bed. She was standing facing the fireplace, looking down into it though there was no fire. She wore a white, lace-trimmed nightgown. Her hair was loose and hung heavy and shining to her waist. He had hoped she would not braid it or try to stuff it beneath a nightcap. She did not turn, though she must have heard his tap and the opening of the door. Her shoulders hunched slightly.

Oh, Lord, he thought, he wanted her. But the knowledge made him feel guilty, though she was his wife and though he fully intended to have her. It should not be so easy for him. He was the guilty one. For her this would be the culmination of all the horrors that had happened to her in the past two days. Except that he knew one small fact about her that might give him a thread of hope. She responded to his physical presence. Slightly and unwillingly, perhaps, but quite unmistakably. She had kissed him in the carriage this morning just as he had kissed her.

"Jennifer." He had stepped up close behind her but found it difficult to touch her.

She turned and looked at him with a pale, set, defiant

face. "Yes," she said. "I am here. I am yours. You will find, I believe, that I know my duty and will perform it without protest."

Lord!

"And without enjoyment," he said.

"Enjoyment?" Color flooded her face, but he saw immediately that it had been brought there more by anger than by embarrassment. She spoke the next words slowly and distinctly. "You are the wrong man to bring me that, my lord Gabriel."

He set his hands on her shoulders, felt the tension there, and massaged them with his hands. "This will not do," he said. "This anger and this bitterness. They are understandable, though I am not as guilty as you believe me to be. But they will only bring you intense unhappiness, Jennifer, and perhaps even destroy you."

"You have done that already," she said.

"Perhaps." He moved his hands in and worked at the taut muscles of her neck. "But I have married you and I am seeing to it that you are not cut off permanently from the people of your own class. And I intend to be gentle with you. Meet me halfway. I am not the man of your choice. You believe that I have trapped you into marriage and you are partly right. But like it or not, you are in the marriage. For life. I cannot give you happiness unless you are prepared to receive it. Don't close your life to it merely in order to punish me."

"I know what is going to happen on that bed," she said, her face pale and set again. She had not given an inch. His massaging hands had met nothing but resistance. "I know just how it is done though it has never been done to me before. Do it, please. Get it over with and leave me to sleep. I am tired."

Deliberately defiant and rather vulgar words, which she could not possibly have spoken just two days ago.

He lowered his head and opened his mouth over hers.

He could feel her lips trembling. They were quite unresponsive, but she did not pull away. He slid one of his arms about her shoulders and the other about her waist and drew her against him. And felt for the first time the slimness of her long legs against his own and her curves against his body. Her full breasts pressed to his chest. *Do it, please. Get it over with . . .* His body clamored to be allowed to give it to her just as she wanted it. His mind ruthlessly imposed control.

He kissed her gently, moving his mouth in a soft, warm caress over her closed lips until the tautness started to go and she leaned into him and her lips relaxed. He licked them lightly with the tip of his tongue, tested the seam of her lips and found it relaxed, prodded through, and licked at the soft moist flesh inside.

Her hands, he realized, had moved up and were gripping the satin collar of his brocaded dressing gown almost at the neck.

He ran his tongue along her teeth until they parted, and then eased it inward. She made a sound in her throat. He took his mouth from hers and kissed her eyes, her temples, her jaw, her chin, her throat. He found fine lace trimming in his way. He kissed her mouth again and found her lips parted.

Her hands, he noticed, were flat on his shoulders, gripping tightly.

He kissed her and opened the buttons of her nightgown. He slipped his hands inside to the warm silky skin of her shoulders and found the tightness gone from her muscles. He moved his hands down over the sides of her breasts and beneath them. He felt suddenly weak at the knees.

But she drew a sharp breath, jerked her head back away from his, and stared at him with wide eyes.

"Beautiful," he murmured to her, gazing back at her through half-closed eyes. "Beautiful, my wife." He stilled his hands. "Kiss me."

She was breathing in jerky gasps, but she brought her mouth obediently back to his. He rather thought that he might have bruises on his shoulders with the imprints of her fingers in the morning.

He stroked her breasts lightly as his tongue circled about hers. He touched his thumbs to her nipples and found them hard and peaked. She gasped, drawing cool air in about his tongue. Lord, he thought, he could not wait. He wanted to be inside her now. He wanted to be thrusting mindlessly toward release. But he needed his mind. Quite desperately. Take her now like a heedless, dominant male and he might forever kill any faint chance they had for some sort of amiable marriage.

"Come." He withdrew his hands from inside her

nightgown and set one arm about her waist. "I think we had better lie down on the bed."

"Yes," she said, looking at it as if it were the executioner's block.

He kept his arm about her waist while he blew out the three candles that stood on the nightstand beside her bed. Then he turned her in the darkness, slid his hands beneath the shoulders of her nightgown again, and lifted away the fabric—off her shoulders, down her arms. It slid to the floor. She made a sound rather like a moan and was silent again.

"Lie down," he told her, edging her back onto the bed. He removed his dressing gown and dropped it to the floor before joining her there.

She was rigid again.

"I am going to love you, Jennifer," he told her, sliding an arm beneath her shoulders and turning her onto her side against him, "not punish or humiliate you. Love in its physical form can be very beautiful." He took her mouth with his again. Could it? He had only ever performed this act to relieve a physical craving. It had only ever been intensely satisfying.

She was incredibly beautiful. He explored her body lightly with his free hand, learning the shape and feel of her naked. And this was not for one night only or for as long as he cared to employ her. This was forever. She was his wife. He would plant his seed in her. She would bear his children. They would grow old together. Strangely, there was nothing frightening in the thought.

"My love," he found himself whispering against her mouth. "My love."

He would not touch her where he most wanted to touch her. Not with his hand. Not yet. She was only just beginning to relax again and accept the fact that the marriage act—for him, at least—involved nakedness and the touching and caressing of every part that modesty had kept hidden through her life. He sensed that he must wait for the more intimate and ultimately more pleasurable touches of full foreplay.

He turned her onto her back and lifted himself over her. He nudged his knees between her thighs and she opened them without further bidding. She was relaxed, acquiescent, heated. He slid his hands beneath her, positioned himself carefully, and mounted her slowly but steadily, moving without pausing beyond the unfamiliar barrier of virginity, though he felt her sudden tension and gasp of pain and panic, until his full length was embedded in her. He held still there, waiting for her body to master the shock of being penetrated for the first time.

God! Dear God in heaven, the urge to let go and to drive on with the act was almost overpowering. He clenched his teeth hard and pressed his face into her hair. She had raised her knees and slid her feet up the bed. He could feel the slim length of her legs against his own. Her body beneath his was soft and warm and intensely feminine.

He drew a few steadying breaths and lifted his weight onto his elbows. His eyes had become accustomed to the darkness and he could see that she lay with her eyes closed, her head thrown back on the pillow, her mouth slightly open.

Lord, he thought, watching her face as he withdrew slowly and as slowly sheathed himself in her again, she was enjoying it. He watched her as he loved her with steady, rhythmic strokes. He would continue the rhythm, he decided, feeling her inner muscles begin to clench involuntarily about him, until she had come to full pleasure. Even if it took another half hour.

And then she opened her eyes. For one moment, so brief that he thought afterward he might have imagined it, they were heavy with passion. Then they were fully open and even in the darkness he could see them fill with tears and he could see the tears spill over. With his body he could feel her first sob even before it became sound. He knew that she was fighting to control both tears and sobs. But she failed miserably.

He closed his own eyes and did what he had been fighting not to do for what had seemed like an eternity. He abandoned control and drove into her swiftly and deeply until he felt the blessed spasms of release and his seed sprang in her.

He lowered his weight onto her body and his face into her hair again. Her sobs sounded as if they were tearing her apart.

He moved to her side, disengaging himself from her body, and brought her with him, his arms locked about her. The very best thing he could do for her at the moment, one part of his mind told him, was to leave her alone. That was what she must want more than anything else in the world. But the instinct to comfort was stronger in him. He cradled her in his arms while she wept, murmuring some nonsense into her ear, stroking his fingers through her hair with light fingertips.

When she quieted eventually, he took a corner of the sheet and dried her eyes and his chest with it. Her eyes were closed, he saw. She made no move to pull away from him. When he drew the bedclothes up about her, she seemed even to cuddle closer to him.

He held her, his mind and his heart numb. He should leave. He should give her privacy for the rest of the night. God, how was he going to be able to come back tomorrow night to do this to her all over again? And yet how could he not? What sort of a nightmare of a marriage were they facing?

Tomorrow morning he would tell her everything, he decided. And yet everything would not exonerate him. Far from it. If she knew everything, she would know she had been only a helpless pawn in a game. That she had been of no importance to either of the players—to either Kersey or himself. How would he convince her then that he would make her the figure of primary importance in the rest of his life?

And would it be enough even if he could convince her?

Numbness did not last nearly long enough sometimes, he thought. He must leave. He must not indulge himself like this with the physical pleasure of holding her warm and naked body while his own relaxed into the physical satiety that followed a vigorous sexual encounter. He must leave.

But even as he made the decision he realized that incredibly she was asleep. The physical and emotional exhaustion of two days had caught up with her and she slept snuggled up to his body like a trusting child.

He felt a tickling in his throat and swallowed. He had not cried for so long that he was not sure he would know how to do it. He swallowed again and tried to blink the moisture from his eyes.

SHE WAS WARM AND relaxed and comfortable. And for a moment—just for the merest moment—she did not know where she was. But then she did, and her very first thought was a treacherous one. She was glad he was still holding her. She was glad he had not gone back to his own room, as Aunt Agatha had assured her he would after he had done that to her. He was warm and solid and she could hear his quiet breathing. Strangely and quite unreasonably she felt safe. She would have gone all to pieces if he had left her.

She kept her eyes closed and grief washed over her again. Grief because this was her wedding night yet he was not Lionel. When she had opened her eyes earlier as he was . . . doing that to her, she had . . . what? Expected to see Lionel? Had she kept her eyes closed imagining that it was he making love to her? No, not really. Not even at all. She had firmly shut her mind to Lionel, not invited his image into her marriage bed. But even so . . .

Oh, the reality of it all had hit her at that moment. She was naked on the bed, spread wide, and her body was being used by someone who was not herself. It belonged to him, to be used for the rest of their lives whenever and however he chose to use it. She was no longer in possession of her own body or of her own person. She had felt in that moment all the total and permanent loss of privacy. Even the inside of her body—there—no longer belonged to her.

And yet she had been enjoying it. The amazing and totally unexpected intimacy of his kiss, the touch of his hands on every part of her body, especially on her breasts, about which she had been self-conscious for several years because they were larger than anyone else's she knew, the feel and smell of his naked body—she had relaxed into the enjoyment of it all. And when he had— well, when he had come inside her, hurting her and then frightening her because she had not thought there would be enough room, and when he had started to move, she had thought she would swoon with the wonder of it.

It was not that she had imagined he was Lionel. It was just that when she had opened her eyes and seen in the darkness that he was not Lionel, but Gabriel, she had felt deep grief. For if she could lose Lionel so cruelly one night and enjoy this just two nights later with the man who had torn her away from him, how could she convince herself that she really loved Lionel? And yet if she did not, then everything she had lived for in the past five years had been an illusion. And if she could be enjoying this with this man, how could she feel moral outrage against him?

She had wept for the weakness of her body and the fickleness of her heart. She had felt all the humiliation and horror of weeping openly while he was still doing that to her, but she had been quite unable to stop herself. She had been at the point of exhaustion.

She had wept because he was not worthy of her liking or her respect. Because he was totally without honor. Because he had cruelly destroyed her and severed her relations with the man she had loved deeply—or perhaps not loved at all—for five years. And because she had enjoyed his two kisses while she was still betrothed to Lionel and was enjoying the deep intimacy of the marriage act with him.

She had wept because her body wanted to love him while her mind and her heart never could. Never.

And yet she was married to him for the rest of her life. She would live with him in the intimacy of daily life unless he chose to give them separate establishments. She would get to know his habits and his preferences and his tastes and perhaps his thoughts just as she now knew Papa's and Samantha's. And she would bear his children. His seed was in her now. He would continue to put more there until she conceived—and she would continue to enjoy the process.

She was a married lady. No longer a virgin. And this was the man who owned her. Not Lionel. Gabriel. He smelled musky, she thought, inhaling slowly and deeply. And sweaty. He smelled wonderfully masculine. She tipped her head back suddenly, alerted perhaps by a change in his breathing. His dark eyes were looking back into hers.

He lifted one hand and stroked the backs of his fingers over her temple. "I am so very sorry, my dear," he said softly. "I know the words are woefully inadequate, but they are the best I can do. It is a damnable mess I have got you into, but there is only one way out. We can only go forward and try to make something workable out of what seems impossible tonight."

She stared at him, remembering the Chisleys' garden and the library and Lady Bromley's orchard. Remembering that she had liked him.

"Can you try?" he asked. "Will you try?"

She really had no choice. She really did not. "I cannot." She closed her eyes. "Gabriel, I cannot bear the thought of you touching your father's wife as you have touched me tonight. I cannot bear the thought that somewhere in Europe you have a child who is both your daughter and your half-sister. It is horrible and obscene. I cannot bear it."

She tried to pull away from him, but his arms tightened. She felt horrified suddenly, and dirty, remembering that she had enjoyed what he did to her.

"Listen to me," he said, his voice stern. "That I am guilty of one offense does not mean that I am therefore guilty of every offense of which I have been accused. You believed me once, Jennifer. I have never touched my stepmother unlawfully. I am not the father of her child. I did not abandon her. I took her away because she was miserable and afraid and desperate. I took her because my father might have done her harm and because the blackguard who had impregn—well, who had impregnated her had taken himself off as soon as it appeared that his fun might bear consequences and then denied all association with her. I took her away to a place where she could bear her child in peace and comfort, and I left her there because she had discovered that it was a place where she could start again and perhaps find respectability and even happiness."

She pressed her face against his chest. She was so naive. She had always believed everything he had told her, despite warnings, despite all the evidence against him. She was believing him now.

"Tomorrow," he said, "we will write to her, Jennifer. Both of us. You will ask for the truth and I will beg her to tell it. You may read my letter before I send it. If that will not satisfy you, I will take you to Switzerland after I have reestablished you here with the *ton*. You will believe it when you see her—and when you see her blond, blue-eyed daughter. Catherine is as dark as I am."

"You do not need to take me or to write," she said. "If you say it is so, I will believe you." Her voice was toneless, but she knew she spoke the truth. If he said it, God help her, she would believe him. She wanted so very, very badly to believe him. The realization startled and rather frightened her.

"No," he said quietly. "We will write so that you will feel not a shadow of a doubt. Of that at least I am not guilty. Just as I am not guilty of writing that letter. The other things, yes, to my shame. I wanted to end your betrothal. I wanted to charm or force you into it. I even went as far as compromising you with that kiss. But I could not have been so wantonly cruel as to write that letter and ensure that it fell into the wrong hands on just that occasion. I could not have done that to you."

The temptation to believe him was strong. But if not he, then who? There was no one else. It would make no sense.

"I think you are right," she said, drawing her head back and looking at him in the darkness again. "I think we have to go on and just hope that time will bring some healing, some—well, something. I think you are right. I am so tired of hating."

His fingers, feathering through her hair, felt soothing. "After a week or two of appearances here," he said, "I will take you to Chalcote, my dear. You will like it there, I believe. There we can learn to be comfortable together."

"Chalcote," she said. "Is that not near Highmoor House?"

"Yes." His hand stilled for a moment. "Just a few miles away."

"That is where—" she said, and broke off. That was where Lionel's uncle lived. That was where Lionel had spent the spring two years ago when she should have been making her come-out and when they should have become officially engaged.

"Yes," he said, seeming to read her thoughts. "Two years ago. Just before I went north to spend the summer with my father. I did not spend the summer as it happened. I left within the month with my stepmother."

She closed her eyes. "Chalcote," she said. "I want to go there. Perhaps there I can forget. Perhaps there we can make something of this marriage after all, Gabriel."

She was giving in to the enemy again. She had no moral fiber at all, she believed. But he had not done that horrible thing with his stepmother. She believed him on that. And he said he had not written that letter. It made no sense, but he was adamant about it while admitting everything else.

Something was nagging at her consciousness. Something that was almost there but not quite. Something that maddeningly refused to present itself to her conscious mind for consideration.

"Jennifer," her husband was saying, "whether you wish it or not, I will be claiming my marital rights each night. I believe it is essential to any hope we have for the future. But only once each night. If I desire you more than once, you will have the right to refuse the second and any succeeding time."

She swallowed and rested her forehead against his chest.

"I desire you now," he said.

She could say no. He was giving her that freedom. That power. She had no idea how long they had slept. But it was still dark. If she wished, she could spend the rest of the night alone. She could have herself back to herself at least until tomorrow night.

She tipped up her face once more. "Then have me," she said. "I am your wife."

She could feel as soon as he drew her close against his length and kissed her that he was very ready for her again. She felt a deep throbbing where she was already sore and wanted him there once more.

She closed her mind to the knowledge that he was the wrong man and that if she had any firm moral convictions at all, she would be fighting with everything she had against this powerful physical attraction she had always felt for him.

"My love," he whispered against her mouth.

She wondered if he meant it.

# 15

*H*E SAT DOWN ALONE TO BREAKFAST. HE WAS considerably later than usual. Although his servants held to their usual impassive expressions, he could almost imagine the smirks and knowing looks they exchanged behind his back. He felt almost embarrassed.

Jennifer had been deeply asleep when he woke up, disoriented, her body pressed to his and entwined with his. It had taken him several minutes to free himself and remove himself from her bed without waking her. Indeed, she must have been deeply asleep not to have woken.

He had covered her to the chin before picking up his dressing gown and going through her dressing room to his. He had been afraid that the chill of the morning and the removal of his body heat would waken her. Or perhaps that strange embarrassment he felt had caused him to cover her so that her maid would not realize that she slept naked. Her maid was going to discover that fact of her mistress's marriage sooner or later anyway.

The post had been delivered already. A small pile of letters was stacked neatly beside his place at the breakfast table, and even a few invitations, he could see, if he was not mistaken. That at least was surprising. He had thought the best he could do was to take Jennifer to those entertainments for which he had already received invitations before the scandal, and to places, like the park and the theater, for which he needed no invitation at all.

He shuffled through the pile and stopped abruptly at one letter. Good Lord, what a strange, strange coincidence. It was a letter from Catherine, the first he had received since his return. He picked it up eagerly, wondering if there was anything in it that might set Jennifer's mind at rest while they waited several weeks, perhaps a few months, for a reply to the letters they would write this morning—or perhaps this afternoon. She had said last night that she believed him, but he could feel the confusion of her mind. He knew that there was a large element of doubt mixed in with the belief, and the fear that he was making her into his dupe.

He read carefully and smiled to himself as he set the letter down and ate his breakfast before tackling the rest of the pile or reading his newspaper.

An hour later he wandered back upstairs, even though this was the time of day he usually spent at White's and there was nothing stopping him from going there today. Indeed, he would probably have to endure merciless teasing and some ribaldry from a few friends and acquaintances if he did not go.

He went into his dressing room, opened the door quietly into his wife's to find it empty, opened the door even more quietly into her bedchamber, and went in.

She was still sleeping, the covers pushed down to her

waist. Her face was half buried in the pillow he had used, one hand pushed beneath it. Her hair, tangled and gloriously rich in color, acted as a kind of blanket but it could not totally hide the creaminess of her skin and the full shapeliness of the breast that was not hidden against the mattress.

Her maid, he noted ruefully, had been in already. There was a cup of chocolate on the nightstand, looking as if it was probably cold. Well, his servants could at least be thoroughly satisfied now that the marriage of their earl and countess had been consummated.

He was glad that she was sleeping so long and so deeply. She must have been totally exhausted in every way. He felt cautiously hopeful this morning. Hopeful that something might be made of the marriage that neither of them had either wanted or expected. She was tired of hating, she had said, though two days ago she had sworn to hate him for the rest of her life. And though she had wept while he was consummating their marriage, doubtless because he was not Kersey, she had allowed him to have her a second time. He had given her the freedom to refuse and she had used that freedom to say yes.

He had loved her with slow thoroughness, and her body had responded, first with relaxation, and then with pleasure. She had said nothing and had kept her eyes closed and her body still. She had kept her arms on the bed at her sides. But he had read the signs of increased body heat and deeper breathing and tautened muscles giving place again to relaxation and a sighing of expelled breath just before he released into her.

There was pleasure to be found together in bed. It was not everything. It was not even perhaps very much when they must live together out of bed all day. But it was something. Perhaps a physical tenderness would in time translate into emotional contentment.

She stirred, stretching in a manner that caused an immediate tightening in his groin. He wondered if he should turn and tiptoe from the room before she awoke fully, but he stayed where he was, watching her. He had called her his love more than once last night while in the process of making love to her. He had not done so deliberately. It had not been part of his plan to show her some tenderness. The words had been spontaneous. Had he meant them? He had never used them to any mistress or casual amour.

Was she his love?

And then she rolled over onto her back, stretched again, her palms pushing against the headboard of the bed, and opened her eyes. Her head turned sharply as she became aware of him standing there.

God, but she was magnificent. His eyes confirmed what his body had felt during the night. He had an unexpected flashing image of his child suckling at one of those breasts. "Good morning, my dear," he said.

He could almost see her mind registering the fact that he was fully dressed while she was naked—and exposed to the waist with her arms raised above her head. She lowered them hastily and jerked the bedcovers up to her chin. She colored rosily. He found the gesture of exaggerated modesty curiously endearing. He had been beneath those covers with her all night and they had twice been as intimate together as man and woman can be.

"Good morning, my l-lor—Gabriel," she said. "What time is it?"

"I believe it lacks a little of noon," he said. He smiled. "But only a very little."

Her eyes widened. "I never sleep late," she said.

"You have never before had a wedding night," he said, and watched her flush deepen. "I have something to show you," he said. "Will you do me the honor of joining me at the breakfast table in half an hour?"

"Do I have a choice?" she asked.

Ah, the night and the physical union and sexual pleasure it had brought them both had not healed many breaches after all. Perhaps none.

"Yes," he said. "You may eat alone if you wish, my dear. Your days may be almost entirely your own, if you so choose, and your nights too except for the one use of my rights I have told you I will insist upon. You are not my prisoner, Jennifer. Only my wife."

He could hear her drawing breath. "Half an hour?" she said.

"I will ring for your maid as I go back through your dressing room," he said. He took a step forward and leaned over her to kiss her fully and somewhat lingeringly on the mouth. "Thank you for the free gift of yourself you made me last night. It was more precious to me than jewels." He had a hand on either side of her head on the pillow.

"I am your wife," she said.

"Yes." He gazed into her eyes. "Are you sore this morning? It was perhaps selfish of me, even with your permission, to use you a second time when your body was newly opened."

He did not believe he was trying to shock her. He did not know what his motive was. To establish some intimacy between them, perhaps, that was not just physical. He felt the strange need to be able to talk with her on even the most intimate of topics. He felt the need for—for a marriage.

"Gabriel." She touched her fingertips to his cheek as he remembered her doing in Lady Bromley's orchard, and then closed her eyes and bit her lip. "Nothing. It does not matter. No, I am not sore." She laughed a little but did not open her eyes. "I suppose I could have used it as an excuse to be free of you tonight and perhaps tomorrow night, could I not? I do not want to be free of you. I cannot be, and I do not want the illusion of freedom. I want to know that this is my life forever after. I want to accustom myself to the knowledge and to the fact. I can only go forward. You were quite right about that. Make me feel married to you, then. Take me as often as you wish, night or day. I want to forget how and why we came together and what I left behind. Make me forget. You can, you know. I believe you must have realized that I find you attractive and always have."

There was enough in her words to chill him for an

eternity and to warm him for as long a time. He stood up and she opened her eyes.

"Yes." He nodded. "We are going to fall in love, Jennifer. We are going to be happy together despite the seemingly insuperable odds. I promise you." He turned and made his way through her dressing room, pulling on the bell rope as he did so, and back to his own. His heart was heavy—and soaring with hope.

ALTHOUGH SHE PULLED HER nightgown back on before going through into her dressing room, she knew that her maid must have seen her naked in bed. She felt intensely embarrassed and could feel herself flush hotly when her maid came bustling into the dressing room carrying a pitcher of steaming water.

Jennifer made her way down the stairs half an hour later, her hair neatly dressed, her morning gown covering her modestly. In some ways it was hard to believe that what had happened during the night had really happened at all, except that even with her previous knowledge and what Aunt Agatha had told her, she could not possibly have dreamed such intimacy and such sensations. And she could feel that it had happened. She was sore, despite what she had told him, but it was not a totally unpleasant feeling.

She was a married lady. She was married to Gabriel, Earl of Thornhill. She drew a deep breath as the footman at whom she had smiled warmly opened the door into what she assumed must be the breakfast room. What must he think, he and all the other servants, of the fact that she was coming down to breakfast well after noon? They would think that she had been kept busy by her bridegroom through much of the night and had caught up with her sleep during the morning, that was what. And they would not be far wrong.

She braced herself for her sight of him again. He really must be the devil or a wizard of some sort. When she could not see him, she could keep her mind partly sane and know him for who and what he was. And yet when she saw him, and especially when he was close to her . . . Well, she had understated the case when she had told him that she found him attractive. She was very much afraid that her body was beginning to crave his and that her mind was being dragged along with it.

And yet these feelings were not wholly unwelcome, she thought, as she entered the room and he hurried toward her from where he had been standing before a window to take her hand and raise it to his lips. Something deep inside her—close to where twice last night he had shared her body—somersaulted and she yearned to forget everything and let herself fall in love with him, mind and soul as well as body. With her body she already loved him, she realized, but she refused to allow her mind to ask her how it could be so when for five years she had loved another.

No, these half-unwilling feelings for him were not unwelcome. She must make the best of the life she had been forced into—by him. The rest of her life, long or short, was all she would ever have, after all.

"Come and sit down," he said, leading her to the place next to the head of the table, and seating her. He signaled to the butler to bring her the hot dishes and to fill her coffee cup. "Will you be pleased to know that we have received invitations this morning to a ball, a concert, and a rout? Addressed to the Earl and Countess of Thornhill, by the way. News travels faster than light in London during the Season."

Each morning usually brought a dizzying number of invitations. Three was a very paltry number. But it was certainly three more than she had expected—or wanted.

"I would prefer to go home to Chalcote," she said, deliberately calling it home, accustoming her mind to the fact that it really was home now because it was his and she was his wife.

"Soon." He covered her hand on the table with his. "We will be seen in all the right places for a week first. As much as anything, I have a mind to show you off and to throw every other male in London into the doldrums because you are mine and beyond anyone else's reach."

He smiled and looked almost boyish in his lightheartedness. But he had made a mistake to remind her of the obsession to have her to himself that was responsible for her being here now with him. Could there be any kinship between obsession and love? Could he ever love her? He had promised earlier in her bedchamber that they would fall in love. Not she, but they. Did he not love her yet, then? It was so hard to understand why he had acted as he had.

"No," he said very quietly after signaling the butler to

leave, "don't look haunted again. I said the wrong thing, did I not? I have a letter to show you when you have finished eating. I think you will be a little happier after you have read it."

She was not hungry. She made to push her plate away from her but his voice stopped her.

"Eat every mouthful," he said. "We will sit here until you have done so. You might have eaten—or not eaten—alone, Jennifer, but you agreed to allow me to join you here. Now you must endure my playing tyrant. You are not going to make yourself ill from lack of food."

She picked up her knife and fork and ate her way doggedly through the food she had allowed the butler to put on her plate. No, she was not going to let it happen either. She was not going to present a wan, skeletal aspect to the world. And if her womb was to house his child for nine months, as it probably would soon, she would make it a warm and welcoming and well-fed place. It would be her child too.

"There," she said, looking up at him with some defiance when she was finished. "Are you satisfied?"

He was smiling at her with what looked to be affection as well as amusement. He chuckled. "Are you planning always to be so obedient?" he asked. "Life with you might just be paradise, my love. I want you to read this letter, if you will. Aloud. It arrived just this morning." He handed her a sheet of paper.

It was covered with closely spaced writing in an elegant hand. *My dearest Gabriel,* she read. Her eyes flew down the page to the signature. *Catherine.* His step-mother!

"Aloud, please," he said again.

" 'My dearest Gabriel,' " she read in a monotone after drawing a deep breath, " 'Time flies along so fast. I fully intended to send a letter speeding after you within a few days of your departure. Forgive the delay. I wanted—and want—to thank you in a more permanent fashion than the words I have already spoken to you for all you have done for me when you might with perfect justification have turned your back on me. I want to thank you for giving me and Eliza more than a year of your life. I will not forget your sacrifice, my dear.' "

Jennifer looked up at him. He was watching her with eyes that seemed to burn.

" 'I dread to think what would have happened to me without your kindness and protection,' " she continued. " 'I know I do not deserve the happiness I feel in this lovely home you found for me, in this beautiful country, in my daughter, and—oh, yes, Gabriel—in the new love I have found, which quite puts into the shade the old love. You said it would happen to me and it has. He is Count Ernst Moritz. I do not believe you met him, though I was acquainted with him before you left. He is very close to a declaration. My woman's intuition assures me of it! But more of that in another letter. This is to be a letter of thanks.

" 'Gabriel, I was so very foolish. I owed your father loyalty, for he was never harsh with me. I was seduced by youth and beauty and a charm that proved selfish and heartless. But no matter, I have Eliza and so I would not change the past. She is so very fair and so wonderfully blue-eyed. It is, perhaps, a pity that she so resembles her father, but I can console myself with the certain knowledge that she will be a great beauty.

" 'I ramble. Has Society accepted you back, Gabriel? I should have insisted, perhaps, that you allow me to announce the truth so that your name would be cleared. I hope at least that HE is not in town this Season. Do not seek revenge if he is. He has given me Eliza and so I was the winner of that encounter. Seek love for yourself, my dear. I cannot think of anyone who more deserves it— though I do not believe the woman exists who deserves you.

" 'I grow sentimental. And I run out of paper! Write to me. I miss your good sense and your cheerfulness. I remain your affectionate Catherine.' "

Jennifer folded the letter carefully back into its original folds and slid it across the table to her husband. She did not look at him.

"Well?" he said. It seemed almost as if there was anxiety in his voice. Perhaps there was.

She looked up at him. "I told you last night that I believed you," she said.

"But you had doubts." His thumb played with the corner of the letter. "Do you have any now?"

She shook her head. "Is he in town?" she asked. "The child's father?"

His hand stilled. She wondered if she imagined that his whole body tensed. He shook his head, but she was not sure if it was a denial or a refusal to discuss the matter. He said nothing.

"I am glad," she said, "that she is happy, that good has come out of evil." His stepmother must have thought that the world had come to an end when she found herself with child by a lover and when that lover cruelly abandoned her though she loved him. She must have wanted to die. At Chalcote. Two years ago. But good had come of it. There was the blond and blue-eyed Elizabeth and the new home and country. And the new beau. Perhaps good would come out of the ending of her world too, she thought.

"Yes," he said. "How would we live with ourselves if we could not feel the assurances that that does happen?"

She wanted to comfort him, Jennifer realized suddenly. She wanted to reach out to touch his hand and to assure him that though he had done a terrible thing, all would be well after all. Until she remembered everything she had lost. Lionel—oh, dear God, Lionel. Her reputation. She remembered that humiliating and painful caning her father had given her just three evenings ago. No, he did not deserve to be forgiven so easily or so soon.

"Will you come with me to the library to write our letters after all?" he asked. "I would like you to introduce yourself to Catherine, and I would like to boast about you and tell her what a fortunate fellow I am."

"Yes." She got to her feet. Catherine had a blond, blue-eyed child. Her own children might have been blond and blue-eyed. But now they would probably have dark hair and dark eyes. She wanted children, she realized, even if they could not be Lionel's. Even if they must be Gabriel's. She hoped she would bear him a son first. She wanted a son.

Something nagged at the edges of her consciousness again as he tucked her arm through his and led her in the direction of the library. She had the same feeling as she had had last night that there was something there just waiting to leap into her conscious mind. But maddeningly it evaded capture.

SAMANTHA HAD HAD A night of broken sleep. Her heart went out to her cousin and the wedding night she was now spending with the man they had called the devil from the first. She wondered with a shudder if he would mistreat Jenny. Surely a man who was capable of such ruthless cruelty as the sending of that letter to Jenny's betrothal ball was incapable of tenderness.

Poor Jenny. Samantha felt terrible guilt for listening with such eager hope to Lionel's protestations of regard and for the elation she had felt at first when she had realized that the betrothal was at an end—an elation that had got all nightmarishly mingled up with horror. Poor Jenny had suffered dreadfully—and innocently, it seemed. First the exposure at the ball, then the beating from Uncle Gerald. He had been persuaded not to send out for a whip, but she and Aunt Aggy had listened at the library door after they had been dismissed. Before fleeing in a panic, Samantha had heard both his command that

Jenny bend over the desk and grip its far edge and the first swish of his cane.

And now—and now perhaps at this very moment that man, Lord Thornhill, was subjecting poor Jenny to unknown indignities. Samantha was not really sure what happened in a marriage bed, but whatever it was would be dreadful indeed with a man one had been forced into marrying.

But not all of Samantha's sleepless thoughts were of her cousin. Some were of the evening just past and the dreadful pain she had felt at seeing Lionel with Horatia Chisley. It was worse—far worse—than seeing him with Jenny had been. At least that had been an attachment that had preceded his acquaintance with her and one that he was trapped in. And at least Jenny was someone she loved dearly. Seeing him with Miss Chisley felt like a dreadful betrayal.

Except that he could not possibly show his true feelings just yet. It would be in dreadfully bad taste. He could not sever his relationship with Jenny one day and escort her cousin to the theater two days later. Not under the circumstances of that severance, anyway. He would have to wait a while. Perhaps a few weeks. Or a month. Or—heaven forbid—he might feel honor-bound to stay away from her for the rest of the Season and start afresh next year.

He would tell her. He would seek her out and make some arrangement with her. She must be patient. She must agree with what he had decided. He was so much older than she—seven years. Sometimes she felt her youth as a dreadful handicap. Sometimes she felt that she knew nothing. She would leave it to Lionel to be wise.

He would let her know. He would arrange a meeting with her somehow at Lady Truscott's ball tomorrow night.

The thought was soothing. And perhaps if the Earl of Thornhill had wanted Jenny so very badly, he would treat her kindly after all. Perhaps all would be well with Jenny. And she would not have been happy for long with Lionel. Sooner or later she would have discovered that he had felt trapped into marrying her by a promise he had made when he was too young to know quite what he was doing. He had been two years older than Samantha was now.

Tomorrow she would talk with him. He would arrange it.

She slept, comforted by the thought.

# 16

THE EARL OF THORNHILL AND HIS NEW COUNT-ess had appeared at the theater the night before and had driven in the park this afternoon, both times accompanied by the eminently respectable Lady Brill and by Miss Samantha Newman, cousin of the countess and one of the more lovely of the new faces of the Season.

On both occasions the newly married couple sat as close as propriety would allow, her hand on his arm, his hand covering hers. And on both occasions they smiled and looked happy. Almost radiantly so, the more kindly disposed were inclined to say. One sour dowager christened them the hussy and the rogue, and her names for them were whispered about and nodded over and chuckled at.

And yet there was something almost romantic about the description. And something almost romantic—though shockingly improper—about the reckless manner in which the earl had wooed and won his bride. Had they fled the capital in shame and humiliation, as they really ought to have done out of deference to decency, they would doubtless have been universally condemned, and the word *romance* would not have occurred to even the most fanciful of minds.

But they had not fled. And they were undoubtedly a young and an extraordinarily handsome pair. And titled and fashionable and wealthy. And apparently happy with what they had so shamelessly accomplished.

Yes, the *ton* whispered with collective reluctance, there was certainly something romantic about the new marriage. They had undoubtedly been extremely naughty and should by rights be expelled from decent society for life. But even the *ton*, jaded as it was as an entity, recognized that young love did sometimes triumph. And the *ton* felt a collective envy to go along with the reluctance.

The *ton* was prepared—with great caution and many reservations—to begin to take the Earl and Countess of Thornhill back to its collective bosom.

Though there was, of course, the fact that the earl had been in deep disgrace even before this scandal.

And there was the fact that Viscount Kersey was nursing a broken heart and was being very brave about it. One might have expected that the poor gentleman would disappear to the country or even overseas to avoid the embarrassment of such public rejection. But he stayed and conducted himself with quiet dignity in company with other gentlemen and with a sweet smiling sadness in that of ladies.

The ladies might have been disdainful of any ordinary gentleman who had been abandoned by his betrothed. But Lord Kersey, with his blond and shining hair and his bluest of blue eyes and his very manly figure, could never be an object of scorn. Especially not with that new air of tragic dignity. He could only be an object of maternal pity to older ladies and one of longing to young ladies and even to many not so young.

The *ton* was constantly a prey to boredom during the Season. Despite the dizzying round of social pleasures, really there was much of a sameness about most of them, and one saw much the same faces wherever one went. Anything even a little out of the ordinary was pounced upon with well-bred glee, especially if there was also something a little scandalous about it. What about this strange and fascinating triangle of three such handsome and—yes—romantic figures? They had all stayed in London. Would Lord Kersey demand satisfaction of Thornhill? Would the countess regret her decision? Would . . . ? Oh, the possibilities were endless. And the chance to watch their development was quite irresistible.

Lady Truscott, whose annual ball was never one of the main squeezes of the Season, was suddenly in the enviable position of seeing her home and her ballroom become the arena for the first formal appearance since their marriage of the Earl and Countess of Thornhill and for the first real encounter of the three protagonists since the scandal broke three evenings before.

Lady Truscott had the unutterably pleasurable gratification of seeing her ballroom so crammed with guests before the dancing even began that it was positively bursting at the seams, as one portly gentleman was heard to remark. Everyone should be paired with someone else, another wag declared in a voice of fashionable boredom, so that they could arrange to take turns breathing.

Lady Truscott's cup of joy ran over.

"SMILE," HER HUSBAND HAD commanded her as soon as he handed her out of the carriage. It was a reminder he did not need to give. She had smiled at the theater last night until she had thought her face would crack, and she had smiled in the park this afternoon so steadily that she feared some might think she must be an imbecile. She would smile tonight even though she must expect no partners except Gabriel. Unless they were turned away from the house, of course. She did not believe she would be able to hold her smile if that happened.

She had a horrible memory as she entered the ball-room on her husband's arm of the last time she had been in a ballroom—just three evenings before. It felt like a lifetime ago. In that ballroom she had been betrothed to Lionel. Now she was married to Gabriel. The unreality of it made her feel slightly dizzy.

She was fully aware, as she had been at the theater last night, of the near hush and then the renewed rush of sound when they entered the ballroom. She was less aware of the unusually crowded nature of the ballroom. She smiled warmly up at her husband and looked determinedly about her.

There were hundreds of eyes she might have met. And perhaps she did meet some of them fleetingly, though most of Lady Truscott's guests were too well bred to be caught gawking at her. But the pair of eyes she did consciously meet, across the full width of the ballroom, were those of Viscount Kersey.

Her heart performed a painful somersault and for many frozen and agonized moments she could not look away. Lionel! As handsome and as elegant as ever. Her Lionel. Her love. The dream that had sustained her through five long and dreary and rather lonely years.

And then she wrenched her eyes away and looked down at the hand she had rested on her husband's arm. She was quite unaware, in her distress, of the intense satisfaction the *ton* was drawing from the scene, though none gazed openly.

The earl took her hand in his free one and raised it to his lips. He was, as she expected, smiling at her with an admirable imitation of adoration in his eyes. She felt a strong wave of hatred again and fought not to let it show.

Someone was bowing before her. Someone was willing to acknowledge her. She looked up in surprise and saw those blue eyes at far closer range. He reached for her hand, and she took it from her husband's and set it in his, without realizing quite what she did. He lifted it and placed his lips against the exact spot where her husband's had just been.

He had never before looked at her like this, one part of her mind told her. With such softness and warmth and tenderness. Never. Oh, he never had, though she had yearned for it and told herself that it would happen as soon as their betrothal had been announced or as soon as they were married.

"Ma'am," he said, his voice soft, though she knew that several people around them, apparently involved in other activities and conversations, would hear what he said, "I would like to offer my sincere good wishes on your marriage. You must know that your happiness has always been my chief and my only goal. I hoped that you could find it with me, but I am glad that you have found it even at the expense of my own. You must not feel guilt." His smile was warm and sad. "Only happiness. It is what I wish you for the rest of your life."

He released her hand, bowed deeply to her, turned away rather jerkily, and hurried from the ballroom.

"The devil!" her husband muttered close to her ear. And then his hand was firm at the back of her waist, propelling her forward. "At last. The first set is to be a waltz, I hear. Come, we will dance it."

She wanted nothing more than to flee into the ladies' withdrawing room and hide in its farthest corner. She stepped forward onto the dancing floor, surprised that her legs would obey the command of her brain.

"Put your hand on my shoulder." His voice was almost harsh as his arm came about her waist and he took her other hand in his. "Now look into my eyes."

She obeyed him woodenly. She rather thought she might entertain the *ton* by fainting in front of them. It was unthinkable.

"Now," he said, "tell me you love me. And when you have done that, smile again."

"I love you," she said.

"Once more." He looked down at her lips. "And with a

little more conviction. And then the smile. Your pallor will be understandable under the circumstances, but it might be misconstrued if it continues."

"I love you," she said and smiled at him.

"Good girl. Keep looking into my eyes for a while," he said.

It was ludicrous. Telling him that she loved him, smiling into his eyes, while both of them knew that she was almost fainting from love of another man. Lionel had been so kind and so very—noble about it. She would have expected him to cut her completely for the rest of her life. He had wished her happy. Even at the expense of his own happiness, he wished for hers. Did he not realize that her heart was aching for him?

Except that treacherously, gazing into her husband's face, she felt that physical pull toward him that she always seemed to feel. And looking at his lips, she thought about his way of kissing and the strange effect the touch of his mouth against her own had on her whole body. She always felt it as much in her toes as on her lips. Her smile broadened with amusement despite herself. And despite herself she found herself thinking about last night, their wedding night, and becoming a little breathless at the knowledge that it was to be repeated tonight. Every night, he had said. At least once and sometimes more if he desired it and she permitted it.

And then her thoughts shifted suddenly and unwillingly to three evenings before and the reading of that letter. Lionel had been with his father. He had been absent from the ballroom with his father, no doubt planning with him what they were to do about the intercepted letter. He had walked at his father's side back into the ballroom and up onto the dais, where he had stood quietly while his father read.

He desired only her happiness, he had just said. How could he have done that, then? How could he have exposed her to such cruel treatment? Even if she had been guilty, it would have been ghastly and unusual punishment. They might as well have stripped her and confined her to a pillory and whipped her. She had felt that helpless, that exposed, that hurt. Of course, the whipping—or the caning—had come later in more privacy.

Even assuming that that letter had shocked and hurt Lionel, how could he have acquiesced in what his father had done? How could any gentleman have done such a thing? Especially a gentleman who had just professed to desire her happiness.

He had just made a gesture so noble that she had almost fainted. But was it really so noble? He had not apologized for his cruelty and lack of gallantry. He had merely—he had made himself look like a gallant martyr to everyone who had watched and listened. She had no doubt that a vast number had watched and that a significant number had listened. His words were probably known to every guest in the ballroom by now.

No, she was doing him an injustice. It was Lionel she was thinking of. Lionel. Her love.

"It was kind of him," she said hesitantly. "It was nobly done."

"It was pure theater," her husband said softly. "He

won the hearts and the sympathy and the deep respect of all of fashionable society, Jennifer. He put you entirely in the wrong."

"But he wished me happy," she said.

"He does not care the snap of two fingers for you," he said. "There is one love and one love only in Kersey's life—and that is Kersey himself. If you did but know it, Jennifer, you are a thousand times better off with me."

She looked at him, startled, her smile slipping for a moment. There was quiet venom in his voice. She would have expected him to feel some shame at the wrong he had done Lionel. But perhaps it was natural to hate the person one has wronged.

And then it was there, full-blown and startlingly unexpected and unbidden—that thought that had been nudging at her consciousness like a maddening irritant. Lionel had been with his sick uncle at Highmoor House two years ago. Catherine, at nearby Chalcote, had had a secret lover two years ago. She had been seduced by youth and beauty and charm, as she had put it in her letter. Her daughter was blond and blue-eyed—like her father. Gabriel, when she had asked if the child's father was in London now, had not really answered her question. Gabriel hated Lionel.

The tumbling thoughts so terrified her that she tried to push them from her back to the place where they had only irritated her.

"Who was your stepmother's lover? Who is Eliza's father?" Horrified, she heard herself whispering the questions.

"No." His hand tightened somewhat at her waist and he twirled her about a corner and then twirled her again. "This is neither the time nor the place, my love. We are dreadfully much on view."

She felt enormous, knee-weakening relief that he had refused to answer, yet she knew that she would not be able to leave it alone. She knew that when they went home she would ask again and that she would not rest until she had heard his answer. Though she knew what the answer would be. And denied it to herself with panicked vehemence.

The set was almost at an end. But it did not end quite soon enough to save her. Even as the music drew to an unmistakable end, the final thought opened the door into her conscious mind and stepped through.

Gabriel hated Lionel. Because Lionel had been Catherine's lover and had abandoned her and denied paternity of her daughter. *Do not seek revenge,* Catherine had written.

But he had sought it.

And he had achieved it, too.

In the crowded and stuffy and stifling hot ballroom, Jennifer suddenly felt freezing cold right through to her heart.

LADY BRILL HAD BEEN very afraid that her one niece's notoriety would reflect on the other. She had feared that Samantha would have no partners at Lady Truscott's ball. She had been quite prepared to use all the power of her influence in order to prevent the disaster of her niece's being a wallflower. The situation might well be irreversible if it once happened. And so Samantha, just like Jennifer, was instructed as soon as she stepped from her uncle's carriage to smile.

But Aunt Agatha need not have worried. Her usual court was about her almost before she had settled in one spot inside the ballroom and she had promised the first three sets. Even some gentlemen who did not normally crowd about her did so this evening. Samantha guessed that she was somehow benefiting from Jennifer's disgrace. Perhaps a few of them hoped that she would say something to feed their thirst for gossip.

She smiled and danced and chattered to gentlemen and to other young ladies of her acquaintance. And she noted with pleased satisfaction that Jenny was not being shunned but that she danced each set. But she could not feel happy. She had witnessed the incredible spectacle of Lionel crossing the ballroom—he had not walked around the edge of the dancing floor as people usually did but right across its emptiness—and kissing Jenny's hand and saying something to her and bowing to her and then hurrying from the room.

While her heart had gone out to him for his courage and nobility in doing something so very difficult to do, the scene had also depressed her. He truly cared for her. She heard those words or words to that effect all about her as people discussed the incident.

Perhaps Lionel had loved Jenny after all.

She watched unhappily for his return to the ballroom and felt mortally depressed at the strong possibility that he had left the house. But he had not. During the second set he returned. He spoke with a group of ladies and danced the third set with one of them.

Samantha waited for him to approach her. Or if not that, for him at least to glance at her. For some sort of signal to pass. Surely he would give some sign. A smile, perhaps. An inclination of the head. Some private promise that he would speak with her openly at a more opportune time.

But there was nothing. He was being very discreet.

Or she was being very foolish?

She could stand it no longer when supper was over and she could see that Lord Graham was about to ask her for the next set. Lionel was standing close to the doorway, talking with two other gentlemen.

"Excuse me, please," Samantha said, and she hurried away after murmuring to Aunt Agatha that she was going to the ladies' withdrawing room. She did not stop to listen to the exasperated question of why she had not gone there when she was passing it a few minutes ago on the way back from the supper room.

Her heart beat painfully as she approached the doorway. She had never in her life contemplated anything so brazenly improper. She bumped awkwardly against Lord Kersey as she hurried past him and stammered an apology as he caught at her upper arms.

"Let me speak with you outside," she whispered, and hurried on past.

A moment later she would have given anything in the world to have those words and that collision back. How could she? Oh, how could she? She stood uncertainly, fanning herself, and decided that after all she would rush for the ladies' room. He would think he had imagined what she had said.

But he came strolling from the ballroom while she still hesitated.

"Ah, Miss Newman," he said, making her an elegant bow and taking her hand to raise to his lips. "I am charmed to see you here. I trust you are enjoying the evening?"

"Oh, yes, my lord, thank you," she said breathlessly, looking anxiously into his face. Let him speak without delay, she thought. There was nothing improper in their exchanging civilities for a few moments. But a few moments were all that propriety would allow.

He was looking at her politely, his eyebrows raised. There was . . . amusement? in his eyes. "Yes, Miss Newman? How may I be of service to you?"

How unspeakably mortifying. Except for that look in his eyes—that knowing look—he might have been addressing a stranger.

"I thought—" she said. "That is— When you were still betrothed to Jenny you said—I—"

He leaned his head a little closer to her as if trying to make sense of a child's meanderings. "I believe," he said, "your extreme youth has led you into a misconception, Miss Newman. You are a lovely young lady, and I have always appreciated loveliness. Perhaps I expressed some gallantry that you misinterpreted?"

She stared at him in disbelief and horror. And realized

in a painful rush everything that her extreme youth had led her into. She had been disturbed by his willingness to speak secretly of love to her when he was promised to Jenny. And she had once suspected that he wanted her to try to end the betrothal by speaking with Jenny. She had been quite right—though she had mistaken his motive. Oh, yes, she had. It was so crystal clear to her now that she felt mortified at her own stupidity. Or at her own childish refusal to listen to her own doubts.

"You wanted your freedom from Jenny," she whispered. "You tried to use me. Oh!"

"My dear Miss Newman." His look was one of avuncular concern. "I believe the heat of the ballroom has been too much for you. May I fetch you a glass of lemonade? And help you to a chair first?"

But another ghastly thought had struck her. Jenny had denied those indiscretions that the letter had listed, and Samantha had known it was almost impossible for her to have had clandestine meetings with the Earl of Thornhill. And Jenny had said the earl had denied writing the letter. Lionel had done nothing to protect Jenny from that dreadfully public disgrace. He might have confronted her privately, put her away from him quietly. But he had not. And now she knew why.

"You wrote the letter." She was still whispering.

"I believe," he said—he was chafing her hand—"I should summon your aunt, Miss Newman, and advise her to take you home."

"No." She snatched her hand away, brushed past him with ungainly haste, almost collided with the Earl of

Thornhill, remembered where she was, and hurried toward the ladies' withdrawing room.

The music had come to an end before she came out again. She would decide tomorrow whether or not she should tell Jenny and Lord Thornhill what she now suspected, though really it was more than suspicion that she felt. Yes, she should tell them. But in the meantime there was the remainder of a ball to be enjoyed and partners to be danced with, and perhaps—yes, perhaps a husband to be chosen.

Although she had been in the ladies' room for only half an hour, she felt as if she had grown up at least five years in that time. She was no longer a naive and innocent girl. She felt quite like a cynical woman of the world.

Never again would she allow herself to be so deceived.

Never again would she love.

# 17

THE EARL OF THORNHILL HAD BEEN DEEPLY AF-
fected by the letter from Switzerland. The very
fact that it had absolved him in Jennifer's eyes of at least
one of the charges against him was no small matter, of
course. But it was not just that. There were two particular points in the letter that had impressed themselves
deeply on his mind.

She had begged him not to seek revenge. Her plea had
come too late, of course. He had already sought revenge
and failed to get it. He had helped rather than hurt
Kersey, he firmly believed. Kersey had been quite happy
to rid himself of the encumbrance of an unwanted betrothal. But the attempt at revenge had not been without
result. Far from it. It had hurt two people—Jennifer and
himself.

And he had been contemplating further and more vicious revenge. He had been half planning Kersey's
death—by provoking him into a duel, perhaps. And yet
Catherine's plea had somehow made him realize that hatred merely breeds hatred and violence. He had made
himself every bit as bad as Kersey in the past month. Yes,
every bit.

It was a chilling realization.

Especially in view of that other thing Catherine had said. *I was the winner of that encounter.* She really had been. It was true that she had suffered dreadfully, but the experience had matured her, and it had led her to find for herself the place and the life that would make her happy. She was about to remarry, it seemed. And most important, she had Eliza, whom she adored.

Yes, Catherine had gained in almost every way, while Kersey was still selfish and rootless and very possibly unhappy.

*I was the winner of that encounter.* The words had haunted him all day. In his efforts to get some measure of revenge, he had severed Kersey's betrothal to Jennifer and had been tricked and trapped into marrying her himself. Was he the loser of the encounter? Was he? Or was he the winner, as Catherine had been?

Was it in fact, in both their cases, a matter of loser take all?

It was a severe provocation when Kersey came to speak to Jennifer at the start of the ball. It was so obviously a well-calculated move. And the Earl of Thornhill would not have been human had he not felt furiously angry and even murderous. But he chose to make his wife his chief concern throughout the evening. He could never atone for what he had done to her in the past. But he could and would do everything in his power to protect her interests and look to her security and contentment in the future. It was all he could do.

He was relieved to find that she was not after all to be a social pariah. Frank, of course, came to pay his respects as soon as the first set had ended and led her into the second set. And at the end of that Bertie brought his blushing and timid betrothed to present—with her mother's permission, Bertie had whispered when the earl had raised his eyebrows and looked pointedly at him. Bertie danced the next set with Jennifer while the earl was forced to lead out the terrified Miss Ogden. It took all of his charm and all of five minutes to draw the first smile from her and another two minutes to draw a giggle. When she relaxed and smiled, she was almost pretty, he thought. She certainly had a considerable amount of sweetness. He must remember to commend Bertie on his choice.

When that set was ended, Colonel Morris strolled over to talk and then bowed in courtly manner to Jennifer and asked for the honor of a dance. And after that the crisis seemed to have passed. It apparently became the fashionable thing to dance with the notorious new Countess of Thornhill.

Such was the fickleness of the *ton,* her husband reflected, watching her and not even trying to hide the admiration in his eyes. He had watched her with deliberate admiration while he had been seeking his revenge. Well, now it had become very real.

And yet all was not perfectly well. Of course it was not. It was only amazing that the evening was proceeding as well as it was. The earl danced the supper dance with her himself even though he had seen two other prospective partners approaching her. He was not quite sure of what would happen at supper and preferred to be at her side to protect her if necessary.

He was very glad he had had the forethought to do so. He had seated her at a table with Bertie and Miss Ogden and two other couples of their acquaintance. The table adjoining theirs was empty, but three older couples were approaching it, among them the Earl and Countess of Rushford. And then the countess, who must have been in the card room all evening, saw them and froze.

"Rushford," she said after a significant pause and in a very distinct voice, "find me another table, if you please." She lifted her head and sniffed the air delicately. "There is something—putrid in the vicinity of this one."

Rushford led her away and the other two couples trailed after them while the Earl of Thornhill lowered his head to his wife's, made some mundane remark to her, and smiled. She smiled back at him.

Before supper was over, everyone in the supper room, and doubtless everyone else who had not come there, would have heard what the countess had said. Many would applaud her wit.

No, all was not yet perfectly well. And it was going to be difficult to forget about revenge when his wife was likely to be the butt of other sallies of wit like that one during the week before he would take her away to the peace and safety of Chalcote.

Henry Chisley danced with her after supper while the earl watched as usual. She was a woman of great strength of character, he thought with an unexpected twinge of pride. She was holding up wonderfully well under circumstances that would have given most other women the vapors long ago and sent them into a permanent decline. Jennifer, he suspected, would not go into a decline even when the full reality of what had happened to her in the past few days finally hit her.

He remembered suddenly her asking him who Catherine's lover had been, who Eliza's father was. Was she suspecting the truth? He drew a slow breath.

But his attention was distracted.

He had been half aware of the fact that Samantha had left her aunt's side and was approaching the doorway. There was nothing very strange about that, but his attention was caught when she stumbled against Kersey of all people. She hurried on past him and out through the doors, but no more than a few seconds later Kersey turned and left too.

The earl frowned. He had not had the chance yet to become well acquainted with Samantha, but she was Jennifer's cousin and even younger than she. He did not see why Kersey would want to have anything to do with Samantha when he had just rid himself of Jennifer. But if he did decide to turn his charm on the girl, her youth and inexperience would doubtless make her easy prey.

He hesitated and looked back to his wife, who was still dancing with Chisley and saying something that had him chuckling. He hesitated a moment longer and then slipped from the room himself.

Yes, Kersey had accosted her and they were talking. He could see only Kersey's back, but she looked considerably agitated. She appeared not to notice him as he strolled closer just in case he was needed. Perhaps he had given up the idea of revenge, but he was not going to stand by while Kersey seduced an innocent young girl.

". . . a lovely young lady," he heard Kersey say, "and I have always appreciated loveliness. Perhaps I expressed some gallantry that you misinterpreted?"

The earl watched agitation give place to horror in Samantha's face. "You wanted your freedom from Jenny," he heard her say, though she spoke almost in a whisper. "You tried to use me. Oh!" The final exclamation was agonized.

It did not take a great deal of intelligence to understand what had happened. Kersey had obviously been playing two games at the same time in the hope that if he did not win the one, he would succeed with the other. And in the process he had quite heartlessly hurt two innocents.

The Earl of Thornhill felt again the murderous urge to get even. He stood where he was until Samantha pushed past Kersey, almost collided with him, and hurried on in the direction of the ladies' withdrawing room. Kersey turned a moment later, a look of amusement on his face. The look disappeared when he saw the earl standing no more than a few feet away.

"Ah," he said, "a soft-footed spy. Must I be looking over my shoulder wherever I go for the rest of the Season, Thornhill?"

"It might be arranged if I thought it would give you a few sleepless nights," the earl said pleasantly. "I will have a word with you now, Kersey."

"Will you?" Viscount Kersey smiled, at his ease again. "I believe I can be expected not to consort with the man who is responsible for my broken heart."

"I shall wait, then," the earl said, unruffled, "for you to return to the ballroom and then slap a glove in your face in defense of the honor of my cousin by marriage, Miss Newman."

"You would simply make an ass of yourself," the viscount said contemptuously.

"We will put it to the test." The earl smiled at him. "I have very little to lose, after all. When reputation is gone, there is nothing much left to guard from public scorn, is there?"

Viscount Kersey looked nettled. "Well?" he said. "What do you have to say?"

"A few things," the earl said, looking about him, "which I would prefer to say in some privacy. By a stroke of good fortune I see that the first anteroom is at this moment being vacated. Shall we go there?"

"Lead the way." Viscount Kersey made him a mocking bow and extended one hand in the direction of the anteroom.

The Truscott mansion had been carefully built for social occasions. There was a whole series of small, cozy anterooms opposite the ballroom, all interlinked by doors that could be closed for privacy or left open for greater sociability. The understanding was that some guests would wish for a quieter place than the ballroom at some point in the evening and yet would be uninterested in cards. The understanding was too that young couples who were involved in the marriage mart, as so many were during the Season, would perhaps wish a moment in which to steal a kiss without being observed by half the *ton*.

Closed doors were not the rule. Closed doors suggested clandestine goings-on and might arouse scandal if left closed for too long a time.

The Earl of Thornhill closed the door into the corridor outside. Viscount Kersey turned to face him, amusement in his face again.

"It is a pity gentlemen gave up the fashion of wearing dress swords a few decades ago, Thornhill," he said. "We might have had a spectacular clash of arms in here, might we not?"

The earl stood just inside the door. He set his hands at his back. "I have to thank you, Kersey," he said, "for making it so easy for me to acquire my wife. She is, I believe, the greatest treasure any man could hope to find."

Lord Kersey laughed. "That good, is she?" he said. "Perhaps I should have tried her out for myself a few times, Thornhill. Broken her in for you and all that."

"Have a care." The earl's voice was very quiet. "Be very careful, Kersey. The lady has been made to suffer indescribable humiliation, for which we are both responsible."

"Come," Lord Kersey said, still laughing, "you must admit that I was a better player than you, Thornhill. The letter was masterly. At least, in the humble opinion of its author it was. I did not expect you to take on a leg-shackle with her, though. That fact will afford me amusement for many a long day."

"I will be brief," the earl said. "I came to say this, Kersey. You debauched my stepmother, you ruined the lady who is now my wife, and you have cruelly toyed with the affections of her cousin, another and even younger innocent. You have nothing to fear from me as I have discovered to my cost since my return from Europe that I have merely reduced myself to your level by seeking to punish you and have hurt innocent people in the process. But if you come near any lady within the sphere of my protection or affection ever again, or if you say or do anything calculated to cause them public humiliation, I will slap that glove I spoke of across your face in the most public place I can find. I will not ask if you understand me. I do not believe imbecility is among your faults."

Viscount Kersey put his head back and roared with laughter. "I am in fear and trembling, Thornhill," he said. "My knees are knocking."

"If they are not now, they will be before this night is out."

Both men turned their heads sharply to look in astonishment at the door to the next anteroom, which now swung open and crashed against the wall behind it. It must not have been quite shut, the Earl of Thornhill realized.

The Earl of Rushford stood there, his eyes ablaze, his face almost purple. Behind him Thornhill had a brief glimpse of the shocked face of the countess. The two gentlemen with whom they had taken supper were hastily ushering their ladies out through the other door into the corridor.

"Father!" Viscount Kersey said.

A well-rehearsed melodrama could not have played itself out with half as much precision, the Earl of Thornhill thought. Well, so much for private rooms and private conversations. He wondered irrelevantly if the sound of a kiss carried from one anteroom to another.

"Rushford," he said curtly, inclining his head. "Ma'am." He did likewise for the countess. "I have had my say here. If you will excuse me."

He turned and left the room, closing the door quietly behind him. The music was just ending, he could hear. Jennifer would need him in the ballroom.

SHE KNEW HERSELF FOR the coward she was before the night was out. Those questions she had asked him during the first waltz, the ones that had gone unanswered, had repeated themselves in her mind over and over again through the rest of the evening. Not that she really needed to have them answered. But as long as they were not, as long as she could not hear the answers in his voice, then perhaps she could convince herself that they were still merely questions, that she did not know the answers.

She would ask again as soon as the ball was over, she decided. And yet she did not ask in the carriage on the way home. They were alone together, and they traveled in silence. It was not that she had no opportunity to ask. But she did not. He sat as far to the right of the seat as he could and she sat as far to the left as she could. But he took her hand in his and held it so tightly throughout that silent journey that her mind became wholly focused on her pain. Or so it seemed. She welcomed the pain because it gave her mind something to focus on.

She would ask him as soon as he came into her bedchamber, she decided when he had escorted her into the house and left her at the door of her dressing room after kissing her briefly and telling her he would be with her shortly. But she did not do so. By the time he came to her she was in her nightgown, and her newly loosened and freshly brushed hair was comfortable against her back, and she could feel only anticipation and desire. If she asked now, a treacherous part of her mind told her, everything would be ruined and he would not make love to her. Or if he did, she would not be able to enjoy it.

And so she decided to ask him afterward, before they fell asleep. But making love took a good deal of time and even more energy. And making love reminded her that she did not want any of it to be true. Any of it, including what she knew beyond all doubt was true. She did not want it to be true because she wanted to love him. And she wanted to be free to enjoy this for the rest of her life. She did not want to have to cringe from him at the once nightly performance of her duty. She did not want it to become nothing but a duty.

"My love," he murmured against her ear when they

were finished at last and she should have been the one talking. "My love, I have not overexhausted you?"

From Aunt Agatha's description and her own previous knowledge, she had not expected it to take longer than a few minutes at the most. And she had expected only a little discomfort to herself, certainly no expenditure of energy. But it had taken many times longer than a few minutes and yes, he had exhausted her and she had exhausted herself. She had not an ounce of energy left with which to utter even a single word. She sighed deeply, cuddled closer, and slept. She was asleep even before she could hear his answering chuckle.

There was a strong suggestion of dawn light in the room when she woke again and realized that it was his lips feathering across one temple and down her cheek that had changed her dream into an erotic one and then waked her. She sighed sleepily against his chest and stretched her legs along his. They were strong, very masculine legs, she decided, and remembered how they felt against her inner thighs.

*All right,* she told herself firmly as full consciousness returned. *This is it. Ask him now. Get it over with. There will be no peace until everything is in the open.*

And then perhaps none ever again!

But the questions must be asked. She took her face away from his chest and tipped her head back. He was smiling at her.

"Good morning, my love," he said. "I did not wake you by any chance, did I?"

"Yes, you did," she said. "What do you mean by it?" *I am smiling*, she thought helplessly. *I am smiling at him.*

"Only to ask humbly," he said, his smile becoming knee-weakeningly tender, "if I might make love to you again, my wife."

"Oh." The body had a frightening power over the mind, she thought briefly. She never would have suspected it before her body had been awakened to pleasure—just last night. Every part of her now leapt into instant arousal. She wanted him. She wanted to feel him—everywhere.

"Only if you wish," he said. "You must say no if you do not."

She realized suddenly and in total amazement that she was seeing his face through a blur. And then she felt a hot tear roll diagonally down her cheek to drip onto his arm.

"Oh, Gabriel," she said, "I do wish it. I do. Make love to me."

When it was over, she said nothing, though she did not immediately sleep and neither did he. They might have talked, but instead they kissed warmly and drowsily with their eyes closed. And she marveled at what she had learned—that he could make love to her with his hand and his fingers and bring her to madness and ecstasy over and over again so that when he came inside at last for his own satisfaction she could be a soft and relaxed cradle for his driving hardness and finally for his seed.

She would ask him the questions tomorrow, or rather

later this morning. Not now. Now was going to be one of the precious memories of her life. She was going to remember tonight as the night she had loved totally. She was going to remember it as the night before love died forever.

But that was tomorrow. This was now. She slipped an arm about his waist and pressed her breasts more comfortingly against his chest. Their kiss was broken for a moment, but they opened their eyes, smiled lazily, and joined mouths again.

# 18

HE WAS GONE AGAIN WHEN SHE WOKE IN THE morning. Though it was not as late as it had been the day before, she was ashamed of the fact that she could sleep so late and had not even stirred when he left her bed.

She felt very married this morning, she thought as she dressed and as her maid styled her hair. It was a curious thought. She had been just as married yesterday morning. Except that yesterday morning she had been embarrassed about meeting her maid's eyes and embarrassed about having to leave her rooms to be seen by other servants, who would know. And except that this morning that somewhat tender feeling in her breasts and the slight soreness—though that was not quite the right word—between her legs, denoting that there was now a man in her life, were more familiar to her. And pleasant. She liked the feeling.

Her eyes, reflected in the looking glass, seemed larger, dreamier. It would be wonderfully pleasant, she thought, to have a marriage free of troubles. She would enjoy having a man as companion and friend during the day and lover during the night. She would love having children of such a marriage.

Lionel. She sighed inwardly and remembered what he had done last night, how his gesture had seemed sadly noble at first until she had analyzed his possible motives for doing such a thing. And until she had begun to wonder about his past. Somehow—and the thought was frightening because it broke a habit of thought she had developed over five years—somehow she did not know if it would ever have been possible to have had Lionel as a companion and friend. There had never been any sort of closeness between them. Whereas with Gabriel . . .

With Gabriel she had always found it easy to talk and easy to listen. If only circumstances were different, they might have been friends. Of course, they already were lovers at night. It was far more wonderful than she had ever imagined it could possibly be. Probably they would continue to be lovers. He had said that he would insist she perform that duty once each night. Except that they would not really be lovers, merely a man exercising his sexual rights and a woman being obedient.

If she was correct, that was. If she asked him again.

She knew she was right.

She was not so sure this morning that she would ask him again. Why not just keep quiet about her knowledge, or her suspicions anyway? Why not let it all slip silently into the past and hope that they could build something of a future at Chalcote? Perhaps she could bring him to love her. She knew he found her desirable already. And she knew he felt responsible for her. He had married her, had he not? And she knew that she loved him.

The admission caught her unaware, and she found herself playing absently with her hairbrush after her maid had set it down. Yes. Oh, yes, it was true.

She drew a deep breath and got to her feet. There was no point in planning what she was going to do or not do. She should know from experience by now the power that Gabriel's presence had on her. She would not know until she was with him again whether she would be able to live with unanswered questions forever festering in her mind or whether she would find it impossible to ask those questions again even if she wanted to.

There was a tap on the door of her dressing room and her maid answered it. His lordship was requesting the presence of her ladyship in the downstairs salon at her earliest convenience, a footman explained.

The downstairs salon was used for visitors, Jennifer had learned the day before in a tour of the house. Who? Aunt Agatha and Sam? It was a little early in the day for them, especially the morning after a ball.

The same footman who had delivered the message and run lightly down the stairs ahead of her opened the salon door, and closed it behind her when she stepped inside.

The room was silent even though it had four occupants. The Countess of Rushford was seated to one side of the fireplace, with her husband standing behind her chair. Viscount Kersey was standing before the fireplace, his back to it. Jennifer turned instinctively to the fourth occupant of the room. Her husband was standing at the window, his body turned toward it, though he had looked over his shoulder at her entrance. She fixed her eyes on him as he hurried toward her.

"My dear." He took her hands in a strong clasp and raised one of them to his lips. He looked as pale as if he had seen a ghost. "Come and have a seat."

He seated her on a chair at the other side of the fireplace and then moved away from her—to stand behind her chair, she believed, though she did not look. She fixed her eyes on the carpet a short distance in front of her feet. They would present what would look like a carefully arranged tableau to anyone now coming through the door, she thought irrelevantly.

"Ma'am." The voice was the Earl of Rushford's. "It was good of you to grant us some of your time. My son has something to say to you."

There was a long silence, which might have been uncomfortable if she had allowed herself to think or to feel atmosphere. And then Viscount Kersey cleared his throat.

"I owe you a deep apology, ma'am," he said. "I did not have the courage to tell either you or my father that a promise made five years ago was no longer appealing to me."

He stopped again and Jennifer thought of that poor naive girl with her dreams of beauty and love and forever after. That girl who had been herself.

"I tried to win my freedom in another way," he continued. "I saw your interest in Thornhill and his in you and I decided to help along your—courtship. I was the author of that letter, ma'am."

His voice was stilted and cold. Jennifer wondered how his father had persuaded him to come and make this confession. Power of the purse, perhaps? Had he threatened to cut off Lionel's funds?

"And the other matter too, if you please," his father said now.

Lord Kersey cleared his throat again. "While I was unofficially betrothed to you, ma'am," he said, "two years ago, I was unfaithful with another lady—with the Countess of Thornhill."

"An ugly reality with which we would not have burdened you, ma'am," the Earl of Rushford said, his voice harsh, "except that it concerns your husband, and you should know that he is not the dishonorable man you might have suspected him of being."

No one filled the silence that followed. The viscount shifted uneasily from one foot to the other.

"We will not distress you further by prolonging our visit, which is not, after all, a social call," Lord Rushford said at last. "We have to make another call, on Viscount Nordal, your father. But you must know, ma'am, that I deeply regret my part in what happened four evenings ago."

"And I mine in what happened last evening," the countess added hurriedly and breathlessly.

"You may be sure," the Earl of Rushford said, "that the *ton* will be informed quite as decisively as they were four evenings ago of the truth of the matter. And you may rest assured that you will not have to suffer the embarrassment of setting eyes on my son for at least the next five years. He will be leaving the country within a few days."

She did not raise her eyes from the carpet as they left, accompanied by her husband. Or after they had gone. Every part of her felt frozen. Mercifully so.

HE HELD UP A staying hand when his footman would have opened the salon door to admit him again. He needed to catch his breath and order his thoughts. He had known that something very similar to this was going to happen. There had been those questions she had asked him at the ball last night. He had known that she would ask them again. He had been thankful that she had not asked them last night. He had wanted last night in which to give her something that she might remember as tenderness after the crisis was over.

But he had known that it would come today. Or tomorrow. Or some time soon.

Well, it was now. He nodded briskly to the footman and stepped inside the room again. He heard the door close quietly at his back.

She was sitting where he had left her. She had not moved. She looked as if she had been turned to marble.

"You had suspected?" he asked her quietly.

"Yes." A mere breath of sound. She did not look up.

"Jennifer," he asked, staying close to the door, clasping his hands behind him, "do you love him? Is your heart quite shattered?"

"I loved the thought of him," she said, addressing the

carpet at her feet, almost as if she were merely thinking aloud. "He was so very handsome and fashionable. He represented the dream of love and romance and exciting living that I suppose most girls who live in the country dream of. For five years he was my life, or at least my hope and my dream. It is shattering, yes, to know that in all that time he did not care for me at all and that this year he was so desperate to be free of me that he would resort to lies and cruelty. It is shattering to feel so very unloved."

"Jennifer—" he said softly.

"It is amazing," she said, "how in the space of a few days one can grow up all in a hurry so that one was a girl one day and is a woman the next. I thought Lionel loved me. I thought you were so obsessed with me that you would resort to dishonorable trickery in order to win me." She laughed softly and at last moved in order to press one hand over her mouth.

"Jennifer, my dear—" he said.

"It was revenge, was it not?" she asked. "You had returned from being with your stepmother and you saw Lionel here and you discovered that he was newly betrothed and you thought to end the betrothal and embarrass and possibly hurt him. That was it, was it not?"

He inhaled slowly. "Yes," he said. He watched her eyes close and then clench tightly above her hand.

"The best way to do it was to make me fall in love with you and break off my own betrothal," she said, "or perhaps cause Lionel to cast me off. And to do it in a rather public manner so that he would look something of a fool. That was it, was it not?"

"Yes."

"I did not matter at all to you," she said. "I was a mere tool. Tools do not have feelings. It did not matter to you that I would be disgraced and probably hurt."

"At first," he said, "I persuaded myself that you would be better off without him. Your life would have been hell with him."

"And now," she said, "it is heaven? You might have written that letter, Gabriel. You were both playing the same game. You might have called it 'Cast-Off Jennifer.' Perhaps you did. But you were both playing it. He out-maneuvered you. He thought of writing that letter before you did. But you might have done it, then or later."

"I might have," he said quietly. "But I did not. I could not."

"Why not?" she asked.

"Because after that . . . kiss," he said, "at the Velgards' costume ball, guilt would no longer allow me to use you. I had come to know it was a person I was using as a pawn. I had come to realize what I was doing to you— and to myself."

"Ah," she said, "the loser's excuse. The noble explanation. And so all must be forgiven. At the last possible moment you had an attack of conscience and put an end to your dastardly scheme. You would have allowed my reputation to recover."

"What I did was inexcusable," he said. "It will be on my conscience until I die, if that is any consolation to you, Jennifer. I can find no excuse whatsoever for what I did. I can find no redeeming feature in my behavior that would give me any right to beg your forgiveness. There is nothing I can say or do."

"You married me." She laughed again and looked at him at last. Her eyes coming to rest on his felt like the flailing of a whip. "You will be able to carry around your guilt for the rest of your life, Gabriel. It will be there every time you look at me. Will you ever make it up to me, do you think?"

"No," he said, "never. And so you must tell me what you wish, Jennifer. If you wish for my protection and perhaps for . . . children, then we will continue to inhabit the same house. I will give you as much freedom as you desire. Or if you would prefer never to set eyes on me again, I will set up a home for you with everything you need and access to a man of business who will handle your concerns so that you will not need to have any deal-ings with me. Think about it for a day or two or for as long as you need. It will be entirely as you wish."

He turned to the door and set a hand on the knob. He wished that he could set her free so that she would not have to bear his name for the rest of her life, so that she could look for a husband to love. He wished it especially now that her name would be cleared in the eyes of the *ton*.

But there was one thing more he must say to her. He turned his head to look back at her. "I suppose for the rest of your life," he said, "it will be a toss-up in your mind which you hate more, Kersey or me. Or perhaps we will be equal in your low esteem. But I must say this, Jennifer. You feel unwanted and unloved. You feel that both men you thought cared about you did not but merely used you. You are wrong. You are both wanted and loved. I did not even realize it until after I had married you. I thought I married you to save you from ruin, and perhaps that was a part of it. But only a part. You are eminently lovable. I love you more than life."

He left the room, directed a footman to see to it that his horse was at the door within ten minutes, and took the stairs up to his dressing room two at a time.

SAMANTHA CALLED DURING THE afternoon, bringing a maid with her. She was wide-eyed with the news that the Earl and Countess of Rushford and Viscount Kersey had come during the morning and been closeted with her uncle for all of half an hour. Aunt Agatha had been summoned after they had left. Jennifer's name—and Lord Thornhill's too—were to be publicly cleared, it seemed.

But Sam still looked unhappy even after hugging Jennifer and telling her how glad she was. And finally she disclosed what she said she had been planning to say today anyway. Lionel had pretended an attachment to her and she had fallen in love with him and then she had discovered how he had used her.

She did not know if Jenny would be able to forgive her.

Jennifer was beyond being hurt more than she had been hurt already. Feeling seemed quite dead in her.

Except feeling for the cousin who had been her closest friend for several years. She did not blame Sam at all. Men were such evil creatures and so powerful when they had looks and charm to combine with ruthlessness and experience.

They walked in the park during the quiet part of the afternoon, arms linked, reflecting on what a difference a few weeks in town had made to their lives—but not at all in the way they had expected.

Jennifer dined alone after word had been brought that her husband would eat at his club. She sat in the dining room feeling the silence, feeling the presence of the servants, eating her way determinedly through at least a small helping of each course.

She spent the evening alone in her private sitting room, stitching at some embroidery. She would have to make an appointment to speak with him, she supposed. She had a feeling that he would keep himself away from the house as much as possible until she had done so and told him what she wanted.

What did she want?

*I love you more than life.* She did not believe him.

She did not know what she wanted. She did not want to think about it yet. At the moment the burdens were too heavy to allow for rational thought. He would have to wait for her decision.

She went to bed early. She was bone-weary. She needed an early night. And so she lay staring up into the darkness, wondering when he would come home and if he would come home—until she heard quiet sounds coming from his dressing room. She had left the door into her own open. And then the sounds stopped. Perhaps it had been only his valet in there.

She could not sleep. For twenty years she had slept in a bed alone. For two nights she had shared her bed. Now she did not know if it would be possible ever again to sleep alone. She could not sleep. She must have been lying in bed for two hours or more.

She sat up and lit a candle. And hugged her knees and stared into space while it burned half down. She could not sleep. Yet she could not get up the energy to pick up one of her books from the shelf below her nightstand. She did not want to read.

There really was only one thing to do. She acknowledged the fact eventually with a sigh and swung her legs over the side of the bed. She left the candle where it was.

SHE DID NOT KNOCK. She just opened the door quietly and stepped inside. She was not even sure that he had come home or that, if he had, he had not gone back downstairs. The curtains were drawn back from the windows, making the room quite light. He was standing by one of the windows, wearing his dressing gown, looking back over his shoulder at her. She walked across the room until she was standing quite close to him.

She could speak only what was in her heart. She had not thought out any plan of what she wanted. But some things were best spoken without prior thought.

"I want our marriage to continue," she told him.

"Very well." His tone was cautious. "It need not take long. Just a few minutes. Shall we do it here? You can go back to your own bed then. With luck and nightly effort I will have you with child very soon. Then you need see me less frequently."

"That is not what I meant," she said.

He stood quiet and still, waiting, looking at her.

"Did you mean it?" she asked him. "Please. Please, please, Gabriel, it must be the truth now. If you said it only because you knew I needed to hear it, and if you say it again now, I will know soon enough. Better by far merely to say that you wish me well and that you want to work with me to a mutually comfortable arrangement. Did you mean it?"

"I love you more than life," he said again.

"Do you?" She set her head on one side and looked closely at his face in the darkness. She had given him a way out without his having to be cruel. But he had said it again. "I think we can make it work, then, Gabriel, because I love you too, you see. I know that I do because you have offered me a comfortable alternative to living with you but I know that I want to go on with you."

He turned his head to look down into the square. It took her a few moments to realize that he was crying.

"Gabriel." She touched his arm, horrified. "Don't."

But he shook his head and turned it even farther from her until he had got control of himself. "You cannot possibly be willing to forgive me for what I did to you, Jennifer," he said. "It would be there between us for the rest of our lives."

"There you are wrong," she said, and she stepped boldly forward to set both arms about his waist. "We say it at church every Sunday when we recite the Lord's Prayer, don't we? But we rarely realize quite what we are saying. But we are all thoughtless sometimes and ride roughshod over the feelings of others. And we all use other people sometimes for our own ends. It is a regrettable part of being human. We are all in need of forgiveness over and over again throughout our lives. The measure of our goodness, I suppose, is the strength of our consciences. I think yours is strong. And apart from the fact that you are hurting now and filled with self-loathing, I am glad all this happened, Gabriel. If it had not, I would have married Lionel and been miserable with him. And I would never have known you or loved you. When I said I wanted our marriage to continue, I meant in every possible way."

His hands were gripping her shoulders. He leaned forward now to rest his forehead against hers. His eyes were closed.

"If it is what you want, of course," she said, suddenly timid again.

"If—" She heard him drawing a deep and slow breath. "I have just spent a day accustoming myself to the thought that I had very probably lost you, wondering how I was to live without you. Hoping that at the very least you would want a child of me before leaving me."

"Ten, please, Gabriel," she said, tipping her head back so that for a moment their mouths met.

"Be careful that I do not take you at your word," he

said, chuckling unexpectedly. "And I have been hoping, Jennifer, I must confess, that the begetting of a child would take a long time."

"For shame," she whispered to him, and she feathered kisses along his jaw to his chin. He must have shaved before coming to her last night and the night before, she realized. He had not shaved tonight.

"I know," he said. "I am incorrigible. Don't do that any more, Jennifer, unless you mean it."

She started along the other side of his jaw. "I have been trying for hours to sleep," she said. "You have done a terrible thing to me, Gabriel. You have spent two nights in my bed and now I do not believe I can sleep without you in it."

"Are you sure it is sleep you have on your mind?" he asked. His hands were at work on the buttons of her nightgown.

She dropped her arms to her sides with a sigh of contentment and a little shiver of something more. "Well, perhaps after and between," she said.

"After and between what?" His hands stilled.

"After you have made love to me and before you do it again and after that before you do it once more and so on," she said.

"Good Lord," he said, "do you want to make an invalid of me?"

Suddenly, amazingly, they were both laughing—with genuine and prolonged amusement and with a deeply shared affection. They wrapped their arms about each other as if they would never let go. They continued to cling together when they were finally quiet again.

"Lord God," he said, sounding shaken. "Oh, dear Lord God."

"Amen," she said. "It really was a prayer, was it not?" She laughed softly.

"Yes," he said. "It really was."

She rubbed her cheek against his.

"I think perhaps," he said, "we should get started, my love. Making love and loving and living and being married in every way it is possible to be. Will my bed do?"

She nodded and gazed up into his face as he nudged her nightgown off her shoulders and slid it down her arms and then dispensed with his dressing gown.

"As long as you are in it with me," she said as he guided her over to the bed and laid her down on it.

He lay down beside her, slid an arm beneath her shoulders, and turned her against him. "That was definitely the idea," he said. "Clever of you to perceive it, my love."

She felt him along the length of her body. She felt the warmth of his mouth against hers and the promise of passion. And she knew she was where she belonged, where she wanted always to be, and where she would not be had it not been for a certain dastardly game.

Life was a strange phenomenon.

But philosophy soon died under the onslaught of passion.

# Lord Carew's Bride

# 1

O H, DO COME WITH US, SAM," THE COUNTESS OF
Thornhill said. "I know it is only a short walk to
the lake, but the setting is lovely and the daffodils are in
bloom. And surely it is better to have company than to
be alone."

There was a look of concern on her face that made her
cousin, Samantha Newman, feel guilty. She would far
*prefer* to be alone.

"The children will not bother you, provided you tell
them quite firmly that you are not to be romped with,"
the countess added.

There were four children, the countess's two and Lady
Boyle's two. They were perfectly normal, well behaved—
though exuberant—children. Samantha was fond of
them and had no objection to being romped with quite
frequently.

"The children never bother me, Jenny," she assured
her cousin. "It is just that I like being alone occasionally.
I like walking long distances to take the air and com-
mune with my own thoughts. You will not be offended,
will you?"

"No," Lady Thornhill said. "Oh, no, of course not,
Sam. You are our guest here and must do as you please.

It is just that you have changed. You used not to like being alone at all."

"It is advancing age," Samantha said, smiling.

"Advancing age!" her cousin said scornfully. "You are four-and-twenty, Sam, and as beautiful as you ever were, and with more admirers than you ever had."

"I think perhaps," Lady Boyle said gently, entering the conversation for the first time, "Samantha is missing Lord Francis."

Samantha hooted inelegantly. "Missing Francis?" she said. "He was here for a week—visiting Gabriel—and left this morning. I always enjoy Francis's company. He teases me about being on the shelf and I tease him about his dandyish appearance. Lavender silk for dinner last evening, indeed, and in the country! But when I am not in his company, I forget him immediately—and I daresay he forgets me, too."

"And yet," the countess said, "he has twice made you a marriage offer, Sam."

"And it would serve him right if I accepted one of these times," Samantha said. "He would die of shock, poor man."

Lady Boyle looked at her in some shock herself and smiled uncertainly at the countess.

"No, if you really do not mind, Jenny, and if you will not be hurt, Rosalie," Samantha said, "I believe I will walk alone this afternoon. Aunt Aggy is having a rest, and this lovely spring weather calls for something brisker than a stroll to the lake."

"You could have gone riding about the estate with

Gabriel and Albert," the countess said. "They would not have minded at all. But here I go, trying to manage your life again. Have a good afternoon, Sam. Come, Rosalie, the children will be climbing the nursery walls in their impatience already."

And so finally Samantha was alone. And feeling guilty for spurning the company that had been offered her. And feeling relieved to have the rest of the afternoon to herself. She drew on a dark blue spencer over her lighter blue dress, tied the ribbons of her bonnet beneath her chin, and set out for her walk.

It was not that she disliked either Jenny or Rosalie or their children. Quite the contrary. She had lived with Jenny and Jenny's father, Viscount Nordal, for four years after her parents died when she was fourteen. She and Jenny had made their come-out together. They had loved the same man. . . . No, that was not to be thought of. Since Jenny's marriage six years before, Samantha had frequently stayed at Chalcote with her and Gabriel. If they were in town during the Season, she often stayed with them there. Jenny was her dearest friend.

And Rosalie, the wife, also for six years, of Gabriel's closest friend, Sir Albert Boyle, was impossible to dislike. She was sweet and shy and gentle and did not have a mean bone in her whole body, Samantha would swear.

The trouble was that they were both very contentedly married. They were both absorbed in affection for their husbands and affection for their children and affection for their homes.

Sometimes Samantha wanted to scream.

And Gabriel and Albert quite clearly shared all those affections with their wives.

Samantha had been at Chalcote since just before Christmas. The Boyles had been there for a month. Aunt Agatha—Lady Brill—Samantha's constant companion, had come with her. Lord Francis Kneller, another of Gabriel's friends, had been there for a week. Everything was so wonderful, so peaceful, so cheerful, so domesticated. Everyone, it seemed, was in the process of living happily ever after.

Oh, yes. Samantha's steps quickened. Sometimes she could scream and scream and scream.

And she felt horribly guilty. No one could be kinder to her than Jenny and Gabriel. At least Jenny was her cousin. Gabriel was nothing to her, and yet he treated her with as much courtesy and even affection as if she were his cousin, too. It was horribly ungrateful to want to scream at their domestic bliss. She did not resent their happiness. Indeed, she was very happy for them. Their marriage had had such an inauspicious beginning. And she had felt that it was partly her fault. . . .

No, it was not that she resented them. It was just that . . . Well, she did not know just what it was. It was not jealousy or even envy. Darkly handsome as Gabriel was, she had never felt attracted to him herself. And she was not in search of a man of her own. She did not believe in love. Not for herself, anyway. And she had no intention of marrying. She wanted to remain free and independent. She was almost both already—Uncle Gerald had not kept firm reins on her since she reached her majority. But when she was five-and-twenty, her parents' small fortune would be hers to manage herself.

She could hardly wait.

Her life was as she wanted it to be. She was not lonely. She had Aunt Aggy all the time, there were always Jenny and Gabriel to be visited, there were numerous other friends. And there was that group of gentlemen whom it pleased Gabriel to call her court. It was flatteringly large, considering her advanced age. She believed it was so large just because all its members knew very well that she intended never to marry. They felt safe flirting with her and sighing over her and sometimes stealing kisses from her, and even occasionally making her marriage offers. Francis had made her two, Sir Robin Talbot one, and Jeremy Nicholson so many that both of them had lost count.

Her life was as she wanted it to be. And yet . . . She could not even complete the thought. She supposed it was the normal human condition never to be quite happy, quite satisfied. She did not know what it was that was missing from her life, if anything. When she turned five-and-twenty, perhaps everything would be finally perfect. And there was not long to wait.

She did not know where she was walking. Except that it was in the opposite direction from the lake. And again she felt guilty. Jenny's Michael and Rosalie's Emily, both five years old, were intelligent and interesting children. Rosalie's Jane, three years old, was a mischief, and Jenny's Mary, aged two, was a sweetheart. Rosalie was in a delicate way again and was due to deliver later in the spring. Perhaps for Jenny's sake Samantha should have gone with them.

She recognized where she was when she came to the line of trees. She was close to the boundary between Chalcote and Highmoor. They were two unusually large estates adjoining each other. Highmoor belonged to the Marquess of Carew, but Samantha had never met him. He was from home a great deal. He was from home now.

She walked among the trees. There was no real sign of spring yet above her head, though the sky was blue and there was definite warmth in the air. The branches were still bare. But soon now there would be buds, and then young leaves, and then a green canopy. There were snowdrops and primroses growing among the trees, though. And there was the stream, which she knew was the exact boundary line, though she had not walked in this particular place before. She strolled to the edge of it and gazed down into the clear water gurgling over the stones at the bottom of the streambed.

Not far to her left she could see broad stepping-stones that would take one safely across to the other side. After strolling toward them and hesitating for only a moment, she crossed them and smiled to find that Highmoor land looked and felt the same as Chalcote land.

She had no wish to turn back yet. If she returned to the house, Aunt Aggy might be up after her rest and Samantha would be obliged to bear her company. Not that she did not love her aunt dearly, but . . . well, sometimes she just liked to be alone. Besides, it was far too lovely an afternoon for part of it to be wasted indoors. The winter had been long enough and cold enough.

Samantha continued on her way through the trees, expecting that soon she would come out into open land again and would be able to see the estate. Perhaps she would be able to glimpse the house, though she did not know if it was close. On such a large estate it might be miles away. Jenny had told her, though, that it was a magnificent house, with features of the old abbey it had once been still visible from the outside.

The trees did not thin out. But the land rose quite steadily and quite steeply. Samantha climbed, pausing a few times to lean one hand against the trunk of a tree. She must be dreadfully out of condition, she thought, panting and feeling the heat of the sun almost as if it were July rather than early March.

But finally she was rewarded for her effort. The land and the forest continued upward—there was even a quite visible path now—but to one side of her the land fell away sharply to open grassland below. And Highmoor Abbey was in the distance, though she had no clear view of it. She moved about a bit, until finally there was almost a clear opening downhill, with only one tree obstructing the view. There was no seeing it quite clearly, it seemed, and the slope looked rather too steep to be scrambled down.

But there was a feeling of magnificence. A feeling of excitement, almost. It looked wilder than Chalcote, more magical.

"Yes, that tree does need to be removed," a voice said

from quite close by, making Samantha jump with alarm. "I was just noticing the same thing."

He was leaning against a tree, one booted foot propped back against it. She felt an instant surging of relief. She had expected to see an arrogant and irate Marquess of Carew—not that she had ever seen him before, of course. It would have been unbearably humiliating to have been caught trespassing and gawking at his ancestral home. Even this was bad enough.

Her first impression that he was a gardener was dismissed even before she reacted to his words. He spoke with cultured English accents, even though he was dressed very informally and not at all elegantly in a brown coat that would have made Weston of Old Bond Street shudder for a week without stopping, breeches that looked as if they were worn for comfort rather than good fit, and top boots that had seen not only better days, but better years.

He was a very ordinary looking gentleman, neither tall nor short, neither herculean nor puny, neither handsome nor ugly. His hair—he was not wearing a hat—was a nondescript brown. His eyes looked gray.

A very unthreatening looking gentleman, she was happy to note. He must be the marquess's steward, or perhaps a minion of the steward.

"I—I do beg your pardon," she said. "I was, um, I was trespassing."

"I will not have the constables sent out to arrest you and haul you before the nearest magistrate," he said. "Not this time, anyway." His eyes were smiling. They were very nice eyes, Samantha decided, definitely a distinguishing feature in an otherwise very ordinary face.

"I am staying at Chalcote," she said, pointing downward through the trees. "With my cousin, the Countess of Thornhill. And her husband, the Earl of Thornhill," she added unnecessarily.

He continued to smile at her with his eyes and she found herself beginning to relax. "Have you never seen Highmoor Abbey before?" he asked. "It is rather splendid, is it not? If that tree were not there, you would have the best view of it from this vantage point. The tree will be moved."

"Moved?" She smiled broadly at him. "Plucked out and planted somewhere else, just like a flower?"

"Yes," he said. "Why kill a tree when it need not die?"

He was serious.

"But it is so huge," she said, laughing.

He pushed away from the tree trunk against which he had been leaning and came toward her. He walked with a decided limp, Samantha noticed. She also noticed that he held his right arm cradled against his side, his wrist and hand turned in against his hip. He was wearing leather gloves.

"Oh, did you hurt yourself?" she asked.

"No." He stopped beside her. He was not a great deal taller than she, and she was considered small. "Not recently, anyway."

She felt herself blushing uncomfortably. How gauche of her. The man was partly crippled and she had asked if he had hurt himself.

"You see?" he said, pointing downward with his good arm. "If the tree is moved, there will be a full frontal view of the abbey from here, perfectly centered between the other trees on the slope. It is all of two miles away, but an artist could not have done better on a canvas, could he? Except to have left that particular tree off the slope. We will be artists and imagine it removed. Soon it will be removed in fact. We can be artists with nature as surely as with watercolors or oils, you see. It is merely a matter of having an eye for the picturesque or the majestic, or merely for what will be visually pleasing."

"Are you the steward here?" she asked.

"No." He turned his head to look at her over his outstretched arm before lowering it.

"I did not think you could be a gardener," she said. "Your accent suggests that you are a gentleman." She blushed again. "I do beg your pardon. It is none of my business, especially as a trespasser." But it struck her suddenly that perhaps he was a trespasser, too.

"I am Hartley Wade," he said, still looking into her face.

"How do you do, Mr. Wade," she said. She extended her right hand to him rather than curtsying—he did not seem the sort of man to whom one would curtsy. "Samantha Newman."

"Miss Newman," he said, "I am pleased to make your acquaintance."

He shook her hand with his right one. She could feel through his glove that his hand was thin and the fingers stiffly bent. She was afraid to exert any pressure and was sorry then for the impulsive gesture of offering the handshake.

"I am considered something of a landscape artist," he said. "I have tramped the estates of many of England's most prominent landowners, giving them advice on how they can make the most of their parks. Many people believe that having well-kept formal gardens before the house and regularly mown lawns is enough."

"And it is not?" she asked.

"Not always. Not often." His eyes were smiling again. "Formal gardens are not always even particularly attractive, especially if the land before the house is unusually flat and there is no possibility of terracing. One would have to be suspended in the sky—in a balloon, perhaps—and looking downward to appreciate the full effect. And usually there is a great deal more to parks than just the house and the mile or so of land directly in front of it. Parks can be extremely pleasant places in which to walk and relax and feast the senses if one exercises just a little care and planning in organizing them."

"Oh," she said, smiling. "And is that what you are doing here? Has the Marquess of Carew employed you to tramp about his park and give him advice?"

"He is about to have one of his trees repositioned at the very least," he said.

"Will he mind?" she asked.

"When someone asks for advice," he said, "he had better be prepared to hear some. A number of things have already been done here to make the most of nature, and to add to it and change it just a little for more pleasing effects. This is not my first visit, you see. But it is always possible to imagine new improvements. As with that tree. I cannot understand how it has escaped my notice before now. Once it is gone, a stone grotto can be erected here so that the marquess and his guests can sit here and enjoy the prospect at their leisure."

"Yes." She looked about her. "It would be the perfect spot, would it not? It would be wonderfully peaceful. If I lived here, I believe I would spend a great deal of time sitting in such a grotto, thinking and dreaming."

"Two very underrated activities," he said. "I am glad you appreciate them, Miss Newman. Or one might be tempted to sit, perhaps, with a special companion, one with whom one can talk or be silent with equal comfort."

She looked at him with sudden understanding. Yes, that was what it was. That was it. That was what was missing. She had felt it and wondered about it and puzzled over it. And here was the answer, so simple that she had not even considered it before. She had no special companion. No one with whom she could be silent in comfort. Even with her dearest relatives, Aunt Aggy and Jenny, she always felt the necessity to converse.

"Yes," she said, a curious ache in her throat. "That would be pleasant. Very pleasant."

"Are you in a hurry to return to Chalcote?" he asked. "Or is there anyone who will be anxious over your absence? A chaperone, perhaps?"

"I have outgrown the need for chaperones, Mr. Wade," she said. "I am four-and-twenty years old."

"You do not look it," he said, smiling. "Would you like to stroll up over the hill, then, and see some of the improvements that have already been made and hear some of my ideas for new ones?"

It was very improper. She was a lady very much alone in a wooded area of the countryside with a strange gentleman, albeit a very ordinary and rather shabby gentleman. She should have turned very firmly in the direction of home. But there was nothing at all threatening about him. He was pleasant. And he had aroused a curiosity in her to see how nature could be manipulated, but not harmed or destroyed, for the pleasure of humans.

"I should like that," she said, looking up the slope.

"I have always thought the marquess was fortunate," he said, "having the hill on his land, while the Earl of Thornhill was left with the flat land. Hills have so many possibilities. Do you need assistance?"

"No." She laughed. "I am just ashamed of my breathlessness. The winter has been endless, and I have been far too long without strenuous exercise."

"We are almost at the top," he said. His limp was quite a bad one, she noticed, but he appeared far more fit than she. "There is a folly there, in a very obvious place. I normally like to be more subtle, but the marquess has assured me that any guests he brings this way are always thankful for the chance to sit and rest there."

Samantha was thankful for it, too. They sat side by side on the stone seat inside the mock temple, looking down over the tops of the trees to the fields and meadows below. The house could be seen over to one side, but it was not as splendid a view as would be that from the top of the slope where she had stood earlier. He pointed out to her places where trees had been removed and replanted in previous years. He indicated two paths down the steeper part of the slope, each leading to a folly that had been carefully placed for the view it afforded. He explained that there was a lake just out of sight that he was particularly working on this year.

"The secret is," he said, "to leave an area looking as if all its beauty and effects are attributable to nature. The lake must look like an area of wild beauty by the time I have finished with it. In reality I will have made several changes. I will take you down there afterward and show you if you wish."

But he made no immediate move to do so. They were sheltered from the slight breeze where they sat, and the sun shone directly on them. It felt almost warm. There were birds singing in the trees, almost invisible except when one rose into the air for some reason before settling back again. And there were all the fresh smells of spring.

They sat in silence for many minutes, though Samantha was largely unaware of the fact. There was no awkwardness, no feeling that the conversation must be picked up again. There was too much of nature to enjoy for it to be missed in conversation.

She sighed at last. "This has been wonderful," she said. "Wonderfully relaxing. I could have gone to the lake at Chalcote with my cousin and Lady Boyle, one of her other guests, and their children. At the risk of offending them, I preferred to be alone."

"And I ruined that attempt," he said.

"No." She turned her head to smile at him. "Being with you has been as good as being alone, Mr. Wade." And then she laughed, only partly embarrassed. "Oh, dear, I did not mean that the way it sounded. I mean I have enjoyed your company and been comfortable with you. Thank you for opening my eyes to what I had not even thought about before."

"It is too late to go down to the lake now," he said. "It must be past teatime, and you will be missed. Perhaps some other time?"

"I would love to," she said. "But you are working. I would not want to waste your time."

"Artists," he said, "and writers and musicians are often accused of being idle when they are staring into space. Often they are hardest at work at such times. I have been sitting here beside you, Miss Newman, having ideas for my—employer's park. I would not have sat here, perhaps, if I had not been with you, and would not therefore have had the ideas. Will you come again? To-morrow, perhaps? Here, at the same time we met today?"

"Yes," she said, coming to a sudden decision. She could not recall an afternoon she had enjoyed more since coming to Chalcote almost three months before. The thought made her feel disloyal to Jenny and Gabriel, who had been so kind to her. "Yes, I will."

"Come," he said, getting to his feet. "I shall escort you

as far as the stream." His eyes smiled at her in that attractive way he had—almost the only thing about him that was actually physically attractive, she thought. "I must see you safely off Carew's property."

She was afraid that all the walking would be hard on his infirmity, but she did not like to mention it again. He limped beside her all the way back down the hill to the stream. They talked the whole while, though she would not have been able to say afterward exactly what they talked about.

"Do be careful," he said as she made her way back across the stones to the other side of the stream, trying not to hold her skirts too high. "Toppling into the water at this time of year might be just too exhilarating an exercise."

She stopped at the other side to smile at him and raise a hand in farewell. One of his arms was behind his back. The other was crooked against his hip. It was his right hand. She wondered if by some miracle he was naturally left-handed.

"Thank you," she said, "for a pleasant afternoon."

"I shall look forward to seeing you again tomorrow, Miss Newman," he said. "Weather permitting."

She was through the trees in no time at all and on her way back across the meadow toward the lawns of Chalcote park. It must indeed be past teatime, she thought. If Jenny and Rosalie were back from the lake, they would wonder what on earth had happened to her.

Would she tell them? That she had walked and sat with a total stranger for well over an hour? That she had made an assignation to meet him again tomorrow? She did not believe she would. It would sound bad in the telling, yet there had been nothing bad about it at all. Quite the contrary. There could not be a more ordinary, pleasant gentleman in existence, or one with whom she could feel so very comfortable. Neither was there a gentleman with whom she had had an encounter less romantic. There had been no physical awareness at all.

If she told, Aunt Aggy would have ideas about coming along with her tomorrow as a chaperone. And then there would be the necessity for conversation among the three of them. It would not be a pleasant afternoon at all.

No, she would not tell. She was four-and-twenty years old. Quite old enough to do some things alone. Quite old enough to have some life of her own.

She would not tell. But she knew she would be looking forward to tomorrow afternoon with pleasure.

# 2

ARTLEY WADE, MARQUESS OF CAREW, WATCHED her go. He stood where he was, on his side of the stream, long after she had gone.

She was the most beautiful woman he had ever seen. By far the most beautiful. She was small and shapely and dainty and graceful. Her hair was honey-blond and worn in short curls. Her bonnet had not hidden its glory. Her eyes were the bluest blue, her lashes long and darker than her hair. Her face was lovely and smiling and animated and intelligent.

He smiled ruefully to himself. For all his seven-and-twenty years, he was reacting like a schoolboy to a rare glimpse of someone from the female world. He was in a fair way to being in love with her.

He turned about to make his way back up the hill through the trees. With the side of his right hand he rubbed at his upper thigh. He was going to suffer tonight from all the walking. Though perhaps not too much. He had not walked a great deal during the past few months, but he had ruthlessly exercised. He smiled anew at the remembered expression on Jackson's face when he had first walked into the famous pugilist's boxing saloon in London three years ago. When he had *limped* in, rather.

Jackson was proud of him now and eager to show him off to some of his other patrons. But the marquess had only ever been there in private and had only ever worked with the master himself. He was no sideshow for a fair.

He arrived at the point close to the top of the hill where he had first seen her—Miss Samantha Newman. Yes, the tree definitely had to go. The view would be quite magnificent.

It had not struck him immediately that she had not realized who he was. Perhaps neither Thornhill nor his lady had described him to her. They were decent people. Perhaps they had not begun any description they might have given of him with the most obvious feature. Perhaps she did not know that the Marquess of Carew was a cripple. That was the label by which he was known, he was well aware, even if it was not strictly true. Had she heard that label, she would surely have realized who he was.

He had given her his name with some reluctance. But even that had meant nothing to her. *How do you do, Mr. Wade,* she had said politely. He had watched for the change in her manner, but it had not come.

The temptation had been overwhelming—the temptation not to enlighten her. And, of course, if she had been given no description of him and if his name meant nothing to her without his title, there was no reason why she should guess his identity—even though he had been roaming his own land. He was dressed for comfort in almost the oldest clothes he possessed. His valet had warned him just that morning that if his lordship insisted on wearing these boots one more time after today, he would send a public notice to all the newspapers that he was not responsible for his master's appearance.

But they were such comfortable boots, and such threats were not by any means new. Hargreaves had been with him, and threatening him, for eleven years.

The marquess continued on his way to the top of the hill and sat on the stone seat he had occupied with Miss Newman earlier. She had conversed with ease and had listened with what had seemed genuine interest. She had sat beside him for what must have been all of fifteen minutes in silence, a silence of remarkable comfort. She had not felt the necessity to speak to hold the silence at bay, nor had she felt the necessity of prompting him into speech.

She had said—what had been her exact words? He thought carefully. *I have enjoyed your company and been comfortable with you.* Her voice had held the ring of truth. Other women had uttered the first part of what she had said. None had ever said the rest. And none had ever spoken with sincerity.

He kept himself from company a great deal these days, though he was no hermit. He avoided female company whenever he could. It had become too demeaning, too hurtful, to see the instant spark of interest and acquisitiveness in female eyes as soon as he was identified and to be fawned over for the rest of that particular social event. His title was an impressive one, he supposed—he was the eighth marquess of his line. And, of course, there was this property in Yorkshire, and the one, almost equally large and prosperous, in Berkshire. He had more wealth than he would ever know what to do with.

He could have lived with the fawning, perhaps. Many gentlemen of his class had to. It was the way of the world. But there was also the disdain he sometimes surprised in female eyes at his unprepossessing appearance. And sometimes it was worse than disdain. Sometimes it was distaste or even disgust at his grotesque limp and his twisted hand. He rarely appeared outside his home now without a glove on at least his right hand.

Lord Byron's limp, of course, had only succeeded in making him more attractive to the ladies. But then the Marquess of Carew did not have either Lord Byron's beauty or his charisma.

He wondered how Samantha Newman would have reacted if he had given her his full name. Would he have seen that familiar gleam of avaricious interest? She had admitted that she was four-and-twenty years old. She was somewhat past the normal marrying age for a woman. Though he could not imagine the reason, even if she was dowryless. She was so very beautiful.

Beauty and the beast, he thought ruefully, resting his left hand flat on the stone seat beside him, where she had sat.

He had not seen disgust in her face. Only concern when she had thought that he had recently hurt himself, and then embarrassment when she had realized her faux pas.

But perhaps the disgust would have been there if she

had known who he was and had seen him as someone whose favor she might court.

No. He closed his eyes and lifted his face to the lowering sun. He did not want to believe that of her. He had liked her. It was not just her looks, though his first sight of her had fairly robbed him of breath. He had *liked* her.

Ah, more than that.

He opened his eyes and got to his feet. It was time to go home. He would not after all go to the lake today to make his plans for improvement. Perhaps she would go there with him tomorrow and he could dream along with her and explain his ideas to her. If the weather held. The clouds gathering in the west did not look promising. He hoped the weather would hold. He looked forward to tomorrow more than he had looked forward to any tomorrow for a long time.

Perhaps by tomorrow she would have discovered his identity for herself. If she described him to Thornhill or his lady, they would tell her with whom she had spent an hour of the afternoon. Or perhaps she simply would not come. Perhaps the afternoon had not meant as much to her as it had to him, and she would not keep their appointment. Tomorrow, if she did come, he would tell her for himself who he was. He would take the risk of seeing her attitude change. But in the meantime he would instruct his servants not to spread the word that he had arrived home unexpectedly yesterday.

He hoped the weather would hold.

He hoped she would come.

Ah, yes. It was more than her beauty. And more than the fact that he had liked her.

He really had reverted to boyhood emotions. He was head over ears in love with her.

Beauty and the beast, indeed!

FOR TWO DAYS IT rained a steady drizzle beyond the windows of Chalcote. Even the men did not venture outside, though the Earl of Thornhill complained that there was estate business to be attended to.

The children were restless and even peevish, and their nurse came close to the end of her tether about how to entertain them. And so the earl, willingly abetted by Sir Albert Boyle, shocked her by taking them on his back and galloping on a cavalry charge all over the house— though she should be past shock by now, she admitted to the housekeeper belowstairs, having had five years of experience of his lordship's unconventional behavior as a father. Lady Boyle was shocked, too, and somewhat charmed, and joined with the rest of the household in a noisy romp of hide-and-seek in which only the kitchens and the outdoors were out-of-bounds. Even Lady Brill participated—though once, when everyone had searched for her for longer than half an hour and had concluded that she must have found that one perfect hiding place none of the rest of them had yet discovered, she was finally found to be stretched out on her own bed, fast asleep.

The game lasted, with brief intervals, for two days.

There were guests for dinner on the second day, neighbors who had visited or been visited several times during the past three months. There were cards and music and conversation after dinner. It was all very pleasant. It was just a pity, the countess said afterward, that the Marquess of Carew had not yet returned to Highmoor Abbey. It would be good to see a different face for a change.

"You would like him, Sam," she said. "He is a very pleasant gentleman, but he never seems to be in residence when you are here. We must plan more carefully next time."

"Samantha does not need to add to her court," the earl said firmly. "It is as large as an army battalion as it is. One more member might turn her head and make her conceited." He winked at his wife when he knew Samantha was looking at him.

It was on the tip of Samantha's tongue to mention the landscape gardener who was staying at Highmoor— Mr. Wade. He was a gentleman, after all. That had been very obvious from his conversation and manners. But perhaps he would be uncomfortable in such elevated company, and perhaps he did not have the clothes to enable him to dine with the likes of Gabriel and Albert. Besides . . . Oh, besides, she wanted to keep him as her own secret companion for the moment. She did not want to see everyone else being polite—though of course both Gabriel and Jenny would be genuinely courteous—to a gentleman who would so obviously be out of his milieu.

She enjoyed the two days. And she fretted at being

confined to the house yet again. She was severely disappointed at being denied the treat of another walk at Highmoor with Mr. Wade. She had enjoyed his company so very much. It had been a great novelty, she had realized after returning to Chalcote and looking back on the hour she had spent with him, to be treated as a person with a mind. She was so accustomed to seeing nothing but admiration and open attraction in men's eyes. That was flattering, of course, but she often had the impression that she was seen only as a pretty face and not as a real person at all.

Mr. Wade had shown no attraction to her. He had merely enjoyed explaining his theories and ideas to her. And he had enjoyed, too, just being with her in lovely surroundings, she believed. Perhaps it was silly to feel so after merely one relatively short encounter, but she had the feeling that she and Mr. Wade could be friends. Companions. She had very few real friends, though she was fortunate enough to have hordes of friendly acquaintances. How had he phrased it? She thought carefully so that she might remember his exact words: . . . *a special companion, one with whom one can talk or be silent with equal comfort.*

She felt again that sense of discovery the words had brought when they were uttered. She did not want love as other women wanted it. Her one experience with love at the age of eighteen had been humiliating and excruciatingly painful. She did not want that feeling ever again. What she really wanted—and she had not realized it until he had put it into words for her—was a special companion.

Mr. Wade could be a special companion, she sensed. Perhaps it was ridiculous to think so when she had met him only once. Perhaps he had forgotten about her as soon as he turned back from the stream that afternoon. Perhaps he would not have kept their appointment even if it had not rained. And perhaps now she would never see him again. Perhaps his work at Highmoor was complete and he had left.

She would be sorry not to see him again.

On the third day the rain had stopped. All morning low clouds threatened more, but by the afternoon they were breaking up and the sun was shining through the gaps.

The earl, with his friend in tow, had ridden off early with the estate steward to sort out some problem with a distant tenant. But they were back soon after noon and announced that it was a perfect afternoon for a family ride, since a walk would only soak boots and hems.

"Rosie will appreciate the rest, will you not, my love?" Sir Albert said, smiling gently at his pregnant wife. "Emmy will be quite safe on the pony Gabe picked out for her when we first arrived, and Jane will ride up with me."

Lady Boyle had a terror of horses and seemed quite thankful that her delicate condition put her joining the riding party quite out of the question.

"You must insist that Michael keep his pony to a sedate walk, Gabriel," the countess said. "Or Emily will feel obliged to try to keep pace with him, and I shall have a heart seizure on the spot, and Rosalie will have one as soon as she hears of it."

The earl winked and grinned at her. "Mary will be up before me begging for a cavalry charge," he said.

His countess tutted. "Then I had better have her up before me," she said. "Sam, you must help me keep this madman in order."

"If you will not mind terribly," Samantha said, "I believe I will go walking."

"Ah, this madman has put terror into her," the earl said. "It is to be a cavalry charge without sabers, Samantha, my dear."

"Then it is to be a charge without purpose," she said, smiling at him. "*Will* you mind?"

"How could you possibly not want to ride with four squealing infants, a mad cavalryman, a scold, and only one normal gentleman?" he asked her. "Some people are very strange. Of course we do not mind, Samantha. You must do what gives you the greatest pleasure. That was why you were invited here."

"Oh, I am *not* a scold," the countess said indignantly. "And do stop winking at me, Gabriel, or I will believe you must have a speck of dust in your eye. Sam, your feet and your hem are going to be *soaked*. But there, I will not scold. And do stop laughing, Gabriel. Sam, I have endured six years of this. Am I an angel or am I not?"

"I am," the earl said. "The angel Gabriel."

Samantha left them when her cousin was tutting again and then chuckling with Albert and Rosalie. She remembered how she and Jenny had called the Earl of Thornhill Lucifer when they first knew him, because of his dark satanic looks. When they learned his given name, it had been an amusing irony, though it had not seemed so amusing at the time. He really had seemed like Lucifer, deliberately bringing to an end Jenny's betrothal to Lionel.

Samantha shuddered. She rarely dredged up that name or the person belonging to it out of her subconscious mind. The devil in angel's garb. The only man she had ever loved—or would ever love. That one sour experience had been more than enough for a lifetime.

She changed into one of her older dresses and pulled on her half boots, though she had hoped that with winter over she would not have to wear them again for a while. She drew on a cloak, since even with the intermittent sunshine it looked chilly outside, and tied the ribbons of a bonnet securely beneath her chin.

He would not be there, she thought as she left the house. Even if he was still at Highmoor, he would not think of keeping an appointment two days late. Besides, pleasant as the afternoon was—though definitely chilly and gusty—the grass underfoot was really quite wet.

He would not be there, but she would enjoy the walk anyway. And surely the stone bench inside the folly at the top of the hill would be dry and sheltered enough so that she could sit there enjoying the view and the solitude for a while. It was better than riding with the others, feeling her loneliness.

The word, verbalized in her mind, took her by surprise.

She was not lonely. Never that. She was almost always in congenial company. Her life was as she wanted it to be. Why had she suddenly described herself as lonely?

She crossed the stepping-stones and strode up the hill, not stopping even once to catch her breath. The air was invigorating, she thought, even better than it had been three days ago. And the sky looked lovely, with white clouds scudding across the blue. She made for the top, trying not to expect to see him there, trying to convince herself that she wanted to be alone there so that she could enjoy the view without distraction.

She stopped when she was within sight of the folly. And felt a surging of happiness, which she did not stop to analyze. She smiled brightly and stepped forward.

He was getting to his feet and smiling with his eyes at her.

"What a climb," she said. "I may never recover my breath."

"Please do," he said. "I am not sure I would fancy having to carry a dead body back down such a steep slope."

Other gentlemen of her acquaintance would have rushed to her assistance, using the excuse to touch her, to take her by the hand, even perhaps to risk setting an arm about her waist. A brisk and quite harmless flirtation would have ensued. Mr. Wade merely motioned to the bench.

"Come and sit down," he said.

She laughed and walked toward him, a new spring in her step despite her breathlessness.

HER CHEEKS AND EVEN the tip of her nose were rosy from the chill and the wind. Her curls were somewhat disheveled beneath her bonnet. The hems of her green walking dress and the gray cloak over it were darkened with moisture to the depth of several inches. Her boots were wet and blades of grass clung to them.

She was even more beautiful than he remembered.

He had been trying to convince himself that she would not come and that he would not particularly mind if she did not. He really was busy with ideas for renovations that would begin as soon as spring was more advanced. He would be able to think and work without distraction if she did not come. He would not wait long, he had told himself when he first arrived at the top of the hill. Just ten minutes.

She came at the end of fifteen. He was somewhat alarmed to realize that he had never felt happier in his life.

"Better?" he asked after she had seated herself beside him. There was a fragrance about her that he had noticed last time. Violets? It was not overpowering. It was very subtle. It seemed to be the smell of her rather than of any perfume she wore.

"I believe so," she said, one hand over her heart. She laughed again, a bright, totally happy sound. "I believe it is almost safe to say that I will survive."

"I am glad," he said. One of those curls would feel soft and silky wrapped about one of his fingers.

"Was not the rain wretched?" she said. "We played hide-and-seek for two days with the children and had to pretend for all of that time not to see them, even when they were perfectly visible behind sheer draperies or beneath desks."

"You were bored?" he asked, a quite improper image of her with an infant at her breast flashing unexpectedly into his mind.

"Not at all," she said. "It was a thoroughly enjoyable romp. I believe I am still a child at heart—an alarming thought. But I was disappointed about our walk. I thought you might not still be at Highmoor. I thought perhaps you would not think of coming today instead. I did not expect to see you here today, but I came anyway." She smiled at him. "Just in case."

She had really wanted to come. She had been disappointed by the rain. She had been anxious today—anxious that he would not come. But she had come anyway. Just in case.

He had planned this part of their meeting—if she came. He was going to turn to her and tell her he was very sorry but he had misled her last time. He had done so, he would say, because she had looked embarrassed to be caught trespassing and he had not wanted to distress her further. But in reality he was more than just Hartley Wade. He was the Marquess of Carew.

That was what he had planned. But she had wanted to meet him. She had come today on the chance that he would be there. She had wanted to spend the afternoon with him just as he was—a sort of cripple of nondescript appearance with not even some of his finery to improve his looks.

She had wanted to be with Hartley Wade, landscape gardener. And she looked pleased to be with him.

How would she react to the knowledge of his real identity? Did he want to find out?

He was enjoying being Hartley Wade. He had never enjoyed anything more in his life. He wanted to continue as he was—just for this afternoon. At the end of it, or next time if there was a next time, he would tell her the truth. But not now.

"I expect to be at Highmoor for a while yet," he said. "There are several plans to make and the marquess to consult when he returns home. And then the work to supervise if he gives his approval and wishes to begin immediately. And I was disappointed, too. And so I came today, as soon as it was not raining. Just in case you would be here also."

She smiled brightly at him. She had white and perfect teeth. Her mouth curved up invitingly at the corners. It was the most kissable mouth he had ever seen.

"Well," she said, "I am recovered, Mr. Wade. Are you going to show me the lake? Is it far? And more to the point, is it all downhill?"

"But uphill on the way back," he said. "No, not far." He got to his feet but did not offer his hand to assist her. He was afraid to touch her. Even if he kept her on his left-hand side, she would be more aware of his limp if she held to his arm. And she might be embarrassed or disgusted. "You will like it. It is the most secluded and the loveliest part of the estate."

"I wonder if the Marquess of Carew appreciates his home," she said. "He is away from it a great deal, is he not? If I were the owner of all this beauty, I am not sure I could bear to leave it."

But there was loneliness to contend with when one lived at home, a loneliness that even houseguests could not quite alleviate. It was when he was at home that he felt most keenly the absence of a woman from his life. And children. But he despaired of ever finding the woman who would love him for himself.

Not that he had ever loved any woman—though he had been fond of the woman who had been his mistress for five years before her sudden death a year and a half ago, the only mistress he had ever employed. But his feelings for her had not had the depth of love.

He suspected that his feelings for Miss Samantha Newman could have such depth, though at the moment he was only very much in love with her.

"He appreciates it," he said, "else why would he be going to such great expense to make it more lovely?"

"Perhaps," she said, "to make of it an even greater showpiece. But that was unkind. Please forgive me. I do not even know the gentleman. But Jenny—my cousin, Lady Thornhill—says that he is a pleasant gentleman."

Bless the earl's lady. She had never been anything but kind and courteous to him, though she was one of this world's beautiful people.

"Here we are," he said. "Mind your step. The slope is

rather steep. I would hate to see you hurtle downward and straight into the water."

"It might forever prejudice my opinion against the place," she said with a laugh.

But she was not laughing a few moments later. She stopped when they were still almost at the top of the slope, when the lake came into view, nestled between the hill on one side and trees on the other. She stood for a few moments, saying nothing.

"Oh," she said at last, her voice hushed. "It must be the loveliest place on earth."

That was the moment when he knew that he was not in love with her, like any schoolboy with any beautiful woman.

That was when he knew, without any doubt and despite such a short acquaintance, that he loved her.

# 3

THERE WAS SOMETHING ALMOST MAGICAL about it. The lake at Chalcote was lovely, with its wide expanse of water and the boathouse and the grassy banks on which the family picnicked and played. But this was different. This was—enchanted.

Perhaps it was the rather steep hill, she thought, and the trees on the other side. They enclosed it, making it seem in a little world of its own. They made the water look deep and still.

"Shall we go down?" he asked. "It is even lovelier from the water's edge."

They descended sedately, though she could see that the slope leveled off before it reached the water so that there was a flat bank on which to stand or sit. She was glad that he did not offer either his hand or his arm. She had noticed that he had never done so. Most gentlemen would have, making her feel frail and ladylike. But touching meant physical awareness. It made one immediately aware that one was of a different gender from one's companion.

She was glad that there was no such awareness with Mr. Wade. It would have spoiled what she thought was a budding friendship. She had never had a gentleman as a friend, she realized. Not really.

Yes, he was right, she thought when they were standing on the bank, looking across the water. "Peace," she said quietly. "Perfect peace. It makes one aware of—oh, of what?"

"The presence of God?" he suggested.

"Yes." She closed her eyes and breathed in the smell of water and damp vegetation. "Yes, there are places like that, are there not? Churches almost always. Sometimes other places. This place."

"I have always liked it wild," he said, "though I would like to give it a touch of—of human appreciation. Perhaps a chapel." He laughed softly. "But that would be an affectation. Certainly nothing suggesting human activity. I did think once of boats and a boathouse, but I dismissed the idea as soon as it came to me. What do you think?"

"No boats," she said.

"A bridge, perhaps," he said, pointing to the narrow end of the lake, where a waterfall down the hillside poured in its waters. "The idea keeps returning to me. But a bridge to nowhere is another affectation, is it not?"

"A stone bridge," she said, "with arches. Three, I think. Leading to a small pavilion or summerhouse."

"Yes." He was silent for a few moments. "Fully enclosed with glass windows on all six or eight sides. Where one can sit and be warm."

"And dry," she said. She laughed. "A rain house. The

lake must look lovely in the rain, with mist on the hills and in the trees."

"A rain house," he said softly. "I like it."

"It could be wonderfully cozy and peaceful," she said. "I believe I would spend a great deal of time there if I lived here."

"A bridge and a rain house," he said. "That is what it will be. I have puzzled for years over exactly what should be done here, and you have helped me solve the problem."

"Perhaps," she said, "you should employ me as your assistant, Mr. Wade."

He turned his head to smile at her. He had one of the loveliest smiles she had ever seen. It went all the way back inside his eyes and drew an answering smile from her.

"Could I afford you?" he asked.

"Probably not," she said. "Will the Marquess of Carew think you are quite mad when you suggest a bridge and a *rain* house here?"

"Quite possibly," he said. "But he has great faith in my judgment. And when he sees the finished products, he will fall in love with them without further ado."

"I hope so," she said. "I would not want them to be neglected."

They stood side by side, looking about them, in perfect harmony, perfect peace.

"I could live here happily for the rest of my life," she said at last with a sigh. But she chuckled at the thought. "If I were just the hermit type."

"Wearing a sackcloth shirt," he said, "and taking your morning plunge into the lake."

"Ugh," she said, shivering, and they both laughed. But she sobered again. "I suppose I should be going back to Chalcote. I must have been here an hour or longer. The time has flown."

"Have you ever seen the inside of the abbey?" he asked.

She shook her head.

"Would you like to?" he asked. "Tomorrow? I would love to show it to you."

"It does not seem proper," she said, "to view a gentleman's home when he is not in residence." It would be even more improper if he were, she thought.

"I would show you only the public rooms," he said. "There are numerous visitors here during the summer. The housekeeper is authorized to show them the parts of the house that are not private—the most magnificent parts. I know them well enough to show them, too."

Highmoor Abbey had looked so very beautiful from a distance. She was very tempted. And his eyes were smiling at her.

"Tomorrow?" he asked.

"Oh." She felt suddenly like a child being denied a treat. "We are going visiting tomorrow. I could not possibly be rude enough to absent myself."

"The day after?" he suggested.

"And the day after we are expecting visitors." She pulled a face and smiled apologetically at him. But she had a sudden idea. "Will you come too? I know that

Gabriel and Jenny—the earl and countess, you know—
would be delighted." And yet as soon as she said it, she
felt sorry. Absurd as it seemed, she did not want to share
her friend with her family.

"I think not," he said quietly. "I had better stay here
and at least pretend to work. But thank you."

They smiled regretfully at each other. She had enjoyed
these two afternoons with him so very much. She
thought he might have spoiled her forever for the normal sort of flirtatious afternoons she sometimes spent
with gentlemen out driving or at garden parties. Friendship was so much more comfortable.

"I could come the afternoon after that," she said
hopefully. "Will you still be here?"

"Yes," he said. "I was not sure you wanted to. It would
be a long walk for you. Do you ride?"

"Yes," she said. "Of course."

"Perhaps I could meet you," he said. "At the gatehouse
to Highmoor? The same time as today?"

She nodded and smiled. "I must go now," she said.
"You need not come with me. It is a long walk to the
stream and back."

"But like last time," he said, "I must make myself personally responsible for seeing all trespassers cleared
from Highmoor property."

They scrambled up the bank together and then up to
the top of the hill and down the slope to the stream and
the stepping-stones to Chalcote land, chatting easily on
a variety of topics. She stopped and turned to him before
crossing to the other side.

"Thank you, Mr. Wade," she said. "This has been so pleasant."

"And for me," he said. "I shall look forward to seeing you three days from now."

After crossing the stones, she turned to wave to him before the trees cut him from her view. He was a gentleman, she thought, a single gentleman. And for longer than an hour on two separate afternoons she had been alone with him in secluded countryside, where they had not seen even one other person. No one knew where she was. And this second time she had deliberately met him. It was almost like a tryst they had arranged. It was dreadfully improper, even for a woman of four-and-twenty. Aunt Aggy would have a fit of the vapors if she knew. Gabriel would frown and look like Lucifer again. Even Jenny would look reproachful.

Why had it not seemed improper at all? Just because there was no flirtation involved, no touching, no romance? Or was it because of his appearance? He was such a very ordinary looking man—except perhaps when he smiled with his eyes, or with his whole face. And so totally unfashionable. And then there was the twisted, gloved hand and the heavy limp. Perhaps it was his appearance. She tried to imagine him as a handsome, perfectly made man. Would she feel the impropriety then? She rather thought she would. She would be attracted to such a man.

She felt no attraction at all to Mr. Wade. Except as a friend. She smiled. Except as a special companion.

THE DAYS CRAWLED BY. His utter solitude was his own fault, of course. If he had only made known his return home, he would have had callers. Thornhill would have been among the first. And he would have called on his neighbors. He would have had invitations to dinner. He would have issued invitations. Oh, yes, it was entirely his own fault that he was so very solitary.

And all because of a little creature so beautiful from the outside of her person right through to her soul that she was as unattainable as a star in a different galaxy. All because he was afraid for her to know who he was, lest he see a change in her, lest he see her humanness. He did not want her to look on him as the immensely wealthy and eligible Marquess of Carew. He wanted her to continue to see him as plain—very plain—Hartley Wade.

Every smile she gave Hartley Wade was a treasure to be stored up for future pleasure, because each smile was guileless and sincere as well as utterly beautiful. Every word she spoke to him had been committed carefully to memory. *It must be the loveliest place on earth. . . . Perhaps you should employ me as your assistant. . . . I could live here happily for the rest of my life. . . . Will you come too? . . . This has been so pleasant.*

He did not want her to know. He wanted the fantasy to continue—for one more afternoon. And so he imposed seclusion on himself, not leaving his land lest he be seen and word should spread. He walked and rode about the park for almost every daylight hour of the two interminable days, thinking about her, dreaming about her, calling himself every abusive name he could think of, from idiot on down.

He could not sleep from thinking of her, and when he did sleep he dreamed of her, dreams in which she was always just beyond the reach of his outstretched arms, and always smiling at him and telling him how pleasant this had been.

One evening, after he had dismissed his valet for the night, he stood in front of a pier glass, dressed only in his shirt and pantaloons, and looked at himself—something he rarely did, apart from careless glances.

He smiled ruefully at his image and then looked downward and closed his eyes. How imbecilic he was being. He set his right hand on his left and massaged his palm with his left thumb, pressing hard over stiff tendons, pushing his fingers straight one by one. She must be the most beautiful little creature ever to have lived. How could any man look at her and not want her and love her? She could choose any man she wanted. She could choose the most handsome man in England. She doubtless had a large court of admirers. The reason she was still unwed at the age of four-and-twenty must be that her choices were legion.

And he dared to want her himself?

He opened his eyes and forced himself to look at his image again. He watched his thin, twisted hand being massaged and exercised—but never brought back quite to full use.

And he dared to love her himself?

If she knew who he was, a demon in his brain told him, perhaps she would want him. Or his title. Or his property. Or his wealth.

No woman could ever want *him*. Though Dorothea had loved him, he remembered. Not at first. He had been merely a man who could afford to pay for her favors and set her up with the security of a prolonged relationship. But she had grown to love him. She had told him so and he had believed her. He would always be grateful to her, poor Dorothea. He had been fond of her.

But Dorothea had been rather plump and plain, ten years his senior, an aging courtesan even when he had first gone to her to lose his virginity.

No other woman could ever want him. Certainly not Miss Samantha Newman. The idea was laughable. He laughed softly, his eyes closed again.

But she had enjoyed their two afternoons together. She had enjoyed his company. And there was to be another. She was going to allow him to show her his greatest treasure, his home. And he was going to have the memory of her there, inside Highmoor Abbey, gazing admiringly at all the state rooms. He was sure she would admire them. And all the while, as unobtrusively as he could, he would admire *her* and commit to memory her every look and gesture and word.

Oh, yes, he was going to remain Mr. Hartley Wade for one more afternoon. He prayed for good weather. In the meanwhile, the days seemed endless and dreary, and the only way he could bring himself any peace was to walk to the lake and stand on the bank staring at the place where the three-arched bridge and the rain house—he smiled at her name for the pavilion—would stand when he had had them constructed later in the year.

But the morning of the appointed day finally came, and then the afternoon. And all his prayers had been answered. Not only was it not raining, but the sun was shining down from a cloudless sky. There was even heat in the air. He gave instructions at the house before he left. Until they saw Miss Newman and drew their own conclusions, his staff would think him mad—first forbidding them to spread word of his return and now forbidding them to use his title for the rest of the day.

He rode down the long, winding driveway toward the gatehouse, from where he would be still out of sight of anyone riding along the road. He tried to persuade himself that he would not be too disappointed if she did not come.

But he knew as soon as he saw her, a scant two minutes after his own arrival, that he would have been very disappointed indeed. Devastated.

She saw him almost immediately and raised a hand in greeting. At the same time, her beautiful face lit up with a happy smile. Yes, happy. She was happy to see him.

She was dressed in a very smart and fashionable riding habit of dark green velvet. She wore an absurd little matching riding hat perched on her blond curls, its paler green feather curling enticingly down over one ear and beneath her chin. His mind searched for a more superlative word than beautiful but could not find one.

"Have you ever known a more glorious spring day?" she called to him gaily when she was within earshot.

"No, never," he said truthfully, smiling at her.

Never. And there would never be another such.

HE DID NOT TAKE her immediately to the house. He took her off the driveway and through old and widely spaced trees.

"It was a tangled, overgrown, ancient forest," he said, "and quite impenetrable except to wild animals of the smaller variety. I had it cleared out so that it could become a deer park and so that it could be walked and ridden in. Of course"—he laughed—"the marquess then decided that there was to be no hunting on his land. The deer have an idyllic life here."

"Oh," she said, "I am so glad. Do you disapprove?" She hoped he did not. She hoped he did not enjoy blood sports. But almost all men did. They saw it as a slur on their manhood to admit otherwise. Her respect for the Marquess of Carew rose.

"No," he said. "I created the deer park only on the understanding that it be in the nature of a preserve. Look." He pointed with his whip. There were five of them, lovely and stately and quite unafraid, though they must have seen and heard the horses and humans no more than a hundred feet away.

"How can anyone want to shoot them?" she said, and he smiled at her with his eyes.

He took her all the way around the more open part of

the park, with the abbey always visible. From the front it still looked as if it might be a cathedral. The other three sides were a strange mixture of architectural designs. Successive marquesses had obviously all made their mark on the building. And yet the result was curiously pleasing. Samantha could not think of a house—and she had seen many of England's most stately—that she admired more.

"Thank you," Mr. Wade said when she told him so.

"Have you had a hand in its design, then?" she asked him.

He looked at her blankly for a moment before laughing. "No," he said. "But I shall pass along your compliment to the marquess. I am merely anticipating his response and expressing it to you while you are able to hear it."

"How absurd you are," she said.

The park was quite unconventionally designed. There were no formal parterre gardens before the house but only a wide cobbled terrace and several large flowerpots, empty at this time of year. But there were flower beds and rock gardens, some of them already full of green shoots; one of them, in a more sheltered area, was overflowing with blooming crocuses and primroses. But there was nothing symmetrical about their design. Most of them were unexpected, in hollows that were hidden from the eye until one was almost on top of them. All of them took careful advantage of the contours of the land.

"It is strange," she said. "But I like it. Is it your work?"

"Not so much my *work*, to be fair to the gardeners," he

said. "But my design. I suppose it is strange. To the human mind, anyway, which demands orderliness and symmetry. Nature makes no such demands. Had you noticed? That tree on the slope where we first met, for example. And sometimes I have to argue a point with nature. But not always. I like to work with nature rather than against it, so that everything in a park looks natural even if it is not so in fact."

"You must have spent a great deal of time here," she said. "The marquess must have a deep respect for your work." Again her respect for the master went up.

"He has no artistic sense himself," he said, a twinkle in his eye. "But he can recognize it and encourage it in others. I have designed several parks in other parts of England. But this is my favorite."

"Do you live close to here?" she asked. It seemed a shame for him to have spent so much time and creative energy dreaming up such beauty if he rarely had the chance to see it all.

"Not too far away," he said. "Shall we take the horses to the stable and go into the abbey?"

"Yes, please," she said. She hoped the interior would not be disappointing. But she desperately wanted to see it for herself, now that she had been so close. She worried a little about what the servants would think. Would they know who she was? Would they be scandalized to see her alone with their master's hired landscape gardener? But she was not going to allow servants to spoil her afternoon. The three-day delay had seemed endless.

And she had felt so happy to see him again, waiting for her at the gatehouse. Her friend.

The hall robbed her of breath. It was two stories high and seemingly all carved stone pillars and great Gothic arches. It felt as though one were walking into a cathedral.

"The oldest and most magnificent part of the house," he said. "Apart from the tiled floor, which my gr—, which my employer's grandfather had put down, this is the entryway almost exactly as it was until the abbey was confiscated by Henry the Eighth."

"Oh!" was the most intelligent comment she could think to make.

A footman bowed to her after Mr. Wade had signaled to him, and took her hat and her whip and the outer jacket of her riding habit. He made a very stiff half-bow to Mr. Wade and, without a word, took his hat and whip. Samantha found herself biting her lower lip at the obvious slight. They must see him here as a servant, little better than themselves, though he was very obviously a gentleman. Servants could be far more discourteous than their betters. But Mr. Wade made no comment. Perhaps he had not noticed.

They spent all of an hour walking about the state rooms—the grand ballroom, the drawing room, the dining room, the reception hall, the bedchamber where King Charles the Second himself had once slept. She looked at Rembrandts and Van Dycks and one magnificent seascape by Mr. Reynolds. It was all more glorious than even she could have pictured.

"Imagine living here," she said to Mr. Wade when they were in the ballroom, stretching her arms wide and twirling twice about. "Imagine all this being your very own."

"Would you like it?" he asked.

"Perhaps not." She stopped twirling. "Surroundings are not everything, are they? There are other things more important." She laughed. "But that will not stop me from *imagining* living here."

"You should marry the Marquess of Carew," he said.

"Indeed." She laughed. "He is a single gentleman, is he not? How old is he? Is he young and handsome? Or is he old and doddering? But no matter. Bring him on and I will set about charming him witless."

"Would you?" He was smiling at her, his head to one side.

"The Marchioness of Carew," she said, waving an imaginary fan languidly before her face. "It has a definite ring to it, does it not? I do believe you should bow to me, sir."

"Do you?" He did not bow.

"I shall have you beheaded for insubordination," she said, raising her chin and looking along the length of her nose at him. "I shall have my husband, the marquess, order it. The marchioness. Of Highmoor Abbey in Yorkshire, you know." She waved a hand before his face for him to kiss.

He did not kiss it.

"I told you I am still a child at heart," she said, reverting to her normal self. "I would not try charming him even if he were the proverbial tall, dark, and handsome gentleman—like Gabriel. I would not exchange my freedom even for all this." She waved an arm about the ballroom without looking away from his face.

"Is your freedom so precious to you, then?" he asked.

"Yes," she said. "Have you wondered why I am unwed at my age? It is because I have decided never to marry."

"Ah," he said. There was a smile in his eyes, but very far back. Most people would not have even realized that it was there. "I think you must have been hurt badly."

She was jolted with surprise. Gentlemen were in the habit of telling her that she was the happiest, sunniest-natured lady of their acquaintance.

"Yes," she said. "A long time ago. It does not matter any longer."

"Except," he said, "that it has blighted your life."

"It has not," she said. "Oh, it has not. What a strange thing to say."

"Forgive me," he said, smiling more fully. "Come to my office and let me order tea. It is the marquess's office, of course, but I have appropriated it for my use while I am here and he is not."

Friends knew each other, she thought. He had seen something that no one else had ever seen. And he had perceived something about her that even she had not perceived—or not admitted, anyway. Had her life been blighted? Had she allowed *him* such power over her?

"Thank you," she said. "Tea would be nice."

# 4

*H*E WAS GLAD HE HAD THOUGHT OF OFFERING her tea in his office rather than in the drawing room. He found the drawing room cold and impersonal unless he was entertaining a large gathering. His office, on the other hand, was where he spent most of his time indoors when he was out of his own apartments. It was a cozy room, not small really, but filled with his own personal treasures and never quite tidy since the maids had learned not to move books—especially ones that lay open.

He seated her in an ancient, comfortable chair to one side of the fire, which his servants always made up as soon as he stepped inside the house, and sat in its twin at the opposite side. His father had been going to have the chairs thrown out years ago, calling them a disgrace to so grand a place as Highmoor Abbey, but he had appropriated them for his study and he did not believe he would ever let them go.

Now he knew that he would not. And he knew that his study would become even more precious to him in the future, because the greatest treasure of his life had been there for tea one afternoon. She looked small and dainty in the chair. She looked comfortable.

He was glad she had made a joke of marrying the Marquess of Carew after some demon in him had made him suggest it as a possibility. But he was sorry that someone had broken her heart. She made light of it now and she always seemed cheerful enough, but he did not believe he had exaggerated in saying that it had blighted her life. Most ladies of her age would have been married long ago and have had children in the nursery by now. Especially ladies as lovely as she was. But there was no other lady as lovely as she. . . .

They talked about books after she had seen some of the titles of those lying on the small table beside her. And about music and opera and the theater. Their tastes were similar, though she had never studied Latin or Greek, as he had, and she had never read the plays she had seen performed. And she preferred a tenor voice to a soprano, unlike him, and a cello to a violin. Both of them preferred the pianoforte to either.

He had never known a woman easier to talk to. But then he had never known a lady who was unaware of his identity. He wondered if it made a difference. She had said in the ballroom that she would not set her cap at the Marquess of Carew even if she had the opportunity to do so. But if she did know that he was the marquess instead of just a gentleman so far down on his luck that he was forced to hire out his services as a landscape gardener— if she did know, would it make a difference? Would she be less comfortable with him? Would she feel the impropriety of their behavior more acutely? She seemed quite unaware of it now. And yet it was even more dreadfully improper for them to be indoors alone together thus than it had been for them to roam the park together.

"What happened?" she asked him quietly. He realized that they had been sitting through one of their silences, which never seemed awkward, and that he had absently fallen into one of his habits. He was massaging his right palm with his left thumb and straightening his fingers one by one. Her eyes were on his hands. "Was it an accident? Or were you born—" Her eyes flew to his face and she blushed. "I am so sorry. It is none of my business. Please forgive me."

It was a measure of the friendship that had grown between them, perhaps, that he could tell her, a virtual stranger, that an unhappy love affair the details of which he did not know had blighted her life, and that she could ask him what had happened to leave his right hand and foot deformed. Good manners would have kept both of them silent on such personal matters had they been merely acquaintances.

"It was an accident." He smiled at her as he told her the lie he had been telling for most of his life. He had never told the truth, even to his parents right after it had happened. There was no point in telling the truth now. "I was six years old. I was out riding my new pony with my cousin." His cousin had been ten. "We had left the groom far behind. I was showing off, showing how I could gallop to match the pace of a cousin four years older than I, and showing how I could jump a fence. But I did not clear it. I crashed very heavily right down onto the fence, breaking bones and tearing ligaments. By some miracle my pony escaped serious harm. The physician told my father that both my leg and my arm would have to be amputated, but fortunately for me my mother had a totally genuine fit of the vapors."

He smiled at her grimace of horror.

"It was a long time ago," he said. "The physician did his best to set the broken bones, but of course there was permanent damage. Both my father and I were told that I would never be able to use either my right leg or my right arm again. But I can be stubborn about some things."

"Courageous," she said. "Determined."

"Stubborn." He laughed. "My mother shrieked when she first saw me limping about and swore that I would do myself dreadful harm. My father merely commented that I would make myself the laughingstock."

"Poor little boy," she said, head to one side, blue eyes large with sympathy. "Children should not have to suffer so."

"Suffering can make all the difference in a person's life," he said. "It can be a definite force for good. At the risk of sounding conceited, I would have to say that I am reasonably happy with the person I have become. Perhaps I would not have liked the person I would have been without the accident." Perhaps he would have always been the sniveling, cringing, self-pitying coward he had been as a young child.

"I am sorry for my unmannerly curiosity," she said. "Please forgive me."

"There is nothing to forgive," he said. "Friends talk

from the heart, do they not? I believe we have become friends. Have we?"

"Yes." She smiled slowly and warmly. "Yes, we have, Mr. Wade."

There was not even the glimmering of a sign in her eyes that they were anything more than that. Of course. How foolish of him even to have dreamed of such a thing, let alone to have hoped. But how unbelievably wonderful it was to see Miss Samantha Newman smiling so kindly at him and agreeing with him that they were friends.

"And this friend," he said, getting reluctantly to his feet, "had better see you on your way back to Chalcote before every constable in the county is called out to search for you. You did not tell Thornhill or his lady where you were going?"

"No." She flushed rather guiltily as she got up herself without his assistance. "They might have thought it improper. My aunt—Lady Brill—might have felt obliged to accompany me as chaperone. I suppose it *is* improper. I suppose I should have a chaperone. But it does not feel wrong, and I do not feel the need of a female protector. And if one cannot exercise a little personal judgment and enjoy a little freedom at such an advanced age as mine, one might as well be shut up inside a cage." She laughed lightly.

"I will ride with you as far as the gatehouse," he said, opening the door of the study for her to precede him from the room. "There is a folly overlooking the lake that I have not shown you yet. And farther back behind the house there is a stretch of rapids where the stream flows downhill. I have ideas for creating a more spectacular series of waterfalls there, but I do not want to spoil the natural beauty. I would like to hear your opinion. Will you walk there with me, perhaps three afternoons from today?"

She turned her head to smile at him as they left the house, her jacket back on and her hat at an even jauntier angle than before. "I would love to," she said, "and will studiously resist all attempts to organize any other entertainment for that afternoon. I shall pray piously for good weather."

"The usual time at the top of the hill?" he asked.

"Yes." She laughed. "By the time I return to London for the Season, I shall be the fittest dancer in any ballroom. I shall smile in sympathy at the ladies and gentlemen wheezing all around me after the first set of country dances."

He wished he could dance. He had always wished it, perhaps because he knew that he never could. He avoided ballrooms. Although he spent almost as much time in London during the year as most other gentlemen, he rarely accepted any of his invitations to the round of social activities that accompanied the Season. He was not very well known, especially by the ladies of the *ton,* despite his rank and fortune and eligible marital status.

"I wish I could be there to see it," he said. They had ridden their horses out of the stable yard and turned in the direction of the gatehouse, a mile or so distant. "This

lawn stretches all the way to the gatehouse. It is tempt-
ingly long and level, is it not? Do you enjoy taking your
horse to a gallop?"

She looked at him and down to his right leg. She
opened her mouth to ask if he was sure he ought to—he
was certain that was what she was about to say. But she
bit her lip instead, and when her eyes came back up to
his, there was mischief dancing in them.

"I will race you," she said, and she was off before he
could recover from his surprise, her laughter almost a
shriek.

He stayed half a length behind her, enjoying her excitement and her exuberance—and also her careful and
excellent horsemanship. Another episode to commit to
memory, he thought as he surged past her when they
were only yards from the gatehouse. He turned his head
to laugh at her chagrin.

"Unfair," she said, her voice breathless. "Oh, unfair.
Gabriel has given me a horse lame in all four legs."

"That is an insulting fib for which you can expect to
fry," he said, looking over the splendid chestnut she
rode. "The Earl of Thornhill keeps the best stables in
these parts—or so I have heard. We did not agree on a
wager."

"Oh," she said, pretending to the sullenness of defeat.
"What do you suppose I owe you?"

"That is a delightful feather in your cap," he said. "Literally, I mean."

"My—" Her laughter was more of a giggle as she removed her hat. "I am not at all sure that it is detachable,

and I would hate to have to give you the whole hat, sir. If there is anything more scandalous than riding about the countryside alone, it is doing so hatless. I would never live down the ignominy if someone were to see me. Ah, here it comes."

And she handed him the curled green feather that had been circling her head and nestling against her ear and beneath her chin.

"Thank you." He inclined his head and chuckled as she pinned the absurd hat back on her hair. "If anyone asks, you will have to say it blew away in the wind."

He raised a hand in farewell as she rode off. He then placed the feather carefully in his right hand before taking up the reins with his left once more and turning back in the direction of home.

He wondered what she would think if she knew that the prize she had just awarded him would be treasured more than any of the costliest of his possessions for the rest of his life.

It was a good thing that one person could not see into another's mind or heart, he thought. What a fool he would appear to her if she could see into his. And how horrified she would be.

Three days. How would he fill them? How would he stop himself from descending to the horribly immature measure of counting the hours?

THE DAY FINALLY CAME and the sun was shining. Still. It had not stopped shining all through every day since the afternoon of her visit to Highmoor Abbey. The law of averages said that it must rain soon, but she had hoped—foolishly, she had even prayed—that it would not be today.

She did not know why she valued Mr. Wade's friendship so dearly. He was a man of very ordinary appearance, and she would guess that though he was a gentleman, he was poor. But then she was not looking at him as a possible suitor, so his appearance and his financial status were of no concern to her at all. That was why she valued him so much, she decided. She had always felt some physical attraction to all the gentlemen who made up her court—she was beginning to describe them to herself by that term, after hearing it from Gabriel so often. She could not have encouraged them and flirted with them and held them always at arm's length if she had not.

She felt no attraction whatsoever to Mr. Wade. No revulsion, either, of course, despite the physical handicaps. Just—oh, just the warmth of friendship. She could not remember the person, man or woman, whose company she had more enjoyed and more yearned for when she was not with him. Even Jenny, she thought disloyally, had never been such a dear friend.

She hoped he would not have to go away soon. He had spoken of planning waterfalls north of the house. He had spoken of seeing the work at the lake started this year. Surely he stayed to oversee his plans brought to fruition when he was designing something new. Would he stay all summer?

But she would not be staying that long, she remembered with a jolt. She would be going to London for the Season. She always went to London for the Season. This would be her seventh—she would wince at the number, perhaps, if she were in search of a husband. Many young ladies considered it an unutterable humiliation to have to go back for a second Season unattached. Jenny and Gabriel were not planning to go this year. They did not always go, being far happier in the country romping with their children. And Jenny had told her in an unguarded moment—and been mortally embarrassed afterward—that they were trying for another.

Perhaps, Samantha thought, she would stay at Chalcote this year, too. But she dismissed the thought immediately. Kind and hospitable as they both were, Jenny and Gabriel needed to have their home to themselves for at least a part of the year. And she and Aunt Aggy had already been here for three months. Too long. Soon—as soon as she had control of her fortune—Samantha was going to set up for herself somewhere so that she would have a home of her own in which to spend those slack months when there was nothing much happening anywhere but in country homes.

No, she could not stay at Chalcote. Soon she and Aunt Aggy must return to London. But she tried to put the thought from her mind. There would be another few weeks first. Another few chances to explore Highmoor land with Mr. Wade. If he wanted to explore them with her, of course. If he did not tire of their friendship.

She did not really understand what the attraction of

the friendship was. She did not try to understand it. She was too busy enjoying it.

But it was not to last much longer after all. She was sitting alone at the breakfast table, staring into space. Gabriel and Albert had gone off riding about some business somewhere, and Jenny was in the nursery with Mary, who had fallen out of bed during the night and bumped her head and was still feeling the need of her mother's soothing words and arms.

Aunt Agatha came into the breakfast room, bringing with her the usual pile of letters from her friends in London. She kissed her niece, exchanged pleasantries with her, took toast and coffee, and settled to reading the latest news and gossip from town after Samantha had assured her that no, of course she did not mind if Aunt Agatha was unsociable for a few minutes.

"Oh, dear," her aunt said after three of those minutes had passed. "Oh, dear, oh, dear. Poor Sophie."

"Is Lady Sophia ill?" Samantha inquired politely.

"An oaf of a coachman ran her down when she was crossing the street," her aunt said, still frowning down at her letter. "He even had the nerve to curse her and to ride off without stopping. She was carried home with a broken leg."

"How nasty," Samantha said, concerned. "I do hope she is not in too much discomfort."

"She is," Lady Brill said. "But worse than that, she is languishing for lack of company, poor Sophie. You know how visiting and exchanging news is the breath of life to her, Samantha, dear."

"Yes." Samantha could not quite suppress a smile. Being confined to her own home with a broken leg must be fairly killing her aunt's closest friend.

But the smile was wiped away almost immediately. "I must go to her," Lady Brill said decisively. "Poor, dear Sophie. And almost no one in town yet to pay her calls. The least I can do, dearest—the very least—is go to sit with her in her hour of need."

Selfishly, the implications for Samantha herself were instantly apparent to her. But so were her obligations.

"When shall we leave?" she asked.

"Oh." Lady Brill looked at her and her frown became worried. "I will be dragging you away from dear Jennifer and Lord Thornhill weeks earlier than we expected. But you cannot stay here, can you, dear? There will be no one with whom to travel back to town next month for the Season. You certainly could not travel alone. Will you mind very, very much? Poor Sophie, you know."

Samantha leaned across the table to set a hand over her aunt's. She minded very much indeed, but for a reason that was quite foolish from any rational consideration. "Of course I will not mind," she said. "I think it very sweet of you to want to return to keep Lady Sophia company. And why should I mind being in town, even if the Season has not yet begun? There is always something to do there. Besides, I need a whole new wardrobe of clothes. I have simply nothing to wear that everyone has not already seen."

"That is very sweet of you, dear," Lady Brill said, looking relieved. "Very sweet indeed. And perhaps this will be the year when you will find the gentleman of your dreams. He will come along, mark my words, even though you keep insisting that you are not even in search of him. I have never heard such nonsense in my life."

Samantha smiled. "When do you want to leave?" she asked. *Please not today. Oh, please, not today.*

"Tomorrow morning?" her aunt asked apologetically. "As early as possible. Will that be too much of a rush for you, dear?"

The door opened at that moment and Lady Thornhill came in. She assured them that Mary, who was not normally a clinging infant, had thoroughly enjoyed her moment of tragedy but could no longer resist the urge to play with Emily and Jane. Michael had gone with the men.

"Oh," she said, looking genuinely dismayed when Lady Brill had given her news and told of their plans, "are we to lose you both so soon, then? I had counted on at least another two or three weeks."

And yet, Samantha thought as she made her way upstairs soon after to give her maid instructions to begin packing for the next day's journey, Jenny must feel some relief, too, to know that soon she was to have Gabriel and her children to herself again. Albert and Rosalie were to leave within the week.

In six years, Samantha had not envied her cousin's married state. She had only pitied her, even though she had always been well aware that Jenny's marriage had quickly developed from its disastrous beginning into a very deep love match. Today for the first time she felt—oh, not envy. No. Nor loneliness. Only—she could not put a word to what she felt.

But she did feel sorrow to know that this afternoon's meeting with Mr. Wade was to be the last. It was very unlikely that she would ever see him again, even though it seemed that he had been to Highmoor several times. It would be just too unrealistic to expect that any future visit of his there would coincide with one of her own to Chalcote. And extremely unlikely that she would encounter him anywhere else.

This afternoon would be their final meeting, then. And she would not even be able to suggest that they correspond, despite the fact that they were friends. They were, after all, a single gentleman and a single lady, who had no ties of blood. They could not correspond. Some things were just too improper to be seriously considered.

She left early for her meeting with him. Yet she hurried toward her destination as if she were late. She hurried with eager footsteps and a heavy heart. She did not want the friendship to end. And she resented the fact that it must end just because social convention frowned heavily on any relationship between a man and a woman that did not lead them in due course to the altar.

It was very foolish.

She had no wish whatsoever to go to the altar with Mr. Wade.

But she had every wish in the world to have him as a friend.

She briefly wondered why.

She was very early at the meeting place. At least half an hour early, she estimated, though she had no watch with her. She was going to have a long wait. She did not want to wait. This afternoon was too precious. Their last together.

But as she approached the temple at the top of the hill, he stood up from the stone bench inside it and waited for her to come up to him. He was as unfashionable and as shabby as ever. He was smiling.

His smile warmed her more than the sun.

"You see?" she called gaily. "I have come all this distance and am hardly out of breath."

"My heartiest congratulations," he said.

# 5

SHE WAS ALL IN PINK, EXCEPT FOR HER STRAW BON-
net, and as pretty as the proverbial picture. She
was flushed and bright-eyed, and it was pleasant for a
moment to imagine that she was a woman hurrying to
meet her lover—him.

Pleasant and absurd.

"Since you are not at all breathless," he said, "you will,
of course, not need to rest here for a while. We will
march onward to the rapids, shall we?"

"Ah," she said, laughing. "How ungentlemanly you
are. You have called my bluff." She went past him and
collapsed with exaggerated exhaustion onto the bench.
"You are early."

"And so are you," he said. "Weather like this is not to
be wasted, is it?" He sat down beside her, careful to leave
a few inches of space between them.

"How long are you planning to be here at Highmoor?"
she asked him. "Long? Or will you be leaving soon?"

She was beginning to feel the impropriety, he
guessed. Perhaps she was finding it increasingly difficult
to give reasonable excuses to her relatives for so many
afternoon absences. She was hoping that he would leave

soon so that she would not have to tell him their meetings must end. He felt infinitely sad.

"I will probably be staying for a while," he said. "But—"

"I am leaving tomorrow," she said hurriedly and breathlessly. Her face was turned toward the sky, but her eyes were tightly closed. "I have to return to London with my aunt. Her friend has been housebound by an accident; Aunt Aggy wants to be with her. We will be leaving early in the morning."

He felt panic coil inside him. "The Season will be beginning soon enough," he said. "I daresay you will be happy to be back in town."

She had opened her eyes and was looking down the hill and across the fields and meadows below.

"Yes," she said. "I have many friends there, and more will be arriving every week. And there is always something to do in town. Sir Albert and Lady Boyle will be leaving Chalcote within the week. Jenny and Gabriel will enjoy having their home to themselves again, though they would be far too polite to admit as much even to each other, I would think. Yes, it will be good to be back. I am looking forward to it."

He was memorizing her profile—long-lashed blue eyes, straight little nose, sweetly curving lips, soft skin with a becoming blush of color on her cheeks, shining blond curls beneath the brim of her bonnet, the very feminine though not voluptuous curve of her bosom.

He wondered if he was being hopelessly fanciful, hopelessly romantic, to believe that he would always remember her, always love her.

She turned her head and smiled at him, and it pleased him to imagine that there was a certain bleakness in her eyes. "And you will be able to work without interruption when I am gone," she said.

"Yes." He dared not think of how he was going to feel after she had gone.

"You really are no gentleman." Her smile deepened. "You are supposed to assure me that I have been no bother at all and that you will miss me when I am gone."

"You have been no bother at all," he said. "I will miss you when you are gone."

"And I will miss you," she said. If there had been any wistfulness in her expression, it vanished instantly. "I have never met a landscape gardener before. I did not realize there were such people. I thought one merely sallied outdoors with a spade and a trowel and some flower seeds and set about creating one's garden."

He laughed.

"I thought follies grew up out of the soil—quite accidentally in the most picturesque places," she said. "And in my naiveté, I thought that all lakes and waterfalls and views were created by nature. I did not know there were men who liked to follow in God's footsteps, correcting his mistakes."

He laughed again. "Is that what I am doing?" he asked her. "It sounds rather dangerous for my chances in the hereafter, does it not? Do you think God will be offended?"

She chuckled with him but failed to take her turn in the conversation. They were left, when the laughter ended, looking at each other, a mere few inches apart. For the first time there was an awkwardness between them, a need to fill the silence.

She filled it first. "Where are the rapids?" she asked.

He scrambled to his feet. "A good march away," he said. "I hope your shoes are comfortable." As well as dainty. She had abandoned her half boots today. Her unshod foot, he thought, would fit on the palm of his hand.

"If I get blisters," she said, "I will have a few days of carriage travel in which to nurse them. What a horrid thought. I hate lengthy carriage journeys. One feels at the end of them that every bone in one's body has been jostled into a different position. One is reluctant to peep into a looking glass for fear that one will be unrecognizable." She laughed gaily.

They laughed a great deal during the rest of the afternoon and talked mostly nonsense. They were comfortable and happy together. Oh, yes, and vastly uncomfortable, too, somewhere beneath the surface of their gaiety. It was always very difficult to live through the last event of a good interlude, he thought. One could not enjoy it. One was too aware of the need to enjoy it to the full because there would be no more.

The afternoon was an agony to him.

He could remember sitting at Dorothea's bedside when she was nearing the end—it had come unbelievably quickly. She had been conscious and able to listen and even to talk a little. It had been so hard to talk to her. There had always been the awareness—*these might be the very last words I will ever speak to her.* And she had been good

to him. He had wanted to say something memorable—
not that she would have long in which to remember.

She was the one who had said it—and he had remembered ever since. *I am so very fortunate,* she had whispered
to him over and over again during what had turned out
to be their last hour together. He thought she had meant
that she was fortunate to die while she was still his mistress, before he tired of her. He had been humbled by her
devotion. And so he had told her the big lie, and had
never been sorry. *I love you, my sweet,* he had whispered
back.

Partings were such wrenchingly dreadful things. He
knew by her manner that Samantha did not look forward to this one, but for her, of course, it was a mere
friendship that was ending. She would feel sorrow rather
than agony. And so he had the extra burden during the
afternoon of hiding his own excruciating pain. For three
days he had counted the hours. Now he was counting
minutes, not knowing exactly how many he had left.

She loved the rapids, with their bare, jutting rocks and
the canopy of trees overhead and the sense—created by
the sound of rushing water—of utter seclusion. The
laughter and the bantering stopped for several minutes
while she wandered slowly up and down the rocky bank
and he gazed at her.

"Not a huge waterfall," she said to him at last. "It
would be too much, too overpowering. It is wildness
that is called for here rather than grandeur. But a series of
smaller falls, yes. It would be an improvement—if this

can be improved upon. Oh, it is lovely, Mr. Wade. How I envy the Marquess of Carew his home."

That had been his thought exactly—a series of falls rather than one great one. Something to stand beside and stroll beside. Something to catch the light and shade at different angles.

"I am sorry," she said, looking at him with contrite eyes. "You are the landscaper. I was merely to approve or disapprove your ideas. Now tell me that you planned a huge waterfall and I shall squirm with embarrassment."

"Your mind must be attuned to mine," he said. "You suggested exactly what I had planned."

She set her head to one side in a characteristic gesture that he would always remember about her. It was something she did when she thought of something particularly important to her. "Yes, that is it," she said. "The reason we are friends. We think alike."

"But you do not like sopranos," he said.

"Yes, I do." She smiled. "But I prefer tenors."

They were back to the lightness and the laughter. And the sadness.

He considered asking her back to the house for tea. But they had spent too long on their walk. Besides, he had the feeling that being indoors with her, sipping on their tea, would be awkward this afternoon. He considered taking her to the folly above the lake he had mentioned to her at the house. But it was too late. And again, sitting in such a quiet, secluded spot, there would be awkwardness. He did not believe that this afternoon they would be able to sit through one of their companionable silences.

"It is time for me to go home," she said quietly, the lightness and laughter gone from her voice again.

"Yes," he said. "They will wonder where you are."

It was a long walk back to the stream. He had the impression that she wanted to stride along quickly. But she had to match her pace to his limp. He could have suggested that they part company before reaching it, as she had suggested on two previous occasions, but he did not do so. He could not let her go before he had to, agonizing as these final minutes were.

They walked in silence.

The sun was sparkling off the water of the stream. There were daffodil buds among the trees on the other side. He had not noticed before that they were almost ready to bloom.

She turned to him. "Thank you for these afternoons," she said with formal politeness. "They have been very pleasant."

"Thank *you*." He made her a half-bow. "I hope you have a safe journey. And a pleasurable Season."

"Thank you," she said. "I hope the Marquess of Carew will approve all the renovations you have planned."

She smiled at him.

He smiled at her.

"Well," she said briskly. "Good-bye, Mr. Wade."

"Good-bye, Miss Newman," he said. He thought that she was going to offer him her hand, but she did not. Perhaps she found the thought of touching his right hand distasteful—though he did not really believe it was that.

She turned and tripped lightly across the stepping-stones, holding her skirt high enough that he had a glimpse of her trim ankles above the dainty shoes. He waited for the final moment, schooled his features for it. He had his smile ready and his left hand ready.

She did not turn back. Within moments she was lost among the trees.

He was left feeling that he had been robbed of something infinitely precious. Something quite, quite irreplaceable. He was left feeling emptiness and panic and a pain deeper than any he had felt before, even if he included the year following his "accident" when he was six. This was not a physical pain and he did not know how it was to be healed. Or whether it could be healed.

He swallowed three times against a gurgling in his throat before turning to make his weary way back to Highmoor Abbey.

SHE HAD HUGGED AND kissed the children and left them in the nursery with their nurse. She had hugged Rosalie, though Albert had warned her to be careful not to squash his new offspring and won for himself a look of gentle reproach from his blushing wife. She had shaken hands with him and with Gabriel and then turned both cheeks for the latter's kiss. He had held onto her hand and told her that she must come back at any time her court could spare her and for as long as she wished.

"You are as close as any sister to Jennifer, my dear," he said. "You must not neglect her out of any mistaken idea that you are imposing on our hospitality."

"Thank you," she whispered to him and squeezed his hand tightly.

She hated good-byes. *Hated* them.

And then, just outside the carriage, she watched as Jenny kissed Aunt Aggy and Gabriel handed the older lady inside. Then Samantha hugged Jenny herself.

"I have had a wonderful time here," she said. "Thank you so much for having me. I do wish you were coming to town for the Season. It is going to seem an age."

"I believe," her cousin whispered to her, "I do believe, Sam, that I have good reason for staying away from the bustle of town life this spring. Keep your fingers crossed for me."

"Are you whispering secrets, my love?" Gabriel asked, looking sternly at his wife. "Is she telling you how we seem about to increase the world's population, Samantha?"

They both blushed while he chuckled.

"Allow me," he said, offering Samantha his hand.

And then she was inside the carriage, sitting next to Aunt Aggy, who was dabbing a handkerchief to her eyes and trying her hardest not to snivel. Samantha patted her knee reassuringly.

They were on their way. They both leaned forward to wave. Jenny and Gabriel were standing together on the terrace, his arm about her waist. Albert and Rosalie were in the doorway, her arm linked through his. Sometimes,

Samantha thought, it was hard to know why she distrusted love and marriage so much. But she saw far more marriages in which there was either mutual indifference or open hostility than unions like these two. And love, she knew from experience, was an extremely unpleasant emotion.

She sat back in her seat and closed her eyes. She drew a slow and deep breath. She hated partings, even those that were only temporary.

"There, that is done," her aunt said briskly, blowing her nose rather loudly and putting her handkerchief away inside her reticule. "I always feel fine once I have made my farewells and driven out of sight. I must say we had a very pleasant stay, dear. It is just a pity that there were so few eligible gentlemen for you to meet."

Aunt Agatha was of the undying opinion that Prince Charming himself was about to make an appearance in her niece's life to sweep her off her feet in true fairy-tale tradition.

"I enjoyed the week Francis was here," Samantha said. "He is always good company."

"And he adores you," Aunt Agatha said. "But I cannot like the idea of your marrying a gentleman who favors lavender coats, Samantha."

Samantha laughed.

"It is a great shame," her aunt said, "that the Marquess of Carew was not in residence—yet again. He is a single gentleman and by no means in his dotage, or so I have heard. I have never met him, which seems strange, really, does it not? I believe he must be somewhat reclusive.

Though if that were true, one would expect him to live at home most of the time. Yet he certainly does not do that."

"Perhaps he is unbelievably handsome," Samantha said, "and if I but met him, I would fall wildly in love with him and he with me and we would be wed within the month." She always enjoyed teasing Aunt Aggy, who did not really have much of a sense of humor—mainly because she did not always recognize that she was being teased.

"Well, dear," she said, "I must confess that has been my hope ever since Jennifer married Lord Thornhill and we first came here and discovered that Chalcote marches right alongside Highmoor land. Maybe next time. Though it is altogether possible that before that you will have found the gentleman you dream of. The Season always brings some new faces to town."

They were passing the imposing stone gateposts leading to Highmoor land. Just beyond them, not quite in sight, was the gatehouse. And a mile or more beyond that, Highmoor Abbey. Behind it—a good way behind it—the trees and the stream and the rapids. And to the right of that, the hills and the lake and then the stream again, forming the border between Chalcote and Highmoor.

There was an ache in Samantha's chest that had been there since the afternoon before. It puzzled her. It was not that she did not know its cause. She did. But the ache, the sense of grief, seemed far in excess of the circumstances.

They had been wonderful afternoons—all four of them. Unconventional, carefree afternoons with a companion whose mind was in tune with her own. Not a handsome or in any way attractive companion—not physically, at least. Nothing that would help explain the depression she was feeling at the knowledge that she would never see him again, that they would never again spend such an afternoon together.

She had not even been able to turn back yesterday after crossing the stream to wave to him, as she had done on the other three afternoons. Stupidly, she had been afraid that she was about to cry.

She wished now that she could go back and wave. Have one last look at him.

She leaned forward suddenly and peered through the window. A hedgerow hid it from sight almost immediately. But she had not been mistaken. For the merest moment she had been able to see the abbey in the distance.

She was surprised and utterly mortified a moment later to hear a great hiccup of an inelegant sob and to realize that it had come from her. She bit her upper lip hard enough to draw blood, but she could not stop the terrible ache in her throat or the tears that spilled over onto her cheeks.

She hoped that Aunt Aggy had fallen asleep. But it was much too soon for that.

"Oh, my poor dear," her aunt said, patting her back as Samantha had patted her knee a few minutes earlier. "You and Jennifer are so close that it is a joy to see.

Though I feel for you now when you are driving away from her. And all because I wanted to give dear Sophie some of my company. You will feel better once we have stopped for luncheon and put some distance between us and Chalcote."

"Yes," Samantha said. "I know I will, Aunt Agatha. I am just being foolish."

She felt very guilty.

LIFE QUICKLY BECAME LESS solitary. He let word seep out that he was at home. There were callers—several of them. Thornhill was first, as he had expected, riding over from Chalcote with his friend, Sir Albert Boyle. They were pleasant company, the two of them. Thornhill and the marquess were in the way of being friends now, though there had been too many years between them when they were growing up for them to have been boyhood chums.

He was invited to Chalcote the following evening for dinner and enjoyed the company of his amiable, kind-hearted hosts and their friends. He was amused to see the terror die out of the eyes of the extremely shy Lady Boyle almost as soon as she had been presented to him and realized that he was not an imposing or a forbidding figure, despite the grandeur of his title. He set himself to putting her even more at her ease and found the subject that loosened her tongue and relaxed her tension. Before the evening was over, he felt that he knew her children as well as anyone, though he had not set eyes on them. He guessed that the third, which she was carrying quite visibly despite the discreetly loose folds of her gown, would be no burden to her.

"What a pity it is that you did not arrive home two days sooner, my lord," Thornhill's lady said. "My aunt and my cousin have just returned to London after a three-month stay. I would have so liked for you to have met them."

"Miss Newman is in possession of both youth and beauty," Thornhill said, amusement in his voice. "I believe my wife has matchmaking tendencies, Carew."

"Oh, you wretch!" his lady said in dismay. "I have no such leanings, my lord. I merely thought it would have been pleasant for them to have met you and for you to have met them. Oh, do stop grinning at me, Gabriel. I do believe I am *blushing*."

The marquess had always liked them as a couple. Courteous and well bred as they undoubtedly were, there were frequent glimpses of the informality and deep affection of their personal relationship.

"What Gabe means," Sir Albert said, "is that Jennifer is very close to her cousin and would love nothing better than to have her established permanently on an adjoining estate."

"Oh," the countess said, outraged, "this is the outside of enough. This is infamous. Now I *know* I am blushing. What will you think of us, my lord?"

He laughed. "I am wishing," he said, "that I might have had a look at this paragon. But, alas, it seems that I am too late. It is the story of my life. Lady Boyle, do you find that your children thrive on Yorkshire air? We York-shiremen have thought of bottling it and sending it south at a profit, you know."

The conversation turned into different channels.

And there were other callers, other invitations. The Ogdens had a niece staying with them and clearly had hopes when he came to dinner and was presented to her. But there was such naked horror in her face when he moved into the room and when his gloved right hand became visible to her that he did not embarrass her by engaging her in conversation during the evening more than strict courtesy dictated, much to the disappointment of his hosts.

The solitariness largely disappeared. It might have vanished completely had he wished. There were invitations for all sorts of daytime activities with his peers, as well as to the more formal evening entertainments. But he had always liked to keep to himself much of the time.

He spent most of his days, when there was no rain and sometimes even when there was, tramping about his park. He wandered many times to the lake, trying to let the peace of the place seep into his mind. But he kept looking at the spot where the bridge would be erected and a pavilion built beyond it. And he kept hearing her voice calling it a rain house. He walked out to the rapids and tried to become a part of the utter seclusion of the scene. But he could see her wandering the bank and telling him that there should be a series of waterfalls there rather than one grand one. And he kept seeing her head tip to one side as she told him that that was why they were friends—because they thought alike.

He sat on the stone bench at the top of the hill and set his hand on the seat beside him. But it was so very empty. And so very cold. And solitariness there became naked loneliness.

He wandered down to the stream and the stepping-stones across to Thornhill's land. He looked across at the blooming daffodils and imagined her disappearing among the trees in her pink dress and spencer and her straw bonnet. But she did not look back. He had smiles to give her and a hand with which to acknowledge her.

But she did not look back.

He sat beside the fire in his study, gazing at the empty chair at the other side. The very empty chair. And he could hear her asking what had happened—had it been an accident, or had he been born this way? But he could not bring her back to tell her the truth, instead of the lie he had always told. Not that he would tell the truth even if she were sitting there now. . . .

He found he could no longer work in his study. He had to take his books upstairs with him. He found that it had not been such a good idea to bring her into the house after all. She haunted it.

He rarely drank, except for a social drink with guests or a host. He could not remember a time when he had been drunk. But he got thoroughly foxed one night, sitting in his study with a decanter of brandy, staring at the empty chair, becoming more bedeviled with self-pity with each mouthful.

Beauty and the beast. The only way he might stand even a remote chance with her was to reveal his identity and hope that it would lure her into an interest for him that went beyond friendship. But then he would despise her—and himself for setting out such lures and taking advantage of them.

Beauty and the beast. She was more lovely than any woman he had seen or dreamed of. It was a beauty that went beyond the merely physical. There was sunshine in her and warmth and intelligence and laughter.

He did not realize he was drunk until he got to his feet to go up to bed and found himself on his hands and knees, the room spinning wildly about him. He did not know the effects of drunkenness until he was lying on his bed—somehow he had called his valet and that astonished individual had helped him upstairs and undressed him—and found himself in imminent danger of spinning off into space. He clung to the outer edges of the mattress with both hands—even his right. Then he disgraced himself utterly by not making it to the close stool in time before retching up all his insides.

It was late the following day—very late—when he made his decision.

He usually stayed away from London during the height of the Season. This year would be an exception. He was going to London. He was going to see her again even if she did not see him. He did not know why he had not thought of it before. Why not torture himself further? The pain surely could not be any worse anyway.

And the Season was about to begin. She had been gone for a whole month.

Yes, he thought, happy now that his life had turned in a definite direction—even if it turned out, as it very likely would, that it was a disastrous direction.

Yes, he was going to London.

## 6

SHE WAS ENJOYING SPRING IN TOWN. SHE ALWAYS did. Life took on its familiar routine and became busier every week, as more and more of her friends and acquaintances arrived from the country for the new session of Parliament and for the Season.

There were visits to modistes and extended sessions for fittings and viewings of fashion plates and the choosing of fabrics. There were shopping trips for slippers and fans and gloves and bonnets and a dozen and one other things. There were visits to the library and the galleries and walks in the parks and drives. There were calls to be paid and received.

· There was her court to receive—she often enjoyed a private smile over Gabriel's description of her admirers. Lord Francis Kneller, the first to call, informed her that after her seventh Season—she had been rash enough to give him the number—a young lady became officially known as a spinster and had to retire to a country cottage with a trunkful of large white mobcaps.

"You had better avoid the ignominy, Samantha," he said languidly, fingering a jeweled snuffbox but deciding against opening it, "and marry me."

"The choice is between a trunkful of mobcaps and

you with your lavender and pink evening clothes, Francis?" she said, tapping her cheek thoughtfully with one finger. "What a shockingly difficult choice. I shall think seriously upon the matter during the Season and give you my answer later. Shall I?"

"The choice will be easier," he said, "once you have seen my new turquoise coat. Satin, you know, with a silver waistcoat and turquoise embroidery. Together, they will bowl you right off your feet."

She laughed and tapped him affectionately on the arm. She wondered how he would react if she accepted his proposal. He would be deeply shocked. Probably horrified. He played the game with her because he knew it was safe. She doubted that Francis would ever marry, unless it was for dynastic reasons. He was too indolent and too frivolous.

"This I can hardly wait to see," she said.

The others all came, too, one by one, as they returned to town. Mr. Wishart came for tea, bringing a large bouquet of spring flowers with him. Mr. Carruthers escorted her to the library and appeared surprised when she took home with her the texts of two plays instead of novels. In Mr. Carruthers's experience ladies read only novels. Sir Robin Talbot took her to the National Gallery and they had a very pleasant afternoon conversing about art. Mr. Nicholson took her driving in the park and made her a marriage offer—again. She refused him—again. He was perhaps the only one of her suitors who seriously wished to marry her, she believed, and yet he always cheerfully accepted defeat. Perhaps he did not really want very badly to marry her. Surely if he did he would have to retire with something of a broken heart after she had refused him so many times.

It was all very pleasant. She was glad to be in London, glad to be busy again, glad to be back in her familiar world. And of course soon the Season would be in full swing, and there would be scarcely a moment in which to wonder if one was happy or sad, enthusiastic or bored, exuberant or exhausted. There would be more invitations to choose among than there were hours in the day.

It was only very occasionally that she literally stopped in her tracks and frowned at a fleeting feeling. She could never quite get her mind around it. It was not a pleasant feeling. It was rather as if the bottom fell out of her stomach—or out of her world—and she was about to fall in after it. And yet she always jolted back to reality before it could happen and before she could even understand what had caused the feeling.

Sometimes if she was walking early in the park, or if she was down by the Serpentine, she would see children tripping along in front of their parents or nurses and the feeling would be there. Was it that she missed Michael and Mary and even Rosalie Boyle's girls? Perhaps. She was fond of them. She did not want children of her own, of course. She did not want that emotional tie. Or sometimes the park was more deserted than usual, and she felt almost as if she were in the country. With a hill and a lake and rapids close by. She was missing Chalcote? Yes, of course she was. It was a beautiful estate, and it was owned by Gabriel and Jenny, two of the dearest people in her life.

Sometimes there were not even clues that strong. Sometimes she was laughing with her friends over some nonsense—she rarely talked seriously with her friends, especially the gentlemen. Or sometimes she was shopping, involved in the purchase of some quite unnecessary frivolity. Or sometimes she just remembered Francis's joke about the seven years and what awaited her afterward.

She never knew what brought on the feeling. It always came quite without warning and disappeared so soon afterward that any person who happened to be with her at the time did not even notice that anything had happened.

She thought sometimes of Highmoor and Mr. Wade. Not often. For some reason she did not stop to analyze, she did not like to remember those afternoons. Doing so depressed her. They had been very pleasant and he had been very pleasant and there was an end to the matter. Those afternoons would never be repeated, and she would never see him again. It did not matter. It was a brief, unimportant episode from her past that should be pleasant to remember but was not. Perhaps later. Perhaps at some other time.

She wished—absurdly, she still wished—that she could go back and change just one moment out of those meetings. She wished she had turned back to wave at the end. If her final memory of him was of seeing him standing at the other side of the stream, his hand raised, his face lit by his lovely smile, perhaps she could put the whole memory away. Perhaps she would not feel slightly distressed every time she remembered.

It seemed that warm friendship was not for her any more than love was. That made her a very—shallow person, did it not?

LADY ROCHESTER'S BALL WAS recognized, by all agreement, as the main opening event of the Season. It was bound to be an impossible squeeze and therefore an unqualified success. Samantha looked forward to it. There was always an excitement about beginning the social whirl yet again. And perhaps there would be someone new. . . . Not that she needed new beaux. It was just that sometimes interest flagged. She felt instantly contrite. Some young ladies of *ton* would give half their fortunes for even one or two of the gentlemen who paid court to Samantha Newman.

Hyde Park was becoming crowded during the afternoons for what was known as the fashionable hour. And the unusually fine weather that they were being graced with was bringing everyone out in force. Perhaps the biggest crowd of all turned out on the afternoon of the day before the Rochester ball. Samantha rode up beside Mr. Nicholson in his new curricle, twirling a confection of a new parasol above her head, smiling gaily and with genuine enjoyment at the people about her. It was a good thing they had not come with serious intentions for a drive, she thought. The press of vehicles and horses about them on the paths was thick, and the intention of most riders was to observe and converse rather than to exercise their horses.

She spoke with friends and acquaintances to whom they could draw close and waved to others who were too far distant.

"How very pleasant this is," she commented to Mr. Nicholson during a brief respite, while one group of acquaintances drew away and another was still approaching. "I am so happy that the Season is starting again."

"My only complaint," he said, "is that I have to share you with the whole world, Miss Newman."

"But I could think of no more congenial companion with whom to make the drive to and from the park, sir," she said. She laughed gaily from sheer exuberance and gave her parasol an exceptionally enthusiastic twirl.

It was at that precise moment that her eyes met those of a gentleman some distance farther on in the crowd and she froze. Utterly. To ice. She forgot to breathe.

The most handsome man in the world, Jenny had once called him. And she had agreed, though she had called him cold. His hair was more blond than her own—almost silver-blond. His eyes were as blue as her own, but a paler shade. His features and his physique were perfect. A Greek god. The angel Gabriel, she and Jenny had called him before they had known that the *other* man—the one they had called his counterpart, Lucifer—had been christened Gabriel. A strange, coincidental irony.

Her eyes met his now across the milling crowd of humanity. He was as beautiful and as dazzling as ever, though she had not set eyes on him in six years. He had been out of the country, banished by his father.

Her eyes met his and held. He looked back appreciatively and touched the brim of his hat with his riding whip.

". . . trying to rival the sun and succeeding quite admirably. Beautiful ladies ought not to be allowed to wear yellow." It was the languid voice of Lord Francis Kneller, who was leaning from his horse's back and draping an arm along the side of the curricle. "I am going to challenge Nicholson to pistols at dawn for luring you into his curricle while the rest of us male mortals must ride alone."

He had disappeared in the crowd. Breath shuddered back into her. "Nonsense, Francis," she said without her usual spirit, unable to think of anything witty to say in return.

He sat upright again and grinned at her. "Crawled out at the wrong side of the bed this morning, did you, pet?" he asked. "*Nonsense, Francis.*" He imitated her sharp tone.

"I say," Lord Hawthorne, his young cousin, exclaimed. He was a young gentleman who had hovered in the outer circle of Samantha's court all last Season, though he must be two or three years her junior. "Frank just pointed out Rushford to me—the notorious Rushford. Did anyone know that he was back?"

Samantha swallowed convulsively. Of course. She had heard that his father had died. But she always thought of Lionel—when she could not stop herself from thinking about him—as Viscount Kersey. He was the Earl of Rushford now, and had been for a couple of years.

"He appeared last week," Mr. Nicholson said. "One would not have thought he would have the nerve. I suppose he is to be admired for having the courage to appear here again after such a shocking scandal. But it must have been years ago."

*Six.* It had been six years ago.

"I hear he is being received," Lord Hawthorne said. "And I hear he has appeared at White's." There was faint envy in his voice. Lord Hawthorne was still waiting for his entrée to the hallowed halls of the most prestigious gentlemen's club in London.

"The ladies will be intrigued," Mr. Nicholson said. "They always are intrigued by the very gentlemen they should spurn. And, of course, he always was a handsome devil. Oh, do beg pardon, Miss Newman. Did you ever meet the Earl of Rushford? He was Viscount Kersey until a year or so ago."

Samantha was feeling somewhat dizzy. She had always wondered—with a fascinated sort of dread—how it would feel to see him again. She had hoped that the shame surrounding his departure from England would keep him away for the rest of his life. But he was back. And she had seen him again. She felt—dizzy.

"It was Miss Newman's cousin—the present Lady Thornhill—who was at the heart of the scandal," Lord

Francis said quietly, without any of the usual bored cynicism in his voice. "I am sure Miss Newman will not wish to be reminded of the gentleman, Ted. Do you suppose that the flowers in Miss Tweedsmuir's bonnet have denuded someone's whole garden? Or do they come from a very large garden, perhaps, and have merely emptied out a corner of it. They must weigh half a ton."

"It is a very modish bonnet, Francis," Samantha said, twirling her parasol again, "and doubtless the envy of half the ladies in the park. She is, after all, drawing a great deal of attention her way, and what more could any lady ask for?" She was deeply grateful for the deliberate change of topic.

"It is a blatant ploy," he said, all ennui again, "to have people look at the bonnet and not at the face beneath it. It is a pity she cannot wear it into ballrooms."

"Francis," Samantha said sharply, "you are wickedly unkind."

"Not to you, my sweet," he said, "except to object to your yellow gown, which makes the sunshine look dim—especially when one looks at the face and figure of the lady inside the gown."

He heaped several more lavish compliments on her during the next minute or so, while Lord Hawthorne looked on in envy and Mr. Nicholson looked impatient to move off. And then they were indeed moving forward, until Lady Penniford and Lord Danton stopped in their barouche to ask Samantha how her aunt and her aunt's friend did.

Samantha no longer looked about her to any distance. She was afraid to look. It took all the effort of her training and experience to keep smiling and conversing, to give Mr. Nicholson and everyone to whom they talked no inkling of the seething upheaval that was churning inside her.

She was home half an hour later, though it seemed ten times as long as that. She ran lightly upstairs, was relieved to find the drawing room empty, was even more relieved to receive no answer to her tap on the door of her aunt's sitting room, and rushed on to her own rooms. Aunt Aggy must still be with Lady Sophia, who was making the most of her invalid state now that there were plenty of friends in town to visit her and sit with her.

Samantha kicked off her slippers in her dressing room and tossed her bonnet in the direction of the nearest chair. She peeled off her gloves and sent them flying after the bonnet. Then she hurried into her bedchamber and threw herself facedown across her bed.

He was back. She clutched fistfuls of the bedcover in both hands and held tight. She had seen him again. And he had seen her. And had acknowledged her. He had not been at all aghast. He had looked at her *appreciatively*. She had seen enough admiration in men's eyes to have recognized it in his.

How dared he.

After what had happened.

He had been Jenny's betrothed. Jenny had been besotted with him, ecstatic to be officially betrothed to him after five years of loving him and having an unofficial understanding with him. Samantha had not particularly liked him. She had always thought that there was a coldness behind the undeniably handsome exterior. Until he had solicited her hand for a set at one ball, that was, and led her outside and down into the garden, presumably because he was upset that Jenny had just spent half an hour with Lord Thornhill. And he had kissed her.

She had been eighteen years old. It had been her first kiss. He had been the most handsome man of her experience. It had been an impossibly tempting combination. She had tumbled into love with him. And had been pained by it, and by his tragic claim to love her while he was bound to marry Jenny, and by guilt because Jenny had loved him so dearly and had been so very happy with her dreams of a future with him. He had suggested that *she* try to do something to end the betrothal, since honor forbade him to do so.

She had been so very naive. She had suppressed her uneasiness, her feeling that it was not very honorable to suggest that the woman he claimed to love do something to end his betrothal to her cousin and closest friend. She had been hopelessly in love, though at least she had not consented to do that for him. He had been forced to do it another way, forging an incriminating letter from Gabriel to Jenny and having the letter read publicly to a whole ballroomful of members of the *ton*. He had brought terrible ruin on Jenny and had forced Gabriel to rush her into a marriage that neither of them wanted— at the time.

Even then, poor, naive girl that she was—though she had not known then of the forgery—Samantha had believed that he would come to claim her. She had maneuvered a brief meeting with him in the hallway outside yet another ballroom—and he had laughed at her and assured her that she must have misunderstood what had been merely gallantry on his part. He had dared to look at her with amused sympathy.

That was the last time she had seen him—until this afternoon. His father had discovered the truth and had forced him to make it publicly known, so that Jenny's reputation might be restored. And then his father had banished him.

She had hated him from that day to this. Hated him for the terrible thing he had done to Jenny, hated him for ruining her own first Season and for toying with the fragile emotions of an innocent and naive young girl. She had hated him for humiliating her so. And she had hated him as a genuinely evil man.

And yet she knew that there was a thin line between hatred and love. For six years she had hated him and feared—deeply feared—that perhaps she still loved him. For six years she had hoped fiercely that her feelings would never be put to the test, that he would never come home to England, that she would never see him again. For six years she had distrusted love, though she had seen signs about her that it could bring happiness. Jenny and Gabriel loved each other and were happy. Rosalie and Albert loved and were happy. But love for her was something to be dreaded, something to be avoided at all costs.

Now she had seen him again, shining and beautiful like an angel, even though she knew that he had the heart of the devil. And her own heart had turned over inside her. She would see him again, she supposed. It was highly probable. And from the way he had looked at her, without withdrawing his eyes hastily and in some confusion, it seemed altogether possible that he would not avoid a direct meeting. They might meet again. He might speak to her.

She was terribly afraid. Afraid of the evil. Afraid that somehow he still had power over her.

She thought fleetingly of returning to Chalcote. Gabriel had said she might go there whenever she wished. Perhaps, she thought . . . perhaps Mr. Wade would still be at Highmoor. But she knew she would not go. Could not go. If he was back in England, this thing must be faced sooner or later. Better sooner than later. Perhaps it would not be as bad as she expected. Perhaps, if she could once meet him face-to-face, she would find that, after all, he was just a gentleman she did not like.

Perhaps if she stayed she could be freed at last.

She knew it was a forlorn hope.

IT HAD BEEN WORTH coming, he convinced himself, despite the fact that he had left Highmoor just at the time of year he usually enjoyed being there most of all. He liked to be there when the fields were being sown on his farms. He liked working alongside his laborers. They had stopped looking at him askance, first because he was an aristocrat and was not expected to soil his hands with real dirt, and second because he was a cripple. They had accepted the fact that he was somewhat eccentric.

And he liked to supervise the work of preparing the park for its summer splendor. This year, more than most others, he had had plans for major renovations that would have taken all summer to effect.

Perhaps next year.

It was time he spent a few months of the spring in London, doing his duty as a member of the House of Lords. And it was pleasant to see faces he had not seen in years—male faces, almost exclusively—and to renew old acquaintances. He even ventured to White's two or three times, though he had never been one to spend his days at a club. It was going to be good to have the chance to enjoy concerts and plays in plenty. It was good to spend some time at Jackson's again to hone his skills, though it was more difficult to schedule times alone with the pugilist himself. And he was able to do some fencing again. He had tried it almost ten years ago now, out of sheer obstinacy, after his father had observed that that was one skill at least that he must never think of mastering. Balance on one's feet was of paramount importance to the exercise, as was skill with one's hands. He was naturally right-handed and had never achieved anything more than an awkward competency with his left. His handwriting looked from a distance like the scrawl of a spider.

But he had persisted and sometimes won bouts against less experienced swordsmen. Never against the best, of course, though he had once surprised one of them with an undeniable hit. But he was able to give even the best of them a run for their money.

It was something he enjoyed. Any conquest against his handicaps was a personal triumph.

No, it had not been a waste of his time to come to town. He did not call upon Samantha, however, though he considered doing so each day of his first week in town. Why not send in his card, after all, and pay a courtesy call on her? He even had cards made that omitted his title. But he never did call.

He saw her once on Bond Street, quite by accident. She was on the arm of a very tall, rather thin, very fashionably dressed gentleman. They were both laughing and looking very merry. The Marquess of Carew ducked into the doorway of a bootmaker's shop and found that his heart was hammering against his ribs and his mind was contemplating murder. She did not see him.

He went home, feeling very foolish.

He caught sight of her another day, coming out of the library with another gentleman, more handsome though not quite as fashionable as the first. Again she was smiling and looking as if she held the sunshine inside herself and was allowing some of it to spill over. Again he managed to duck out of sight before she saw him.

He considered going back home on the evening of that day. But he had made the long journey only days before, and the Season had not even started yet. He could not be so cowardly.

His arrival in town had been noted. A small but steady trickle of invitations had begun to arrive. He had been invited to Lady Rochester's ball. Friends had told him that it was expected to be the first great squeeze of the Season. Would not everyone be surprised and even shocked if he were to turn up at a *ball*! Though he knew of many gentlemen and even a few ladies who attended balls without ever intending to dance at them. There were always rooms for cards and rooms for sitting and gossiping or for eating and drinking.

She would almost certainly be at the ball.

If it was a great squeeze, it would be possible for him to go there and see her without being seen. He would be able to see her dressed in all the finery of a *ton* ball. He would be able to watch her dance. Without himself being seen.

But he dismissed the thought. Those other two times, though he had hidden from sight, had been accidental encounters. He had not planned to see her. If he went to the ball deliberately to see her and hide from her, he would be in the nature of a spy, a peeping Tom, a stalker. It was not a pleasant notion.

No, if he went to the ball . . . *if*? Was he seriously considering it, then? If he went, it must be with the intention of letting her see him, of greeting her, of letting her know who he was. It would be better than calling on her at Lady Brill's house. It would be a briefer meeting—he could not, after all, ask her to dance and ensure that he would have her to himself for half an hour. It would be a more public meeting. It would be ideal.

And she should know who he was. Perhaps she had already forgotten him, but he felt guilty for having deceived her.

If she knew who he was and if he continued to appear at some of the *ton* events of the Season, perhaps they could continue their friendship. Perhaps occasionally he could call on her, take her for a drive, invite her to sit in his box at the theater with him.

Perhaps life need not be as bleak as he had thought for the last month and a half that it must be.

But would it be enough—even assuming she would be willing to continue the acquaintance? Would it not be better to have nothing of her than to have an occasional and casual friendship?

And what if his earlier fears were confirmed? What if she showed another type of interest in him once she knew his real identity? But it was a fear unworthy of him. It was not something she would do. He must trust his good opinion of her.

How would he be able to stand seeing her sparkle at other, more handsome gentlemen? How would he cope with the jealousy?

He would cope because he was a mature man, he thought, and because his eyes were open to reality. He would cope because he must.

Yes, he decided finally just the evening before the Rochester ball, when a couple of friends asked him teasingly if he had accepted his invitation. Yes, he was going to go. He was going to see her. And he was going to let her see him.

"Yes, of course," he said to a grinning Lord Gerson and an interested Duke of Bridgwater. "I would not miss it for worlds."

Lord Gerson slapped the duke on the back and roared with laughter. "This I must see," he said. "All the mamas with eligible hopefuls will fall off their chairs, Carew."

"Now this is fascinating," his grace said, raising his quizzing glass and having the gall to peer through it at the marquess. "One might almost imagine that there was one particular eligible hopeful, Hart, my dear chap."

"This is rich." Lord Gerson launched into renewed guffaws of mirth.

"I shall call here with my carriage?" his grace suggested. "We must go together, the three of us. Moral support and all that."

"Yes," the marquess said, quelling the ridiculous, schoolboyish panic. "Yes, do that, Bridge, will you?"

## 7

*A*SQUEEZE IT WAS INDEED. THEY KNEW AS SOON as they approached Hanover Square that Lady Rochester's ball must already be pronounced an unqualified success. They could not even get onto the square with the carriage, but must sit and wait a full twenty minutes while it crawled forward behind a long line of others. An equally long line soon formed behind them.

"Louisa will be very gratified," Lady Brill said, uttering probably the understatement of the evening. Lady Rochester would be more than ecstatic.

There was a special excitement about arriving at a *ton* ball that never quite faded, even at the beginning of a seventh year, Samantha found. Even the tedious wait merely built the feeling of anticipation, that breathless, heart-pounding notion that tonight might be the beginning of the rest of one's life, that something might happen during the coming hours to change the course of one's life.

It almost never happened that way, of course. One saw the same faces, conversed with the same people, danced the same dances every time. But the feeling never quite went away.

Every window of the mansion appeared to be brightly

lit. A carpet had been rolled out, down the shallow stone steps and across the pavement, so that those alighting from their carriages might have the illusion of never having had to step outdoors. There were smartly liveried footmen everywhere, discreetly busy. And so much finery and priceless jewelry displayed on so many elegant and not-so-elegant persons of *ton* that one immediately lost any pretensions to personal conceit.

Samantha smiled and stepped out of the carriage. She was in her own milieu and felt thoroughly at home in it. But she could not help remembering her very first ball during her first Season. There had been so much excitement, so much anxiety, so much hope. So much innocence. She would not go back, she thought now, even if she could. There were crowds of people in the hall, talking rather too loudly and laughing rather too heartily. And there was a solid line of people on the stairs, waiting to ascend and pass along the receiving line into the ballroom. There were numerous young girls in the crowd, dressed in the uniform of virginal white gown and white accessories. The most extravagant jewelry any of them wore was a string of pearls. They looked everything she had once been—the poor girls.

"We do not need to go to the ladies' withdrawing room," Lady Brill said after looking over her charge—if the term still applied to a lady of four-and-twenty. "You look quite as handsome as you have ever looked, my dear. I do not know how you do it. I like the colors."

Samantha did too. The silver lace overdress sparkled in the light of candles and gave a smoky hue to the dark green silk gown beneath it. Apart from three ruffles at the hem, her low-necked, short-sleeved gown was unadorned. She had learned from experience that beautiful fabrics and skilled workmanship ought to be left to speak for themselves. She always avoided plumes in her hair, too, though they were very fashionable and Aunt Aggy had told her that she needed the height they would lend her. But she preferred the simplicity of a few flowers in her hair or a ribbon threaded through her curls. Tonight it was a silver ribbon. And silver gloves and slippers. And a fan that by happy chance matched the green of her gown.

"You ought not to have been issued an invitation, Samantha," a familiar, rather bored voice said from behind her shoulder. "Lady Rochester should have more wisdom. You will outshine every other lady present and ruin the evening for every last one of them."

She smiled in amusement as she turned. "Oh," she said appreciatively, "you were quite right, Francis. The turquoise is quite, quite splendid. I am impressed."

He made her an elegant bow. "And would you marry a man who wears turquoise?" he asked, causing a large dowager to turn her head, adorned with six nodding purple plumes, sharply in his direction.

"Definitely not," Samantha said. "I should be afraid of being outshone, Francis. Besides, you might always backslide into pink or lavender, and I should feel cheated. Are you going to offer us your arms and keep us company on the stairs?"

"How could I resist making myself the envy of every

male in the house by having the two loveliest ladies to escort?" he asked, offering one arm to Samantha and the other to Lady Brill.

Samantha laughed gaily. Lady Brill tutted and took the offered arm.

Another fifteen minutes passed before they finally stepped into the ballroom. It was the usual scene. The floor itself was empty, in anticipation of the dancing. Crowds lined all four walls, talking and gossiping and laughing. Several people, mostly in couples, promenaded about, looking for acquaintances or merely hoping to be seen and admired. The members of the orchestra were tuning their instruments. The floral decorations, all in varying shades of pink, were hardly noticeable in comparison with the gorgeous clothes and jewels of the gathered guests.

Samantha was soon in conversation with two of her lady friends and a gathering army of gentlemen acquaintances. Hers was the usual court, though Mr. Bains brought with him a neighbor from the country, a tall gentleman who was handsome even without the distinguishing feature of bright red hair. He bowed to all three ladies, but somehow maneuvered matters that he was soon in conversation with Samantha and signing her card for a quadrille later in the evening.

Perhaps the Season would have something new to offer, she thought. A new beau. Did she need a new beau? She never knew quite what to do with the old ones, beyond teasing them and flirting with them and making it quite clear to all of them that it was just a game they played, that she was not in the business of seeking a husband. She never had any wish to lead a man on only to dash his honest and sincere hopes.

She was a little apprehensive tonight. Well, perhaps more than a little. She was afraid that Lionel, Lord Rushford, would be there. But surely not. Somehow he had found the impudence—or the courage, depending how one looked upon it—to return to London and even to ride in Hyde Park during the fashionable hour. But those things he was free to do. There had never been any criminal charges against him, after all. No one could forbid him to live and move about in England. His father was dead now and no longer held the purse strings. But surely he would not receive any invitations to *ton* events. . . .

*I hear he is being received.*

She could hear Lord Hawthorne saying those words. But surely not by most people, and surely in no very public manner.

Even if he had been invited and even if he had accepted, he would surely keep his distance from her. He would not wish for the embarrassment of a reacquaintance. He had not approached her in the park yesterday, after all. Even though he had looked his fill.

She need not feel apprehensive, she had been telling herself all day. But she was. It was a great relief to glance all about the ballroom and see beyond any doubt that he was not there. There was no possibility that she could have missed him if he had been there. He was so very blond and so very beautiful. One could not miss Lionel even in the largest crowd.

She danced the opening set of country dances with Sir Robin Talbot. He was a skilled, graceful dancer. She always enjoyed being partnered by him. It was an energetic dance. She was breathless and felt flushed at the end of it. Briefly she remembered her boast that after all the walking and hill climbing at Highmoor she would be fitter than anyone else in a London ballroom. But she pushed the thought aside again before she could even smile over it. It brought on one of those feelings of falling into a deep depression.

She fanned herself as she talked with a crowd of acquaintances between sets. She was laughing at poor Lord Hawthorne, whom Francis was teasing because he had just danced with a particularly pretty young lady who was making her debut this year. Lord Hawthorne was blushing behind his exaggeratedly high starched collar points and assuring his cousin that indeed he did not have intentions of offering for the chit tomorrow morning. How absurd!

"Though she is uncommonly pretty, Frank," he added, causing a fresh burst of laughter from the group.

Someone touched Samantha lightly on her gloved arm. Even as she turned with a smile to greet the new arrival, she felt Francis's hand close protectively about her other elbow and heard him utter a muffled oath.

"It *is*," a startlingly familiar voice said. "I could scarce believe that after so many years you could be even more lovely than you were as a girl."

She had the sensation of falling into his pale blue eyes as they gazed into hers with open appreciation. There was almost no other sensation at all. Other sounds and sights around her receded, and with them all awareness of where she was. There were only his eyes. Only him.

"Rushford," a voice said in coldly courteous acknowledgment from a long way away. "A famous squeeze, is it not? This is my set, I believe, Samantha."

*Lionel.*

He inclined his head to her without removing his eyes from hers. "Samantha," he said. "How are you?"

She heard someone speak. A female voice, quite cool, quite in possession of itself. "I am quite well, I thank you, my lord."

"I saw you in the park yesterday," he said. "I could not believe it was you. But now I can see that indeed it was. And is."

"Samantha?" It was Francis's voice, unusually curt. "The sets are forming."

"You are engaged to dance with Miss Crowther," she heard herself say.

"Devil take it," Francis said, and then apologized to the ladies for his language and released her arm to stride away.

"Dare I hope," Lionel, Lord Rushford asked, "that you have this set free, Samantha? Will you honor me by dancing it with me?"

"Thank you," she said. Even though she was still looking into his eyes and the world was still in recession, her mind somehow told her that she had not indeed promised the set to anyone, though one of her court was bound to lead her out. She never had to miss any dances at any ball.

She had placed her hand in his and stepped away from the group before the world came jolting back. A world that seemed focused all on her. Or on him, rather, she supposed. It had been a very public humiliation, though she had not been there to see it. His father, who had read publicly the letter Gabriel was supposed to have written to Jenny while she was betrothed to Lionel, had made his son read an equally public confession and apology before leaving for the Continent.

He was the focus now of fascinated stares and of an excited buzz of conversation. And she had agreed to dance with him. It was a waltz. Of all the dances it might have been, it was a waltz. She wondered how many people would remember that it had been her cousin who had been at the heart of the scandal with him. Yet she was according him the public courtesy of dancing with him.

"You are more lovely than you were," he said as he set one hand against the back of her waist and clasped her hand with his. "Far more lovely, Samantha. You are a woman now. I cannot take my eyes off you."

She could feel his hands on her. She could feel his body heat, though they touched nowhere else. She felt surrounded by him. Suddenly she felt suffocated by him. She smiled from sheer instinct.

"Thank you," she said curtly. She tried to look about

her, to detach herself from the aura of his powerful presence, but everywhere about her she met curious eyes. She stopped looking.

"I came home," he said. "I had to come."

"I daresay one would become homesick after being out of the country for a number of years," she said. "It is only natural."

"I was homesick," he said softly, tightening his hand almost imperceptibly against her back. "But for people more than places. For one particular person, whom I treated unpardonably because I would not have her share my disgrace. For one person I have never forgotten for a single day, Samantha."

She looked into his eyes in shock, forgetting for one moment to smile. His silver-blond hair seemed thicker and shinier than ever. For the first time she noticed that he was dressed in pale blue and silver and white and looked like a prince from a fairy tale. But his words and their obvious meaning had jolted her finally out of the spell his sudden appearance had cast on her. She felt a welcoming fury build inside her as she smiled again.

"How gratified that person will be, my lord," she said, "if she is able to forgive you and if she has not long forgotten you."

His eyes became almost warm. "Ah," he said, and the word was almost a caress. "Yes. You have grown up indeed, Samantha. I had hoped for it. You are angry and unforgiving and I am glad of it. You should not forgive me easily."

"Or ever?" She made her eyes sparkle.

He smiled back, something Lionel had rarely done in those weeks when she had seen him frequently in his capacity as Jenny's betrothed. Treacherously, she felt a lurching of desire deep in her womb. And an equal recoiling in horror. Could he really believe her naive enough to become entangled in his web again? When she knew how cruel and callous and self-serving he was?

Had he set himself that challenge?

And was there any possibility at all that he would win?

She grew cold with terror.

They danced in silence after that—for twenty interminable minutes. He waltzed superbly, never missing a step, never allowing her to collide with any other dancer, never slowing their progress about the perimeter of the ballroom or missing the sweep of a full twirl. His hand was firm and steady in hers. His shoulder was firmly muscled. His cologne was subtle and faultlessly masculine. She could remember his kiss—her first—openmouthed, skilled, persuasive. He was the only man she had ever kissed who had used his tongue as well as his lips. A practiced seducer. Was it any wonder that she had fallen hard for him and had her heart quite shattered by his ultimate rejection? She had been a mere girl, inexperienced and naive.

No longer.

She danced and smiled. And tried to think of her beaux and her friends and of Jenny and the much-wanted third child she and Gabriel were now definitely expecting and of Lady Sophia, whose leg was miraculously healing now that the Season was beginning and there was much to be seen and done beyond the confines of her own home. She tried to think of Highmoor and the view from the hill to the abbey, spoiled only by the presence of a single tree on the slope. She thought of Mr. Wade and pushed the image away again, or she tried to.

And she felt Lionel's magnificence and his attractiveness. She knew she hated him and despised him—despised him anew since their brief conversation at the beginning of the waltz. But she also wondered in fascination and dread how his kiss would feel now that she had had more experience herself. And how his body would feel against her own slightly more knowledgeable one—though only slightly. She was still woefully ignorant for a woman of her age. She wondered . . . No, no she did not. She did not wonder that at all. She was not given to lascivious thoughts.

She wondered if the waltz would ever end.

It did. But by the end of it she felt breathless and bruised and bewildered and unhappy. Desperately unhappy. Unhappy to the point of tears. He returned her to her group—Aunt Aggy was away in the card room, the necessity for close chaperonage long in the past—and bowed over her hand before thanking her for the honor and taking his leave of her.

Francis was looking uncommonly belligerent but showed his good breeding by resisting talking about what he clearly wanted to talk about. Francis, of course,

had been a close friend of Gabriel's at the time of the ca-
tastrophe. It was only later that he had become one of
her beaux—though only because she was safe to flirt
with and propose marriage to occasionally, she knew.

"The Earl of Rushford?" Helena Cox said, her eyes as
wide as the proverbial saucers. "I have heard all about
him. And you *danced* with him, Sam? I do not care what
they say of him." She giggled. "He is *gorgeous*."

Mr. Wishart coughed and Helena giggled again. "Oh,
and you too, sir," she said. "Of course."

"Gorgeous Wishart," Sir Robin said. "It sounds altogether more distinguished than mere George Wishart,
does it not? We must let it be generally known that
George has officially changed his name."

"You asked for it, Gorgeous," Francis said in a falsetto
voice when Mr. Wishart protested hotly.

She could stand it no longer. There was no air left in
the ballroom, and what little there was was hot and per-
fumed and nauseating. There was no space in which to
move. And the noise was deafening. She would faint—or
worse, vomit—if she stood where she was for a moment
longer.

"Excuse me," she said hastily and turned to hurry
away. She wormed her way through the crowds, occasionally having a brief path cleared by someone who saw
her coming, once or twice having to stop for a moment
to return the greeting of an acquaintance. The doors
seemed a mile away.

She reached them eventually and hurried out into the

comparative coolness and emptiness of the landing beyond. And was forced to stop when someone stepped into her path and did not move out of it. She looked up into his face, not very far above her own.

Never, never in her whole life had she felt such a rush of pure happiness.

LORD GERSON AND THE Duke of Bridgwater were greeted with refined enthusiasm by Lady Rochester, who had stayed on with her husband at the entrance to the ballroom to greet latecomers. She smiled with bland courtesy at the Marquess of Carew until his name was mentioned. Then her eyes widened and filled with interest.

"The elusive marquess," she said. "Welcome." But she made the mistake of extending her hand to him instead of merely curtsying. She glanced down in hasty, quickly veiled shock at the thin, gloved, hooked hand that shook her own. He did not see how she reacted to his limp as he followed his friends into the ballroom.

He felt shy, a rather ridiculous emotion for a man of seven-and-twenty to feel. And awkward and conspicuous. His friends wanted to promenade about the edge of the ballroom to find out whom they knew, to examine the new faces—young and female, of course—of the Season. But he wanted to stand still. He wanted only to look about him to see if she was there. He was no longer sure that he wished to make himself known to her. If she was there, he would not hide from her, he thought. But if she did not see him, then he would be content merely to watch her. *If* she was there. He hated the thought that he might have put himself through this torture for nothing.

His friends stayed with him for a while, the duke teasing him about being as skittish as the freshest female recruit from the schoolroom, Gerson finding every remark hilarious.

"Is she here?" his grace asked, making free with his quizzing glass as he gazed about at the milling masses.

"She?" the marquess said. He had not yet had the time or the courage to make a thorough examination of the room.

"I hope she is worthy of this devotion of yours," the duke said. "Pretty, is she, Hart? Young? Supple? Mouthwatering? And panting to become a marchioness?"

"This is rich," Lord Gerson said. "You must point her out to us, Carew. You really must."

But his grace's elegant sweep of the room with his glass halted abruptly and he pursed his lips. He whistled softly. "Look at that," he said quietly. "Pretty, young, supple, did I say? And mouthwatering? And bedworthy, too. Deliciously bedworthy. Not a day over eighteen, if my eyes do not deceive me."

"Muir's chit," Lord Gerson said, following the direction of his friend's quizzing glass. "Maybe only half a day over, Bridge. With a dowry to lend her beauty even if she were not already overendowed."

"You know him?" his grace asked. "Present me, Gerson, there's a good chap. I have to have a closer look.

And feel, if it is only the girl's hand. What would you wager that her card is already overflowing?"

Lord Gerson laughed heartily, and the two of them began to make their slow way toward the pretty young lady in white who was making a pathetic attempt to appear fashionably bored with all that was proceeding about her. The marquess smiled in sympathy for the girl.

But Bridge was going to have to wait for his introduction. The next set was about to begin and a handsome young fresh-faced lad was talking to the girl. But not leading her out. Of course, the marquess thought as soon as the music began. It was a waltz. She would not be allowed to dance it, since it was obvious she had only just made her come-out and she must have permission from one of the patronesses of Almack's before she could dance the scandalous waltz. Perhaps later in the Season, if she was fortunate. Perhaps not until next year.

He had never seen the waltz performed, though he had heard of it. It had sounded to him like a marvelously romantic dance, each couple a unit unto itself, the man and his partner dancing face-to-face through the whole of it, able to look at each other and converse with each other for the full half hour.

And indeed it looked as wonderful as it had sounded. He watched for a few moments, enviously.

He had been aware during the five minutes or so he had been inside the ballroom that he had almost deliberately avoided looking about him for Samantha. He was not quite sure why. Was it because he was afraid she would not be there? Or because he was afraid she would?

In the event, he did not have to search for her. She waltzed into his line of vision. His heart lurched. She shimmered in a delightfully simple gown that looked both green and silver from this distance. She waltzed with grace and beauty. She smiled with pleasure.

His eyes followed her with love and with longing for several moments before he spared a glance for her partner. But when he did so, his eyes became riveted.

And his blood ran cold.

# 8

*H*E HAD LIED SO CONSISTENTLY AND SO OFTEN about the events of that morning when he was six years old that sometimes—not often, it was true—he almost forgot himself that it was a lie.

That his accident had been no accident at all.

He had been a disappointment to his father. Born five years after his father and mother's marriage, it had seemed that he was probably to be the only child of the union. And while his father might have been glad that he had at least begotten a son, he had deplored the weakness of that son. He had been a small and sickly child, the darling of his mother, overprotected and coddled. A sniveling coward, his father had called him contemptuously on one occasion—it was when at the age of five he had gone running home crying because some village boys had chanted names at him and he had thought they were going to attack him.

Sometimes his father was not even glad about his gender. For had he not been his father's heir, then his father's nephew would have been heir to at least part of his property and fortune. And his father adored his nephew, his sister's son, four years Hartley's senior. Lionel, Viscount Kersey, he had been then. A handsome, charming, fearless boy, who had basked in his uncle's favor and had taunted his cousin—except in the hearing of his aunt.

Hartley had adored him and feared him, had ached for his visits to Highmoor and then longed for his departures.

Sometimes Lionel had deliberately tried—usually successfully—to make him cry, pushing him painfully against doorways with a surreptitiously jabbed elbow, jumping out at him from dark corners at night, spilling his milk at table when his nurse was not looking—he had been endlessly inventive.

One thing Hartley had been good at was riding. Even his father had grudgingly admitted that he had a good seat and a firm hand on the reins. He had loved galloping his pony over permitted stretches of land and jumping over specially constructed fences—ones that would collapse easily if he did not clear them.

Vanity and the need to impress Lionel had made him rash one morning. Lionel had dared him to gallop with him across a forbidden meadow, one with ground that was too uneven and that had too many rabbit holes to be on the permitted route. He had accepted the dare, and they had left behind the startled groom who always rode with them. Before the man could catch up, they had been across the field and approaching a low, solid gate. Quite jumpable. Even so, he would not have jumped it if Lionel had not shouted a challenge. But Lionel had shouted and he had jumped.

He would have cleared the obstacle without any trouble at all—even in his need to impress, he had not been *that* rash. But Lionel had chosen to jump it at the same moment. He had been laughing. And one arm had shot out, its hand balled into a fist, and struck Hartley on the hip.

He had been midway through his jump. He had crashed down right onto the gate, smashing both it and himself in his fall. By some miracle his horse had cleared the gate and landed safely on the other side. By another miracle—though it did not seem a miracle for many months afterward—he himself had lived.

He had been conscious when the groom galloped up, his face contorted with terror, and then galloped off again to fetch help. Lionel had knelt over him, his face ashen, telling him over and over again that it had been an accident and he had better not forget it or make up stories that would shift the blame to someone else. That it was Hartley who had suggested both the gallop and the jump. Lionel had come after him to try to stop him.

During the few minutes of blessedly numbing shock before the weeks and months of truly hellish pain had set in, he had assured Lionel that he would never tell. Never, never, never. Even in those moments there had been the necessity to appear noble in his cousin's eyes.

"There is nothing to tell, you bleeding little worm," Lionel had hissed at him. For some reason those words had remained indelibly etched on his brain ever since.

And he never had told.

There were precious few good effects of what had happened that day. One of them was that he had stopped worshiping or even liking Lionel. Another was that he developed an iron will, a strong determination to conquer his disabilities. Although his mother lived for another four years after his accident, he never allowed her after that day to coddle him, to protect him. He knew almost from the start, despite what the physician told his father in his hearing, that he would walk again, that he would use his right arm and hand again, that he would learn to compensate for their stiffness by using his left hand, that he would make of his body the fittest, strongest instrument it could possibly be.

And he had learned to like himself, to accept himself for what he was. He was human, of course. It was not that he never envied other men or longed to be what he was not. But he did not allow envy or bitterness to gnaw away at him. He lived with reality.

Lionel had been ten years old. A mere child. Hartley forgave him when he was well past that age himself and looked back. He never liked him, but he forgave him and accepted him as his basically cold, selfish cousin.

But dislike had intensified into something much stronger again. His father had been ill. The physician had thought for a while that he would not recover. Lionel had come. There had always been a strong bond between uncle and nephew.

And he had begun an affair with the Countess of Thornhill—the former countess, young stepmother of the present earl. Hartley, young and romantic, had adored her from afar for several years. She was very beautiful and very kind and not many years his senior.

But he would not have presumed to treat her or even to think of her with disrespect.

Lionel had become her lover and had regaled his cousin's unwilling ears with lurid, graphic descriptions of exactly what he did to her and what she did to show her appreciation—and her love. It had been a great joke to Lionel that she claimed to love him.

Hartley had thought he was making it all up—until the countess disappeared with the present earl and the story became too strong to be entirely disbelieved that they had run away to the Continent together because she was with child by her own stepson. Hartley disbelieved the one part of that story, of course. The child was Lionel's—Lionel himself had disappeared in fright some weeks before the countess left with Gabriel.

She was living now in Switzerland with her daughter and her second husband. He believed there were a few more children from that second marriage. Once, on the only occasion he had asked the present Thornhill about her, he had been told that she was happy. He was glad of that. He had liked her. And of course it was understandable that she had fallen for Lionel's charms. He was undoubtedly one of the handsomest men in England. She had been years younger than her husband, and the late earl had always been sickly. When older and wiser, the Marquess of Carew realized that it was probable the two of them had never had a regular marital relationship. She must have been lonely.

His dislike of Lionel had grown into something resembling hatred. Certainly he despised him heartily.

And he had heard a garbled version of how Lionel had locked horns with the present Thornhill after the latter returned from Switzerland, leaving his stepmother behind. Somehow Lionel had tricked Thornhill into marrying his lady. She had been betrothed to Lionel himself at the time. But the marquess could not believe that Lionel had won any great victory there. Thornhill's lady was well rid of the blackguard, and there could be little doubt that her marriage to Thornhill was now a love match, however it had started.

He would have been happy if he could have avoided all contact with Lionel, now the Earl of Rushford, for the rest of his life.

SAMANTHA NEWMAN WAS WALTZING with Lionel.

The Marquess of Carew's blood ran cold.

His one hand was splayed against her delicately arched back while the other held hers. Her left hand was on his shoulder.

Suddenly the waltz seemed the most obscenely intimate dance ever invented.

They were beautiful together. Quite spectacularly, heart-stoppingly beautiful.

The devil and his prey.

The marquess had not even heard that Lionel was back in England. Yet there he was, obviously using his considerable charm—and succeeding. She was smiling and not looking about her as many of the other dancers were. She seemed totally absorbed in her partner, though she was not talking to him or he to her. An ominous sign. Were they well acquainted, then? So well acquainted that they did not even feel the need to make conversation?

His heart sank like lead within him. He could remember being with her himself in companionable silence.

And now she was with Lionel.

Instinct told him to get out of there. Out of the ballroom and out of the Rochester mansion. To go back to his town house. Back to Highmoor. To forget about her. He must forget about her. He had been foolish to come after her like a lovesick puppy.

But he could not move. Even though his attention was focused on the waltzing couple, he was not unaware of the curious glances he was receiving from some people close to him and of some nudging elbows and murmuring voices. He did not want to walk away—limp away—in their sight. Besides, he had the foolish notion that she might need him. He could not leave her alone with Lionel—alone with him and a few hundred other people, he thought in self-mockery.

But he could not leave her alone. Perhaps she did not know about Lionel—though she was Lady Thornhill's cousin. Perhaps she was being charmed. Perhaps she would be the next to disappear to Switzerland. His left hand balled into a fist at his side.

And so he remained where he was, watching her, watching *him*, torturing himself with the possibility that they were an item, a couple, that perhaps at the age of thirty-one and with the weight of an earl's title on his shoulders, Lionel was at last in search of a bride. And what lovelier bride could he choose than Samantha Newman?

It was an interminable half hour. Half an hour of excruciating torture. When the music came to an end, he watched Lionel escort her to a group of young people—the marquess recognized only Lord Francis Kneller, whom he had met a few times at Chalcote. He was a friend of Thornhill's, a pleasant if somewhat dandified fellow. Lionel bowed over her hand and took his leave of her.

Perhaps after all, then, it was not as bad as he had feared. Perhaps they were merely distant acquaintances who had shared a dance. That was what a ball was for, after all.

But he felt no wish to stay longer. He did not want to see her dance with any other gentleman. He did not wish for her to see him. He looked about for his two friends, but they were both deep in conversation—Bridge with Muir while Muir's pretty daughter hovered close by—at the far side of the ballroom. He would leave without them. He would walk home. It was no great distance.

But when he reached the doorway, he could not resist one last look back. She was no longer with the group. His searching eyes found her making her way rather slowly through the crowd toward the door, smiling, exchanging greetings with several people as she passed. She was coming in his direction, though he did not believe she had seen him.

He took several steps back so that he was no longer in

the ballroom but was on the landing beyond. He was about to turn to flee as fast as he could down the stairs before she reached the doors herself and saw him. But he stopped. What would be the harm in greeting her himself, in seeing recognition in her eyes, in being the recipient of her smile once more? One last time. Tomorrow he would start on his return journey to Yorkshire. He should never have left.

He stopped and waited for her.

She came through the doors in a rush. She looked a little bewildered, dazzled perhaps by the dancing and the crowds. She had not seen him, though she was only feet away from him. He stepped into her path. For a moment he thought she was going to move around him without even looking at him, but she did look.

And stopped in her tracks.

And her face lit up with such bright and total delight that all else about him faded into oblivion.

"Mr. Wade!" Her voice was all astonishment and warm welcome. "How wonderful. Oh, how *happy* I am to see you." She stretched out both hands to him.

He took them, noticed fleetingly that she did not flinch at all from the touch of his right hand in its silk glove, and found himself grinning foolishly back at her.

"Hello, Miss Newman," he said.

SHE COULD SCARCELY BELIEVE the evidence of her own eyes. What was he doing here? Did he know someone who had somehow wangled him an invitation? He was smartly though conservatively dressed in brown and dull gold and white. But it did not matter how the miracle had happened. What was important was that it had. If there was anyone she could have hoped would be waiting for her beyond the ballroom doors, it would have been he.

She did not stop to ponder that strange thought.

"What are you *doing* here?" she asked. But she did not wait for his answer. "I never dreamed . . . You are the last person . . . Oh, but this is so *wonderful*. I am so happy to see you again."

She had been distraught over the encounter with Lionel. All that pent-up emotion now came bursting out of her as happiness in seeing her dearest friend, when she had thought never to see him again. And just at the moment when she most needed him.

"It is so hot in here and so stuffy and so crowded," she said. "Come outside for a moment? Come and stroll with me." She had never felt a greater need to get away from the gathered *ton*.

"It will be my pleasure," he said, offering her his left arm and favoring her with that dear smile of the eyes that always warmed her right down to her toes.

Despite the miles they had walked together at Highmoor, this was the first time, she realized, that she had taken his arm. She was far more aware than she had been at Highmoor of his heavy limp and rather slow progress. They had to descend the stairs to reach the door to the garden. He steadied himself against the banister with the outside of his right wrist.

He was drawing some attention. Curious eyes looked at him and then looked hastily away again. A few gentlemen nodded to him in recognition. One of them, she noticed, then proceeded to whisper into his wife's ear.

She had her right arm linked through his. She rested her left hand on his arm, too, feeling a tender sort of protectiveness toward him. Maybe he was a nobody in the eyes of the *ton* and many people would feel that he had no business being here, but he was her dear friend. Let any of them just try to say something to him. They would have her to contend with.

The garden had been lit for the occasion with colored lanterns strung in the trees and lamps lit on the terrace. It was a small garden, but it had been cleverly landscaped to look larger and deceptively secluded. It was hard to believe that they were in the middle of the largest and busiest city in England. Perhaps in all the world, for all she knew.

She had a sudden thought and laughed softly. "Did you landscape this garden, by any chance?" she asked.

"I did, actually." He laughed too. "It was several years ago, one of my first projects. I drew up the plans for the old baron, the present Rochester's father. He completed the work only just before his death."

She laughed again. "I might have known," she said. "And so that is how you came by your invitation. But you did not tell me you were planning to come to London. How unkind of you! Were you hoping that I would not see you and never know? And I thought we were friends."

She spoke lightly, but there was a heavy feeling deep inside, a fear that perhaps that was exactly it.

"I did not know I was coming here until very recently," he said. "And I did hope to see you. I came tonight with the intention of saying hello to you and discovering if you remembered me or not."

"Did you?" She was strangely touched that he would take time away from whatever job had brought him here just to say hello to her. And even if he had landscaped this garden, he had still been only an employee of a man now dead. It must not have been easy to wangle an invitation to this ball. He was a gentleman, but that fact alone did not ensure him entrée to *ton* events. "Of course I remember you. Those afternoons were among the loveliest I have ever spent."

They were, too. If she cast her mind back over all the picnics and excursions and Venetian breakfasts and garden parties she had ever attended, none of them had left her with such warm memories as those four afternoons spent at Highmoor.

There were not many people in the garden. It was not a cold evening, but neither was it warm. It felt wonderfully refreshing to Samantha. She breathed in fresh air and closed her eyes. And stopped walking. They were beneath the low boughs of a beech tree.

"I could almost imagine that we were back in the country," she said. "I was never more reluctant to come back to town than I was this spring."

"The early springtime was unusually lovely at Highmoor this year," he said.

She felt a wave of intense nostalgia for those afternoons. She thought of seeing Lionel in the park yesterday and of the dread his appreciative look had aroused in her—a dread that he would try to renew their acquaintance, a dread that she would somehow respond. And she thought of waltzing with him just a short while ago and of his impudent, seductive words. And of the desire and horror she had felt. She felt them again now, both coiled and throbbing deep in her womb.

"I have missed you so much," she heard herself say in a thin, distressed voice. She felt instant embarrassment—and the need for arms to hold her.

She was never sure afterward whether he had felt her need and responded to it or whether she had moved to satisfy her own need. But his arms were there where she wanted and needed them. They were about her and holding her comfortingly against his surprisingly strong and well-muscled body. His left arm was tight about her waist.

She rested her cheek against his shoulder as her arms wrapped themselves about his waist, and she breathed in the smell of—what? Not cologne. Soap. A comforting, clean smell. She felt sheltered, comforted. Wonderfully comforted. She fit against him much more cozily than she did against any of the beaux she had allowed to embrace her. She was usually so much smaller than the gentlemen who escorted her.

Another thing she was never sure of afterward. Did he nudge his shoulder in order to get her to raise her head? Or did she raise it for herself? In all truth she thought it must have been the latter. But however it was, neither loosened their hold on the other, and so they looked into each other's eyes with no more than a few inches separating them. His gray eyes looked kindly and seriously back into hers.

"Kiss me." It was a whisper, but in an unmistakably feminine voice. That at least was quite embarrassingly clear in her memory afterward.

His kiss surprised her. Most men of her experience kissed with closed lips, only the pressure against her own denoting their ardor. Those few who had dared to part their lips had done so with lascivious intent and had all been swiftly put in their places—all except Lionel.

Mr. Wade kissed with parted lips. She felt the warmth and moisture of his mouth against her own. But he kissed gently, softly, almost tenderly. He kissed wonderfully. She kissed him back in the same way and felt relaxation and a healing sort of peace seep back into her body and into her soul.

He was very dear to her, she thought. A very dear friend. Not that they should be kissing—especially with mouths rather than lips. Friends did not kiss, not like this anyway. But she had needed his arms and even his mouth to take away the rawness of the injury Lionel had inflicted on her. And he had felt her need and was giving her comfort in the way she needed it.

That was what friends were for.

She turned her head when the kiss was over and nestled her cheek against his shoulder. His right arm was lightly about her. His left hand was gently massaging the back of her head. Her hair was going to be disheveled, she thought, without caring in the least.

She sighed with contentment. "Oh, I do love you so very, very much," she said. And froze. Had she really said those exact words? But she could hear the echo of them as clearly as if they were still being spoken. How mortifying in the extreme. He would think she had windmills in her head.

She whipped her head up and dropped her arms from about his waist. Whatever was she doing, clinging to him and kissing him and telling him she loved him, just as if he were her lover?

She looked at him in confusion. "I am so sorry," she said. "I did not mean . . . Whatever will you think . . ."

But he set one finger against her lips and pressed. His eyes were smiling. He shook his head. "You need not be embarrassed," he said, his voice so gentle and so sane that she relaxed instantly. That was another good thing about friends. One could utter any idiocy and they would understand. "I think I had better take you back inside."

Her eyes widened. "Oh, dear," she said. "I have promised this set. It must have started already. How unspeakably ill-mannered of me."

But she turned to him when they were indoors and at the top of the staircase again. She could both see and hear that the set had indeed begun. It would be impossible now to join it. The next set was free. She must sit with Mr. Hancock through what remained of this and ask if she might grant him the next set instead.

"Will I see you later?" she asked. "I have a few sets free after supper."

"I must leave," he said. "I have another engagement."

"Oh." She was disappointed. She wanted to ask him when she would see him again, but she had been inexcusably forward in her behavior to him more than once already this evening. She did not ask the question and he did not volunteer the information. "Good night, then. Thank you. Thank you for . . ." For holding her? And kissing her? "I am glad you came."

"So am I," he said. "Good night."

He waited until she had turned away. She hurried back into the ballroom to find and make her apologies to Mr. Hancock. She felt better, she thought, except that she did not know when or even if she would ever see him again.

The wonder of it struck her. Had he really been here? Had she walked with him and talked with him and been comforted by his arms and his kiss?

There was a certain panic in the thought that she might never see him again.

The first person she saw when she returned to the ballroom was Lionel, Earl of Rushford. He was looking at her with appreciative and lustful eyes across the width of the ballroom.

She wished she had gone with Mr. Wade. Anywhere with him.

She was afraid again.

# 9

$I$T WAS A LONG WALK HOME, ESPECIALLY FOR ONE
who did not walk easily. It was a chilly evening.
And a dark one, for a gentleman walking the streets of
London unaccompanied and unarmed.

He did not think of any of it. He hardly even noticed
his surroundings. He entered his town house, handed his
cloak, hat, and gloves to the butler, climbed the stairs to
his room, dismissed his valet, and stretched out fully
clothed on his bed. He stared upward at the silk-lined
canopy.

He could not quite believe that it had happened. All
the way home he had avoided thinking about it or reliving any of it. He was afraid now to think of it. He was
afraid to pinch himself, lest he wake up and find that it
had all been a dream.

But he could not stop the memories.

Her face lighting up with unmistakable joy at seeing
him.

Her assurance, undeniably genuine, that she was so
very happy to see him.

Her suggestion that they walk outdoors together for
a while, though it had turned out later that she had

promised the coming set to another man. She had totally forgotten it in her happiness at seeing him.

The way both her hands had rested on his arm as they went downstairs and outside into the garden.

The nostalgia with which she had talked of those afternoons at Highmoor.

He tried to stop thinking. Surely if he really thought about them, the next memories would crumble away and he would realize that they had been a fabrication of his imagination. A foolish fabrication. They could not possibly have happened in reality.

But thought could not always be stopped at will. And there they were—real memories of what had really happened.

She had stepped into his arms and set her own about his waist and her head against his shoulder.

God. Oh, God, it had really happened. He could feel her again. He could feel her warm, soft curves all along the length of his body. He could feel her arms tight about him. He could feel her curls soft and tickly against his cheek. He could smell her hair and that elusive violet smell he had noticed at Highmoor.

And then—ah, God, then.

She had lifted her head and gazed with soft warmth and *love*—even then he had thought it was love and had not believed the evidence of his own senses—into his eyes.

*Kiss me.* He shut his eyes very tightly, listening to her soft whisper again. Yearning—there had been yearning in her voice. And in her eyes.

And so he had kissed her. And she had kissed him back with warm and parted lips. She had kissed him with gentleness and tenderness. His mind had not found those words at the time, but his body and his heart had felt them.

She had missed him. She had said that, earlier, before the kiss.

He did not want to think beyond the kiss. It had happened, he knew. But it was too much. Too great a gift. Too far beyond belief and acceptance.

*I do love you so very, very much.*

No, no. She could not have meant it quite that way. What she had meant was that she felt an affection for him. He must not read too much into her words. Perhaps that was why he had laid a finger against her lips when she had been embarrassed at blurting out so stark a truth and had tried to explain. Perhaps he was afraid that it was not the truth.

*I do love you so very, very much.*

Friends—a man and a woman—did not talk thus to each other. Only lovers. Even Dorothea had not said that to him until close to the end.

No, he would not believe it too deeply. She was unbelievably beautiful and—perfect. He had seen her with three different men since his arrival in London, all handsome and young and fashionable. How could she have meant what she had said to him tonight? The idea was absurd.

"She loves me." He whispered the words into the

candlelit darkness and felt foolish, even though there was no one to hear except him.

"She loves me," he said aloud and more firmly. He felt even more foolish. "Very, very much."

Was he going to set out on his return to Yorkshire tomorrow? Or was he going to try to see her again? How? By haunting fashionable areas during the daytime in the hope of catching a glimpse of her? By attending some other evening function in the hope of having a few words with her?

By calling on her? She was living at Lady Brill's. He knew that.

Dared he call on her? Would it not be an occasion of amusement to Lady Brill and others—and even perhaps to Samantha—if he went calling on her? But why should he not? He was the Marquess of Carew; for the first time he realized that he had not after all told her of that fact this evening. And she had been glad to see him tonight. More than glad.

*I love you so very, very much.*

He closed his eyes tightly again. He had to believe it. It had not been just the words themselves. Everything in that whole incredible encounter had led up to those words and confirmed them as true.

The miracle had happened.

She loved him.

THEY HAD NOT LET it be known that they would be at home to visitors. Their plan was to spend the afternoon visiting. Their intention was to take Lady Sophia with them—her first outing since her accident. Samantha was supposed to drive in the park later with Lord Francis, but it was raining. He had sent a note to ask if she wished to join the world of the ducks, in which case he would don his oilskins and accompany her, or if she would prefer to honor him with her company on the morrow, weather permitting. She wrote back that she had checked but had discovered that she did not have webbed feet and that, yes, she would be delighted to drive out with him tomorrow.

And then a note had arrived from Lady Sophia, who considered that wet weather was not good for a recently broken limb, and would Agatha and Miss Newman humor her with a visit later in the afternoon? She was going to have a rest after luncheon, another adverse effect of the wet weather, it seemed.

And so they had an unexpectedly free half an afternoon and settled in Lady Brill's sitting room with their embroidery to have a cozy chat about last night's ball. Samantha allowed her aunt to do most of the talking. She preferred not to think about last night's ball. She could hardly believe that she had behaved with such dreadful forwardness toward Mr. Wade, who was, when all was said and done, practically a stranger. And she felt depressed about the fact that it was likely to be their only meeting in town. They would hardly move in the same circles there. And she did not want to think about Lionel and the strange, repellent attraction she had felt for him.

She had dreamed about him during the night. A horrible, shocking dream. He had been on the bed with her, looming over her, his body braced on his two arms on either side of her head. He had been looking at her with burning eyes and moistened lips. He had been telling her, his voice soft and persuasive, that of course she wanted him and it was silly to fight the feeling.

*You are a woman now. I cannot take my eyes off you.*

There had been that feeling in her womb again, and she had known that she was about to give in, to admit defeat. She *did* want him. There—close to her womb. But then she had felt nauseated with a revulsion at least equal to the desire and had pushed at his chest, desperate for air.

His right arm had collapsed and he had tumbled down on top of her. And had turned into Mr. Wade.

*You need not be embarrassed,* he had said, his voice gentle.

She had sobbed with relief and wrapped her arms tightly about him and relaxed and gone back to sleep.

She had woken with a pillow hugged tightly to her.

It was not a dream she enjoyed remembering.

Fortunately Aunt Aggy appeared not to have heard that Lionel was at the ball. She sighed after they had been sitting for almost an hour. "I suppose that soon we had better get ready to go," she said. "There is something about a rainy day that makes one wish to stay indoors, is there not, dear? But poor, dear Sophie will be lonely if I do not go to see her."

But there was a tap on the door at that moment, and Aunt Agatha's butler came in with a card on a silver tray.

"Did you not say we were not receiving this afternoon?" she asked him.

"I did, ma'am," he said. "But the gentleman wished me to ask if you would make an exception in his case."

Aunt Agatha picked up the card and glanced at it. Her eyebrows shot up and then drew together.

"You will never believe this, Samantha," she said. "The gall of the man. I had no idea he was back in England. And he is calling on us?"

*Lionel.* Samantha's stomach performed a somersault.

"The Earl of Rushford," Lady Brill said scornfully. "You may tell him we are not at home." She looked fiercely at her butler. "You may tell him we do not plan to be at home for the rest of the Season."

"He danced with me last evening," Samantha said quietly.

Her aunt turned her fierce gaze on her, and the butler paused in the doorway.

"He took me by surprise," Samantha said. "And he was very civil. It would have seemed ill-mannered . . ." She folded her embroidery without conscious thought and set it beside her on the chair. "I danced with him."

"Gracious," her aunt said. "After the scandal of six years ago, Samantha? After he disgraced dear Jennifer with such deliberate malice? Her own father caned her as a result!"

Samantha bit her lip. She hated the memory of listening outside Uncle Gerald's study door with Aunt Aggy and hearing his command to Jenny to bend over his desk and then the first two whistling strokes of his cane.

"Very well," her aunt said after a pause, "we will be *civil* to him, Samantha. Show him up." She looked at her butler again. "After all, it was six years ago. A man can sometimes learn wisdom in six years."

It was hard to believe that she had not fought against his admission, especially when Aunt Aggy herself had been reluctant to admit him. But she knew why. Of course she knew. Why keep denying it to herself? Why keep pretending?

She had never forgotten him. She had never stopped being fascinated by him. She had known last night that there was still something that drew her to him. She had known then that her life seemed destined for ugliness, not beauty, for pain, not happiness.

The only question that remained was whether she was going to continue to fight. What was the alternative to fighting? Oh, dear God, what was it?

And then he was in the room, filling it with his good looks and his charm and his charisma. He was bowing over Aunt Aggy's hand and assuring her that she was in remarkable good looks and that he would cherish the honor she had done him by admitting him on an afternoon when she was not officially receiving.

He was dressed in a coat of dark green superfine, Weston's finest, with buff pantaloons and sparkling Hessians. His linen was crisply white. He was even more breathtakingly handsome now than he had been six years ago, if that were possible.

And then he was turning to Samantha and bowing elegantly and gazing at her with burning eyes—oh, dear God, she had seen his eyes like that in her dream—and thanking her for the honor she had paid him in dancing a set with him last evening.

"I came, Miss Newman, ma'am," he said, including them both in his bow, "to make a more private and certainly more sincere apology for my part in the events of six years ago that caused such distress to your family."

"Well." Samantha noticed that her aunt melted without further ado. "Well, that is most civil of you, my lord, I am sure. I was just remarking to Samantha that a man can sometimes learn wisdom in six years."

"Thank you, ma'am," he said. "I believe I have."

Lady Brill ordered tea and they sat for twenty minutes, engaged in an amiable conversation, during which he told them about his travels and asked after the health and happiness of Lady Thornhill.

"I have always wished her happy," he said. "I was young and fearful, as most young men are, of matrimony. But I never wished her harm and have been deeply ashamed of the distress I caused her." He looked at Samantha, his eyes warmly contrite.

He had never wished her harm? And yet he had maliciously caused that letter to be written and to be read aloud, a letter suggesting that Jenny and Lord Thornhill were lovers and intended to continue as lovers. If Gabriel had not married her, Jenny would have lived out her life in deep disgrace. Oh, yes, it would be a sin to try to forget—Uncle Gerald had caned her after that letter was read to the *ton*. And Lionel had never wished her harm? He had not even had the excuse of youth. He had been five-and-twenty at the time.

And he had pretended a passion for her, Samantha, in the hope that she would tell Jenny and Jenny would end their betrothal. And then, when the betrothal was ended anyway, he had laughed at her and told her that she must have misunderstood what was only gallantry.

Had he changed so much in six years? Was it possible? Or was he still the snake he had been then? But even more suave.

How could she even fear that she still loved him? But if it was not love, what was it that bound her to him despite the horror she felt at being so bound?

"You are very quiet, Miss Newman," he said at last, bringing her attention back to the conversation. "Do you find me impossible to forgive? I could hardly blame you if you do."

Good manners dictated that she give him the answer he wanted. But she felt again the fury that had rescued her the evening before. He was playing with them, manipulating them. For what reason, she did not know. Perhaps for simple amusement.

Or perhaps he was sincere.

"Perhaps not impossible, my lord," she said carefully.

He got to his feet. "It is time I took my leave," he said, bowing to them again. He looked at Samantha. "I shall study to win your forgiveness before the Season is out, Miss Newman."

It had been *Samantha* the evening before, when Aunt

Aggy had not been within hearing distance, she remembered. She nodded her head curtly.

"Would you do me the honor of walking to the door with me?" he asked.

Samantha's eyes flew to her aunt. But Lady Brill merely raised her eyebrows and shrugged almost imperceptibly. Samantha was no girl, and he had not asked for a private visit with her, after all.

She preceded him from the room but took his offered arm to walk downstairs. Although it was higher above her own, it was not so very different from Mr. Wade's arm, she thought. It did not feel any stronger or any more firmly muscled despite the overall splendor of his physique.

"I know how difficult you find it to forgive me," he said quietly. "You have more to forgive me for than Lady Brill, and more than she knows of. But I will win your trust."

Perhaps he was sincere. How did one know if a man was sincere? She had not known this man for six years. It was a long time.

"I loved you even then," he said. "But it was hopeless. You too would have been ruined in the scandal, and I would have died sooner than ruin you. I still would. I never forgot you. I came home because I could no longer live without . . . Well, I do not want to sound like a bad melodrama."

But he did. How did one know if a man was sincere? Perhaps the way he remembered—or distorted—the past was a key. He had *not* loved her. And the scandal had not yet touched him when he had spurned her. If he would have died rather than ruin her, would he not have died rather than viciously humiliate and hurt her?

She did not know what his game was. But game it was.

"I came home, you know," he said, "because it is time I took a countess. And I wanted an English countess. An English rose—one more beautiful than any other." He took her hand from his arm and raised it to his lips without removing his eyes from hers. "Will you drive with me in the park tomorrow afternoon?"

"I have a prior appointment," she said.

"Tell me the man's name," he said, "so that I may slap a glove in his face." His eyes were burning into hers again.

He *was* still a snake. This was too polished a performance to be real. And not a pleasant performance.

"He is a man I like and admire," she said. "I would drive with him any day he asked, my lord. He is also a man I trust."

He sighed and released her hand. "And you do not trust me," he said. "I cannot blame you. But that will change. My honor on it."

She almost laughed and asked him the obvious question—*What honor?* But she could feel no amusement, and she did not want to prolong their conversation.

He made her an elegant bow and took his leave.

Aunt Aggy was still in her sitting room.

"Well," she said when Samantha returned there. "I

have never seen such a transformation in my life. He has become a thoroughly amiable young man."

"Are you sure, Aunt?" Samantha asked her. "It was not all artifice? He was not laughing at us?"

"But to what purpose?" Her aunt's eyebrows shot up again. "It must have been extremely difficult, Samantha, for him to come here and say what he did. I honor his courage."

"He wanted me to drive with him tomorrow," Samantha said. "I was very glad that I am to drive with Francis."

"I believe," Lady Brill said, smiling archly, "he is smitten with you, Samantha. And it would hardly be surprising. You are as lovely now as when you made your come-out. Lovelier. You have a self-assurance now that is quite becoming."

Samantha did not feel self-assured. Not any longer. Not now that he had come back.

"He was very complimentary," she said. "But I could not think him sincere, Aunt."

Lady Brill clucked her tongue. "I begin to despair of ever persuading you to step up to the altar with a presentable gentleman," she said. "But we must not stand here arguing. Poor Sophie will be despairing of our coming."

"Will you mind a great deal if I stay at home?" Samantha asked. She smiled. "The two of you can have a more comfortable coze if I am not there, anyway."

"What utter nonsense," her aunt said, but she made no attempt to persuade Samantha to accompany her after all.

It was a relief to be alone again, Samantha thought, retiring to her own room and sitting down at her escritoire to write a letter to Jenny. But no matter how many times she dipped her quill pen in the inkwell, she could not make a start on the letter beyond writing "My dear Jenny."

What would Jenny and Gabriel say if they were in town this year and knew what had happened in the last two days? She could almost imagine their horror. Imagining it helped. It helped her see that renewing an acquaintance with Lionel just would not do. They would not be fooled, as Aunt Aggy had been fooled, into thinking that he truly regretted the past. If he did regret it, surely he would pay her the courtesy of remaining out of her life.

She was four-and-twenty years old, she reminded herself. She prided herself on her maturity and her worldly wisdom. After six years of being "out," she believed she knew a great deal about human nature in general and about gentlemen in particular. For several years she had felt very much in charge of her own life and emotions.

Was she to revert now to the naiveté of her eighteen-year-old self? She had been able to excuse her own gullibility then because she had known no better. She had been in search of love and marriage and had known nothing about either. Would she ever be able to excuse herself for making the same mistake now?

What if he was sincere? But even if he was, it would be

unpardonable to have anything to do with him. What would Jenny and Gabriel think?

She found herself drawing geometric patterns with her pen below the "My dear Jenny" on the page.

He was going to remain in London for the Season. Of that she had little doubt. And he was going to pursue her for that time. For what reason she did not know. Perhaps—there was a slim chance—he was sincere. Or perhaps it merely amused him to discover whether he could do to her again what he had done six years ago.

She was not sure she would be able to endure it.

Part of her was still foolishly fascinated by him, as she had admitted to herself before his visit. Part of her had never been able to let him go and get on with her life. She had thought she had done so. But if she had, why had she never been able to love any other man? Why had she never been able to marry?

He had a hold on her emotions that she neither welcomed nor understood. She could only admit it.

She set her pen down when there was a tap on her door.

"Come in," she called.

It was the butler again, bearing another card on his tray. Surely he had not come back, she thought. Surely he had not waited until Aunt Aggy left and then returned. She would not put such subterfuge past him. But she certainly would not receive him. The very idea!

She looked down at the card and then picked it up and closed her eyes as she brought her hand unconsciously to her lips.

"Where is he?" she asked.

"I put him in the salon downstairs, miss," the butler said. "He said only if it was not too much trouble to you."

Samantha got to her feet. She was smiling.

"It is no trouble at all," she said, and she brushed past him in the doorway and went running lightly down the stairs. She did not wait for him to come after her to open the door to the salon. She opened it herself and rushed inside with quite undignified eagerness. Her smile had widened.

"You came," she said, closing the door behind her and leaning back against it. "I wanted so badly last evening to ask when I would see you again, but it seemed presumptuous, and I had said and done so much else that was presumptuous before we said good night. I hope I did not give you a great disgust of me."

His eyes glowed as he smiled at her and she felt her first real happiness of the day.

"I came," he said.

# 10

*H*E HAD ALMOST TALKED HIMSELF OUT OF COM-
ing. In the gloomy light of a rainy day the events
of last evening had seemed unreal. But the only alternative to coming was to go home, back to Highmoor, and
know that he would never see her again. It was an alternative he could not contemplate.

All the way here his stomach had been tied in knots.
He had tried to think of excuses for giving his coachman
instructions to take a different direction. It was rather
late in the afternoon. She would doubtless be from
home. She would have other visitors. He should have
written asking permission to call. But he had come, and
his coachman had knocked on the door, and he had
handed his card to Lady Brill's butler and asked if it
might be taken to Miss Newman and if he might see
her—but only if it was no trouble to her to see him.

The butler had looked with well-bred condescension
on a babbling Mr. Hartley Wade.

He had paced the small salon with its heavy, rather
old-fashioned furniture, wondering if it was too late to
escape, hoping that she would send back some excuse
not to see him.

And yet the moment the door burst open again and

she hurried inside, closed the door and leaned back against it, and delivered her opening speech far faster and more breathlessly than she usually spoke, his nervousness and uncertainty fled. She was smiling. Her eyes were shining. And he listened to the words she spoke.

The miracle really had happened.

"I came," he said.

She laughed. "But you have avoided admitting that I gave you a disgust of me," she said. "I am so ashamed. If I had told Aunt Aggy how I behaved last night, she would have had a fit of the vapors. Do please forgive me."

"I wish you would not apologize," he said. "I was not disgusted." She looked delightfully pretty in sprigged muslin, he thought. She looked like a girl. Though perhaps that was no great compliment. She had all the allure and fascination of a woman.

"You are kind." Her smile softened. "As always. I am sorry my aunt is from home. But I will ring for tea here if you do not feel it would be too improper a tête-à-tête. We did not care about that at Highmoor, though, did we?"

"I'll not stay long," he said, quelling the temptation to be drawn into a mere social half hour, chatting about inconsequential matters. "Please don't bother with tea."

"Oh." She looked disappointed.

"I came to ask you something," he said. "I suppose I should lead up to it by gradual degrees, but I do not know how. I would rather just ask and hear your reply."

"I am intrigued," she said. She was still leaning back

against the door, he noticed, her hands behind her, prob-ably holding the door handle. "But I do hope the ques-tion is not that I will drive in the park with you tomorrow afternoon. If so, you will be the third to ask and I accepted the first. But I will be sorry if that is what you want. Perhaps—"

"I wondered," he said, "if you would marry me."

Her smile disappeared and she stared at him mutely, her eyes huge, her lips slightly parted.

It had been a disastrous way to ask. Baldly abrupt. To-tally lacking in grace or courtliness. He wished he could withdraw the words and try again.

"I could try it on one knee," he said, smiling, "but I am afraid you might have to help haul me back to my feet again."

She did not smile. "What?" she said, her voice and her face bewildered.

He swallowed. It was too soon. He should have spent some time courting her first. Or perhaps he had been to-tally mistaken. But it was too late to retreat now.

"I would like to marry you," he said. "If you wish to marry me, that is. I know I am not much—" No, he must not apologize for his lack of stature and looks, for his de-formed hand and foot. He was as he was. And she had told him she loved him. He had believed her.

Her eyes had focused on him again. "Don't belittle yourself," she said quietly, having obviously completed his sentence for herself. "You are wonderful just the way you are. Far more wonderful than any other man of my acquaintance."

They stared at each other, their eyes roaming each other's face, no real awkwardness between them.

"I thought never to marry," she said. "I have not given it serious consideration for a long time."

"Someone hurt you," he said gently. It hurt him to know that another man had hurt her—obviously very badly. "But life is not all pain. I would never hurt you. You would be quite safe with me." They were not the romantic words he had dreamed of saying and had tried to rehearse, but they were the words needed by the moment.

"I know I would," she said softly. "I always feel wonderfully safe and—and happy when I am with you. Do you with me? I—"

"Yes," he said. "Always."

She set her head back against the door and looked at him. "I would not have dreamed of feeling this tempted," she said.

"But only tempted?" He felt as if he were holding his breath. "Would you like time to consider?"

"Yes," she said. And then very quickly, she changed her mind. "No. I do not need time. Time only confuses the mind. I will marry you."

Despite his hopes and his dreams and even his expectations, he was stunned. He stared at her, not sure that he had heard right. But she was coming toward him, and she reached out both her hands when she was close.

"Thank you," she said, and there were tears shining in her eyes. "Oh, thank you."

He took her hands in his, not even conscious for once

of the deformity of his right. He laughed, his voice breathless with relief.

"I muddled it horribly," he said. "I am so sorry. I have never done this before."

"I hope," she said, "since it has so embarrassed you, that you will not have to do it ever again. I will be a good wife to you, I promise. Oh, I do promise that. I shall make you—contented."

He rather thought that she would make him delirious, as she was making him now. He looked at her, so exquisitely pretty and dainty and warmhearted, and could not for the moment believe that she was his. His love. His betrothed. She was going to be his wife, the mother of his children.

"You already have," he said. "And I promise to see to it that you never regret the decision you have made today."

Two tears spilled over and trickled down her cheeks. She bit her lip and laughed. "Oh, dear," she said. "Is this really happening? I feared I would never see you again after last evening."

For answer he leaned forward and kissed her swiftly on both cheeks, brushing away the salt tears with his lips. "Is there anyone I must ask?" he said. "Even just for courtesy's sake? You do not still have a guardian, do you?"

"My uncle has control of my fortune until my next birthday," she said. "Viscount Nordal, Jenny's father. But it will be released to me immediately on my marriage. It is quite a respectable fortune. Perhaps you are marrying me for my money." She laughed lightly and breathlessly.

That was when he remembered. Oh, yes, he really had made a mess of things. He had done everything quite the wrong way around.

She laughed again. "It was a bad joke," she said. "It was a *joke*. But very tasteless. I know you could never be mercenary. Forgive me."

He squeezed her right hand with his left.

"I will call on your uncle," he said. "And I will see about having the banns started. Next Sunday? Am I rushing you? I am almost ready to suggest a special license, but I want you to have a *wedding*. I want the whole world to see you as a bride. Just as soon as the banns can be read. Would you prefer to wait a while? Until summer, perhaps?"

"No." She shook her head slowly. "No, let's not wait. I want to be your wife—now, as soon as possible. I want to be with you. If you wish to reconsider the special license . . ."

But he shook his head, dizzying as the thought was of having her as his wife within the next couple of days. No, he would rather wait. He wanted to show her off to the whole *ton*. He wanted a wedding to remember. At St. George's, in Hanover Square.

"No," he said. "We must do this properly."

"Yes, sir." Her smile became almost impish. "I will practice wifely obedience, you see."

He laughed. "You will not find me a hard taskmaster," he said. "I must take my leave." He let go of her hands regretfully. "Your aunt's servants will be scandalized if I stay longer."

"Yes, sir," she said meekly. "When will I see you again? You must meet my aunt. Will you come tomorrow afternoon?"

"Yes." He had crossed the room to the door. He looked back, his hand on the handle. No, he could not leave like this. It would be unpardonable. He had put it off long enough. Too long. And even that was an understatement.

"There is something I have not told you," he said quietly.

"You are a convicted murderer," she said. "You have had six wives and have murdered them all. Worse even than Henry the Eighth." She smiled merrily. "What have you not told me?"

He licked dry lips. "When I gave you my name at Highmoor," he said, "I thought you would recognize it and fill in what was missing. When you did not, I was tempted by the novelty of being just an itinerant landscape gardener. It seemed harmless at the time. I did not know that the day would come soon when I would want to ask you to marry me."

She merely stared at him. He thought her face had paled.

"Hartley Wade is not my complete name," he said. He swallowed. "I am Carew."

Her face was drained of every vestige of color. "The *Marquess* of Carew?" she said in an unnaturally high-pitched voice after the silence had stretched.

He nodded.

She opened her mouth more than once to speak. "You lied to me," she said at last.

"No," he said quickly. "I merely withheld the full truth. Though *merely* is a damning word, I must admit. And I suppose I did lie. We talked about me a few times in the third person, did we not? I pretended that he was someone other than myself."

"Why?" The word was whispered. She had closed her eyes very tightly, as if to shut off what was happening.

"You were there on the hill," he said, "so unexpected and so—pretty and so flustered at being caught trespassing. I expected to see you become stiff and formal and even more embarrassed when I gave you my name. Instead, you did not make the connection. And I was tempted. You would not understand, perhaps, the barrier my title puts between me and new acquaintances. I wanted to talk with you. I wanted you to admire my home and my park. I did not want to see that barrier go up."

"Oh," she said. She had looked at him while he spoke, but now her eyes closed again. "The things I said in the ballroom at Highmoor. In *your* ballroom." She spread her hands over her face.

He would have smiled at the memory, but he was too tense with fear.

"Does it make a difference?" he asked. "Will you wish to withdraw your acceptance of my offer? I am deeply sorry. Once one has deceived another, it is incredibly difficult to find the courage to undeceive her. But that is no excuse. Does it make a difference?"

He waited tensely for his world to end.

"I will not be just plain Mrs. Hartley Wade, then, will I?" she said.

"No." He did not dare hope. "You would be the Marchioness of Carew."

"Grand," she said. "Very grand. And Highmoor will be my home."

"Yes." *Will*, she had said, not *would*.

She laughed unexpectedly against her hands. "Perhaps I am marrying you for *your* money," she said. "Have you thought of that?"

"You did not know of it," he said. "But I know you well enough to trust that my title and wealth would have done nothing to sway you. I will always cherish the memory of your accepting me when you thought me an impoverished landscape gardener. Will you now accept me, knowing that I am the almost indecently wealthy Marquess of Carew?"

She sighed and lowered her hands before looking at him rather wanly. "Yes," she said. "How could I possibly resist the lure of Highmoor? *Have* you ever done any landscaping?"

He nodded. "Except in that one particular," he said, "I have always spoken the truth to you."

"Well," she said. "You will come tomorrow, *my lord*?" She smiled rather uncertainly at him.

"I would be honored," he said, "if you will call me Hartley. And if you will see me no differently than you ever have. Yes, I will come tomorrow."

They exchanged a look that was not quite a smile, and

he let himself out of the room. He took his cloak and hat from the butler, who must have been hovering in the hall all the time, and allowed the man to open the outer door for him.

A few moments later he was in his carriage on the way home, the rain beating against the windows. It was done, he thought, setting his head back against the squabs and closing his eyes. And she had accepted him—both as Mr. Wade and as the Marquess of Carew. She had accepted him.

She was going to be his wife.

*I love you so very, very much.*

They had not spoken of love this afternoon. He supposed he should have made that declaration a part of his marriage offer. He had been very gauche. But the words had not needed to be spoken. They were only words, after all. They loved each other. It had been there in every look and word they had exchanged. She had been willing to marry him just for himself. She had said yes, believing that he had nothing but himself to offer. Not that he had deliberately put her to the test. But he would always be able to remember that.

And soon—within a month—she would be his by both civil and church law. She would be his wife. He would be able to make love to her as well as loving her.

God. Ah, God. Happiness sometimes felt almost like agony.

"WHAT?" LORD FRANCIS KNELLER almost fell off the seat of his high-perch phaeton and jerked on the ribbons sufficiently to cause one of his horses to snort and jerk its head and threaten mutiny. He skillfully brought it under control.

"I am going to marry the Marquess of Carew," she repeated. "Exactly four weeks from today. I do not believe I will be able to drive out with you like this again, Francis. But I do thank you for your friendship during the past five years."

"Friendship?" He glanced at her incredulously before giving the road leading to the park his attention again. "*Friendship,* Samantha? Good God, woman, I *love* you."

She gazed at him in shock.

"Francis," she said, "what a dreadful bouncer."

"Sorry," he muttered. "No, it was no lie, but it ought not to have been said. But Carew, Samantha. *Carew?* He is a crip— Oh, dash it. I am sorry—again."

"He is not," she said. "He had an accident. He manages very well. And he never complains."

"Where did you meet him?" he asked. She noticed that he had taken his phaeton past the gates into the park. "At Chalcote, I suppose. That bloody Gabe—sorry! I'll draw his cork when I see him next. And I suppose you were dazzled by his title and his fortune and Highmoor—dratted splendid place. I cannot think of any other reason why you would be marrying him. Good God, Samantha, you could do a thousand times better than him."

"Please take me home," she said quietly.

He drew a deep breath and blew it out through puffed cheeks. "Your trouble, Samantha," he said, "is that you are blind in one eye and keep the other firmly closed. You do not realize, do you, that all of us, all your blood— your *blessed* court, are head over boots for you. And you do not care the snap of two fingers for any of us. But Carew! I—words fail me. Yes, home it is." He turned a corner sharply enough to arouse shouts of protest and some profanities from other drivers. "You do not have to demand it again. Carew! Good Lord."

"I care for him," she said quietly.

"The man is the next thing to a recluse," he said. "He has nothing to recommend him to someone like you."

"And you do?" she asked him. "Francis, you never said—"

"Because I knew—or thought—you did not want to hear it," he said. "I wanted to try to trick you into caring for me. I thought perhaps time would do it. The devil and his pitchfork! How long have you known him?"

"Since the day you left Chalcote," she said. "I walked onto Highmoor property and he was there."

He swore. And did not even apologize afterward.

"Francis." She set a hand lightly on his arm, but he flinched and jerked away from her. "I am sorry. But I do care for him, you know. I care very much."

"He must be worth at least fifty thousand a year," he said. "At least! I suppose I would care very much, too, Samantha, if I was a woman."

She said no more and they proceeded in silence—

a distressed silence on her part, an angry, frustrated one on his.

"Francis," she said as they drew nearer to Lady Brill's, "I do not want to lose your friendship."

"It never was friendship," he said.

"Yes, it was," she said. "It was always—fun. I always enjoyed your teasing insults. I always enjoyed matching wits with you. I thought that was all. I had no idea I would—hurt you by marrying someone else."

"I thought it was going to be Rushford, if anyone," he said, his jaw tightening. "I thought I saw a spark there, Samantha. More than a spark. I am glad at least it is not him. I would have fought dirty if he had tried anything, and if you had not had the sense to send him packing."

"No," she said. "There was nothing there, Francis. He merely took me by surprise and I danced with him. But there was nothing. I care for the Marquess of Carew. I am going to marry him. I am going to give him contentment. He is going to keep me safe."

"This would make a riveting romance, Samantha," he said. "I'll wager my hat you will make him contented. And from what is he to keep you safe, pray? Wolves like myself?"

"No," she said. "It was just a manner of speaking. He is going to—to keep me safe, that is all. We are to be wed at St. George's. It is what he wants. I was going to invite you. But perhaps you would rather I did not. I have written to Jenny and Gabriel, but I do not know if they will come. Jenny is—well, she is in delicate health again."

"Is she?" he said. "I thought Gabe was contented with two."

"I am hoping they will come," she said. "Will you if I invite you?"

"Carew would just adore seeing all your court in attendance at his wedding," he said.

"My friends," she said. "You are all my friends, Francis. Don't distress me with that other nonsense. It is nonsense, you know. We are all just friends."

"Someone should give you a looking glass for a gift sometime, Samantha," he said. "Though that would not be quite sufficient, either. It is not just looks with you. Can Carew see beyond your looks? I'll bloody kill him if—"

"Francis." She spoke sharply to him. "That is enough. I have heard enough such words from you to last a lifetime. I will hear your apology, if you please."

He grinned for the first time. "Spoken like a true marchioness," he said. "When you are considerably older, your ladyship, you will have to invest in a jeweled lorgnette. You will wither everyone you turn it on. It would help, of course, if your nose was longer. Perhaps it will grow in time. I am sorry. I have been a perfect bounder over this whole thing, I must confess. You should have given me some sort of warning, Samantha. If you had written a note, I could have blackened both my valet's eyes and broken his nose and smashed all his remaining teeth, and by the time I saw you I would have been perfectly civil and amiable. My apologies. Forgive me?"

"Of course," she said. "But, Francis, you did not mean all that nonsense, did you? Not really. You were just trying to tease me into feeling rotten, you idiot, and you succeeded."

"Well, then," he said lightly, "my day is made, Samantha. You really care for him, then? I'll have to see for myself at your wedding."

"You will come?" She turned her head to smile brightly at him. "Oh, thank you, Francis. I am going to be very happy, you know. I am going to be very—"

"—safe," he said. "Yes, I know. The pinnacle of any maiden's dreams. To marry and live—safely ever after. Do you want to go back to the park? For once there would be something truly spectacular to announce there."

"No," she said. "Hartley is to announce our betrothal in tomorrow's papers. I would not say anything before then. Only to you, because you are my friend and I was engaged to drive out with you."

"Hartley," he said quietly. "*Do* you want to go back to the park?"

"I think I would rather not, if you do not mind very much, Francis," she said.

They were at Lady Brill's already. He descended nimbly from the high seat and lifted her to the ground. He kept his hands at her waist for a brief moment.

"I hope he keeps you very—safe, Samantha," he said. "And I hope you will be very happy, too. He is a lucky devil."

"Thank you," she said, smiling at him. "Thank you, Francis."

He waited until she had been admitted to the house by the butler, who appeared surprised to see her return so soon. Then he climbed back to his seat and drove away.

His valet had better not look sideways or any other ways at him for an hour or two after he returned home, he thought, or those two black eyes and that broken nose and those smashed teeth might well become a reality.

Carew! He had met the man at Chalcote the year before last and again last year. A pleasant enough fellow, quiet and unassuming. But he appeared to have nothing beyond his title and fortune to recommend him to any woman, least of all to someone of Samantha's beauty and charm. And yet she was the last person he would have expected to succumb to such temptation.

Lord Francis Kneller swore under his breath. And then, realizing that he no longer had an audience that might demand an apology, he swore more vehemently and marginally more satisfyingly.

# 11

*H*E FINISHED HIS TOAST AND SIPPED ON HIS SEC-
ond cup of coffee. He was almost reluctant to
get up from the breakfast table in order to dress for the
outdoors before the Duke of Bridgwater arrived. He had
promised to accompany his friend to Tattersall's. Bridge
was in search of a pair of grays grand enough to comple-
ment his new curricle.

The Marquess of Carew looked down yet again at the
*Morning Post* open on the table beside him. He set his left
hand on it and touched the announcement with two fingers. He smiled. Now at last it was real to him. They were
betrothed. The whole fashionable world would know it
this morning.

Everyone would assume that it was a loveless match,
that she was marrying him for his position and fortune,
that he was marrying her for her beauty.

Only he and she would know. It was enough. It was a
delicious secret, in fact. It did not matter what the world
thought. He would take her home to Highmoor soon
after the wedding and live with her there for the rest of
their lives, with only the occasional visit elsewhere. She
loved Highmoor already. They would raise their children

there. It did not matter if no one else ever realized that they loved.

Viscount Nordal had been first surprised and then gratified. The girl had been difficult, he had explained, talking about Samantha as if she were still fresh from the schoolroom. She had refused more marriage offers than enough. But of course she would have to have windmills in her head to have refused the Marquess of Carew.

The marquess had smiled secretly at the assumption that she could have had only one reason for accepting his offer.

Lady Brill, too, had looked surprised when she first saw him. She knew, of course, that he had proposed marriage to her niece and had been accepted. She had been very civil to him during tea while Samantha had been quiet, looking with an endearing mixture of eagerness and anxiety from him to her aunt. He believed that Lady Brill had liked him by the time he rose to take his leave.

He wondered if Samantha had told her aunt that she was marrying him because she loved him. But it did not matter.

He took a few more sips of his coffee, his eyes still on the newspaper. He could hear the knocker banging against the outer door. Bridge was early. But then he heard voices outside the breakfast room, one of them raised confidently.

"No, no," the voice said. "No need to announce me. I shall announce myself."

It was a voice the marquess had not heard for a number of years, but there was no mistaking it. He pursed his lips and took one last rueful look down at the *Post*.

Lionel, Earl of Rushford, opened the door himself and sauntered inside, glancing about him as he did so. He was looking as if he had just stepped out of Weston's. He was immaculately dressed in the best tradition of Beau Brummell, with nothing overstated. Nothing that Lionel might wear needed overstatement, of course. He looked as if his splendid body had been poured into his clothes.

The marquess did not rise.

"Good morning, Lionel," he said. "Come and join me for breakfast." He gestured toward an empty chair.

"You have made changes," his cousin said.

"Yes, as you see." He had not admired his father's preference for heavy draperies and ponderous furniture. He had made extensive changes both here and at Highmoor. His eye for beauty as a landscape gardener sometimes extended indoors, too.

"Uncle would turn over in his grave," Lionel said. He was at the sideboard, helping himself to something from each of the hot plates. The words were not spoken with any apparent rancor, but they did not need to be. Even after all these years, the marquess recognized the tone. He was his uncle's favorite, the words had suggested, more favored than the son his uncle had been ashamed of.

The suggestion could no longer hurt. Any pain he might have felt had been swallowed up in a far greater pain when he was six years old. But because he had never responded to taunts since then, he guessed that Lionel still thought he had the power to wound.

"You do not seem particularly surprised to see me," Lionel said, seating himself at the table—but not on the chair the marquess had indicated—and tucking into his breakfast.

"I saw you at the Rochester ball," the marquess said.

"But did not come near even to exchange civilities?" Lionel said. "Were you too busy tripping the light fantastic, Hart? That must have been a sight for sore eyes."

"You were dancing with Miss Newman," the marquess said.

"Ah." Lionel set down his knife and fork. "Yes, that. The reason I came. I understand congratulations are in order."

The marquess inclined his head.

"Samantha is exquisitely lovely," Lionel said. "Enough to set any male mouth to watering. You are a fortunate man, Hart."

It was not lost upon the marquess that his betrothed had been referred to by the name that even he had not used aloud yet. Perhaps deliberately so? Yes, probably.

"I am well aware of my good fortune, Lionel," he said. "Thank you."

" 'My face is my fortune, sir, she said.' " Lionel sang through the whole verse of the old song before chuckling. "But no longer, eh, Hart? Now she will exchange it for a far greater fortune. Yes, you are a lucky man indeed. Not that I am suggesting, of course, that she is marrying you for that alone. I am sure your—person offers other inducements. I do believe you have fine eyes."

He spoke with the greatest good nature. Anyone listening would have laughed with him and taken his words for light teasing. The Marquess of Carew was not deceived.

Or ruffled.

"I thank you for your congratulations, Lionel," he said, smiling. "You will, of course, come to the wedding?"

"I would not miss it for worlds," his cousin said. "I am almost your only remaining relative, am I not? In the absence of your mother and my uncle, I must be there myself. It will be affecting to watch you—walk up the aisle with the lovely Samantha."

He was a master at the art of innuendo, the marquess thought. A mere pause between words could speak volumes with Lionel.

"Thank you," he said. "I shall look forward to seeing you there."

"Doubtless you will be taking her back to Highmoor as soon as the wedding breakfast has been consumed," Lionel said. "I would if I were you, Hart. Incarcerate her there. You would not want her running around town once she is married, would you? You know what is said of married ladies. And every man wants to be quite sure of the paternity of at least his firstborn son, after all."

The fingers of the marquess's left hand curled about his napkin. He lifted it to his lips when he saw that Lionel had noted the action.

"A joke, of course," Lionel said, chuckling. "She has a spotless reputation and will doubtless be true to you. What woman would not?" He pushed his chair away and got to his feet, even though his plate was still half-full. "I can see that you are finished, Hart. You doubtless have plans for the morning. I will not keep you. I just felt compelled to come to assure you of a cousin's good wishes."

"Thank you." The marquess stayed where he was. "That was good of you, Lionel. You can show yourself out?"

He stayed where he was for a few minutes after his cousin had left. He smiled again at the announcement still spread on the table beside his plate. Lionel did not know, of course, that it was impossible to put doubts in his mind this morning. Not that he would have allowed himself to be goaded, anyway.

But there was annoyance nevertheless. Perhaps more than annoyance, if he was perfectly honest with himself. Fury. No, fury was an uncontrolled emotion, and his was quite under control. A steely anger, then.

*Samantha*. Lionel had deliberately called her by her given name to suggest a familiarity with her. He had suggested that she was capable of being unfaithful to him after marriage. He had suggested that she would be capable of conceiving another man's child and passing it off as his own.

He did not mind the insult such slurs cast upon himself and his ability to attract and to please and to control a wife. Lionel's opinion meant less than nothing to him.

But he had better not try such insinuations on anyone else.

Let him breathe one breath of an insult on Samantha and there would be trouble. Lionel might yet learn a thing or two about letting the proverbial sleeping dog lie. This dog might not prove to be such an abject weakling as he doubtless thought.

Samantha was his. His possession after their marriage, though he did not believe he would ever be able to think of her in quite such terms. She was his by virtue of the facts that she loved him and he loved her and they were to be married. She was his.

He would protect what was his own.

SHE FELT SAFE. AND cheerful and at peace with herself. She knew she had done the right thing, despite the reactions of other people.

"I was more gratified than I can say," Uncle Gerald had said when he called at Lady Brill's, "to learn that you could be so wise, Samantha. Carew is worth seventy thousand a year, you know, and has made very generous provision indeed for you and any children of the marriage in the event that he should predecease you. The first boy, of course, will inherit."

It did not matter to her that half the members of the *ton*, or maybe a great deal more than half, would believe that she was marrying Hartley for his position and wealth. It was enough that she knew she was marrying him for friendship and safety. Because she liked him more than any other man she had known.

"You could have knocked me down with a feather," Aunt Aggy said after Hartley's afternoon call. "He is not at all the type of young man one would have expected you to choose. And I know, of course, that his title and his fortune did not weigh with you at all. I am happy to have this proof that you have acquired the wisdom to see beyond outer appearances to the man within. He is a very pleasant young man, dear. And I know you would not marry for anything less than love. I believe you have done very well for yourself."

She did not correct her aunt. What she and Hartley had was better than love. Far better. There would be none of the deceptive highs and shattering lows of love in their relationship. Only friendship and gentleness and kindness and—oh, and safety. She clung to the word and the idea more than to any other.

She wondered if it would be a normal marriage. She could not imagine anything more than friendship between them. It seemed almost embarrassing to think of more—until she remembered the kiss they had shared at the Rochester ball. That had been a wonderful kiss, warm and comforting. Perhaps the marriage bed would be like that, too. And she wanted the marriage bed, she realized, even though she had put marriage from her mind years ago and had never felt any great craving for what she would miss as a spinster.

There was no reason to believe that he had been suggesting a mere platonic relationship. He was a marquess—

it was still difficult to adjust her mind to that reality—and would want an heir.

She wanted children. Now that she had made the quite unexpected and impulsive decision to marry—so that she would feel safe from the raw emotions that had threatened her with Lionel's return—she wanted all that marriage could offer her. Except love. Love terrified her. She was deeply thankful that Mr. Wade—Hartley—was just her friend. And soon to be her husband. The man who would initiate her in his own quiet way into the secrets of the marriage bed. Despite her age and her worldly wisdom, she knew only the essential fact of what would happen there.

She wanted it—with him. Without any extreme of emotion. With just—affection. There was affection between them, she believed.

Her "court" surprised her. None as much as Francis, it was true—she had been dreadfully upset over his quite uncharacteristic reaction to her announcement, until she met him at a soirée two evenings later and he was his old self, right down to the notorious lavender coat and to the indolent, teasing manner as he asked her if he had succeeded in squeezing a tear from her eye during the afternoon they had not gone to the park.

"Pray do not disappoint me by telling me that I did not succeed with my superior acting skills, Samantha," he said. "You deserved a little punishment for your defection, after all. Now whom am I expected to flirt with without running the danger of finding myself caught in parson's mousetrap?"

She was enormously relieved to learn that it had all been an act. At least, she chose to believe that it had been. She did not like to think that she really had hurt him.

A few of her former beaux quietly disappeared. Some of them expressed disappointment, with varying degrees of intensity. One or two of them were hearty in their congratulations.

All of them believed the worst of her motives for betrothing herself to the Marquess of Carew. She did not care. But she did try to look at him through the eyes of the *ton,* many of whose members either had never seen him before he started to escort her to some evening entertainments or else were virtual strangers to him.

She saw a gentleman of little more than average height and of only average build—though she knew from the one occasion when her body had rested along the length of his that there was strength in his muscles. She saw a man who had no great claim to good looks, though there was nothing ugly about his face. And of course, she saw a man whose right arm was usually held stiffly to his side, the hand, always gloved, curled inward against his hip. And a man whose permanent limp jarred his whole body when he walked.

She could hardly blame people for the conclusions they must have drawn about her motives for marrying him. But she did not care. She could no longer see him as other people saw him unless she deliberately tried—she was not sure that she had ever seen him as others saw him. To her he was Hartley Wade, more recently the

Marquess of Carew, her dear friend. Her savior—the word did not seem too extravagant.

He had saved her from herself.

She saw Lionel twice when she was with Hartley, once at the theater and once at a private concert, but neither time did he approach them, to her great relief. She did not still love him, she had decided. Of course she did not. She had more sense than that. It was just the eternal pull of the human will to what was undeniably attractive and evil.

Hartley had saved her from that. She had settled for friendship and contentment. And Lionel would have no further interest in whatever game he had been playing with her now that she was betrothed to another man.

She was safe.

But she attended a ball with her aunt one evening, two weeks after her betrothal. It was an invitation she had accepted long ago and felt obliged to honor. Besides, she loved to dance, and Hartley had urged her not to stop dancing because of him.

This time Lionel did not keep his distance. He approached her before the opening set began—her court was somewhat thinner about her than it had always been—and signed his name in her card next to the first waltz.

He did not speak for the first few minutes after their set began. He merely danced with her and gazed at her, a half smile on his lips. She could not tell if it was mocking or wistful.

"You did not believe me, did you?" he asked her at last,

his voice low, intimate, although they were surrounded by dancers.

She looked up into his pale blue eyes.

"You did not trust me," he said. "You thought I would break your heart again, as I did six years ago."

When he looked and spoke like this, it was difficult not to forget all else except him and the feelings she had once had for him.

"I should not say anything more, should I?" he said. "It would be the honorable thing for me to step back in silence now that you are betrothed to someone else."

"Yes," she managed to whisper.

"You knew," he said, "that I was going to ask you to be my countess. Because I love you. Because I have always loved you."

Why was he doing it if he was not sincere? What could he hope to gain now? She looked into his eyes and saw nothing but sincerity and sadness.

*It would be the honorable thing for me to step back in silence . . .*

Why was he not doing the honorable thing? If he loved her, as he said he did, why was he trying to cause her distress? Francis, after his first outburst when she had taken him totally by surprise, had gone out of his way to release her from the burden of believing that she had hurt him. He had acted honorably, like the gentleman he was—despite a tendency toward dandyism, even foppishness.

But what if Lionel really loved her? What if he had really intended to offer for her? She might have been his wife. Lionel's instead of Hartley's. She felt the now almost familiar stabbing of desire in her womb.

But she would still be better off as Hartley's wife.

"Someone else asked me," she said. "And I accepted him. Because I wanted to."

"Because you love him?" He moved his head a little closer to hers. His eyes dropped to her lips. "Can you say those words, Samantha? *Because I love the Marquess of Carew.*"

"My feelings for my betrothed are none of your concern, my lord," she said.

"And for me?" he said. "Can you tell me in all honesty, Samantha, that you do not love me?"

"The question is impertinent," she said.

"You cannot, can you?" His eyes pleaded with her.

She clamped her lips together.

The encounter upset her for several days. But she was within two weeks of her wedding. She set her mind on it and the preparations that were being made for it. She longed for it.

Jenny and Gabriel were not coming. Samantha was both disappointed and relieved when she had her cousin's letter. She hated to think of their not being at her wedding, but she had dreaded, too, that if they came they would encounter Lionel somewhere in London.

Jenny herself was very disappointed. But Gabriel was always unwilling for her to travel during the early—and the late—months of her pregnancies, she explained. He was always terrified that she would miscarry and ruin her own health as well as losing their child. But he was disappointed, too.

"He says he is vastly impressed by your good sense, Sam," Jenny wrote. "And by that he does not mean your sense in marrying a man even wealthier than himself, I hasten to add. He means your sense in choosing a man of Lord Carew's kindness and good nature.

"I would choose stronger words myself. How naughty of you to have met him at Highmoor before you left for London and not to have told us. For shame! And I was so chagrined when he arrived home apparently the day after you left. I had great matchmaking hopes for the two of you, though I would never admit as much to Gabriel. He would crow with triumph and never let me forget it.

"Sam, how very *romantic*. I sigh with vicarious bliss. Clandestine meetings in Highmoor Park, the heartrending separation, and the heartsick lover going after you to claim your hand. And they were married and lived happily ever after—sigh! You see what being in an 'interesting condition' does to me? Oh, I *wish* we could be there at your wedding. I like him enormously, Sam, and of course I *love* you. And we are to be neighbors. I become delirious."

She had continued with strict instructions for Samantha to use her newfound influence—"all new husbands wrap very comfortably about one's little finger, Sam"—to persuade Lord Carew to bring her home immediately following the wedding night.

"And do not—I repeat, *do not*—listen with more than

half an ear to the lecture Aunt Aggy will give you the night before your wedding," she had written in conclusion. "She will have you quaking in your slippers, Sam, with admonitions about duty and pain and discomfort and enduring for a mere few minutes each night and all the advantages accruing from marriage that quite offset such an unpalatable duty. Performing that particular duty is beautiful and wonderful and utterly pleasurable, Sam—I speak from personal experience, though I blush even as I write—when one loves the man concerned. So enjoy, my dear, your wedding night and every night following it—my blush deepens."

Even Jenny did not know their real reason for marrying. But it did not matter. Love had worked for her and Gabriel. But happy love was a rare commodity. Samantha was happier to settle for something else.

She waited for her wedding day with longing and a thinly veiled impatience. Once she was married, everything would finally be settled in her life. She could proceed to live contentedly ever after.

Sometimes it felt as if the day would never come.

# 12

S T. GEORGE'S, HANOVER SQUARE—THE FASHION-
able church in which to wed. The first day of
June—the fashionable time to marry. The weather was
kind. More than kind—there was not a cloud in the sky,
and the morning was hot without being oppressively so.
The church was filled with modishly dressed members
of the *ton*.

If he had ever had a dream of the beginning of wedded
bliss, the Marquess of Carew thought as he waited rather
nervously at the front of the church with an unusually
solemn Duke of Bridgwater, then this was it. There was a
great deal to be said for the quiet intimacy of a private
ceremony, with only family and very close friends in attendance, but it was not what he wanted for himself.

He wanted the whole world to see their happiness. He
wanted the whole world to know what a lucky fellow he
was. He had never dreamed of winning for himself such
a sweet and beautiful bride, and one, moreover, who had
chosen him entirely for himself. He had never expected
to find a bride who would love him. And although he
had dreamed of loving a woman, he had never really expected to feel that love so powerfully and to have it returned.

To be marrying the woman he loved and the woman who loved him, especially when she happened to be the most beautiful woman in all England—oh, yes, it was an occasion to be celebrated with his peers and hers.

Brides were always late. There were some who would say that it was ill-bred for them to arrive early, or even on time. It showed an overeagerness, something a lady must never show for anyone or anything.

Samantha was on time. If he had been able to smile at that particular moment, the marquess would have smiled. If she was overeager, then his happiness could only be more complete. But he could not smile. At first he was so nervous that he was afraid when he got to his feet his legs would not hold him up. And then he saw her.

He was aware only that she was so beautiful his breath caught in his throat. He did not really see the delicate pink muslin high-waisted dress, as simply and elegantly styled as most of her clothes, or the flowers woven into her blond curls, or the simple posy of flowers she carried in one hand. He did not notice Viscount Nordal, on whose arm she walked down the aisle of the church toward him.

He saw only Samantha. His bride.

She was looking pale and rather frightened. She looked neither to left nor to right at the gathered congregation, though everyone, perhaps without exception, was looking at her. She was looking—at him. And he recognized the slight curving of her lips as an attempt at a smile. He smiled back, though he was not sure that his face responded to his will. He hoped she would know from his eyes that he was smiling at her, encouraging her, welcoming her.

And then they were there beside him and he knew, almost as if he had not yet realized it, that this was their wedding day, that in a matter of minutes they would be married. Irrevocably. For life. Lady Brill, he noticed, was already sniveling in the front pew.

"Dearly beloved, we are gathered . . ."

The familiar words. The familiar ceremony. So very familiar. And yet new and wonderful. Because this time the words were being spoken and the ceremony was being performed for them—for him and his own dearly beloved.

Such a very short ceremony, he thought, promising to love and to cherish and to keep her through all the vicissitudes of life, listening to her promise to love, honor, and obey him—though he would never, ever demand obedience of his love against her will. So short and yet so momentous.

In those few minutes and with very few words, two lives were being changed forever. Two lives were being interwoven, being made one. Man and wife. One body, one soul.

Bridge's hand, as he passed him the ring, was slightly unsteady, he noticed. His own was no longer so. He slid the ring onto her finger. The visual symbol of the endlessness of their union and their love.

"With this ring I thee wed . . ."

*And with my body I thee worship,* he said with his heart and his eyes as well as with his lips. My *beloved.*

And it was over. Almost before his mind had begun to comprehend that this was it, the most important event of his life. It was over.

"—I now pronounce you man and wife together . . ."

She was still pale. Her eyes, luminous and trusting, gazed into his.

He kissed her, very lightly, very briefly, on the lips. And while the congregation murmured with what sounded like a collective sigh, he smiled at her. His facial muscles obeyed his will this time. He smiled at his bride, his wife.

And she smiled back.

Sometimes happiness could be almost an agony, he had discovered on the day she had accepted his offer. But sometimes it could be such a welling of pure joy that it seemed impossible that one human frame could contain it without exploding into a million fragments.

There was the register to sign. And then the organ was pealing out a glorious anthem as he set his bride's right arm on his left and took her back along the aisle she had descended such a short while ago with her uncle. She was smiling, he saw, looking across at her, and there was color in her cheeks again. He smiled about him at the gathered *ton,* only a few of whom he knew well, but most of whom he had met within the past month. There was Lady Brill, with red-rimmed eyes and watery smile. And Gerson, grinning and winking. And Lionel, with an unfathomable expression.

They were outside on the pavement, the sounds of the organ suddenly faint behind them, a small crowd of the curious standing at a little distance from the waiting carriages. Soon the congregation would spill outside and there would be a damnable crush. He reached across with his stiff right hand and set it lightly on top of hers.

"Samantha Wade, Marchioness of Carew," he said. He wanted to be the first—after the rector—to say it aloud. "You look more beautiful than there are words to describe you."

"Oh, I do sound very grand." She laughed breathlessly. "And you look splendidly handsome, Hartley."

She was looking through the eyes of love, he thought fondly.

Their one moment of near privacy was at an end.

THE BALLROOM AT CAREW House, Stanhope Gate, was large. Even so, it appeared crowded, with tables set up along its whole length and the cream of the *ton* seated for the wedding breakfast. Samantha, sitting beside her husband, still felt numb, as she had done since waking up from a fitful sleep. It was hard to grasp that it was over, that it was done. She was married. Hartley was her husband.

All yesterday she had been sick with indecision. Literally sick. She had vomited three separate times and had noticed her aunt's look of startled speculation.

But the vomiting had been caused entirely by nerves and last-minute doubts. Was it right to marry just for convenience—for *safety*? What if, after all, life had love to offer her? It would be too late to discover that it did after tomorrow.

She had told Aunt Aggy only about the nerves. She had had to say *something* after her aunt had asked her straight out if it was possible she was increasing.

"Because if you had been," Aunt Aggy had said with a sigh after she had been assured that it was no such thing—she had sounded almost disappointed, "I would not have to proceed to instruct you on what you must expect of your wedding night. I have no wish to add to your fears, dear, but it is as well to be prepared."

She had proceeded with the lecture Jenny had warned about. Samantha had blushed at the graphic and quite dispassionate description of the physical process— some of it she had not known before. But part of her mind had been elsewhere, unwillingly turning over her doubts once more.

Lionel had danced with her twice in the past two weeks. Each time he had been pale and restrained and serious and, of course, impossibly handsome. He had made no further reference to her betrothal. In fact, he had spoken very little—with his voice. His blue eyes had spoken volumes. And somehow she had found it difficult during those sets—waltzes, of course—to stop herself from looking into his eyes.

He had behaved honorably for the past two weeks. As honorably as Francis and Jeremy and Sir Robin and all the rest of her gentlemen friends. She would have preferred it if he had been more obviously snakelike.

She had begun to doubt again. To doubt her own judgment of him. Six years was a long time. He had spent those years traveling abroad. He had aged during those years from five-and-twenty to one-and-thirty. From young manhood to maturity.

What if he had been sincere all the time? He had told her that he had wanted her as his countess. She might have known with him again the heights of romantic love.

And perhaps the depths, too. Perhaps he was not sincere. And even if he had really wanted to marry her and had done so, would he have remained faithful to her for the rest of their lives? Would she have known again the misery that was the exact antithesis of the joy of love?

She was doing the right thing. The sort of affection she and Hartley felt for each other—she did not believe she was using too strong a word—would remain constant. He would always be kind and gentle with her. They would always be friends. She need never fear that he would be unfaithful. And she—she would devote herself to him once they were married. She would hope that there would be a child soon—surely he meant for it to be a normal marriage. She would be safe.

But the doubts had started again and had continued all day and on through the night—a constant cycle of fear and panic and reassurance and good sense.

And now it was all over. Now she could let the doubts rest. It was too late now to doubt. They were married.

The wedding ceremony had affected her far more deeply than she had expected. It had seemed up until she had seen him this morning, looking smart and even handsome in a new blue coat with gray breeches and very white linen, that it was a practical and sensible alliance they were contracting. But in the event it had turned out to be—a marriage. He was not just a friend she had decided to live with for the rest of her life. He was her husband.

She shivered with the finality of it.

He touched her hand with light fingertips and leaned toward her. "You have eaten very little," he said.

She smiled at him. "Would it not amaze everyone if the bride ate heartily?" she asked.

She loved the way his eyes smiled. She could almost fall in love with that smile, she thought, startled.

"Tomorrow," he said. "Tomorrow you will be able to eat again."

She felt herself blushing. And yet she did not dread the coming night, despite Aunt Aggy's warnings and her new realization that there was more than the mere penetration of her body to be expected. But she did not dread it. She was only a little embarrassed at the thought of doing it with a friend rather than with a lover.

They had been greeted by a dizzying number of people outside the church, almost all of whom had kissed her cheeks and squeezed her hand and pumped Hartley's hand—he had offered his left, she noticed—and kissed him, too, if they happened to be female. But even so, she had not seen everyone. And even now, she had been sitting and eating—or not eating—in such a daze that she had not looked at each separate guest. There were a few—friends of Hartley's—that she did not even know or knew only very vaguely by sight.

He had presented her to Lord Gerson, one of his particular friends, a couple of weeks ago at an afternoon fête. She smiled at the man now and he winked at her. He seemed to find the marriage of his friend a huge joke. In fact, he had remarked to her at that fête that he had never seen Hartley in town during the Season before and had known that there must be a woman behind his appearance this time.

"And, by Jove, everything is as clear as daylight to me now that I have clapped eyes on you, Miss Newman," he had said. "Carew is a lucky dog."

There was Lord Hawthorne toward the back of the ballroom, not far from Francis. Francis was looking quite eye-catching in a lemon-yellow coat with pale turquoise waistcoat. It looked as if he were flirting with the ladies on either side of him. He was certainly doing a great deal of smiling and laughing.

Had he been serious? Probably not. He seemed to have recovered very nicely. She hoped he had not been serious. She was fond of him.

And there was —oh, dear God. Dear God! Had he been there all the time? He was seated in the middle of the ballroom, looking so startlingly conspicuous that she could not believe he had not suddenly appeared there from nowhere. Had he been at the church? What was he doing here? He had certainly not been on her guest list. And not on Hartley's, either, though he had told her that he had issued some verbal invitations and not bothered to add them to his written list. But Hartley could not have invited *him*.

Her eyes met his and he looked steadily and gravely at her before she snatched her eyes away. She had not noticed how hot the room had become, how heavy the air was with a hundred different perfumes. She breathed slowly through her mouth, determined not to pant.

There were speeches and toasts and applause and laughter. Hartley got up to speak and she smiled and touched his arm, aware that he was saying something complimentary about her and something about his own good fortune.

He was very sweet. Did he not realize that she was the fortunate one? She felt a sudden wave of gladness—that it was all over and doubts were at rest, that she was safe at last. With a man she trusted and liked.

Those who had not greeted them personally outside the church did so after the breakfast. Guests milled about the ballroom while servants discreetly tried to clear the tables. Guests wandered into the hall and the drawing room and out onto the terrace and into the garden. Samantha was separated from her husband, who was dragged off to the drawing room by someone she scarcely knew to meet an elderly dowager who had known his grandfather. Samantha was led into the garden by several of her lady friends, two of whom linked arms with her.

There she received the homage of her court—she

could almost hear Gabriel's voice describing the scene thus and smiled, though she suddenly missed him and Jenny dreadfully.

Francis told her that they were all going to go into deep mourning the next day and into a permanent decline after that. But she tapped him sharply on the arm and reminded him that his behavior at table earlier had hardly been that of a man planning to pine away from unrequited love.

He grinned at her and squeezed both her hands and kissed both her cheeks. Sir Robin followed suit and then Jeremy Nicholson and several others.

She must go and find Hartley, she thought. It felt wrong to be without him.

"Oh, dear," she said suddenly, as her eyes blurred and tears spilled over onto her cheeks. Talking thus with all her old friends and suitors, she had realized anew that her life had changed irrevocably today, that she was a bride and a wife. And that the thought was a pleasing one. "Oh, dear, how foolish I am."

"You see, Samantha?" Sir Robin said. "You are grieving along with us. But for which one of us in particular? That is the intriguing question." He smiled kindly at her while Francis handed her a large linen handkerchief.

She dabbed at her eyes with it and then clutched it in her hand. Francis had turned away, his attention called by one of the ladies who had sat beside him at breakfast.

"Something old and something new," a quiet voice said into her ear, and she spun around, effectively cutting herself off from the small group that still lingered about her. "The pearls are the ones you had as a girl. Your mother's, at a guess. The dress is new and very lovely."

"Thank you," she said, smiling uncertainly at Lionel. She did not like to ask him what he did there. She feared he must have brazened his way in without an invitation. But why?

"Something borrowed," he said, one long, well-manicured finger flicking at the handkerchief she held clutched in one hand. "But nothing blue, Samantha?"

"I did not think of it," she said, gazing into his blue eyes. They looked sad.

"I did," he said. "I brought you a wedding gift. A family heirloom. It has always been very precious to me. I wanted to give it to you on the occasion of your wedding." The shadow of a frown crossed his brow for one moment, but he smiled as he reached into a pocket and brought out a small box. He did not hand it to her but opened it and showed her the contents. His eyes looked into her face the whole while.

She breathed in deeply. The sapphire stone of the brooch was surrounded by diamonds in a pleasingly old-fashioned setting.

"Something blue," he said.

"Oh, my lord," she said, in deep distress. It was such a beautiful, personal gift. "I could not."

"No," he said softly, "you could not refuse a wedding gift, could you? As a token of my—esteem, Samantha?"

"No." She still shook her head. "It is too—personal, my lord. I do thank you. Truly I do. But I could not accept it."

"Whatever would Hartley say if you refused it?" he asked.

"H—Hartley?" She looked at him, frowning.

He laughed suddenly. "My cousin," he said. "My cousin Hartley. We practically grew up together. Has he not told you? And I have not, either, until now, have I? There are some things one assumes another must know; but there is no reason you should have. I am sorry. My mother and his father were sister and brother. I spent a large part of my youth in Yorkshire, at Highmoor."

She could remember that one year, when Jenny was to have made her come-out and her engagement to Lionel was to become official, it had all been postponed because Lionel was in Yorkshire attending his uncle, who was gravely ill. And she remembered that it was some ghastly personal feud between Lionel and Gabriel that had thrown Jenny into the midst of such a dreadful scandal and had forced her to marry Gabriel. But she had never known or asked for all the details. Lionel was Hartley's *cousin*?

"The idea has taken you by surprise," he said. He was unpinning the brooch from its small velvet cushion inside the box. "But you see, you and I are cousins by marriage. And this is a *family* heirloom. You will not refuse it now, will you? And you really must have something blue."

"Yes," she said uncertainly. "Thank you, my lord."

She watched rather unhappily as he took the brooch from the box and reached across to pin it himself on her dress, just above her left breast. The pin was stiff. His fingers lingered for what seemed an eternity and burned her flesh through the thin muslin of her dress. One of his hands brushed downward over her breast, touching the sensitive nipple, when he was finished and was examining the effect of his handiwork.

"Yes," he said softly. "I knew this was where it belonged, Samantha. I could only wish that circumstances had been different, that you had been someone else's bride today. But I wish you every happiness, my dear." He made her an elegant bow, his eyes holding hers.

"Thank you, Lionel," she said, realizing only when it was too late that she had used his given name, something she had not done in six years. "I must go and find my husband."

"Your husband," he echoed. The sadness was back in his eyes. She turned and hurried in the direction of the house, though she was stopped and kissed by wedding guests no fewer than three times before she stepped indoors.

HE HAD SOMEHOW GOT himself cornered by five elderly ladies, all of whom seemed pleased to reminisce about his father or his grandfather—"that handsome devil"—and all of whom agreed that it had been extremely naughty of him to hide himself away from the public gaze for most of his life.

"We will just have to hope that dear Lady Carew will effect a change in you," one lady said, startling him with the use of Samantha's new name.

"And really, you know," another said with unashamed lack of tact, "you need not hide away on account of a limp and a withered hand, Carew. Many of our war heroes have fared far worse. Young Waters, my sister's grandson, came home without one leg and with the other sawn off to the knee."

It was a great relief to see Samantha in the drawing room doorway, looking about her until she spotted him. Everyone she passed on the way wanted to talk to her and kiss her, but in five minutes' time she was at his side and smiling and talking easily with the dowagers, two of whom were not above giving her rather earthy advice about the coming night and then cackling at their own wit and her blushes—as well as his own.

Samantha had the social skills to extricate them easily from the situation after a mere few minutes. He headed into the hall with her, where some of their guests were finally taking their leave. They had no time for private words for some time to come.

He longed for privacy. He was the one who had wanted a large wedding, and indeed he was not sorry. This would be a day to remember for the rest of their lives. But he longed to be alone with her. Even though there was a large part of the day left and he would not be tasteless enough to try taking her to bed before it was time, nevertheless he longed for just her company, just the two of them talking together or perhaps even silently sitting together.

He felt a sudden nostalgia for those afternoons at

Highmoor. Soon. Within a week they would be back there and would proceed to live happily ever after.

He took her out to the garden eventually, past the thinning crowds of their guests. He breathed in fresh air, tucked her arm through his, and walked with her toward a small rose arbor, which he hoped would give them a few moments of privacy. Fortunately there was no one there. He seated her on a wrought-iron seat and sat at her left.

"Someone should have told me," he said, "that the person one sees the very least on one's wedding day is one's bride."

"But this has all been so very pleasant, Hartley," she said, turning to smile at him.

That was when he saw it for the first time. His eyes fixed on it and he felt the blood drain from his head.

"Where did you get that?" he whispered.

"What?" She frowned. But her eyes followed the line of his and she flushed and covered it with her hand. "Lionel—L-Lord Rushford gave it to me as a wedding present," she said. "He said it was a family heirloom. Of *your* family. He said—I did not know he was your cousin, Hartley. I did not know you were close. He implied that you would want me to have it. He made a joke about it being something blue. I had the other three things—my mother's pearls, my new dress, Lord Francis Kneller's borrowed handkerchief. I— Do you recognize it?"

It had been his mother's. One of her precious possessions, given her by his father on their wedding day—as "something blue," she had always said. She had worn it almost constantly. She had told him when she was dying that he was to have it and give it to his own bride one day. For some reason that had stuck in his mind more than anything after she died, and he had hunted for the brooch, asked his father about it, asked his aunt, Lionel's mother, about it, grieved over it almost as much, it had sometimes seemed, as he had grieved over his mother.

He had never found it.

Lionel had had it. Perhaps he had taken it, or perhaps it had been given him. But no one had ever told him, Hartley. He had been left to search, far beyond the bounds of reason, for years.

And now the brooch had been given to his bride after all—by Lionel.

"Yes, I recognize it," he said. "It was my mother's."

"Oh." She sounded enormously relieved. "Then it was a very kind gesture, was it not, Hartley, for him to give it to me? To give it back to you through me. It is a wedding gift for both of us. It is yours as much as it is mine."

"It is yours, Samantha," he said, "just as it was my mother's. It looks good on you."

She smiled at him and fingered the brooch again. But he felt a deep and impotent fury—partly against himself. Apart from her wedding ring, he had not yet bought her a gift, he realized. His mother's lovely sapphire brooch, the "something blue" for the wedding day, had been a gift from Lionel.

What the devil had he meant by it?

Was it a peace offering?

The marquess did not for one moment believe it.

## 13

SHE HAD OFTEN BEEN A GUEST IN OTHER PEOPLE'S homes. She was accustomed to sleeping in strange bedchambers. Indeed, it could be said that she had had no real home of her own for a number of years. It was hard now to grasp the reality of the fact that this room was her own. She belonged here at Carew House as she belonged at Highmoor Abbey by virtue of the fact that she was married to the owner of both.

She wrapped her arms about herself, though she was not cold, as she gazed about the large square room with its high coved ceiling, painted with an idyllic pastoral scene, its warm carpet underfoot, its elegant furniture, its large, silk-canopied bed.

It seemed it was to be a normal marriage—there was no reason at all why it would not be, of course. He had said he would join her here shortly. Her mind touched on what Aunt Aggy had told her yesterday and on what Jenny had said in her letter. But she did not expect either extreme from her wedding night. She did not expect to find it fearsome and distasteful. Neither did she expect to find it beautiful and wonderful. She expected—she hoped—to find it pleasant.

She had been pacing, she realized when there was a

tap on the door and she stopped. She did not call to him to come in. He opened the door and stepped inside and closed the door behind him. He was wearing a wine-colored brocaded dressing gown with a satin collar. He was smiling at her as he came across the room toward her, his hands reaching out for hers.

"I thought this moment would never come," he said. "I have been shamelessly looking forward to it all day. All month."

He was not wearing a glove. She found herself glancing down at his right hand as it clasped hers. It was paler than the left and thinner. His fingers were bent sharply at the joints. His wrist was bent.

"I wish I could be whole for you," he said.

"Whole?" She looked into his eyes. "You mean because of your accident? Do you think that makes a difference to me? Because you limp? And because you have lost some of the use of your hand? You are whole in every way that could possibly be of importance to me. I regret these things only in that they cause you distress."

She lifted his right hand to rub her cheek against his fingers. She turned her head to kiss them.

"Thank you," he said. "I was a little afraid."

She smiled at him—and blushed.

"You are nervous?" he asked.

"Not really," she said. "Just a little—embarrassed, perhaps." She laughed. "And I suppose nervous, too. But not afraid or reluctant."

He took a step closer so that he was almost touching her and set the backs of the fingers of his left hand against her cheek. "I have some experience," he said. "Which I say not as a boast but as some reassurance. I know how to relax you and how to give you pleasure. And I believe I will be able to minimize the pain of this first encounter for you."

He kissed her.

She was rather surprised, despite the fact that this was their wedding night and he had just come to her bed-chamber, and despite the fact that he had kissed her at the Rochester ball—at her request. She had not expected him to kiss her tonight. Kissing was somehow sugges-tive of love and romance.

But she was glad. She set her arms about his neck and leaned into him. He was warm and comfortable and somehow familiar. He had said he knew how to relax her. He was doing it now. It would not have been relax-ing to have been led immediately to the bed and to have been taken into the marriage act without further ado. She parted her lips as he had done and felt the increased warmth and intimacy of the meeting of inner flesh. She felt his tongue stroking the soft inside of her mouth.

She kept her eyes closed as he kissed them and her temples and her chin and her throat. His hair was soft and silky between her fingers. He intended for them to be lovers, she thought in some wonder, as well as friends and man and wife who had conjugal relations.

His mouth returned to hers. His hands were stroking up and down her back, relaxing her further. His left hand came forward to circle gently over the side of her breast. She turned slightly without conscious thought until her breast was cupped in his hand and his thumb was rubbing very lightly over the nipple.

Oh, he felt very good. She had known that he would feel good. How wrong Aunt Aggy had been—had her own marriage been so dreadful? This was lovely. Though this, of course, was not the marriage act.

"We will be more comfortable lying down," he said against her lips, as if he had read her thoughts.

She wondered if the time would come—she supposed it must—when all of this would be so routine that she would hardly think about it at all. But suddenly, as she lay down on the bed and watched him blow out the candles and waited for him to join her, she was glad this was the first time. Two of the most momentous experiences of her life—her wedding and her first sexual encounter—were happening today, and she wanted to remember them for the rest of her life as also two of the most pleasant experiences of her life.

He slid his right arm beneath her head and drew her against him before kissing her again. He was wearing only a nightshirt now, she could feel. He was very warm. She snuggled into his warmth. He felt solid and dependable. She was so glad it was he. She was so glad this was not an experience of wild passion and love. She would have been terrified. This she could enjoy. Thoroughly enjoy.

"Yes," she whispered when he touched her breast again. "That feels good, Hartley." His hand moved to the other breast.

She fell into a waking dream of contented pleasure.

She was almost unaware that after a short while he undid the buttons at the front of her nightgown and slipped his hand inside so that he could stroke her naked breasts. Certainly there was no embarrassment.

"Beautiful," he murmured against her mouth. "Softer than silk."

She was a little more aware when he lifted her nightgown to her hips. But she was curiously unembarrassed. Had the time come, then? She was ready for it. But he did not do what she expected. His fingertips stroked lightly up the inner thigh of one of her legs and the backs of his fingers stroked down the other thigh. It was exquisitely pleasurable. She parted her legs slightly.

And then his hand moved higher and his fingers touched secret places, parting folds, stroking lightly through them. She tensed only slightly before relaxing again. He was her husband. He had the right. And really it felt very good. She would never have expected it. And then she tensed again as she both felt and heard wetness.

"No, no," he said against her ear. "You must not take fright. This is quite natural. This will help ease any discomfort. It is your body preparing itself for mine."

Aunt Aggy had not mentioned this. She relaxed. Though it was not quite relaxation, either. She felt— desire? No, not quite that, perhaps. She had no wish to feel desire or anything suggestive of passion. Her body had prepared itself for his and was waiting for his. Yes, he had described it well. Her body was ready.

And so, when he lifted himself over her and onto her, she welcomed his weight and his legs widening her own.

Her breath quickened. She pressed her palms hard into the mattress on either side of her.

He was against her. And coming slowly and firmly into her.

It was—yes, it was by far the most wonderful experience of the day. Perhaps of her life. How foolish Aunt Aggy's warnings seemed now. There was no pain, except for one brief moment when she thought there would not be enough room and then felt him breaking through and realized that it had just been the loss of her virginity. There was no other pain, even though there was an unexpected tightness and stretching. He was far bigger than her imagination had anticipated. When he was finally fully embedded in her, she felt very—married, although she knew that this was not all.

"Have I hurt you?" His warm breath tickled her ear.

"No." She moved her arms to wrap them about his waist. "It feels good, Hartley."

"Slide your feet up the bed," he said. "You will be more comfortable. Wrap your legs about mine later if you wish."

*Later.* Just a few seconds there would be, Aunt Aggy had said, of movement that could be intensely unpleasant for the woman. It was best to hold one's breath and count slowly to ten—beyond, if necessary. Jenny had disagreed.

She bent her legs and braced her feet against the mattress on either side of his legs.

He began to move. Very slowly out and in again until a rhythm had been established. She could hear wetness but could understand now how it created ease of movement for him and pleasure instead of pain or discomfort for her.

It lasted a long time. When his pace increased slightly she remembered what he had suggested and twined her legs about his. His right thigh was as powerfully muscled as his left, she thought idly before her new position made her part of his rhythm and she gave herself up to pure enjoyment again.

She was sorry when she sensed that it was about to end. As far as she was concerned, it could have gone on all night. But he had slowed and his inward pushes had deepened. He strained against her while she tightened her legs about his, pulling him deeper, and even contracted inner muscles that she had been unaware of until now.

And then she felt a hot flow deep inside and knew that his seed had been released into her womb. He sighed against the side of her face and she sighed with contentment at the same moment. She was now in every way his wife. It was a lovely feeling, far lovelier than she had imagined. It was possible, she thought, to be lovers without feeling any powerful or destructive passion for each other.

Just this warm—uniting. She felt one with him at that moment and thought how accurate were the words of the wedding service. *One flesh.*

She was sorry it was over until tomorrow night. She did not want him to go away. She did not want to be alone again, even though she was tired. He was warm and relaxed and heavy on her. She wanted him to be asleep so that she could hold the comfort and the pleasure of her wedding day to her for a while longer.

But he was not sleeping deeply. After a mere couple of minutes he stirred.

"I am sorry," he said, lifting himself away from her. "I must be squashing you."

He did not immediately get out of bed. He lay on his side beside her. She turned to face him and smiled at him. She could see him quite clearly in the darkness. He slid his arm beneath her head again and smiled back.

"That was—"

"I did not know—"

They spoke together and stopped together. She waited for him to resume, snuggling close into his warmth again.

"I did not know it was possible to love so deeply," he said, "or to be loved so tenderly."

Love? Was he talking merely about the act they had just performed?

"I can still hardly believe it," he said. His voice was sleepy. "That you love me. I fell in love with you as soon as I set eyes on you, of course. You looked so lovely and so peaceful and so much as if you belonged, gazing down at the abbey from the hill. And then so startled and so guilty when I spoke. But then you are naturally beautiful and desirable—I have not failed to notice how many men here admire you. I will never cease to be amazed and grateful that you came to love me of all men. I am so very ordinary."

"You are not—"

But he laid a finger on her lips. "I am not fishing for compliments," he said. "I followed you to London because life at Highmoor without you was too empty and too painful. I thought that perhaps if I just saw you once more and perhaps spoke with you once more I would find ease for the pain in my heart. When I saw the gladness in your face and when you asked me to kiss you and told me you loved me . . . No, I cannot tell you how I felt, my love. There are not words to describe the joy."

Oh, dear Lord. Oh, dear Lord. No. Please, no. She would lose him. She was going to lose him. Feelings like that could not last. And feelings like that could not subside into affection or friendship. Only into hatred and pain. And despair.

He drew her closer until his lips almost touched hers.

"I love you," he whispered. "I am not sure I have ever said those words aloud to you, have I? They are strangely difficult to say. What a precious gift they were when you said them to me. I love you. I love you."

She gulped rather noisily and hid her face against his shoulder. "Hartley," she said. "Oh, Hartley." She was crying then, loudly and wetly, and could seem to do nothing about it. Everything was ruined. She had had no idea. If only she had. She could have prevented this from happening. But now it was too late. Why had she assumed that he felt as she did? He had never told her why he wanted to marry her. Only now did she realize that. And she had married him to escape from the terrors and insecurities of passion.

"Sweetheart." He was holding her very tightly, but his voice was gentle. "Darling, I know. Sometimes the heart is so full that it spills itself in surprising ways. It has been an emotion-filled day for you. Did I hurt you when I loved you?"

"N—no," she said. "It was good, Hartley. I enjoyed it." They seemed inadequate words. But she did not want to use or feel anything more superlative. It *had* been good. She *had* enjoyed it.

She did not want him to love her. Not in the way he had just described. Romantic, delirious, passionate love. She remembered the feelings and the corresponding agony when they had let her down. If she had wanted passion again, she could have married Lionel and shared the feeling with him—for a while. Until it was over again.

"It will get even better," he said. "I wanted you to become comfortable with what happens this first time, my love. I wanted you to find it pleasant. But there is more. There is so much more for you to experience. So much more I want to teach you—and be taught by you. It will work both ways, you know, even if you do not realize it now. And we have the rest of our lives ahead of us."

*Hartley*, she thought, her eyes closed against his shoulder, *don't love me. I don't want you to love me.*

"Just a moment," he said as she sniffed rather wetly. "I have a handkerchief in the pocket of my dressing gown." He left the bed and felt around in the darkness. He sat on the edge of the bed as she wiped her eyes and blew her nose in his handkerchief.

"Don't leave me," she said, suddenly fearful. Though she did not quite know if she was talking about now, this moment, or about some vague future time in their lives. She had felt so safe with him. Now she felt bewildered and rather frightened.

"Leave you?" He bent toward her and tucked an errant curl behind her ear. "I married you at least partly so that I might sleep with you, my love. And I use the word not just as a euphemism for making love, though that, too." He smiled. "I want to sleep with you in my arms all night and every night. I want to feel married to you. But we are both very tired. I think we should sleep, don't you? Together?"

"Yes, please," she said. She lifted her head as he lay down again so that his arm could come beneath her. She curled in against him and breathed in the warm smell of him. She felt almost safe again.

"Hartley." She could give him only one thing at the moment. "I did not cry because it was not good. I cried because it was very good. Because this whole day has been very good."

"I know, love." He lifted her chin and kissed her softly. "Do you think your body did not tell me your feelings? I know it was good. Sleep now."

She was bone weary, she realized. She felt herself falling immediately toward sleep. She was in this marriage now, was one of her last thoughts. And she could not be as sorry as she should be. Perhaps she could make him so firmly her friend that he would never leave her or hurt her, even when the love he now felt had died.

HE HAD NEVER BELIEVED in happily-ever-afters. They
were fine for stories intended for the delight of children.
Children needed the security of a belief in lifelong happiness. He knew that in reality life for most people was a
series of peaks and valleys, and that the best one could
hope for was that there would be more peaks than valleys and that they would be higher than the valleys were
deep.

Perhaps he still did not believe in happily-ever-afters.
If he had stopped, really, to consider the matter, basic
good sense would have forced him to admit that at some
future time there would be troubles and problems and
sadnesses in his life again. But he was so firmly on one of
life's highest pinnacles that it seemed to him for two
whole days after his wedding that he would never have
to suffer again.

And he would never let his wife suffer. For the rest of
his days, he would devote himself to her happiness.

It was an immature assessment of the future, he realized later. But it was understandable. He was in love with
a woman who loved him and they were newly married.
What more could life offer, except endless years together
and children of their bodies?

He believed—though he had never discussed the matter openly with anyone—that it was considered deco-
rous to love one's wife once a night and perhaps not even
that often. What was a pleasure for men was said to be
an unpleasant duty for women. If one needed a woman

more often than decorum allowed, then there were women enough who were only too glad to provide a service for a suitable fee.

He cared nothing for decorum. Allowing him his marital rights was no unpleasant duty to Samantha—he had known that from the very first time. And he had no wish for any other woman but his wife for the rest of their lives. It was not so much that he needed a woman more often than strict decorum allowed. It was that he wanted his wife constantly.

On their wedding night, tired as they both had been when they fell asleep, they woke together just before dawn, smiled sleepily at each other, and sank toward sleep again. But desire had kept him awake, and he had made love to her once more after she had assured him that she was not sore. He had made it long and almost languorous, all interior play with no foreplay. He had held back his release until he felt her relaxed pleasure.

They went walking in the park during the morning, when it was almost deserted, keeping to the quieter paths that gave the illusion of being in the country rather than in the middle of a city. There were even deer grazing among the trees, as there were at Highmoor. They held hands when it seemed they would be unobserved, and talked about their surroundings and about Highmoor. It was always so easy to talk with Samantha. He was fortunate, he thought, to have a friend as well as a lover in his wife. She glowed when she talked to him and smiled a great deal. She *liked* him as well as she loved him, he thought, and derived amusement from the rather peculiar thought.

They drove out into the country in an open carriage during the afternoon, taking a direction that would be unlikely to bring them into company with others. They sat with clasped hands and talked very little as they gazed about at the wonders of nature. And that was another thing about Samantha, he thought. They could sit silently together for hours and still be comfortable. It seemed almost as if their minds worked along the same lines, though they rarely compared notes to be sure.

The *ton* would have been shocked at what he did when they arrived home at teatime. They did have tea, but then he took her to bed and loved her again. Of course it was not in bad taste, she assured him with a smile that was almost impish when he suggested it. She was his wife. She was his for the asking. And he certainly would not have to beg.

He loved her twice during that night. The next day followed much the pattern of the day before, except that it rained soon after luncheon and they spent the whole afternoon in bed, first loving, then sleeping, then talking about Highmoor and what they would do there during the summer. The day after tomorrow they would start their journey, he told her. He had intended starting back earlier, but he did not want to end this idyll with her too soon. Travel was tedious and inn beds not nearly as comfortable for love as this bed was.

He loved her three times during the night. He really

must allow her some rest in the coming day and the following night, he decided with a smile as he held her and watched dawn lighten the room while she slept. Not that making love was a great deal of exertion for her. She enjoyed physical love with him. He did not doubt that. But so far hers had been a largely passive role. She had lain quiet and receptive as he worked in her.

He could bring her to climax. He could arouse passion in her and build it to a crescendo and then coax her over the edge. He could teach her to be as active in their lovemaking as he was. He could teach her to make love to him and in the process intensify her own pleasure. And he would do it. He longed for it.

But not yet. She was not ready yet for passion. He would not have been able to put into words how he knew. It was something he sensed. Because he loved her. Because he knew her well despite the fact that they had been acquainted for a relatively short time. Because— Dorothea had once told him this—he had the rare skill of being able to read the messages of a woman's body.

He knew that his wife was not yet ready for passion.

And so he waited patiently for her. It was no hardship. They loved dearly. And they both drew deep enjoyment from their sexual encounters.

For the three days and nights that started with his wedding day, the Marquess of Carew would have said that he was living happily ever after, even if a part of him would have known that there is no such thing in this life.

All of him knew it the next day.

# 14

THEY WERE TO LEAVE FOR HIGHMOOR THE NEXT day. Samantha could hardly wait. To go back there and know it was to be her home—the thought was still unreal. She would not believe it until she was there. And all of the summer would remain to wander about the park, to see perhaps the construction of the bridge over the lake—Hartley had said he would start with that. And there would be Jenny and Gabriel and the children to see again. She was to be their close neighbor. And Hartley had said they were his friends.

She longed to be on the way. The sooner they left, the sooner they would arrive. But there was one bad part about leaving so soon. The honeymoon was at an end. She had several people to call on in order to take her leave of them. Hartley had similar errands and some business to do. And so they went their separate ways that day after a late and lingering breakfast together.

Some of her fears had been allayed. He had talked of love that first night and had frequently told her since that he loved her. He almost always called her by some endearment rather than by her name. But he was invariably kind to her and gentle, and they were still friends.

They could still talk and laugh together endlessly, or be silent together without any awkwardness or boredom.

Perhaps, after all, she had nothing to fear. Perhaps she was safe. After all, Jenny and Gabriel loved, and they still seemed perfectly happy—and each other's friend—even after six years of marriage.

Perhaps she need no longer punish herself for the sin of kissing and of falling in love with Jenny's betrothed all those years ago. And for wishing that the betrothal could somehow be ended. And for being secretly glad when it was, despite the terrible suffering and humiliation Jenny had had to face.

Perhaps, after all, she could allow herself to be loved.

She had been happy for three days—and three nights. Wonderfully, unexpectedly happy. He was the friend and companion she had hoped for when she had agreed to marry him. And as a lover he was—oh, how could she use any superlative? She had no one with whom to compare him. He was gentle and considerate and patient and thorough. He was good—he was very good. She had come to adore his body and the skilled way he used it to give her pleasure. She never minded being wakened during the night, tired as she might be—and sometimes she was the one to do the waking, though she did not believe he realized it yet. And she never minded being taken to bed during the day, even though it was very obvious to her that the servants *knew*. Let them know. Let them be envious.

She had looked forward to the physical side of marriage and had hoped that it would at least be pleasant. It was far more than pleasant. It bound them together in a tie deeper than mere friendship. She could not put a word to the bond. But after three days she felt very much his wife. And she hugged the feeling to herself as perhaps her most precious possession, even if it was intangible.

She called on Lady Brill first and the two of them made a round of calls. Her uncle told her that he had been pleased to discover that, after all, she had a wise and sensible head on her shoulders in choosing a husband with a superior title and seventy thousand a year. Her lady friends hugged her and lamented the fact that she would be gone for the rest of the Season and wished her well. Some of them looked faintly envious. One of them—though she had never been a close friend—remarked apropos of nothing, or so it seemed, that it was a pity the richest men never seemed to be also the handsomest men.

"Not that I was insinuating—" she said, looking at Samantha in dismay, one hand flying to her mouth.

Samantha merely smiled.

Lady Sophia, her newly mended leg elevated on a satin pouf, looked Samantha over from head to foot and nodded in satisfaction.

"She is looking like the cat that got locked in with the cream pot, Aggy," she said. "Carew must have done his job on her and done it well." She cackled at her own joke and Samantha's hot blush.

"You are in need of exercise and fresh air, Sophie," Lady Brill said briskly.

And so they drove in the park, the three of them. The weather was warm and sunny again after yesterday's rain. The *ton* was out in force. The barouche in which they rode moved at snail's pace, when it was moving at all. People came to inquire after Lady Sophia's health. Friends came to greet and chat with Lady Brill. And Samantha drew quite as much attention as she had ever done. Perhaps more today. She fancied that everyone was looking at her with curiosity and interest. It was doubtless her imagination, she told herself, but the knowledge of how she had been spending her nights—and her afternoons—since the *ton* saw her last set her to blushing a great deal of the time.

Lord Francis, dashing in puce riding coat and skintight black leather pantaloons and hessians, rode up to her side of the carriage, distracting her attention from the conversation the other two ladies were holding with a couple at the other side. He leaned one arm on the door of the carriage and looked at her closely and apprecia-tively.

"Well, Samantha," he said quietly, "never let it be said that marriage disagrees with you."

"*I* certainly would begin no such rumor, Francis," she said. But she could not prevent the telltale blush.

"Lucky dog," he said, more to himself than to her. "You love him, then, Sam?"

It was the first time he had used Jenny's name for her. But his question jolted her. There must be something in her face. But what could show in her face apart from her blush?

"Why else would I have married him, Francis?" she asked. She had meant the question to be lightly, teasingly phrased. She heard too late the earnestness in her voice. She wanted him to believe that she had married for love, she realized. Hartley deserved that. "Of course I love him."

"Yes, Sam," he said, his smile slow in coming. "It is there in your eyes for all to see, my dear. And so I must begin the search for another incomparable to inspire my devotion. You will be hard to replace."

"Oh, nonsense, Francis," she said, but fortunately Lord Hawthorne rode up at that moment and the couple who had been talking with her aunt and Lady Sophia drove away. The privateness of the moment was gone.

Was there really something about her eyes? Samantha wondered in some alarm as they drove from the park a short while later. She could not think what it could be, except perhaps a certain vacantness occasioned by the fact that her mind kept wandering to Hartley, wondering how he was spending his day, wondering if he would be home when she returned, hoping that he would be, longing to see him again, dreaming about the past three days—and nights.

She must not start daydreaming. It had never been one of her shortcomings. And it was very ungenteel to daydream in the presence of others about her husband.

Finally her own carriage set her down outside Carew House and she hurried inside with eager steps. It was after six already. The day was gone. She hoped he would be home. She hoped some of his friends had not persuaded him to dine at one of the clubs on his last evening in town. How dreary it would be to have to dine alone and wait until perhaps late into the night for his return. And then perhaps he would be foxed, though she had never known him to drink to excess. Or else he would sleep in his own bed because of the lateness of the hour and his reluctance to wake her.

Her foolish fears fled faster than they had crowded in upon her as soon as she stepped into the hall. He was standing at the far side of it, his left arm behind his back, his feet braced slightly apart. He looked—handsome, she thought, smiling. The library door was open behind him. He must have heard the carriage and come out to greet her. But he had not hurried toward her. And so, just in time, she checked her impulse to rush toward him and offer her mouth to be kissed. There were two footmen in the hall, and despite what they must know, all open signs of affection must be reserved until he and she were behind closed doors.

"Hartley," she said, untying the strings of her bonnet, pulling it off, and shaking out her flattened curls, "did you have a good day?"

*Tell me you missed me. No, wait until we are alone.*

"Thank you, yes," he said. "Will you join me in the library?"

*So that we can close the door and put our arms about each other and bemoan the waste of a day apart?*

She pulled off her gloves. "Give me time to wash my hands and comb my hair?" she asked, still smiling. *So that I can be beautiful for you.*

He inclined his head to her.

"Will you order tea?" she asked, hurrying toward the staircase. "I am parched."

She turned her head to look down at him as she climbed the stairs. And stopped for a moment. What was it? He looked his usual self, neat and tidy, but not in the first stare of fashion. He was watching her with no particular expression on his face.

*What is wrong?* she was about to ask. But there were the servants. She would wait until she came back down and they were in the library.

Her steps quickened. She would be as fast as she could. She did not even bother to ring for her maid. She washed her hands and face in cold water and brushed quickly at her curls to bring the spring back into them. The need to hurry, to waste not one more moment than was necessary, was strong on her.

But the brush paused as she caught herself feeling the urgency. The need to be with him. In his arms.

What was happening?

She peered suspiciously at her eyes in the looking glass. *Were* they different from usual? They looked like the same old eyes to her. She grinned at herself.

And went hurrying from the room and running lightly down the stairs. A footman crossed to the library door and held it open for her. She smiled at him in passing.

————

HE WENT TO WHITE'S with Bridgwater for luncheon, and they were joined by Gerson and a few other acquaintances. It was a very pleasant way to spend his last day in town, even though he had missed Samantha from the moment of handing her into his carriage and waving her on the way to Lady Brill's.

He endured a great deal of teasing, much of it decidedly ribald. It was all good-natured, he knew, and perhaps fueled by a degree of envy. Besides, he admitted to himself that he really was feeling rather smug. No one else, after all, had just married the loveliest lady in London. No one else was loved by her. And, truth to tell, he had been every bit as randy during the past three days as his friends accused him of being, though he had been more respectful of his wife's body than a few of them dared to suggest.

They were enjoying a few drinks after luncheon, and he was trying to calculate in his mind the earliest hour he could expect to find Samantha at home, when Lionel appeared in the doorway of the dining room, paused there, and came inside.

"Hart," he said, walking toward him, right hand extended, his smile warm. "How is the new bridegroom? Retreated to your club to recuperate from certain, ah, exertions, have you?"

He squeezed the marquess's right hand rather painfully while the others chuckled and offered their own answers to the question. Friends, it seemed, never tired of reminding a newly married man of how his nights had suddenly changed for the better, even if they had become more sleepless.

The marquess got to his feet and drew his cousin a little apart from the crowd. The noise there was getting louder in direct proportion to the amount of alcohol that was being consumed. He swallowed his dislike of Lionel and smiled back at him. Perhaps it was time. They were grown men. The stupidities of boyhood and the excesses of young manhood were behind them. At least he must believe so. He was rather ashamed of his reaction to Samantha's wedding gift.

"I have to thank you, Lionel," he said. "It was a kind and generous gesture."

Lionel's handsome brows rose. There was some amusement in his eyes, the marquess thought.

"The brooch," the marquess said. "You must know that it is more precious to me than just its market value. Mother always wore it and it is somehow associated with my fondest memories of her. I suppose Father gave it to you as a memento after her death, not realizing that she had intended . . . But it does not matter. It was a precious wedding gift you gave us. I thank you."

"Perhaps you misunderstood, Hart." There was definite amusement in Lionel's eyes now. "It was a gift for your bride alone. A gift from me to her. In appreciative memory of times past. Did you not know about us?"

The very thought of Lionel and Samantha's being referred to as "us" was somehow nauseating.

"We were an item six years ago," Lionel said. "Indeed we were indiscreet enough to be a partial cause of the breakup of my betrothal to her cousin—Lady Thornhill, you know, your neighbor. We were what you might call in love, Hart. Deeply, head over ears in love. I had to abandon her because Papa had the notion that my absence was more desirable than my presence, and I would not embroil her in my disgrace. She was still an innocent, you see. I am sure you found her satisfyingly virgin on your wedding night?"

He raised his eyebrows but did not wait long for an answer.

"I do believe I broke her heart," he said. "I rather fancy that she blamed me. And perhaps she was right. It is a shameful thing for a man to be responsible for breaking his own engagement, is it not? She would have nothing to do with me when I returned this spring. And yet she was frightened by the power of the feelings she still had for me. Strange, is it not, Hart, that a woman of such exquisite beauty was still unmarried at her age? You came along at the right moment, old chap. She ran to your arms, where I daresay she feels safe. Rightfully so, I would imagine. You are looking after her well, I presume? But of course you would."

Regrettably it was not a story he could brush off as a product of a malicious imagination. Though the intent in telling it was utterly malicious, of course.

"Yes, I am looking after her well, Lionel," he said quietly. "You will, of course, leave what is past in the past from this moment on."

"Why, Hart," Lionel said, chuckling, "if I did not know

you better, I could almost imagine that that was a threat."

"You were doubtless on your way somewhere when you spotted me through the doorway," the marquess said. "I will not delay you any longer, Lionel. Thank you for your good wishes."

"Ah, yes," Lionel said. "You remind me of my manners, Hart. My good wishes for your continued happiness."

He smiled warmly at his cousin and at the noisy group of men still gathered about the table, then left the room.

"It is time for me to leave, too," the marquess said to his friends, dredging up a smile from somewhere inside.

"The bride must not be left to pine alone for one moment longer than necessary," a tipsy voice said from the midst of the throng. "A toast to you, Carew. A toast to your continued stamina. Still able to get to your feet after three days. Jolly good show, my good fellow."

"But flat on his stomach again as soon as he has raced home," someone else said, raising his glass in acknowledgment of the toast.

"I'll come with you, Hart," the Duke of Bridgwater said, getting to his feet.

"There is no need," the marquess said. "I am going directly home."

But his friend clapped a hand on his shoulder and accompanied him downstairs, where they retrieved their hats and canes, and out onto the pavement.

"I overheard," he said. "I did not mean to eavesdrop,

Hart. At first I did not realize it was a private conversation."

"Hardly a conversation," the marquess said.

"He was always a scoundrel," the duke said, falling into step beside him and adjusting his stride to the more halting one of his friend. "And for what he did to Lady Thornhill—and to Thornhill, too—he deserved to be shot. Thornhill showed great but lamentable restraint in not calling him out. The lady had been put through enough distress already, of course. I have been glad to see since then, whenever they have been in town, that the two of them seem contented enough with each other."

"More than that," the marquess said. "I never did know quite what happened, Bridge. And I do not want to know now. It was a long time in the past."

"Except that the scoundrel has managed to bring it into the present," the duke said. "There was never a breath of scandal surrounding Lady Carew's name, Hart. I would advise you not to give any credence to anything he said. He obviously fancied her himself this year and was annoyed when she chose you—London is full of men who are annoyed about exactly the same thing. Fortunately all the others are honorable men. Kneller, for example. He has been wearing his heart on his sleeve for more than one Season. She chose you, Hart. She might have chosen any of a dozen others, all almost as well set up as you."

The marquess smiled. "You do not have to plead my wife's case, Bridge," he said. "I am married to the lady. I know why she married me. I respect her and trust her. And I do not choose to discuss the matter further with you. Marriage is a private business between two people."

"And I would not intrude," his friend said unhappily. "But if you could see your face, Hart."

"I am going home," the marquess said. "I would take you out of your way if you came any farther, Bridge."

His grace stopped walking. "And I would not be invited inside if I did come farther," he said ruefully. "Well, Hart." He extended his left hand. "Have a safe journey and a good summer. Give Lady Carew my regards."

They shook hands before the marquess turned and limped away.

He tried not to think. He had known from the age of six on that Lionel was not worth one moment of suffering. For some reason—he supposed the reasons were pretty obvious—Lionel had marked him as a victim ever since they were young children together. Nothing had changed. Lionel would do anything and everything in his power to hurt him or belittle him. But Lionel could have that power only if it was given him. The Marquess of Carew had done no giving since the vicious "accident" that had left him partly crippled.

He was not going to reverse the lesson of a lifetime now. It was as Bridge had said. Lionel had returned to London, set his sights on Samantha—whether for marriage or mere dalliance only he knew—and had been severely humiliated when she would have none of him. Humiliation had turned to spite and the vicious need for revenge when she had married his far less personable cousin, the apparent weakling who had always been his victim.

But thought could not be kept at bay. He retired to his library as soon as he reached home, with the instruction to the footmen on duty that Lady Carew was to be asked to join him there on her return. He paced as he waited for her. But it was a wait of three hours.

She had been hurt in the past. He had known that. He had even spoken of it to her. Six years ago she would have been eighteen. Probably in her first Season. A ripe age for a romance with a man of Lionel's looks and practiced charms. And of course she would have met him on a number of occasions. He had been betrothed to her cousin at the time. And she had been living with her uncle, Lady Thornhill's father.

She had been hurt so deeply that in six years she had not married, though he knew that she had spent each Season in London, and since his arrival this year he had seen that she had a following unrivaled by any other young lady of *ton*. He had seen, too, that a number of those followers—yes, Lord Francis Kneller was among them—had a serious attachment to her. But she had not married.

It must have been a far worse than ordinary heartbreak. If she had been partly responsible for the breakup of her cousin's engagement . . . She loved her cousin. And it seemed from the little he knew that the incident had brought terrible and painful scandal to Lady Thornhill. And if then, after it all, the object of her love had left the country, abandoned her . . . Yes, for someone as sweet and sensitive as his wife, such events might keep her from love and marriage for six years.

And inexplicably this year she had fallen headlong in love with him. With a man who was apparently no more than a traveling landscape gardener. With a man about whose looks the kindest thing that could be said was that he was not quite ugly. With a man who limped so badly that sometimes people turned their heads away in embarrassment. With a man with a claw for a right hand.

What a gullible wretch, he would have said of himself if the story had been told to him of someone else. What a romantic fool!

Lionel had returned to England this year. Perhaps—no, *probably*—that had been their first meeting, at the Rochester ball. They had been waltzing together, looking incredibly beautiful together. He would have used his charm on her again—Lionel would have been unable to resist the temptation to exert power over a beautiful woman who had once loved him when he was forbidden territory. And she would have felt a resurgence of her long-suppressed feelings for him. She would have tried to resist them. She would have been very upset.

If she had rushed from the ballroom after the set was over, rushed onto the landing outside the ballroom and run into someone she had never expected to see again, someone with whom she had struck up a friendship a month or two earlier, she would have greeted him with delight and relief. She would have seen him almost as a savior. She would have begged him to take her outside where there was air. She would have tried to forget with him. She would have asked him to kiss her. She would have told him she loved him. . . .

And if she was still upset the following day, and if the friend called upon her to make her an offer, having mistaken the cause of her ardor the night before, she might have impulsively accepted him. She might have tried to escape from herself and to have avoided having her fragile heart rebroken by accepting the offer of someone safe.

She had never once since their marriage, he thought, told him that she loved him. He had said the words to her numerous times. She had never shown any sign that she wanted passion with him.

He was her friend. No less and no more than that.

He wondered how far off the mark all his guesses were. Not far, he believed. As far as the sun is from the earth, he hoped.

He could not bring himself to hope.

She came, finally. He heard the carriage and stepped into the hall. She was like a little piece of the summer sky in her pale blue muslin dress and straw bonnet trimmed with yellow flowers. She was flushed and smiling.

*Something blue,* he thought.

And even then he had to wait. She wanted to go upstairs and wash her hands and comb her hair, though it looked lovely enough to him. She paused on the stairs and looked down at him. But she continued on her way.

She could have been no longer than ten minutes. It seemed like ten hours. But he heard the door of the library open behind him eventually and turned as she came in. Fresh and lovely and still smiling.

His wife. His love.

The door closed behind her and she stopped suddenly. He had thought she was going to walk right across the room into his arms.

"What is it?" she asked him, her head tipping to one side and her smile dying. "What is the matter, Hartley?"

"Why did you marry me?" he asked her.

He watched her eyes widen with surprise and—with something else.

# 15

THE LIGHT WENT OUT OF THE DAY. SHE DID NOT understand the question—and yet she understood one thing very well. She understood that the dream was fading, that she was waking up. That she was being forced to wake up.

"What?" she asked. She was not sure that any sound got past her lips.

"Why did you marry me?" he asked again. "Because you love me, Samantha?"

The ready lie sprang to her lips but did not make it past them this time. She stared at him, the man above all others whom she would protect from hurt if she could. "What has happened?" she asked him.

"You counter one question with another," he said. "Was mine so difficult to answer, Samantha? A simple yes or no would have sufficed."

The light that had been in his eyes since the night of the Rochester ball had died. Oh, fool not to have realized before it was too late that it was the light of love. It was gone.

"Tell me something," he said. "And let there be honesty between us. Do you still love him?"

Something died inside her. Something that had been

blooming unnamed and almost unnoticed since her wedding day.

"What has he been telling you?" she asked.

His eyes grew bleaker, if that was possible. "I notice," he said, "that you do not ask to whom I refer."

"What has he been telling you?" Her hands sought and found the handle of the door behind her back. She clung to it and moved back against it as if it could protect her from pain.

"About six years ago," he said. "And about this year."

"And you believe him?" she asked.

"I will believe *you*," he said. "Tell me what happened six years ago."

She closed her eyes for a few moments and drew deep breaths. What did six years ago have to do with this moment? But of course it had everything to do with it.

"I was very young," she said, "and fresh from the schoolroom. And he was handsome, charming, experienced. I did not like him. I thought him cold. I even told Jenny so. But that was before he kissed me one evening and declared his passion for me. There was nothing else except melting looks from him and fiercely unhappy glances and the suggestion that if we were ever to know happiness together, I should speak with Jenny and have her end the betrothal. He could not do so as an honorable gentleman."

"Did you think him honorable, Samantha?" he asked quietly.

"No!" she said sharply. "But I thought him unhappy and in love and desperate."

"As you were?" he asked.

"I would not do as he asked," she said. "I fought my feelings for him. And I felt sick for Jenny, about to marry a man who did not love her. I prayed for an ending of the betrothal so that she could be saved and he and I could be together, but when it happened it was horrible. Oh, dear God, it was horrible. The terribly public disgrace for Jenny. Uncle Gerald caning her and preparing to send her away. And worst of all—or so it seemed at the time—Gabriel forcing her into marriage. And it was all my fault."

"But it was not," he said.

"No." She had her hands over her face. She drew a deep breath again. "But I have never been able to stop feeling guilty. If I had not presented Lionel with the idea of a way out . . . He did not love me. He had tried to use me. He laughed at me when I approached him after Jenny's hasty marriage. He made me feel like a silly child, which is just what I was, of course. I have hated him ever since."

"Hated," he said. "Hatred is a powerful emotion, Samantha. Akin to love, it is said."

"Yes." Her voice was dull. "So it is said. I still hate him. Today more than ever. Why would he want to hurt his own cousin?"

"It amuses Lionel to hurt people," he said. "Tell me about this spring."

"There is nothing to tell," she said. "I saw him in the park the day before the Rochester ball. I had not known he was back in England. I was terrified. And then he appeared at the ball and asked me to waltz with him. I did. That was all. Oh, and he called on my aunt and me the next afternoon."

"Before I called?" he asked.

"Yes."

"You were terrified," he said. "Of what? That he would harm you?"

"No." She felt suddenly weary. She would have liked nothing better than to sink to the floor and fall asleep. But there was the necessity to talk. He was not going to let it go. And now she must reap one of the rewards of the friendship she had wanted with him. Friends were open and honest with each other. "No, not that he would harm me. That he— That I would find that my hatred—"

"—was merely a mask for love?"

"Yes." Her hands had found the handle of the door again.

"And was it?" he asked.

"No," she said more firmly. "For a while I thought it just possible that he was sincere. He tried to persuade me that he had loved me all the time, that he had hurt me in order to protect me from his own disgrace, that he had come back with the intention of wooing me again and making me his countess. I was confused. And afraid. But I did not want to believe him or love him. I did not trust him and would never have been able to. I know now that my instinct was right, that he is still as contemptible as he ever was. Why did he want to hurt you?"

"When you asked me to walk in the garden with you," he said, "and when you asked me to kiss you and told me that you loved me, you were reacting to the turmoil of emotions he had aroused in you, Samantha? And the next afternoon when I came to offer you marriage, the same thing?"

"Oh." She gazed at him unhappily. "I was so very happy to see you. Those afternoons at Highmoor with you had been among the happiest times in my life."

"With plain, ordinary Mr. Wade," he said. "Who had defects to add to his ordinariness. Who was the very antithesis of a Don Juan. Who would never confuse you or hurt or abandon you. Who would be your little puppy dog. You would be very safe with him. And so you married him."

The horrifying thing was that there was truth in his words. But only some of the truth. Not all of it.

"Hartley." Her grip on the doorknob became painful. "Don't belittle yourself. Oh, please don't do this."

"Then suppose you tell me," he said, "why you married me. Tell me, Samantha."

"Because I wanted to," she said. "Because you were sweet and kind and, and—"

"—and very rich?" His voice was hardly recognizable. She had never heard sarcasm in it before.

His face swam before her eyes, and her jaw felt suddenly cold as a hot tear dripped off it onto her dress. "Oh, don't, Hartley," she begged him. "Please don't. You *know* that I was unaware of that fact. I married you because I wanted to, because I liked you more than any other man I have ever known, because I felt s—"

"—safe with me." There was harshness in his voice. "I

would be so ecstatic to win such beauty for myself that I would be unlikely ever to stray from you. Well, you were right there, Samantha. I have what is perhaps an unfortunate belief in fidelity in marriage—on both sides. No mistresses for me, no lovers for you."

"Hartley—"

"Listen to me, Samantha," he said. There was a harsh command in his voice that frightened and distressed her. "You lied to me. You let me marry you believing that lie. And it was a momentous lie. I have never wanted a loveless marriage, and yet now it seems I am irrevocably in one. But it *is* a marriage. Never forget that. You are *my wife.* You had better sort out your feelings for *my cousin* once and for all. If it is love, put it from your heart. If it is hatred, let it go. I will not have you always afraid to see him lest you find yourself in love with him. And I will not have you beneath me on our bed, dreaming that I am he."

"Hartley!" Her mouth fell open and she gasped for air.

"There may never be love between us," he said. "It is strange how my own has shriveled to nothing in the course of a few hours. But there will never be shadows. Or secrets. Is that understood?"

"You are being unfair," she said. "You are being cruel. I have never—"

"I *asked* if you understood." His face was stony, his eyes opaque. He was unrecognizable. She did not know this man.

"Yes," she said.

"If your maid has started packing your things," he

said, "you may tell her to unpack again. We will be staying here."

"No." She was shaking her head against the door. "I want to go home, Hartley. Please let us go home. Oh, please."

"We will be staying here," he said. "You can enjoy the rest of the Season, as you usually do. I can occupy myself in any number of useful and useless ways. We need not be in each other's company any more than either of us would wish."

"I want to go home," she whispered. But she knew it was useless. He was implacable, this stranger who still stood across the room from her, his back to the empty fireplace.

"If you have taken leave of all your friends," he said, "you may now boast, Samantha, that you begged to stay and that your besotted bridegroom bowed to your wishes. I will not contradict you. It is late. You will wish to change for dinner. If you will excuse me, my lady, I will be taking dinner at my club."

She turned without another word and fumbled at the handle of the door before getting it open. She hurried, head down so that the footmen would not see her face, up the stairs to her room.

It was all ruined, she thought. Her marriage. Her life. Everything.

It seemed she had been wrong to forgive herself at last.

There was to be no happiness for her.

Only three days and three nights. Pure joy, now worth

less than nothing. Yes, less. It would have been far better if she had never known it.

She did not know how she was going to live through the pain. It was worse than the last time. Oh, far worse. Because this time she—

Well, this time she was the one who had done most of the hurting. And therefore her own pain was inconsolable.

HE LIFTED HIS LEFT arm to the mantel and rested his forehead on it. He did not know himself or this strange, unexpected anger that had had him lashing out to hurt as badly as he was hurt. He had intended only to talk with her, to have the truth in the open so that somehow they could patch something together out of their marriage and move on.

He had not intended to become angry—he *never* lost his temper. Never until today. And with the person he loved most dearly. And he had never felt the desire to hurt. Until today. He wanted to put a bullet between Lionel's eyes— No, that was too quick and probably painless. He wanted to pound him to a bloody pulp. And he had wanted just now to reduce Samantha to tears, to have her begging for what he would not grant.

He had succeeded admirably.

He drew a deep and ragged breath through his nose. But it was no use. He wept with painful, chest-wrenching sobs.

He froze when the door opened behind him again. He

kept his head where it was. She came close to him before speaking.

"Hartley." Her voice was very quiet, very calm. If she had touched him at that moment, he would have gathered her to him with such force that he would have crushed every bone in her body. "I want you to return it to Lord Rushford, if you please. Or if you wish to keep it because it was your mother's and is precious to you, then please do so. But I do not want it and I don't want ever to see it again. This 'something blue' has ruined my marriage."

He lifted his head and looked at his mother's sapphire brooch in her palm. He took it without a word.

He felt her looking into his half-lowered face for several silent moments before she turned and left the room again.

He closed his fingers over the brooch and tightened them until the diamonds cut into his hand rather painfully.

HE WAS LATE COMING home. She lay on her back, staring up into the darkness beneath the canopy of her bed as she had done for several hours, listening to the sound of the door to his room opening and closing more than once, to the distant hum of his voice and his valet's. To silence.

She gazed upward and imagined him leaning against the tree on the hill at Highmoor, watching her look downward toward the abbey, catching her trespassing. If only she had turned and hurried away at that moment. Back to Chalcote and safety.

But she had not.

Her dressing room door opened softly and a faint beam of candlelight shone across the room, across the lower half of her bed. She did not move her head or close her eyes. He came and stood beside the bed.

"You are awake, then," he said after a few moments. His eyes must not be as accustomed to the darkness as hers were.

"Yes."

*Please talk to me. Please tell me you did not mean those cruel things. Tell me I did not really lie to you. Take me home tomorrow.*

She did not move. She continued to stare upward.

He was removing his dressing gown and climbing into bed beside her. And turning to her and starting to make love to her.

*Say something. Not in silence like this.*

He was slow and gentle and patient. His hands—not his mouth—worked their skilled magic on her body, until they both knew she was ready for him. And then he came inside her and slowly, skillfully worked the same magic there, until she was wonderfully relaxed and strangely aching all at the same time. He released his seed, hot and deep inside her.

It was all right, she told herself. Everything was going to be all right. But she knew that nothing at all was right.

He had loved her as he usually did, though there was never a sameness about his loving. But there was something missing. Something undefinable. Something essential.

She could smell liquor on his breath, though she did not believe he was foxed.

She held him against her, her legs still twined about his, willing him to sleep. But he never slept on her for more than a minute or two at the longest. He was too considerate of her comfort to squash her beneath his full weight for too long. He lifted himself away.

And up to sit on the side of the bed. He got to his feet after a few moments and put his dressing gown back on. He looked down at her in the darkness.

"Thank you," he said. "Good night, Samantha."

She was too miserable to reply. She gazed upward again. Moments later the beam of light from the doorway narrowed and disappeared. She was in darkness once more.

Ah, dear God, she was in eternal darkness.

LADY CAREW, THE TON were soon agreed, had got just exactly what she wanted. She had made a brilliant match to a wealthy and indulgent husband who was willing to cater to her every whim. He had been about to drag the poor lady back to his own dull life at remote Highmoor in the middle of the Season. But she had easily talked him out of that foolishness. And so they had remained, she to dazzle society with more charm and wit than ever, he to follow in her wake or to pursue his own quieter pleasures until summer came.

It appeared to be a thoroughly successful marriage. They were both happy—no one had ever seen Lady Carew more vivacious than she was in the weeks following her marriage, and no one had ever seen as much of her husband. He was almost always smiling.

Lucky dog, the gentlemen of the *ton* thought, looking with some envy and some surreptitious lust at his wife. There was more than one thing to be said for being worth upward of fifty thousand a year.

Fortunate woman, the ladies of the *ton* thought. Her husband was not much of a man, perhaps, but he was wealthy and besotted and kept her on a very loose leash—if there was a leash at all. Give her a year to produce his heir and next spring they would watch with interest to see whom she would take as her first lover. She could hardly have done better for herself.

Samantha was pregnant already. She knew it, even though she was only one week late and her newness to sexual activity might be the reason for the irregularity. But she knew she was pregnant. There was something relaxed—she could not quite put a word to the feeling— deep inside her, rather like the feeling she always had at the end of the marriage act. She knew it was their child starting life in her womb.

She did not know how she would tell him when the time came. She did not know how he would feel about it.

He would be glad, she supposed, as she was. She would be able to stay at Highmoor. He would not be able to force her to come back next year for the torture of another Season. Perhaps, if he continued relations with her after the birth of the child, she would conceive again. And again. Perhaps she would be able to stay at Highmoor for the rest of her life.

It seemed to her, perhaps irrationally, that Highmoor was her only hope for any measure of happiness. No, never that. Of peace. She could live out her life if only she could find some peace.

They spent a fair amount of time together, almost all of it in company with other people. Almost the only time they spent alone together was the half hour or so he took to make love to her each night. A silent half hour except for the courteous thanks at the end of it. Thanks for services rendered.

He accompanied her to most evening entertainments. Even balls. He would see her into the ballroom, stand with her until the first set began and she had taken the floor with her first partner, and then disappear into the card room or somewhere else until it was time to escort her home.

He always smiled in public. She always sparkled.

The perfect couple, perfectly in love but perfectly well bred—they did not live in each other's pockets.

They saw Lionel almost wherever they went. They avoided him and he seemed content to look alternatively amused and lovelorn—the latter if he caught her eye across a room when Hartley was not with her. She perfected the art of moving out of a room or attaching herself to another gentleman—usually poor Francis—if she suspected he was moving her way.

She hated him. And despised him. And she was no longer afraid of the hatred. She knew that it was just that and that it was poles away from love.

She hated him, not so much for what he had done to her—innocent as she had been, she had partly asked for it—but for what he had done to Hartley. His own cousin.

For what he had done to Hartley she could cheerfully kill him. With slow torture.

She did not know how to put right what was wrong with her marriage. If only they could go home to Highmoor, she thought. Somehow it seemed as if everything would be fine if only they could go there. And there would be a baby early in the new year. A new start for them, perhaps. But he had not said anything more about going home.

And she was afraid to ask again. Or perhaps too proud to ask.


THEY WERE TO HAVE attended Lady Gregory's ball. The invitation had been accepted. But he did not feel like going. He was weary of the constant going, the constant pretense. He told Samantha that he would stay at home, that she should pen a note to Lady Brill to accompany her and he would have it sent over.

He went into the library after dinner—she had gone

to dine with Lady Brill. He sat in his favorite chair beside the fire, a book in his hands though he did not open it. He set his head back against the chair and closed his eyes.

He was so weary. He wanted to go home. He did not know what to do about his marriage. It had all been his fault, this estrangement. Perhaps she had not married him for love, but the lie had been inadvertent. And he had not told her of his own feelings until their wedding night. Many people married for reasons other than love and had perfectly successful marriages. And theirs had started well. She had enjoyed his company and his love-making—he had ignored those facts in the first hours of blinding hurt. She was not the sort of woman who would give less than her whole devotion to a marriage. She would have been a good wife to him for the rest of their lives if he had not ruined things.

He did not know how to put things right. He did not know if things *could* be put right. Perhaps all was ruined forever.

He wanted to go home. Perhaps things would be better there. He would tell her tomorrow to pack again. No, he would *ask* her. Perhaps she no longer wanted to go there herself. She always seemed happiest when they were in company.

He turned his head when the door opened without there having been a knock. It was Samantha, dressed neatly in an evening dress but not in a ball gown. She was carrying her embroidery bag.

"I did not want to go to the ball," she said, not quite

looking at him. "Do you mind if I sit in here with you, Hartley?"

"Please do," he said. He felt almost like crying when she sat quietly across from him and drew her work from her bag and began to sew. He had dreamed of evenings like this. Evenings of quiet domestic contentment with his wife. He wanted to say something to her, but he could not think of anything meaningful to say. He pretended to read.

It was only when she got up from her place some time later and left the room without a word that he realized he had been staring into the fire, rubbing his right palm with the thumb of his left hand, straightening the fingers one by one. His hand was stiff and aching.

He should have talked to her. Perhaps she would have stayed. What was the matter with him? Was he determined to drive her away even when she had been perhaps offering an olive branch? But she had left her embroidery and her workbag behind.

And then she returned, something in her hand. She did not say anything to him or even look at him. But she drew a footstool up beside him on his right side, undid the top of the little bottle of oil he could see now in her hand, poured some of it into her palm, and rubbed her hands together. She reached out and took his right hand in her own and began gently massaging the oil into his palm and out along his fingers. Her touch was firm and sure despite the gentleness. He put his head back and closed his eyes.

He thought she was finished, but she was just applying more oil to her hands. The massage was incredibly soothing. No one had ever done that for him before. Not even his mother. His mother had not been able to bear to touch his wounded parts. Or even to look at them. She was the one who had first made him gloves.

Incredibly, he was almost half-asleep when he felt his hand being lifted and felt the softness of her cheek against the back of it. She must have thought him fully asleep. She turned her head and kissed his knuckles. And kept his hand where it was.

She did not move when he rested his left hand very lightly on her curls. He gently smoothed his fingers over her head beneath her hair.

"Samantha," he said. "Forgive me."

"You have done nothing," she said. "It was me."

"No," he said. "You were good to me during those three days, and have been patient and gentle since. And you were right—I *was* cruel. Forgive me."

"I married you," she said, "because I wanted to. I really wanted to, Hartley."

"Shh," he said. "You never gave me reason to believe otherwise. Shall we go home?"

"To Highmoor?" She looked up at him then, her eyes shining with tears.

He nodded. "Home. Shall we go?"

"Yes." She smiled at him. "Yes, let's go home, Hartley."

"As soon as possible. Three days," he said. "There are a few things we are really obligated to attend. Three days and then home." He closed the gap between their mouths and kissed her softly—for the first time in several weeks.

"Thank you, Hartley," she said, and laid her cheek against the back of his hand again. It no longer ached or felt stiff, he noticed.

# 16

*L*ADY STEBBINS WAS THE DUKE OF BRIDGWATER'S aunt. Her ball, always one of the great squeezes of the Season, was one they felt obligated to attend, though neither wished to go. They did not say so to each other— he knew that she enjoyed dancing, and she knew that the duke was a particular friend of his. His grace had been best man at their wedding. They both knew, though, that their longing to be home was mutual. They talked about Highmoor frequently again—it had scarcely been mentioned in the weeks that had succeeded their all-too-short honeymoon.

One more ball could be endured, they both thought, quite separately.

Word had spread once more that they were leaving London early in order to return to Yorkshire. Word always spread among the *ton*, even if one confided the news to almost no one.

A few people commiserated with Samantha.

"Alas," Mr. Wishart said. "Have you lost your influence with your husband already, Lady Carew? Is he forcing you to miss what is left of the Season? It is a downright shameful thing."

"I have not lost my influence at all," she said, laughing

lightly—it was easy to laugh these days. "Why do you think we are going to Highmoor, sir?"

"*You* want to go?" he asked in some astonishment.

"*I* want to go," she said. "Hartley has bowed to my wishes."

He was no longer in the ballroom. He had gone to observe the proceedings in the card room, as he usually did. But he had not left before signing his name in her card next to the supper dance. She had raised her eyebrows and smiled at him.

"No, I am not going to make a spectacle of myself," he said, returning her smile. "But I want to be the man to lead you in to supper, Samantha. Will you mind sitting out a set? Or *walking* it out? Shall we stroll in the garden? The evening is warm."

"I will look forward to it," she had said. It would remind her of their first meeting in London—how long ago that seemed now. Perhaps they could relive it with better results. Perhaps she would find a quiet spot to lead him to and would ask him to kiss her again. And perhaps she would—oh, perhaps she would repeat the words she had spoken to him then.

She would mean them. Not quite in the way that she thought of as love, perhaps. But there were many kinds of love. And one of those kinds described her feelings for Hartley. Perhaps she would tell him.

He had kissed her hand in a courtly gesture that she knew was being observed by many people around them. She was glad. She wanted everyone to know that they had a close relationship. She had told herself that she did not mind that people believed she had married for position and wealth, and in many ways she did not mind. But for Hartley's sake, she would like it to be known that she cared for him. Not for any of his possessions, but only for him.

Sometimes she wished she had told the story of the rather shabby landscape gardener who had come calling and proposed marriage to her. It would have amused the *ton*. Especially the part about her accepting before she discovered her mistake.

"I will meet you outside?" he had said.

She had nodded and he had taken his leave.

Lionel arrived late. She was dancing a country dance with Jeremy Nicholson at the time and inadvertently met Lionel's eyes across the room. He gave her a burning glance. She looked hastily away. The next set was a waltz, she knew. A dangerous dance. As soon as Jeremy had escorted her back to the group, she linked her arm through Francis's and smiled brightly at him.

"Our waltz next?" she said, though in fact no one had yet solicited her hand.

He looked casually about the ballroom. "Ah, yes," he said lazily. "I would have been out of sorts for the rest of the year if you had forgotten, Samantha."

"Thank you," she said later when they were safely dancing.

"If you were my wife," he said, "I would have challenged the bastard to pistols at dawn long before this, Samantha. Pardon the language."

"But why?" she asked. "He has done nothing but

hover ever since my marriage, Francis. You do look splendid, though a little shocking, in that particular shade of pink, by the way."

"I wanted to powder my hair the same color," he said, "but my valet threatened to leave without notice. He is too good a man to squander. I can see my face in my boots when he polishes them."

"How pleasant for you," she said, grinning at him.

"Saucy wench," he said. "And clever wench. You can always divert my thoughts by appealing to my vanity. I do not like the looks he gives you, Samantha. Is Carew willing to tolerate them?"

"We are going home the day after tomorrow," she said.

"Running away?" he asked.

"How dare you, Francis!" she said indignantly.

"Sorry," he said. "I am sorry, Sam. Truly. It is none of my business."

"No," she said, "it is not. How could you make your hair pink when it is so dark a brown?"

He chuckled. "With a couple of tons of powder," he said. "I think it rather a shame that we have outlived those days. Men of a few decades ago used to know how to dress, by Jove. I abhor the trend toward black. Ugh!" He shuddered theatrically and almost lost his step.

Samantha laughed. "You almost have me believing you," she said. "For shame!"

He looked at her with pursed lips, then threw back his head and laughed. "Pink hair," he said. "And you almost believed me. Sam, Sam."

The evening seemed interminable. Perhaps if Hartley's name had not been scrawled—his left-handed writing was anything but elegant—in her card for her to see every time she glanced at it, she could have lived through the evening with greater patience. As things were, she looked forward to their stroll and to having supper with him just as if she were a girl planning her first rendezvous with her first beau. He was her husband of more than a month. She was increasing with his child—surely she could not be wrong about that. There was still no sign of bleeding.

She did not wait for the supper dance to begin. As soon as Mr. Carruthers had led her off the floor following a quadrille, she made an excuse to her group and dashed from the ballroom out onto the balcony and down the steps into the garden. There was no one down there, even though it was quite well lit. Everyone would want to dance the supper dance, she supposed, and stroll outside afterward before the dancing resumed.

Hartley had not come out yet. She found herself smiling in some glee. She would find her secluded spot now and lure him to it as soon as he came down the steps. She would greet him with open arms and ask for his kiss. Would he realize what she was doing? Would he know that she was obliterating old memories and replacing them with new? Would he know that she meant it this time, that she would not be in any way motivated by an upheaval of emotions?

There was a small stone fountain, the water shooting out of the mouth of a fat cherub, in the middle of the garden. A willow tree overhung it on one side. It was the perfect spot. She moved into the shade of the drooping branches and turned to watch the steps from the balcony, just visible from where she stood.

But she had already missed him. He must have come down the steps when she was still moving into her hiding place. He came up almost behind her. She whirled around to face him, a smile on her lips, mischief in her eyes. She half lifted her arms.

"An invitation I have long dreamed of," he said, his voice husky with mingled amusement and desire. "And one I have had the patience to wait for."

Her smile froze. She took one step back, but that one step brought the backs of her legs up against the stone wall of the fountain.

"Go away," she said. "Go away."

"I believe it is time you stopped fighting it, Samantha," Lionel said. "It has been me from the start, has it not? You married Hartley because you were afraid of your feelings for me. But you must have grown mortally tired of him after more than a month of marriage. He is not much of a man, is he? I cannot imagine he has what it takes to satisfy someone of your passions. You need someone like me for that."

She could not lean back far enough to avoid his long finger stroking along her jaw.

"Go away," she said.

"After you led me out here?" He laughed softly. "It was in a garden such as this that we shared our first kiss, Samantha. It is time we repeated it."

"I will vomit," she said, "if you come any closer."

For once he looked nonplussed. "You and Hartley," he said. "I do believe you deserve each other, Samantha. I seem to remember that six years ago, too, you lacked the courage to reach out for what you wanted. I must taste, though, what you have been giving my cousin for the past month."

He had her backed up against the fountain. She could go no farther. But she was boiling with rage. It had been a foolish threat. Though she might *feel* like vomiting, and it would serve him right if she did it all over him, it was not something she could do at will. But she was not going to let such a snake steal any kisses without putting up a decent fight.

She brought her knee up sharply before he got quite close enough to make it impossible. He grunted with pain and surprise and folded over, presenting his face as a tempting target before he dipped too low.

"That was for Hartley," she said, feeling a wonderful sense of exhilaration. "And this is for Jenny." She stung her hand so sharply across his face that she almost cried out in pain herself. But she was not quite done. "And this one is for me." She snapped his head the other way with a slap to the other cheek. "Now, what was that you had to say about tasting?"

"I think," a quiet voice said from the shadows, "my wife has made herself perfectly clear, Lionel."

Lionel was a little too preoccupied with his pain to respond.

Samantha turned her head, the exhilaration dying as

quickly as it had come. "I did not arrange a meeting with him," she said. "I came out here to meet *you,* Hartley."

"I know," he said.

"Do you need any help here, Carew?" another voice asked from a short distance away.

They both turned to see Lord Francis Kneller.

"I saw him follow Samantha—Lady Carew—outside," he said. "I thought she might need my protection."

"You may escort her inside, if you will, Kneller," the marquess said.

"No, Hartley," she said quickly. "Take me home. I want to go home now."

"My lady?" Francis was offering her his arm, just as if she had not spoken.

"Go with him, Samantha," her husband said.

What was he planning to do? Lionel was already straightening up. Obviously she had not done a great deal of damage. Lionel would pluck Hartley limb from limb. She opened her mouth to argue. And snapped her teeth together again. She had recognized the tone. She guessed she would hear it from time to time down the years, and her children, too. It was the tone that said he was to be obeyed without question. And she could not argue with that tone before witnesses. She could not humiliate him like that.

She took Francis's arm and he led her with firm steps toward the ballroom. Music was playing, she realized. The supper waltz was in progress. Everything at the ball was normal. No one else appeared to be down in the garden.

"Francis." She pulled on his arm. "What is happening? He is not being foolish, is he?"

"Good Lord, Samantha," he said, "I hope not."

Which was about as ambiguous an answer as anyone had given to any of the questions she had ever asked.

"Smile," he said, smiling down at her. "We are about to be on view, Samantha."

Her teeth were beginning to chatter. Her hands were stinging. Hartley was out there being murdered, at the very least.

She smiled.

"WELL, HART." LIONEL LEANED a hand on the wall of the fountain and clenched the other hand in an obvious attempt to control his pain. "You have taken an admirably heroic stand. I am sure Samantha and Kneller were marvelously impressed. Are you about to slap a glove in my face? Or would you prefer to keep it on, to hide your deformity?"

"I'll meet you at Jackson's tomorrow morning at eleven," the marquess said quietly. "Be there, Lionel. And come prepared to fight. Until one of us is insensible."

Lionel looked at him incredulously for a few moments and then threw back his head and burst into laughter.

"By God, Hart," he said when he finally had his amusement under control, "I hope you invite a large audience. It is going to be more amusing than a public hanging. Someone will be lugging raw meat back to Samantha's arms."

"Perhaps," the marquess said curtly. "And then again, perhaps not. Choose your second and bring him with you. Though I daresay Jackson himself will set down the rules and see to it that we abide by them. It will be just as well. I might kill you, else."

His words occasioned another roar of laughter.

"You had better reconsider before morning, Hart," Lionel said, still chuckling. "Before this reaches a point from which you cannot back down. I will think no worse of you. I will hold you in the same esteem I have always held you in. You had better go inside now and tell Samantha and Kneller that you wagged your finger at me and scolded me roundly for trying to steal a kiss from your wife, and that you left me drowning in tears of remorse. Tomorrow you can crawl home to the safety of Highmoor and live there happily ever after. I'll not come after you—or Samantha. I thought it would be amusing to revive old emotions, and I was right. It was. But she bores me now. She is all yours, Hart, my boy. Run away now like a good little boy."

The marquess inclined his head. "Good night to you, Lionel," he said with quiet courtesy. "I shall see you tomorrow morning. At eleven sharp." He turned and made his way back to the ballroom.

Lionel's laughter followed him.

He made his way as quickly and unobtrusively as he could around the edge of the floor—amazingly, the supper dance was still in progress—and out through the nearest door. He found the Duke of Bridgwater in the card room, watching a game in progress. He sent up a silent prayer of thanks that his friend was not dancing, as he had been most of the evening.

"Bridge." He touched the duke on the sleeve and drew him to one side. "I need your services."

His friend grinned. "I thought you were slinking off into the garden for a secret tryst with Lady Carew," he said.

"I need a second tomorrow at Jackson's saloon," the marquess said. "I have challenged Rushford to a bout—until one of us is unconscious, if Jackson will allow it. Will you stand by me?"

His friend merely stared at him.

"He was molesting Samantha in the garden," the marquess said. "She gave a good account of herself, but it was not enough."

"No," his friend said quietly. "No, it would not be. Yes, you can count on me, Hart."

"And on me." The marquess had been half-aware of Lord Francis Kneller entering the room and coming to stand a short distance away. "I'll second you, too, Carew, if I may."

"Thank you." His lordship nodded curtly. "Where is Samantha?"

"Dancing with Stebbins," Francis said. "He led her out despite the fact that the set had already begun and he was wheezing and as red as a lobster from the evening's exertions."

"My uncle could never resist treading a measure," his grace said, "especially with a pretty partner."

"She is smiling and sparkling and holding up like a trouper," Francis said. "What time tomorrow, Carew?"

"Eleven," he said. "If you will excuse me, I'll catch the end of the waltz and then take Samantha home. It has been a trying evening for her."

His friend and Samantha's stood where they were as he limped away. Then their eyes met.

"It is going to be a massacre," Francis said. "But he had no choice."

"I am not so sure," the duke said, frowning. "About the massacre, I mean. He will be beaten, of course, but maybe not quite as badly as one might think. For the last few years he has been having private sessions with Jackson. Jackson would not waste his time on nothing, would he? I have no idea what has been going on between the two of them, but it appears that tomorrow morning we will find out."

"I'll respect him in future," Francis said, "however humiliating the outcome is for him tomorrow. I must confess I have thought him a weakling. That bastard has been stalking Lady Carew since he came back to England."

"No, not a weakling, Kneller," his grace said. "Hartley has a quiet dignity that does not need to assert itself in swashbuckling. But he has a wife now whom he loves. He is not the type to stand by and see her insulted."

"Good," Francis said. "If he had not challenged

Rushford, you know, then I would have. And that would not have been quite the thing, would it?"

"Most unwise, my dear chap," his grace said. He raised one eyebrow. "Though I am sure that if you look hard enough you will find some other lady with quite equal charms who would welcome your gallantry and your devotion and your willingness to rush to her defense."

"By Jove," Francis said, "I do believe you are warning me, Bridgwater."

"My dear fellow," the duke said, rearranging the lace folds of his cuffs over the backs of his hands, "I would not dream of it. I am merely suggesting that you avoid, ah, making an ass of yourself, shall we say? She is very lovely, but then so are many of the ladies who grace our ballrooms and drawing rooms if we but take the trouble to look. I am famished. Shall we make an early sortie into the supper room?"

"Lead the way," Francis said, brushing an invisible speck from his pink arm.

"HARTLEY?" SHE LEANED ACROSS her empty breakfast plate and set her hand flat on the table, close to his.

He had been glancing through the morning paper. He looked up, set it aside, and smiled at her.

"Hartley," she said, her best wheedling look on her face and a matching tone in her voice, "I have been thinking. My trunks are almost packed and I daresay yours are, too. The weather is good. Do we need to waste another day? Could we not start on our way home this morning?"

She wanted to be out of London. She did not believe she would ever want to come back, though she supposed that feeling might pass in time. She wanted to be home, back in that wonderful place where it had all started—her love affair with friendship. And with Hartley. She could not bear the thought of waiting even another day.

He covered her hand with his own—his right one, thin and crooked and ungloved. She had asked him not to wear his glove at home. There was no need, she had assured him, taking his hand in her own and raising it to her cheek and kissing it, the morning after she had massaged it for the first time. She had done so each day since.

"It will have to wait one more day," he said. "I have a couple of pieces of business to attend to first. Tomorrow will come eventually, my love. And then we will have Highmoor and the summer to look forward to."

She sighed. "And no one else can attend to this business for you?" she asked.

"I am afraid not." He patted her hand. "And you will wish to say good-bye to Lady Brill."

"I seem to have done nothing but say good-bye to her in the past month or so," she said.

"Poor Samantha." He smiled at her. "Take her shopping with you. Buy her something pretty, and yourself, too, and have the bills sent to me. Lady Thornhill has been known to complain, you know, even in my hearing, that there is nothing fashionable to be bought in York-shire."

"You will be sorry," she said. "I will spend your whole fortune."

He chuckled and got to his feet before offering her his hand. "I will have to be going," he said. "I have an appointment for which I cannot possibly be late."

She pulled a face. "And so a mere wife has been put firmly in her place," she said. "All she is good for is tripping out to shop for baubles."

He chuckled again. "Scold me all day tomorrow," he said. "You will have a captive audience in the carriage. Now I really must be going."

Men and their mysterious "appointments," she thought a few minutes later, alone with her maid in her room, preparing to call on her aunt. He had probably promised to meet the Duke of Bridgwater and Lord Gerson at White's for luncheon, and that was more important than making an early start for home. Or than giving in to a wife's best wheedling.

She did not really want to go out today. She dreaded that she would perhaps run into Lionel. Not that she would stay indoors merely to hide away from him. She had been rather proud of the way she had handled him the evening before—and enormously relieved to see later that Hartley was unharmed. She had rather expected a shattered nose and two black eyes, at the very least.

He had been very reticent about what had happened out in the garden after he and Francis between them had removed her from the scene of her triumph. He had merely assured her that she need not worry about Lionel's harassing her ever again.

He had not—as she had half expected—asked her if she had finally got her feelings for Lionel sorted out. Perhaps her actions in the garden had spoken louder than any words.

And he had not—it had been a terrible disappointment—come to her bed last night. It had been the first time since their wedding. She had shed a few tears of self-pity and anger—he *did* believe she had gone out there to meet Lionel, despite what he had said at the time. Why had he not *said* so, then? She had done the unthinkable eventually. She had gone through to his room—she had never even set foot in it before—and stood by the side of his bed, shuffling and clearing her throat until he woke up. He had been *sleeping*.

"What is it?" he had asked, sitting up.

"I went out there to meet *you*," she had said, her voice more abject than she had intended. "I was finding a secluded spot so that you could *kiss* me there."

"Ah. I know, love," he had said. And he had reached out and lifted her bodily over him and onto the bed beside him. There had appeared to be no lack of strength in his right arm. He had covered her with the blankets. His bed was soft and warm. "I did not doubt you for even a moment."

"Then why—?" she had asked.

"I thought you would be as tired as I was," he had said. "I did not realize my not coming would upset you."

"It did not—" she had begun, but he had shushed her and then kissed her.

He had not made love to her.

It had not mattered. She had been asleep within minutes.

Well, she would go out, she thought now. The day would crawl by if she stayed at home. She would do as he had suggested and take Aunt Aggy shopping. She smiled and met her maid's eyes in the looking glass. The girl smiled back. And she would spend a fortune, too. She was *never* a spendthrift. But today she would be. She would punish him horribly.

"No, my straw bonnet," she said when her maid handed her a more subdued and more elegant one.

This was going to be a day of gaiety. She was going to enjoy her last day in London. Her last day for maybe a long, long time. This time next year she was going to be nursing a baby—no wet nurses for her, even if Hartley tried using his I-must-be-obeyed-without-question voice. And the year after next—well, she was sure the nursery at Highmoor must be far too large for one child. Probably even for two.

# 17

*H*E WAS GAZING DOWNWARD, TRYING TO BLOCK out both sight and sound, trying to concentrate. It was not easy. This particular sparring room in Jackson's boxing saloon was crowded with eager spectators. He had told no one and Bridge and Kneller had just assured him that they had not. But Lionel, of course, would have no reason for keeping quiet about the fight and every reason to publicize it.

Barefoot and stripped to the waist, he felt woefully inadequate. He knew that in appearance, even apart from his twisted foot and hand, he was laughably inferior to Lionel, tall and splendidly built and beautiful in his corner with Viscount Birchley, his second. He was flashing his grin on all comers and loudly greeting every new arrival.

"It is a good thing you are punctual," he called gaily to someone who had just arrived. "It will not be a lengthy entertainment. But then neither is a hanging."

He had obviously liked that analogy the evening before and had thought it worthy of repetition.

Jackson had agreed—reluctantly—to a fight that would end only with the unconsciousness of one or other of the combatants. Normally very strict and very gentlemanly rules applied to the sparring bouts at his establishment. He had just finished explaining to both of them and their seconds and anyone else who cared to listen—there had been a dead hush in the room—that there would be a limitless number of rounds, each to last three minutes. There were to be no hits after he had called the end of a round or before he had called for the beginning of the next. All hits were to be cleanly above the waist.

"Pipe down, Jackson," someone had called from the back of the room. "Your instructions are taking longer than the fight will last."

Gentleman Jackson had fixed the offender with an iron stare and invited him to take his leave. It was a measure of the power he wielded within the doors of his saloon that Mr. Smithers rather sheepishly slipped away through the door and did not come back.

And now the fight was about to begin. The Marquess of Carew tried to concentrate, to remember everything he had learned over the past three years—though he had never expected to be using his skills in actual combat.

"Defend with your right and attack with your left," Lord Francis Kneller advised him rather urgently. "Protect your head."

"You will need to get in close, Hart," the Duke of Bridgwater said. "He has a longer reach than yours and powerful fists. But protect your head. Keep your chin tucked in."

"Go get him," Lord Francis said. "Think of your wife." Poor advice. Very poor. He tried to concentrate on the fight itself. A fight he could not win, perhaps. But one in which he must give a good account of himself.

"Round one," Jackson said. "Begin, gentlemen."

The marquess looked up and stepped forward to a swell of sound from the onlookers.

"Daniel and one of the lions," some wit said.

"David and Goliath, more like," someone else shouted from the other side of the room.

Lionel was grinning and dancing and waving his fists in a most unsportsmanlike way. He was making very little pretense of defending himself.

"Time to draw your slingshot from your belt, Hart," he said. "See if you can get me right between the eyes."

The next moment he was flat on his back on the floor while a roar of mingled astonishment and amusement went up from the crowd. And then murmurings of outrage and calls of "Foul!" and "Shame!"

Lionel roared with wrath as he scrambled to his knees. "What the bloody hell!" he shouted.

"Disqualification, Jackson," Viscount Birchley cried. "The verdict goes to Rushford."

"By God, Hart, splendid hit, old chap," the duke said.

The bout appeared to have stopped.

"You were not listening, gentlemen," Jackson said crisply. "The rule was that no hit was to be below the belt. That hit was full on the chin. The rule did not state that hits can be made only with the fists. The foot is a permitted weapon within the rules of today's bout. Proceed, gentlemen."

"I am not fighting a bloody contortionist," Lionel said scornfully.

Since he was still on his knees, it took the marquess little effort at all to twist his right leg high enough to poke Lionel on the chin again hard enough to send him sprawling.

"Then yield," he said coldly, "while you are still conscious. Before all these witnesses of yours, Rushford. And be stripped of what little honor you have remaining."

Lionel scrambled to his feet and put himself in a far more respectful attitude of defense than before.

"Come on, Carew," he said. "If one of us can kick, the other can, too. If you choose to fight dirty, then dirty it will be. But do not expect mercy of me. I might have spared—"

His speech was cut short when the sole of the marquess's foot caught him on the shoulder and sent him reeling, though he managed to keep his feet this time.

Before the end of round one it became obvious that the Earl of Rushford was not going to be able to use his feet in the fight. The only time he tried it he kicked his cousin almost in the groin and received a severe warning from Jackson. He swore again about contortionists, but he had not had the hours of exercise and practice that the marquess had had in turning his body and throwing out his leg to the height of his own head. Nor had he had the training and experience of using that leg and foot as a weapon quite as powerful as a fist.

There had been little if any betting before the start of

the bout. What was the point of betting when the outcome was a foregone conclusion? The only betting there had been was on how many seconds the fight would last. At the end of the first round the real betting began. At the end of round two it was as fast and furious as the round itself had been.

After four rounds the marquess was feeling sore on every square inch of his body and weary in every muscle, even muscles he had not known he possessed. He had been down twice, Lionel three times, not counting those first two falls in the first round. Lionel had succeeded a few times in grabbing his leg and twisting it, throwing him off balance and causing excruciating pain. But Jackson had warned him about holding and it had not happened in the last round.

Lord Francis was squeezing a sponge of cold water over his head and down his back. It felt delicious. Bridge was waving a towel energetically before his face.

"Keep it up, Hart," he said. "Show him a thing or two, old chap."

"Think of your wife, Carew," Lord Francis said quietly.

He had begun to think of her. Of the innocent, eager eighteen-year-old who had fallen prey to Lionel's cynical scheming. Of the heartbreak his cruel rejection had caused her and—worse—the guilt that had been left behind to blight her life for six years. Of the woman of four-and-twenty who had feared that he would still have a power over her she would be unable to resist and who had turned to him—to Hartley Wade—to protect her and keep her safe from ugly passions for the rest of her life. He thought of her last night, lashing out with her knee and her hands and even then lingering to throw defiance in Lionel's teeth. He thought of her beside his bed last night, miserable because she thought *he* had rejected her, too. He had been refraining from sexual relations in order to conserve his energy for this morning.

He had promised her last night that she would never have to fear Lionel again. And there was only one way to ensure that. He knew that he had won the respect of his peers this morning, even if he was rendered unconscious in the very next round. And perhaps he had won his own respect, too, finally doing more than just enduring Lionel's taunts, finally challenging him and facing him man-to-man.

But it was not enough. It was no longer enough merely to give a good account of himself in this fight. He had to win it.

He *had* to win it. And it no longer seemed an impossibility. Lionel was sitting across from him, in the opposite corner, gazing at him from one open eye and one swollen and half-closed one. His breathing was labored. And for once—and at last—he was looking with quite open and naked hatred.

"Time, gentlemen. Round five," Gentleman Jackson said. "Begin."

It was easier, of course, to tell oneself that one had to win than to do it. In round nine the marquess finally knew that he not only could do it, but would. Lionel was swaying on his feet. His guard was low, so it was possible to punish his face with both left fist and right foot. One of his eyes was a mere slit in swollen flesh. The other was half closed. His nose looked as if it were broken.

His own strength had all but been used up. He was proceeding on sheer willpower and determination. And on the image of Samantha's face that constantly swam before his tired vision.

There was very little noise now in the room, though it appeared that no one had left except the unfortunate Smithers.

"Think of her, Carew. Think of her," Lord Francis said to him insistently at the end of the round, as he had said at the end of the round before, and the round before that. He was squeezing a sponge down over his chest. "Think of her, dammit, and don't you dare let up."

Kneller was in love with Samantha, he thought sluggishly. He had known that all along. But Kneller was an honorable man. Well, he would avenge her for both of them.

"It has to be this round, old chap," the duke said, still vigorously fanning as he had between all rounds. "You are close to exhaustion. You will collapse in round eleven. This is round ten. This is the one, Hart. Go to it. There is not a man here, with the possible exception of those two opposite, who is not pulling for you. *This* round, Hart."

It took him two and a half minutes to do it. But finally Lionel was swaying on boneless legs, his hands in very loose fists at his sides, looking at him—though perhaps not really seeing him—with implacable hatred. He would have fallen unaided and been unconscious by the time he hit the floor. And it was tempting even then to have a modicum of mercy on him.

But the marquess saw an image of himself at the age of six, his child's body shattered and in indescribable pain. And an image of his mother, who could not endure the sight of pain, especially when it was being suffered by her beloved only son. And of Samantha begging him to kiss her, telling him she loved him—and *meaning* it at the moment she spoke—because she had been frightened by Lionel's reappearance in a life he had made unhappy for six years.

He gathered together his last remaining shreds of strength and jabbed out with his right leg. His last blow, like the first, landed squarely on Lionel's chin, snapping back his head and sending him crashing backward.

He groaned once and then lay still.

There was noise then. Deafening noise. Men talking to him, laughing, thumping him on the back before Bridge roared at them all to keep their distance and Kneller swore at them to stand back and give Carew air or he would start laying about him with his own fists.

"Well, lad," Jackson was saying from somewhere above him—someone had pulled him down onto the stool in his corner, "I feel compelled to say that you are perhaps my best ever pupil. But if you had just remembered to keep up that right hand—how many *times* have I told you?—your face would not be looking quite as raw as it does. Some people are a glutton for punishment."

Viscount Birchley was fanning Lionel, who was prone

on the floor, and yelling for someone to fetch some water. No one was taking a great deal of notice.

"Go and give him a hand, Bridge," the marquess said, not even daring yet to flex sore muscles or to try to get to his feet. His legs had turned to rubber.

The duke gave him a speaking glance, which he did not even see, and went.

Lionel was still on the floor, groaning with returning consciousness as Birchley sponged his face carefully and the Duke of Bridgwater waved the inevitable towel before his face, when the marquess finally got to his feet with Lord Francis Kneller's help and limped stiffly from the room to retrieve his clothes and make his way back home.

There was going to be no keeping the morning's events from Samantha as he had hoped to do, he thought ruefully. He did not think any story of walking into a door was going to convince her. Well, perhaps she would be happy to know that he had avenged her.

Perhaps she would even be proud of him.


SHE HAD SPENT A veritable fortune—far more, at least, than she had ever spent in a single day before. And she did not feel even a moment's guilt. If he had taken her home today as she had asked, she would not have spent a single penny. He would not have had anything to grumble about. Not that Hartley would grumble anyway. She could not quite imagine him grumbling about anything.

Besides, he had told her to go out and buy Aunt Aggy and herself something pretty. Like a good little wife she had obeyed.

She bought her aunt a delicate ivory fan, laughing at Aunt Aggy's protests that she was too old for such a pretty little trinket. And she bought her a pair of kid gloves, too, since her aunt had been saying all spring that she simply must buy herself new ones. She bought Hartley a snuffbox, though he never took snuff, because it was pretty and irresistible and because the silver lid was inlaid with sapphires and she had the sudden idea of giving it to him as a belated wedding present—though he was going to pay for it. It would be their "something blue" to replace the other horrid thing. She had not asked if he had kept it or given it back. She did not want to know.

She almost forgot to buy herself something, but remembered just in time and bought some silk stockings and a new bonnet so bedecked with ribbons and flowers that she half expected that her neck would disappear into her chest when she tried it on. But it was as light as a feather and looked so dashing and so very—extravagant that she had to buy it, though she was not sure if it was the type of bonnet she would wear in Yorkshire. She also visualized herself wearing it when she was huge with child and had to swallow her laughter lest she have to explain to Aunt Aggy and the milliner.

Despite herself, she was enjoying her last day in London.

And then, after they had stopped for luncheon—

although Aunt Aggy had protested that it was extravagant to eat out and not quite proper without a gentleman to escort them—Samantha spotted Francis farther down Oxford Street and lifted her hand gaily and waved to him and smiled.

He came hurrying toward them.

"Samantha," he said. "Lady Brill." But he turned back to the former. "Were you not at home when Carew arrived?"

"Now?" she said. "Recently? Is he at home already? I thought his business was to keep him out all day."

He took her arm and lowered his voice. "I believe he may need you," he said.

The tone of his voice and the look on his face alerted her. "Why?" she asked fearfully. "What has happened? Lionel? Did—?"

"Yes," he said.

Her eyes widened in terror. "Hartley *challenged* him last night? Is he *dead*?" But even as she clutched at his sleeve she remembered his just saying that Hartley might need her. Would a dead man have need of her?

"No," he said. "Deuce take it, but I have bungled this. It was fisticuffs, Samantha. At Jackson's. And your husband *won*."

"Your timing and your sensibilities leave something to be desired, my lord," Lady Brill said as Samantha clung to his sleeve with both hands. "She is all but fainting. Come. Help her to the carriage. I will convey her to Stanhope Gate without any further delay. Carew won, did you say? But against whom, pray? And in what cause? It will be a story worth listening to, at any rate. And I do not doubt it will be the *on dit* by this evening. There, dear, in you go. Lord Francis will help you."

Samantha smiled rather wanly down at him after she was seated. "No, do not apologize, Francis," she said. "Thank you. I might not have heard, otherwise. I might have been gone all day. Oh, Hartley." She fumbled in her reticule for a handkerchief.

"He may be battered and bruised, Samantha," he said, "but you may tell him from me that he is the most fortunate man in England. And more worthy of you than any other man I know. Good-bye."

He closed the door before she could make any response more than a rather watery smile.

HE HAD BATHED AND changed, and his valet—looking quite smug and satisfied—had rubbed ointment into the rawer of his wounds. And he had limped his way downstairs to the library to sit by the fire he had had lit despite the warmness of the day outside. There was probably not a joint or a muscle in his body that was not screaming at him. Miraculously, both eyes had escaped, but they were about the only part of him that had.

He wished Samantha would come home and massage his hand.

He wished he did not have to face her for a week.

He had won. He set his head back and closed his eyes, but the euphoria built in him like an expanding balloon of excitement. He had *won*. He had set the score right. He had avenged her—and himself, too. He allowed himself a smile of pride. He had never realized that a smile could physically hurt.

And then the door crashed inward. He turned in time to see a little whirlwind rush inside, the yellow flowers on its straw bonnet nodding violently. But she snatched the bonnet from her head even as he watched and hurled it to one side without even checking to see that there was somewhere other than the floor for it to land. Someone closed the door quietly from the outside.

"I could *kill* you," she said. "With my bare hands. Hartley! You did not even *tell* me. Business indeed. Business to attend to. He might have *killed* you. I could kill you."

"Perhaps it is as well," he said, "that a man can die only once."

"Hartley." She came to stand in front of him and then went down on her knees and rested her hands on his knees. "Oh, Hartley, your poor face. Why did you do it? Oh, I know why. You did it for me. You should never have done anything so foolhardy. But thank you. Oh, thank you. I do love you so."

"For those words alone it was all worth it," he said, smiling carefully. "It was partly for me, too, Samantha."

"Because in insulting me he insulted you?" she asked, gazing up at his shiny, reddened face.

He was never a handsome man, he thought, but now he must look grotesque. And yet she was gazing with something that looked almost like adoration in her face.

"Yes," he said. "And because of this, Samantha." He held up his right hand. "And my foot. He was the cause of both. It was no accident. He pushed me—a child of six."

Her eyes brightened with tears. "Oh, Hartley," she whispered. "Oh, my poor love. Francis said that you won. Does Lionel look worse than you?"

"Considerably," he said. "He will spend the rest of his life with a crooked nose, and I would wager his eyes will be invisible and blind for at least the next week."

"How delicious," she said, grinning unexpectedly. "I am so glad. Well done, sir."

"Bloodthirsty woman," he said.

"Hartley." She rested her chin on his knees and continued to gaze up at him. "I have been terribly foolish. I have realized it only during the past few days, and only last night and today has it become fully apparent to me. I have been mistaking the meaning of a word."

He chuckled. "Foolish indeed," he said. "What word?"

"I think you are in terrible pain," she said. "Would it be quite impossible to sit on your lap?"

He was in pain. Even the pressure on his knees hurt. He reached his arms down to her. She curled up against him, her head on his shoulder.

"It is the word 'like,'" she said. "I did not know that what I had always thought was liking was really love. I have been very foolish."

He felt rather as if someone had just punched him in the stomach again. He felt robbed of breath.

"Give me an example," he said, risking further pain by lowering his cheek to the top of her head.

"When I met you at Highmoor," she said, "I liked you

so terribly much, Hartley. After each meeting I lived for the next time, and when I had to leave early with Aunt Aggy, there was a dreadful emptiness in my life where you had been. I thought you my best friend in the world, and I thought I would never know such friendship again. Town and the Season were flat because I did not have my friend to share them with. And then when I saw you again, I was so *happy* that I thought I would burst. I wanted you to kiss me and I wanted to say what I said to you afterward and I wanted to marry you—because I liked you so much. After we were married, for those three days, I—I have never been so happy in my life. I was delirious with happiness. Because I liked you so much. And afterward I wanted to die, I wanted the world to end because I thought you did not like me any longer."

"Ah, love," he said.

"Have I given you enough examples?" she asked. "Do you see what I mean?"

He swallowed and rubbed his cheek against her hair.

"You see," she said, "when I went through that horrid experience during my first Season, I called it love. I thought that was what it was, that horrible obsession, the dreadful guilt, the—oh, everything. And all I have clung to since is the conviction that I wanted nothing more to do with love. I saw Jenny and Gabriel together and other people, too, but I did not believe in it for myself. So when I met you, I think I was afraid to call my feelings what they were. I thought everything would turn ugly. I wanted to like you and you to like me so that we could be happy together."

"I like you, sweetheart," he said.

"And I *love* you," she said. "You see? I have said it and no thunderbolt has fallen on our heads. Hartley, you are everything in the world to me. Everything and more. You always have been, from the moment I first saw you. You put sunshine back into my life."

He swallowed again, and then, without thinking of the pain he was going to cause himself, he moved his head, found her mouth with his own, and kissed her.

"It is not too late?" she whispered.

"It is never too late," he said. "I love you."

She sighed and reached for another kiss. But she broke off after a few moments and smiled at him. "I have a gift for you," she said. "I bought it and have had the bill sent to you." She laughed gaily. "And it is not even something you use, Hartley. But it was so pretty that I could not resist it. And it is blue. Something blue. A belated wedding gift." She leaned down from his lap and retrieved the reticule she had dropped to the floor.

"I have a gift for you, too," he said. "It was the first matter of business I spoke of at breakfast this morning." He chuckled. "It is something blue. To help you forget the other." He had slipped it into a pocket before coming downstairs. He reached for it now.

"Oh," she said, looking at her sapphire ring a few moments later. "Oh, Hartley, it is beautiful. Oh, my love, thank you." She held out her hand to him and he slipped the ring on next to her wedding band. She held the hand farther away, fingers spread, to admire the effect.

He smiled down at his snuffbox. "Shall I take up the habit," he asked, "and learn to sneeze all over you?"

"You do not like it?" she asked doubtfully. "It was a foolish idea, was it not?"

"I shall wear it next to my heart for the rest of my life," he said. "I shall treasure it as much as a certain green feather I once won. Thank you, Samantha."

"Do you want another gift?" she asked. "It is not blue or a green feather and cannot be put in your hands—yet. But I think you will like it." She was looking at him with luminous eyes.

"What?" He smiled and set his head back against the chair.

"I think . . . ," she said. "Actually, I am almost sure. I think we are going to have a baby, Hartley."

He was glad his head was back. He closed his eyes briefly. "Oh, my love," he said.

"I think it must be so," she said. "In fact, I feel that it must be so. I want to go home to Highmoor, Hartley. The baby will be born in the new year and I will nurse him or her next spring and summer, and then before you can have ideas to bring me back here to enjoy another silly Season, we will have another and squash the possibility again. That is my plan, anyway." She was smiling warmly, a little impishly at him. "Do you not think it a wonderful plan?"

He smiled at her and cupped her cheek with his right hand. "I think *you* are wonderful," he said. "I cannot grasp this reality yet. I am to be a father? Am I really that clever?"

"Yes, you are," she said. "Hartley? Do you remember telling me there was more to learn? That you would teach me and that I would teach you?"

"Yes," he said.

"I do not know what I could possibly teach you," she said, "but will you help me to learn?" Her eyes were warm, wistful, full of love. "And to teach? I want everything there can be with you. And I want to give you every happiness there is."

He drew her head down to his shoulder again and nestled his cheek against her head. "Starting tonight, love," he said. "And continuing through the rest of our lives."

There was a contented silence for no longer than a few moments.

"What is wrong with this afternoon?" she asked him.

Nothing except a whole bodyful of aching joints and sore muscles and raw flesh. Absolutely nothing whatsoever.

"Nothing that I can think of," he said. "Your room or mine, my love?"

"Yours," she said, springing to her feet and reaching down a hand for his. "For a change. Your bed felt deliciously soft last night, Hartley, even though all we did was *sleep* in it."

"Well," he said, hauling himself somehow to his feet and offering her his left arm, "we will certainly have to rectify that little omission before another hour has passed. Never let it be said that all I ever did in my own bed with my wife was sleep with her."

She chuckled merrily and laid her arm along the top of his, just as if he were about to lead her into a dance.

"This is certainly going to be more enjoyable than shopping," she said. "Thank heaven I ran into Francis. Oh, by the way, I am to tell you from him that you are the most fortunate man in the world."

"Amen to that," he said, opening the door and leading her through to the hall and up the stairs.

"I, of course," she said, "am the luckiest woman in the whole *universe*. I am in love with and married to my dearest friend. My *special companion*."

Get ready to be entranced
by the fourth book in Mary Balogh's
series featuring the extraordinary
Huxtable family. *Seducing an Angel*
spotlights brother Stephen, the young
earl whose innocent façade hides
the determination within.

# Seducing an Angel

## STEPHEN'S STORY

Available now

Turn the page for a sneak peek inside.

# MARY BALOGH

*New York Times* Bestselling Author of
*At Last Comes Love*

# Seducing an Angel

# Seducing an Angel

## On sale now

STEPHEN was turning as he spoke and did not finish his sentence because he almost collided with someone who was passing close behind him. Sheer instinct caused him to grasp her by the upper arms so that she would not be bowled entirely over.

"I do beg your pardon," he said, and found himself almost toe-to-toe and eye-to-eye with Lady Paget. "I ought to have been looking where I was going."

She was in no hurry to step back. Her fan was in her hand—it looked ivory with a fine filigree design across its surface—and she wafted it slowly before her face.

Oh, Lord, her eyes almost matched her gown. He had never seen such green eyes, and they did indeed slant upward ever so slightly at the outer corners. Viewed against the background of her red hair, they were simply stunning. Her eyelashes were thick and darker than her hair—as were her eyebrows. She was wearing some unidentifiable perfume, which was floral but neither overstrong nor oversweet.

"You are pardoned," she said in such a low-pitched velvet voice that Stephen felt a shiver along his spine.

He had noticed earlier that the ballroom was warm despite the fact that all the windows had been thrown wide. He had not noticed until now that the room was also airless.

Her lips curled into a faint suggestion of a smile, and her eyes remained on his.

He expected her to continue on her way to wherever she had been going. She did not do so. Perhaps because—oh. Perhaps because he was still clutching her arms. He released them with another apology.

"I saw you looking at me earlier," she said. "I was looking at you, of course, or I would not have noticed. Have we met somewhere before?"

She must know they had not. Unless—

"I saw you in Hyde Park yesterday afternoon," he said. "Perhaps I look familiar because you saw me there too but do not quite recall doing so. You were dressed in widow's weeds."

"How clever of you," she said. "I thought they made me quite unidentifiable."

There was amusement in her eyes. He was not sure if it was occasioned by real humor or by a certain inexplicable sort of scorn.

"I do recall," she said. "I did as soon as I saw you again tonight. How could I have forgotten you? I thought you looked like an angel then, and I think it again tonight."

"Oh, I say." Stephen laughed with a mingling of embarrassment and amusement. He seemed particularly inarticulate this evening. "Looks can deceive, I am afraid, ma'am."

"Yes," she said, "they can. Perhaps on further acquaintance I will change my mind about you—or would if there *were* any further acquaintance."

He wished her bosom were not quite so exposed or that she were not standing quite so close. But he would feel foolish taking a step back now when he ought to have thought to do so as soon as he let go of her arms. He felt it imperative to keep his eyes on her face.

Her lips were full, her mouth on the wide side. It was probably one of the most kissable mouths his eyes had ever dwelled upon. No, it was definitely *the* most kissable. It was one more feature to add to a beauty that was already perfect.

"I beg your pardon," he said, stepping back at last so that he could make her a slight bow. "I am Merton, at your service, ma'am."

"I knew that," she said. "When one sees an angel, one must waste no time in discovering his identity. I do not need to tell you mine."

"You are Lady Paget," he said. "I am pleased to make your acquaintance, ma'am."

"Are you?" Her eyelids had drooped half over her eyes, and she was regarding him from beneath them. Her eyes were still amused.

Over her shoulder he could see couples taking their places on the dance floor. The musicians were tuning their instruments.

"Lady Paget," he said, "would you care to waltz?"

"I would indeed care to," she said, "if I had a partner."

And she smiled fully and with such dazzling force that Stephen almost took another step back.

"Shall I try that again?" he said. "Lady Paget, would you care to waltz *with me*?"

"I would indeed, Lord Merton," she said. "Why do you think I collided with you?"

Good Lord.

Well, *good Lord*!

He held out his arm for her hand.

It was a long-fingered hand encased in a white glove. It might never have wielded an axe, Stephen thought. It might never have wielded any weapon with deadly force. But it was very dangerous nonetheless.

*She* was very dangerous.

The trouble was, he really did not know what his mind meant by telling him that.

He was going to waltz with the notorious Lady Paget—and lead her in to supper afterward.

He would swear his wrist was tingling where her hand rested on his sleeve.

He felt stupidly young and gauche and naive—none of which he was to any marked degree.


The Earl of Merton was taller than Cassandra had thought—half a head or more taller than she. He was broad-shouldered, and his chest and arms were well muscled. There was no need of any padding with his figure. His waist and hips were slender, his legs long and shapely. His eyes were intensely blue and seemed to smile even when his face was in repose. His mouth was wide and good-humored. She had always thought that dark-haired men had a strong advantage when it came to male attractiveness. But this man was golden blond and physically perfect.

He smelled of maleness and something subtle and musky.

He was surely younger than she. He was also—and not at all surprisingly—very popular with the ladies. She had seen how those who were not dancing had followed him wistfully with their eyes during the last two sets—and even a few of those who *were* dancing. She had seen a few glance his way with growing agitation, as the time to take partners for the waltz grew close. Several, she suspected, had waited until the last possible moment before accepting other, less desirable partners.

There was an air of openness about him, almost of innocence.

Cassandra set one hand on his shoulder and the other in his as his right arm came about her waist and the music began.

She was not responsible for guarding his innocence. She had been quite open with him. She had told him she remembered seeing him yesterday. She had told him she had deliberately discovered his identity and just as deliberately collided with him a short while ago so that he would dance with her. That was warning enough. If he was fool enough after the waltz was over to continue to consort with the notorious Lady Paget—axe murderer, husband killer—then on his own head be the consequences.

She closed her eyes briefly as he spun her into the first twirl of the dance. She gave in to a moment of wistfulness. How lovely it would be to relax for half an hour and enjoy herself. It seemed to her that her life had been devoid of enjoyment for a long, long time.

But relaxation and enjoyment were luxuries she could not afford.

She looked into Lord Merton's eyes. They were smiling back at her.

"You waltz well," he said.

Did she? She had waltzed once in London a number of years ago and a few times at country assemblies. She did not consider herself accomplished in the steps.

"Of course I do," she said, "when I have a partner who waltzes even better."

"The youngest of my sisters would be delighted to take the credit," he said. "She taught me years ago, when I was a boy with two left feet who thought dancing was for girls and wished to be out climbing trees and swimming in streams instead."

"Your sister was wise," she said. "She realized that boys grow up into men who understand that waltzing is a necessary prelude to courtship."

He raised his eyebrows.

"Or," she added, "to seduction."

His blue eyes met hers, but he said nothing for a moment.

"I am not trying to seduce you, Lady Paget," he said. "I do beg your pardon if—"

"I do believe," she said, interrupting him, "you are the perfect gentleman, Lord Merton. I know you are not trying to seduce me. It is the other way around. *I* am trying to seduce *you*. And determined to succeed, I may add."

They danced in silence. It was a lovely, lilting tune that the orchestra played. They twirled about the perimeter of the ballroom with all the other dancers. The gowns of the other ladies were a kaleidoscope of color, the candles in the wall sconces a swirl of light. Behind the sound of the music there were voices raised in conversation and laughter.

She could feel his heat flowing into her hands from his shoulder and palm, radiating into her bosom and stomach and thighs from his body.

"Why?" he asked quietly after some time had elapsed.

She tipped back her head and smiled fully at him.

"Because you are beautiful, Lord Merton," she said, "and because I have no interest in enticing you into a courtship, as most of the very young ladies here tonight do. I have been married once, and that was quite enough for this lifetime."

He had not responded to her smile. He gazed at her with intense eyes while they danced. And then his eyes softened and smiled again, and his lips curved attractively upward at the corners.

"I believe, Lady Paget," he said, "you enjoy being outrageous."

She lifted her shoulders and held the shrug, knowing that by doing so she was revealing even more of her bosom. He really had been the perfect gentleman so far. His eyes had not strayed below the level of her chin. But he glanced down now and a slight flush reddened his cheeks.

"Are *you* ready for marriage?" she asked him. "Are you actively seeking a bride? Are you looking forward to settling down and setting up your nursery?"

The music had stopped, and they stood facing each other, waiting for another waltz tune to begin the second dance of the set.

"I am not, ma'am," he said gravely. "The answer to all your questions is no. Not yet. I am sorry, but—"

"It is as I thought, then," she said. "How old are you, Lord Merton?"

The music began again, a slightly faster tune this time. He looked suddenly amused.

"I am twenty-five," he told her.

"I am twenty-eight," she said. "And for the first time in my life I am free. There is a marvelous freedom in being a widow, Lord Merton. At last I owe no allegiance to any man, whether father or husband. At last I can do what I want with my life, unrestrained by the rules of the very male-dominated society in which we live."

Perhaps her words would be truer if she were not so utterly destitute. And if three other persons, through no fault of their own, were not so totally dependent upon her. Her boast sounded good anyway. Freedom and independence always sounded good.

He was smiling again.

"I am no threat to you, you see, Lord Merton," she said. "I would not marry you if you were to approach me on bended knee every day for a year and send me a daily bouquet of two dozen red roses."

"But you *would* seduce me," he said.

"Only if it were necessary," she said, smiling back at him. "If you were unwilling or hesitant, that is. You are so very beautiful, you see, and if I am to exercise my freedom from all restraints, I would rather share my bed with someone who is perfect than with someone who is not."

"Then you are doomed, ma'am," he said, his eyes dancing with merriment. "No man is perfect."

"And he would be insufferably dull if he were," she said. "But there *are* men who are perfectly handsome and perfectly attractive. At least, I suppose their number is plural. I have seen only one such for myself. And perhaps there really are no more than you. Perhaps you are unique."

He laughed out loud, and for the first time Cassandra was aware that they were the focus of much attention, just as she and the Earl of Sheringford had been during the last set.

She had thought of the Earl of Merton and Mr. Huxtable yesterday as angel and devil. Probably the *ton* gathered here this evening were seeing him and her in the same way.

"You *are* outrageous, Lady Paget," he said. "I believe

you must be enjoying yourself enormously. I also believe we ought to concentrate upon the steps of the dance for a while now."

"Ah," she said, lowering her voice, "I perceive that you are afraid. You are afraid that I am serious. Or that I am not. Or perhaps you are simply afraid that I will cleave your skull with an axe one night while it rests asleep upon the pillow beside mine."

"None of the three, Lady Paget," he said. "But I *am* afraid that I will lose my step and crush your toes and utterly disgrace myself if we continue such a conversation. My sister taught me to count my steps as I dance, but I find it impossible to count while at the same time conducting a risqué discussion with a beautiful temptress."

"Ah," she said. "Count away, then, Lord Merton."

He really did not know if she was serious or if she joked, she thought as they danced in silence—as she had intended.

But he was attracted—intrigued and attracted. *As she had intended.*

Now all she needed to do was persuade him to reserve the final set of the evening with her, and *then* he would discover which it was—serious or not.

But good fortune was on her side and offered something even better than having to wait. They danced for a long while without talking to each other. She looked at him as the music drew to a close and drew breath to speak, but he spoke first.

"This was the supper dance, Lady Paget," he said,

"which gives me the privilege of taking you into the dining room and seating you beside me—if you will grant it to me, that is. Will you?"

"But of course," she said, looking at him through her eyelashes. "How else am I to complete my plan to seduce you?"

He smiled and then chuckled softly.